PRAISE FOR FARRA[illegible]

THE HOOKUP PLAN

"It [is] impossible not to fall in love with this smart story."

—*Publishers Weekly*

THE DATING PLAYBOOK

USA *Today* Best Rom-Coms of the Year
NPR Best Romances of the Year
Vulture: Best Romance Novels of the Year
***Kirkus* Best Romances of the Year**

"Deeply felt and hilarious...a winning playbook. Grade: A."

—*Entertainment Weekly*

"A total knockout: funny, sexy, and full of heart."

—*Kirkus*, Starred Review

"Fun, heartfelt, and totally relatable."

—Abby Jimenez, *New York Times* bestselling author

"A fun and thoughtful summer read." —*USA Today*

"A swoo[illegible] —PopSugar

"An absolute romp, packed with humor, brilliant banter, and—of course—sex appeal.... Rochon's central love story comes through beautifully with inspiration, heart, and soul."—NPR

"Such a joyful reading experience... With smoking hot chemistry, next to no angst, and a friend group that is literally squad goals, Rochon has written another winner."

—Vulture

"This emotional romance is sure to win hearts."

—*Publishers Weekly*

"Filled with lovable characters and swoon-worthy moments."

—*Woman's World*

THE BOYFRIEND PROJECT

NPR's Favorite Books of the Year
***Cosmopolitan*: Best Romance Novels of the Year**
Insider: Best Romance Books of the Year

"*The Boyfriend Project* is rom-com joy... Rochon is incisively funny, gifted at winging between laugh-out-loud scenarios, crackling banter, and pointed social commentary. Grade: A."

—*Entertainment Weekly*

"There's so much to love in this—smart, highly competent and sexy romantic leads, strong female friendships and a dose of intrigue—and it kicks off what promises to be an excellent series."

—NPR

"A prime example of how complex and insightful romances can be. Farrah Rochon deftly explores what it means to go viral, the unique joys of strong female friendships, and the particular struggles of Black women in the workplace, all within a great love story."

—Jasmine Guillory, *New York Times* bestselling author of *While We Were Dating*

"Farrah Rochon writes intensely real characters with flaws and gifts in equal measure."

—Nalini Singh, *New York Times* bestselling author

"*The Boyfriend Project* is a wonderful mix of what I love in romance: romantic tenderness, great chemistry, bright individuals, expertise in their jobs, deep friendships with secondary characters, and excellent conflict between them leading to great trust-building." —Frolic

"Rochon is a romance master who adeptly writes interesting and dynamic characters." —*Kirkus*

Also by Farrah Rochon

The Boyfriend Project

The Dating Playbook

FARRAH ROCHON

FOREVER
New York Boston

This book is a work of fiction. Names, characters, places, and incidents are the product of the author's imagination or are used fictitiously. Any resemblance to actual events, locales, or persons, living or dead, is coincidental.

Cover design by Daniela Medina
Cover illustration by Elizabeth Turner Stokes

Grand Central Publishing
Hachette Book Group
1290 Avenue of the Americas, New York, NY 10104
grandcentralpublishing.com
twitter.com/grandcentralpub

First Edition: August 2022

Grand Central Publishing is a division of Hachette Book Group, Inc. The Grand Central Publishing name and logo is a trademark of Hachette Book Group, Inc.

Library of Congress Cataloging-in-Publication Data
Names: Rochon, Farrah, author.
Title: The hookup plan / Farrah Rochon.
Description: First Edition. | New York : Forever, 2022.
Identifiers: LCCN 2022004311 | ISBN 9781538716687 (trade paperback) | ISBN 9781538716700 (ebook)
Subjects: LCGFT: Novels.
Classification: LCC PS3618.O346 H66 2022 | DDC 813/.6—dc23
LC record available at https://lccn.loc.gov/2022004311

ISBN: 9781538716687 (trade paperback), 9781538716700 (ebook)

Printed in the United States of America

LSC-C

Printing 2, 2022

To my favorite registered nurse, my goddaughter,
Kia Roybiskie.

Thank you for being a lifesaver,
in more ways than one.

1

London Kelley struggled to pinpoint the source of the persistent throb assaulting the base of her skull. It could've been the strobe lights bouncing off the Moroccan-themed decorations strewn about the ballroom where her fifteen-year high school reunion was being held. Or maybe it was the clamor of three hundred voices shouting over the blaring music.

The volume lowered a smidge before the DJ called out his next challenge to the crowd.

"All right, Class of 2007, let's see if you remember this one."

London took another sip of her rum and Coke. She'd started her own private drinking game, tossing back a hit whenever the DJ reminded them how long it had been since they'd graduated from high school.

It was also possible the alcohol was to blame for her headache.

The chatter subsided for a moment before erupting into hoots and hollers as the intro to Flo Rida's "Low" began to play.

It would appear the class of 2007 did indeed remember this one.

Although it looked to London as if some of her classmates

had forgotten they were wearing cocktail dresses instead of Apple Bottom jeans. The amount of underwear being flashed as they all got low, low, low, low rivaled the Victoria's Secret fashion show.

As she glanced around the ballroom, her eyes landed on the current bane of her existence: that ridiculous chocolate fountain.

"Not again," London growled.

She took a hasty sip from her glass before setting it on a passing waiter's tray, then hurried toward the dessert table. Instead of a flowing curtain of silky milk chocolate, uneven clumps dripped from the three tiers, plopping into the pool at the fountain's base. She was *so* over this thing.

She searched for the banquet manager, but the short blonde was nowhere to be seen.

Recalling what had been done the last time it jammed—not even twenty minutes ago—London reached underneath the table skirt and unplugged the fountain. She used a skewered pineapple spear to swirl the chocolate, breaking up the blobs that had collected in the bowl until all was smooth.

"Oh no, did it stop working again?" called a voice from several feet away. It was Yvette, the banquet manager.

"It did, but I took care of it," London said as she grabbed the plug and reinserted it.

"Wait! Not yet!" Yvette screeched a second too late.

The machine let out a loud whirr as bands of chocolate whipped from it, slashing across the table and landing on everything within a three-foot radius. Including London.

"Shit!" she hissed.

The banquet manager rushed to her side. "You have to turn it back to level one before starting it up again," she said, quickly shutting down the fountain. "Or else you get... well... this." She gestured to the mess before them.

"That's good to know for the next time it jams," London said. Hopefully the crowd's roar from the DJ's newest song drowned out her sarcasm. It wasn't Yvette's fault that she'd taken it upon herself to fix this stupid fountain.

London held her arms out, assessing the damage. She'd dodged the brunt of the fountain's assault, incurring only a few streaks across her forearms and the front of her jumpsuit. She looked like those fancy strawberries with chocolate drizzled across them.

Several people dancing near the dessert table gawked at her, but they were too busy getting hot in herre with Nelly to help a fellow classmate in distress.

"Let me ask the bartender for a towel," Yvette offered.

"Don't worry about it. I'll go wash up in a minute. I just need to check the buffet line to make sure we're not running out of anything."

"I'll take care of that," Yvette said.

"I can—"

"It's my job," the banquet manager stated, a tinge of annoyance in her voice. "It's why you're paying me."

"You're right." London held up both hands and took a step back. "Yes, of course. I just... just want everything to be the way I envisioned it."

Because even though she barely had time to take a breath these days, she'd felt compelled as class president to take over planning this reunion. Which meant that everything had to be perfect.

She really needed to get a handle on her control issues. And the perfectionism. And sleep. Another hour or so every night would do her wonders.

Hell, if she was adding things to her need-to-do list, she'd just as well add sex. Lord knows she needed that.

"If we are running low on anything, please add it to my tab," London said. "I'll settle the bill with you later tonight."

Yvette nodded and took off in the direction of the buffet table.

Just as London started for the restroom, she heard, "Well, if it isn't my co-valedictorian."

Her eyelids slid closed at the sound of that voice. It was deeper than it had been fifteen years ago, but unmistakable. And it still grated on her very last nerve.

"In over your head as usual, huh, London?" Drew Sullivan asked.

You're a grown woman. Do not *take the bait.*

She turned and smiled.

"Well, if it isn't the guy who maintained his 4.0 GPA by taking an extra PE class while I took advanced chemistry," London replied. She'd aimed for cordiality but missed the mark by at least ten miles.

Drew stood a couple of feet away, his amused smile revealing straight white teeth that shone bright against his dark brown skin. Meticulously trimmed facial hair covered his strong jaw and framed his mouth. As far as mouths went, it was a nice one. A *very* nice one. Too bad it belonged to Drew freaking Sullivan.

"You know," Drew continued, lifting several napkins from a stack at the end of the table, "if you wanted all the chocolate to yourself, you could have just had the DJ announce it. I doubt any of our classmates would mind."

She accepted the napkins he offered and cleaned her arms with them. "Do you mean to tell me that in all these years you couldn't find a sense of humor?"

"I'm still working on it," Drew said, wiping the chocolate that streaked the tablecloth.

"You're making a mess." London moved his hand out of the way. But when she started scrubbing the tablecloth, she smeared it even more.

"Some things never change," Drew said.

She looked up to find him smirking at her. "What are you talking about?"

He gestured at the table. "You thought you could do a better job than me."

His smile widened and London had to fight the urge to fling chocolate at him.

She braced her hands on the table and leaned forward. "Make no mistake, I have *always* been a step ahead of you. But unlike fifteen years ago, I'm not going to waste my time trying to prove it."

"Like you did in calculus? Oh, wait. We had the same grade in that class, didn't we? Same with world history. Hmm…as a matter of fact, we both ended the year with straight As in all the classes that counted."

"Still a cocky bastard," she said.

"Only because I can back it up." Drew leaned toward her. "Admit it, you loved going toe to toe with me back then."

London narrowed her eyes. She wanted to laugh so damn bad, but she would rip her own lips off before she gave Drew the satisfaction. He'd had enough laughs at her expense fifteen years ago, during the many times he'd bested her over the course of their senior year.

Instead, she rounded the table, intending to go to the restroom to finish cleaning up, only to find herself clasped in a bear hug.

"London Kelley? Oh my God, how are you?"

Anika Harvey—now Anika Sanderson—smiled up at her, the top of her head barely reaching London's chin.

"Anika. How . . . uh . . . how are you?" She disengaged from the woman's hold, surveying her clothes to make sure she hadn't smeared any of the chocolate on her. "How are Marcus and the kids?"

Anika had married Marcus Sanderson, the guy whose braces had cut London's bottom lip during her very first kiss back in the ninth grade.

"Oh, everyone is just fine. Marcus is here somewhere." Anika gestured at the dance floor, then she winked at London. "So, that Craig guy was something else, wasn't he? Have you heard from him since the drama that went down at the sushi place?"

London tried not to roll her eyes at yet another person asking about Craig.

The only thing she had been known for back in high school was getting all As, being class president, and being the reluctant teacher's pet. She would have killed someone—okay, maybe only maimed someone—for the attention she'd garnered tonight. And all because six months ago she'd been one of three women at the center of a video that had gone viral online after discovering they had all been duped by the same three-timing creep.

The most ironic part in all of this? She'd started dating said creep only in the hopes of having a date for this very reunion. The prospect of showing up to yet another function alone and fending off questions about why she wasn't settled with a husband and kids had prompted her to accept a date from the first warm body with a pulse who'd swiped right.

Just then, the banquet manager reappeared with the promised washcloth.

"Thank you." London accepted it and ran the damp towel along her forearms. She returned her attention to Anika. "Social media blew up that thing with Craig. It really wasn't as serious as people made it out to be."

She could tell by Anika's frown that she was hoping for more inside dirt, but London was done providing fodder for the rumor mill. There had to be another classmate whose crappy love life had gone viral online.

"That's too bad," Anika said. "You and those other two girls should have pitched it as a reality TV show, like the Real Housewives."

As if she had time to star in a TV show. She barely had time to *watch* TV.

She hunched her shoulders in a *what are you gonna do* gesture as Anika walked off. London glanced over to find Drew observing her with a curious expression.

"Do not even think about it," she said. She didn't know for sure that he was going to ask her about Craig, but whatever it was, she didn't want to hear it. Especially from Drew.

He held his hands up. "I didn't say anything."

"But it's on the tip of your tongue," London accused.

That grin reappeared. "If it's my tongue that interests you—"

"Shut up, Drew," she said, cutting him off. "I knew it was smart to steer clear of you tonight."

"So you *have* been avoiding me."

"Damn right I have," she said.

She had done her best to dodge him, but this was the Hilton, not Cowboys Stadium—or whatever they called that behemoth of a dome up there in Arlington now. There were only so many places in this ballroom for a girl to hide.

What was he even doing here? As far as London knew, Drew had left Austin soon after graduation and hadn't looked back.

Not that she kept tabs on the bastard or anything. It was just that Drew Sullivan and his millions of dollars were all any of her classmates ever talked about.

"So, what are you doing here, Drew?" she decided to ask as she dabbed at the remaining chocolate on her red sequined jumpsuit with the towel. "Your name wasn't on the list of attendees. I know because I triple-checked."

"I paid at the door. I hadn't planned on being in Austin for the reunion, but since I'm in town on business, I figured why not?"

"Business, huh? What do you do again? Accountant?"

"Hedge fund manager."

She knew exactly what he did for a living. That smug arch of his brow told her that *he* knew that *she* knew. Whatever.

"Ah, that's right. Drew Sullivan, the multimillionaire hedge fund manager." She tipped her head to the side. "Didn't you get caught up in some type of money-laundering scheme?"

"Nope." He grinned. "I earned it all through hard work, the same way I did with my grades back in high school. You know, the grades that earned me co-valedictorian status?"

"Oh, there you are!" called a high-pitched voice.

London looked over her shoulder just as Tabitha Rawlings walked up to them. The former cheerleader was as perky as ever. She wore her hair in microbraids that reached her behind and still had those sculpted cheekbones that London had coveted when they were teenagers. Okay, so she still coveted those cheekbones.

Tabitha held out a glossy magazine to Drew. "I kept it in my car on the off chance you'd be here tonight," she said. "Can you sign it for me?"

London let her nosiness get the better of her and peered over at the magazine.

"Have you seen the spread in *Dwellings*?" Tabitha asked, her perkiness dialed up several notches. "There's a four-page feature on Drew's amazing apartment in New York. He can see Central Park from his bathroom!"

"Quite the selling point. Is that how the real estate broker reeled you in?" London asked.

Drew flashed her another of those grins that were much too devastating for her peace of mind as he scribbled his name across Tabitha's magazine.

"The magazine calls it the quintessential bachelor pad. Although, I must say that I'm surprised you're still a bachelor, Drew," Tabitha said, heavy on the eye smolder.

It took every modicum of restraint London had not to gag.

"Here you go," Drew said, handing the magazine to Tabitha.

Once their classmate had gone off with her prized possession, he turned his attention back to London. Hooking a thumb in Tabitha's direction, he said, "If you want a copy of the magazine, I can get you one. It really is a nice spread."

"Maybe once the weather gets a little colder. I can use it as kindling in my fireplace."

He slapped his hand to his chest. "Still slinging those daggers, huh?"

"When you're good at something..." She shrugged. "And as much as I would love to stand here shooting the shit with you all night—not—I need to make sure that no one is taking more than one favor. By the way, I only ordered enough for those who preregistered for the reunion, so you can't have one."

"But those blue-and-orange mugs match my kitchen so well," he said.

London rolled her eyes. "Once a smart-ass, always a smart-ass."

"Takes one to know one."

She started to leave, but Drew stopped her.

"The favors are fine," he said. "Take a minute to breathe. You can't be everywhere at once."

"What makes you think—"

He cut her off. "It's been fifteen years, but I *know* you, London Kelley. You probably haven't stopped moving all night. Just chill for a minute. Tell me how things have been going for you."

"Why do you even want to know?"

"Because this is a class reunion and you're a former classmate. That's what people do at these things, right?"

Sure, that's why he wanted to catch up. London was tempted to play along just to see how long it took him to throw his outrageous success in her face. She could totally see him pretending to answer a text just so he could inadvertently click onto his banking app and "mistakenly" show her his bank balance.

Instead, it was *her* phone that buzzed with a text. London slipped it from her pocket and swiped her thumb across the screen. Her eyes grew wide as she read the text from her coworker, Dr. Aleshia Williams.

Oh. My. God.

"Don't go keeping all the good news to yourself," Drew said.

London jerked her phone away, even though there was no way he could see the screen from where he stood. "How did you know it was good news?"

"Because you just told me." His arrogant smile was both irritating and kind of cute.

Ugh. She always hated the fact that she found Drew attractive. She'd tried to convince herself that he looked good only if she was tired and squinted her eyes a little, but facts were facts. This bastard was gorgeous.

"And also because your eyes lit up as you read the text," Drew continued. "What has you grinning? I'm not used to seeing a smile on your face."

"You haven't seen me in fifteen years. You're not used to seeing my face. Period."

He lifted his brow in a look that said he was becoming bored with this conversation. "Are you going to share your news, or what?"

"Fine. Nosy ass," London muttered. She shot a quick reply to her colleague, then slipped her phone back into her pocket. "You know that I'm a pediatric surgeon, right?"

"You don't have to rub it in," he said.

"I wasn't rubbing anything in, you delicate little snowflake. Besides, you never wanted to go into medicine."

"You're right. Blood." He grimaced and gave an exaggerated shiver.

"Anyway," London continued, trying her hardest not to laugh. "For months, the administration at my hospital has been hinting at going the privatization route, but one of my colleagues just texted me a bit of inside scoop that makes me think that they've decided against the sale. She said the board is calling a meeting on Monday and they're going to make an announcement."

He paused for a moment before asking, "Why are you against the hospital being sold? I know several firms that broker those types of deals. It's not always a bad thing."

"Spoken like someone strictly interested in the money end of such deals," London said. "I'm concerned about the medicine. I'm in the final year of a five-year residency at this hospital, and I think I know better than you what's best for it. And it is definitely *not* a sale to the highest bidder."

"A person can be concerned about the medicine and the money," Drew said.

"And, as usual, we disagree. Good to know some things never change." London slipped a glass of sparkling wine from a passing waiter's tray. "But, you know what? I'm so happy right now that I don't even mind trading barbs with you."

"How about dancing with me?" he asked.

London drew up short. Narrowing her eyes at him, she asked, "What's *really* going on here?"

"What? Everyone else is dancing."

"Yeah, but I don't trust you," she said. "Never have."

"I'm just trying to get my hardworking classmate to have a little fun at the reunion she worked so hard to plan," he said. "Is there something wrong with that?"

London picked up a strawberry from the fruit platter.

"I'll pass on the dance," she told him. "But, to my surprise, it actually wasn't all that bad to see you again, Drew. Let's do this again in another fifteen years."

She slipped the strawberry in her mouth and left him standing at the dessert table.

2

Drew stood next to a horseshoe-shaped archway, like those he'd seen on his recent trip to Marrakesh. He shifted his attention between his phone, the projector screen that featured a slideshow of snapshots from high school, and a group of his former basketball teammates he now regretted approaching.

As he listened to them, Drew was reminded why he rarely kept in touch with anyone from this crew. Most of them hadn't matured past their high school days. Still cracking the same lame jokes and jockeying for position as the big man on campus.

He remained quiet. His success spoke for itself; he didn't have anything to prove to these guys. Then again, he had never been one to seek validation from anyone other than his mother or uncle. And London Kelley.

Drew looked to where he'd last seen her, fussing with the four-foot-tall Moroccan-inspired lantern being used as one of the photo props. She was easy to spot. Unlike some women who resented the fact that they were tall, London had always embraced her height. Those sexy-as-hell heels she wore made her even more imposing.

She was *stunning*.

Her once gangly frame had filled out in all the best ways. She was now svelte and graceful, with the barest suggestion of curves underneath the flowing fabric of that fire-red jumpsuit that only London could pull off. Even though it was now streaked with chocolate.

His lips tipped up in a grin as he thought back to their conversation a little while ago. Drew could have spent the rest of the evening going back and forth with her, but after discovering her opposition to the changes happening at Travis County Hospital, he decided it would be best if he kept his distance. For a moment, he'd contemplated telling her that the board meeting she'd gotten the scoop on was to announce an audit of the hospital pending its potential acquisition. An audit performed by Trident Health Management Systems. *His* company.

But then he'd thought better of it. Why spoil their night with talk about work? She would find out soon enough.

A heated debate about this year's NBA playoffs broke out among the basketball crew, signaling Drew's cue to leave. He returned to the dessert table. Not because he was overly fond of cream puffs, but because it provided the best vantage point to view the entire ballroom.

He sought London out again, his heart rate accelerating as he spotted her heading straight toward him.

"Back so soon?" Drew asked casually as she approached.

"What can I say, I just couldn't stay away from you," she deadpanned. She snagged a melon ball from the fruit display. "I meant to ask earlier. Who does the apartment in that magazine belong to?"

"What do you mean? It's my apartment."

"Well, who decorated your apartment for that spread? I

don't believe for a second that you live in a place with only white furniture. No one lives that way."

Whip smart, as always.

"It was a company that does staging for estate sales and stuff like that," Drew admitted. "I checked into a hotel for three nights while they got the apartment ready and took those photos. But Tabitha is right, I *can* see Central Park from my bathroom."

She snorted. "Life of the rich and famous."

"Between the two of us, I think *you're* the one with more fame," he said.

She glanced over, serving him serious side-eye. "You're going to bring up that stupid video with Craig, aren't you?"

"I'm pretty proud of myself for holding out this long before asking you about it," he said. "That video was everywhere. And, for the record, you were way out of that guy's league. He was lucky you gave him the time of day."

Her eyes teemed with suspicion even as they sparkled with mirth.

"That was very sweet of you," she said. "It makes me uneasy."

"That's not fair," Drew said. "You've been trying to make me out to be the bad guy since high school. I haven't given you a single reason not to trust me."

"I guess you're right," she said, her expression still wary. "You're definitely no Craig Johnson." She blew out a sigh. "I don't even know why I'm telling you this, but..."

"But what?" Drew urged when she didn't go further.

"I only went out with Craig so that I wouldn't have to come to this reunion stag. Oh, the irony." She laughed. "Just look at me. I still ended up here by myself, only now I've brought even *more* attention to the fact that I don't have a date."

Drew shrugged. "Who cares that you're here alone. I don't have a date either."

"Yeah, but that's to be expected." She winced. "That was mean even for me, wasn't it?"

"Extremely mean."

"Sorry." She hunched her shoulders, an irresistible smile playing at the corners of her lips. "Old habits die hard. And needling you has always been a favorite pastime."

He huffed out a laugh. "I knew you got a special thrill out of making my life hell back in high school, but—"

"*Excuse* me?" She cut him off. "I made *your* life hell? Are you serious?"

"You were horrible to me!"

"I don't know what kind of revisionist history is going on inside that head of yours, but don't expect me to just forget the shit you pulled in high school, Drew Sullivan. You did everything within your power to show me up whenever you could."

"Because you thought you were better than everyone else."

"Not better, just smarter."

Drew did his best to hold back his grin. That sass got him every damn time.

"I hate to be the one to remind you, but on paper, we're equals. No one cares that you took advanced physics while I took PE."

"It was advanced chemistry."

He didn't bother to hide his smile this time. "What if I officially renounced my co-valedictorian status? I'll do it right here, right now. Would that make you happy?"

"Nope." She picked up another melon ball and popped it in her mouth. "I'd rather go on blaming you for ruining my senior year for the rest of eternity. It's more fun."

"I did not ruin your senior year. If we're being honest here, it's the opposite. You never gave me the credit I deserve."

"Credit for what?"

"For pushing you to work harder," he said. "You were so far ahead of everybody else in our class that you probably would have started slacking by the time senior year rolled around. Who knows if you would have even gotten into medical school if I hadn't been there to provide you competition? Face it, Dr. Kelley, if it wasn't for me, you may not be a doctor at all."

She threw her head back and released a full-throated laugh. She probably hadn't intended for it to be sexy, but damn if it wasn't.

"You are so full of shit, Drew. Then again, that doesn't surprise me. You've always been full of shit." She pointed at him. "But you are right. You did push me to work harder. Getting the better of you in every single class was my sole mission in life fifteen years ago."

"Told you," Drew said. "You owe me."

She picked up a toothpick, stabbed a cube of marbled cheese from the fruit display, and held it up to him. "Here's some cheese to go with all that whine. Don't say I never gave you anything."

Now it was his turn to laugh.

Drew had decided to attend tonight's reunion only because it was being held in the same hotel where he was staying these first few nights in Austin. If the executive apartment he'd rented had been move-in ready, he doubted he would be in this ballroom right now.

If he'd known he would spend half the night going back and forth with London, he would have sent in his registration for the reunion when he'd first received—and promptly deleted—the email. Even after fifteen years, it was more than obvious that she had no idea that he'd crushed on her from the minute he arrived at Barbara Jordan High halfway through their junior year.

How could she know? She'd been too busy scheming his demise for swooping in and encroaching on her territory as smartest person in the class.

"So, tell me, London, what's been going on with you these days?" Drew asked. "Outside of working at the hospital."

He knew all about her job. Before his mom passed away last year, she would occasionally text him about that smart, pretty girl with the nice teeth he went to high school with, and how she was now a doctor who was sometimes interviewed on the local news.

"That's pretty much all there is to me," London said. "My job doesn't leave much time for anything else."

"You mean besides planning class reunions and going viral online?"

"Yeah, besides those things," she said. "Oh, and I crochet now. It's a new thing I'm trying. You know, broadening my horizons and all that good stuff."

"Crochet, huh? Do you play bridge and take in stray cats too?"

"Hey, fiber art is the new hip thing, Drew Sullivan."

"I would believe that if you'd used any word other than *hip*."

"Shut up." She laughed.

"Why do you have to make goading you so much fun?"

"Because—"

A high-pitched squeal came from the area of the DJ's table. Tabitha Rawlings had taken control of the microphone.

"Okay, fellow Trojans, it's time for the class roll call!" Tabitha said.

"What the hell?" London's brow dipped in disapproval. "There isn't supposed to be any class roll call. The reunion committee never discussed this."

"Maybe they discussed it when you weren't there?"

She gave him the death glare.

Drew held up his hands. "Or, maybe not."

Tabitha started with the Class Clown, Reginald Brown, who also won Best Personality, Most School Spirit, and Best Dressed. She went through the list, calling out several more "Most Likely To" categories, and then moved on to couples.

"Is she just pulling these out of her ass?" London asked. "They didn't even take votes."

"Yes, they did," Drew said. "I was given a form to fill out when I arrived."

"You were?" She jerked her head around. "No one told me about any form."

"It sounds as if the rest of the committee kept it from you. They probably knew you'd be pissed." He leaned toward her and, in a stage whisper, said, "I voted for you as Most Likely to Succeed, by the way."

Tabitha called out Most Popular Girl and Guy, then corrected herself, changing it to *persons* out of respect for the nonbinary members of their graduating class.

"We originally had two members of the class of 2007 who were voted Most Likely to Succeed," Tabitha said. She clapped her hands together. "And wouldn't you know, those same two people are once again in a tie! Come on up, Drew and London!"

"This is pathetic," London groused.

"Where's your school spirit?" Drew tipped his head toward the center of the room. "Your fellow classmates are waiting for you."

She rolled her eyes. "I should have just gone to work tonight and skipped this reunion altogether."

But then she pasted on a brilliant smile, took Drew by the hand, and dragged him with her to accept accolades from the rest of their class.

After awarding Reginald Brown with Most Unique, Most Changed, and Best Attitude, Tabitha ended the roll with Best Dancer, which also went to—surprise, surprise—Reginald Brown.

London leaned over and whispered in Drew's ear, "Reginald must have spent the entire night campaigning."

"Nah, Reggie's a good egg," Drew said. "Although I don't think he can touch me when it comes to dancing."

He did a hip thrust, à la Michael Jackson, and London burst out laughing.

"Better watch it there," she said. "You don't want to break anything."

Drew scoffed. "You must not remember me at those school dances. Oh, wait." He pointed at her. "You didn't go to any of the school dances because you were too busy studying nonstop so that you could keep up with me in class."

She flashed him her middle finger.

"Okay, folks!" Tabitha shouted into the microphone. "We all know that Reggie was the best dancer back in high school, but there's only one way to find out who that title truly belongs to now." She shot her fist in the air. "Dance-off!"

"Oh, hell no," London said. She turned, but Drew caught

her before she could take a step. She shot him an annoyed look. "I told you already, I am *not* dancing."

The entire ballroom broke out in excited cheers when Soulja Boy's "Crank That" spilled out from the speakers.

"You sure about that?" Drew asked. He spread his arms out like Superman and did three bounce jumps to the right.

London stood in the middle of the dance floor with her arms folded and the barest hint of a smile playing at the corners of her mouth. Her eyes followed him as he executed dance moves he hadn't done in fifteen years, pumping his fists and hopping on one leg.

Drew knew the moment he crisscrossed his feet that he'd gone too far.

"Shit!" he hissed as pain shot through his ankle. He hopped around on one leg again, but it had nothing to do with Soulja Boy's directives.

"What did you do?" London asked. She wrapped an arm around his waist and guided him to a chair just off the dance floor. "See what happens when the over-thirty crowd tries to relive their teenage years?"

"Hey, I was doing okay until that second Superman move."

She rolled her eyes as she settled in the chair next to his and patted her lap. "Up here, Clark Kent."

He shook his head. "Nah, I'm good."

"Drew Sullivan, let me see your damn ankle."

"I don't go around showing skin to just anybody, Ms. Kelley."

"*Dr.* Kelley," she reminded him. "Now, let me see it."

Drew relinquished his ankle to her, gingerly setting it in her lap. He looked on as she rolled up the hem of his tailored pants and rolled down his sock, exposing his ankle. Using both index fingers and thumbs, she lightly pressed on the joint.

"How does that feel?" she asked.

He studied her profile. "It feels like you know what you're doing," Drew murmured.

She looked up at him, their eyes locking. After several moments passed, she said, "I think you'll be okay."

She carefully lifted his foot from her lap and slipped from the chair, setting his foot down on the seat she'd just vacated. "Why don't you sit here for the next three hours, just to be sure?"

He grinned. "Will you come back to check on me?"

"Hmm, I don't think so. After all, I'm a pediatric surgeon. I wouldn't want to...how did you describe it? Get in over my head?"

She winked and walked away.

3

Drew had already removed his necktie and jacket before he walked through the door of his executive suite. He headed straight for the wet bar, but set down the decanter of bourbon he'd ordered without ever removing the crystal stopper. If he was going to have a drink, he'd rather have it at the bar downstairs instead of in his hotel room. Being alone held little appeal after being surrounded by his classmates tonight. And to think he'd almost skipped the reunion.

He didn't bother with the tie, but slipped his jacket back on before leaving the room and heading for the elevators. It stopped on the eighth floor and a group of twentysomethings boarded. They wore matching bright pink T-shirts with SHANNA'S BACHELORETTE WEEKEND written across the chest. Their hair matched the T-shirts.

"Catching the bars on Sixth Street in all this rain?" Drew asked in an effort to make small talk.

"All night long!" the women answered in obviously practiced unison. They cheered and high-fived each other until the elevator made it to the first floor.

As if their youth and exuberance hadn't already made him

feel old, Drew heard himself say, "Be safe out there," as they exited the elevator.

When had he gone from being the guy asking to join a group of beautiful women on their barhopping adventure to the guy issuing warnings like a concerned dad? If he wasn't careful, he'd find himself crocheting alongside London.

Drew did a double take as he looked toward the bar and spotted her. He was surprised to see her still here, since the reunion had ended a half hour ago. These days, the class of 2007 was more concerned with making it home to their kids than partying past midnight.

He walked up to where she stood with both elbows on the bar. "You're still here?" he asked.

Was that a flash of interest he saw in her eyes when she looked over at him, or was that just wishful thinking on his part?

"Yes, I am." She held up a silver credit card. "I have to square away the remainder of the bill for tonight."

"With your personal credit card?"

She shrugged. "I added a few things that weren't agreed upon by the committee. It's only right that I cover it."

"Let me take care of that." Drew pulled out his wallet from inside his jacket pocket.

"Put that away," London admonished. "I may not be a rich hedge fund manager, but my little job down at the county hospital pays me well enough to cover a few dozen bacon-wrapped shrimp and fried ravioli."

"But you've already put in enough of your time planning this reunion, you shouldn't have to come out of your pocket," Drew said. "And don't try to deny that you put most of this together. Tonight had the London Kelley hand stamp all over it."

"It was my job as class president," she said.

"I call bullshit on that. You just wanted to make sure things were done your way," he said. Drew raised his brows as she remained silent. "What? No rebuttal?"

"Shut up, Drew." She laughed. She jutted her chin at his leg. "How's the ankle?"

He stretched his foot out and rotated it. "Good as new." He put his credit card back in his wallet and tucked it away. "If you won't let me cover the balance for the reunion, you can at least let me buy you a drink." He pointed to the tall, smoke-gray windows. The storm raging outside made it nearly impossible to see anything beyond the sidewalk. "There's no way you're going anywhere anytime soon."

The woman Drew had noticed London talking to earlier at the reunion—the banquet manager, he presumed—came over, and London handed her the card.

"I'll have this back to you in just a few," the woman said.

"Thanks, Yvette." London glanced at the windows, then turned her gaze on him. Her eyes traveled from his head to his feet, as if sizing him up, or trying to figure out what kind of game he was running.

"It's just a drink," Drew said. "Something to do while you wait out the rain."

She thought about it for a moment before answering, "Fine." She turned to the bartender. "A Tom Collins. Use that Hendrick's Midsummer Solstice up there." She glanced back at Drew. "He can afford it."

Drew grinned. "Whatever the lady wants." He pointed to the glass enclosure that held a single bottle of bourbon behind lock and key. "I'll take a shot of the Willett."

"I'll need payment beforehand," the bartender said.

Drew noticed the way London's eyes narrowed in confusion as he passed the bartender his credit card.

"What kind of drink requires prepayment?" she asked.

"Bourbon," he answered.

The bartender handed the shot glass to Drew.

"This is the first time I've gotten to pour this one in the two years that I've been working here," he said. "Enjoy!"

Drew threw back the ninety-dollar shot in one swallow. "You want to try it?" he asked London.

She looked to the glass-encased Willett and shook her head. Taking her drink from the bartender with a smile and a thank-you, she told Drew, "I'll stick to my gin."

She tipped her glass toward him in salute before taking a sip. "Thanks for the drink," she said, then turned and started for the seating that ran along the far wall of the bar area. Just as she approached one of the plush couches, a group of college-aged kids, drenched from the rain, invaded the bar. They were raucous and unruly and a reminder of everything Drew hated about college towns.

London stood with her drink in the middle of the bar. There wasn't an open seat anywhere.

Drew walked up alongside her. "Before you get the wrong idea, this is only an offer to sit out the rain," he started. "But you are more than welcome to bring this drink up to my room."

Her reply was quick. "I don't think so."

One of the college kids struck a John Travolta pose, à la *Saturday Night Fever*, and the rest of the crew broke out into boisterous laughter.

"On second thought," London said.

The banquet manager returned with the credit card, then London followed Drew to the bank of elevators. They took one up to the twenty-seventh floor. Once in the suite, London headed straight for the span of windows, which afforded a spectacular view of downtown Austin. The jagged crown of the Frost Bank Tower, one of the most recognizable structures in the city, sparkled despite the deluge taking place outside.

"Goodness, but it's coming down out there. I should have checked my phone to see when this rain is forecast to end," she said.

Drew slipped his out of his pocket and did just that. He grimaced as he held it up to her. "You may want to get comfortable," he said.

London squinted at the phone and released another of those long-suffering sighs. She held her glass out to him. "Can you hold this for a minute?" She stepped out of her heels, kicked them to the side, and reclaimed her glass. "Thanks."

She turned and moved away from the windows. Heeding his advice to make herself comfortable, London folded her long legs underneath her as she sat on the couch.

Drew walked over to the wet bar and poured himself another bourbon. He wasn't expecting much after that shot of Willett he'd had downstairs, but it was pretty decent. He returned to London, taking a seat in one of the chairs instead of on the couch. He kicked his shoes off and stretched his legs out in front of him.

"So what are you *really* doing back in Austin, Drew?" she asked.

"This is home, isn't it?"

"Yes, but it hasn't been your home in a long time."

He cocked a brow. "Have you been keeping tabs on me, Dr. Kelley?"

"Stop flattering yourself." She rolled her eyes, but amusement played at the corners of her lips. "Your classmates are obsessed with you," she continued. "You went to some fancy party a few months back, and the reunion committee spent the first half hour of the meeting fawning over your glamorous life."

"Sounds as if you weren't part of the fawning crowd."

She shrugged. "Celebrity doesn't impress me. And after having a small taste of notoriety, I know for certain that I do not want anything to do with it. I much prefer the humdrum existence of becoming a world-class doctor who saves the lives of sick children."

Her cheeky smile was, without a doubt, the most enchanting thing Drew had seen tonight.

"From what I've gleaned over the years, you're pretty damn good at saving the lives of sick children," he said. "Although I'll admit that I'm surprised you work at County."

"Well, I'm surprised you're staying at the Hilton and not the Driskill," she countered. "And, for your information, County is a wonderful hospital." Her affronted scowl told him everything he needed to know about the pride she took in working at Travis County Hospital. He stored away that tidbit for later.

"All the suites at the Driskill were taken," Drew said. "And I just assumed a doctor of your caliber would be at some world-renowned hospital, like Dell Children's here in Austin. Your talent seems...I don't know...*wasted* doesn't seem like the right word."

"That is *definitely* not the right word," she said. "The patients at Travis County Hospital deserve the same caliber of care as those at any other hospital."

Drew sat back and took another sip of his bourbon. "If you approach patient care with even half the passion that you had toward your schoolwork, I have no doubt they're getting all the care they need."

"Is that your way of complimenting me?"

"I never had a problem complimenting you, London. You had an issue with *accepting* compliments. Is that still the case?"

"I don't know." She swirled the ice in her tumbler, that hint of a smile returning to her lips. "Why don't you take another shot at it?"

He stared at her over the rim of his highball glass. "You're wearing the hell out of that jumpsuit. It's stunning."

"Hmm." She took a sip from her drink. "It appears I *have* gotten better at accepting compliments. Thank you." She gestured to him. "The suit is nice."

"You can work on your delivery, but I'll take it."

She looked over at him, and they both burst out laughing.

Drew was surprised by how at ease she seemed. The London Kelley he remembered from fifteen years ago would have never accepted an invitation up to his room, let alone feel relaxed enough to lounge barefoot on his couch.

"The slideshow that played throughout the reunion brought back some pretty wild memories," Drew mused. "There was one picture from School Spirit Week I wish I'd grabbed a shot of."

"I have them all on my phone."

Of course she did.

"Come on." She motioned for him to join her on the couch. "You should see the ones that *didn't* make the cut for the slideshow."

Drew halted in the middle of rising from his chair. "Tell me you don't have that picture from when the basketball team got our hair cut to spell out TROJANS."

She scrolled for a second before holding up the phone.

Drew groaned. "I'll pay you a million dollars to delete that."

"Your money can't buy me off." She practically cackled. "I do believe your barber intentionally cut that *O* to look like a condom."

"I later found out he graduated from Anderson High," Drew said as he sat beside her. London's knee brushed against his thigh and his pulse skyrocketed.

It suddenly occurred to him that reducing the distance between himself and the woman he'd been halfway in love with in high school wasn't his smartest decision of the night. But he refused to move. London Kelley was in his hotel room, joking around with him like an old friend. He would savor every second of this.

They browsed through the photos, pointing out who had changed the most—and the least—in their graduating class, then they got into a heated but hilarious debate about his favorite math teacher. London was adamant that Mrs. Wallace had it out for her, which she claimed was the only reason Drew had ended the year with the better grade.

"You're delusional, Dr. Kelley."

"That woman hated me," London said. "And, of course, she absolutely *loved* you, just like all the other teachers."

"Mrs. Wallace didn't hate you. She was intimidated by you. You can't really blame her."

She arched a brow. "Were *you* intimidated by me?"

He was fascinated by her back then. He still was.

"Nah," he answered. "Not after I discovered your weak spot." Her brow arched higher. "You had to control everything," Drew continued. "And if you didn't, it drove you out of your mind. Do you think I actually *wanted* to be president of the Beta Club and the debate team?" He shook his head. "I only ran for those things to keep you from winning."

"I knew it, you bastard!" She took one of the stiff throw pillows and lobbed it at his head. "This is the real reason you're here alone, because no woman in her right mind would put up with someone like you."

Close enough. Although it was his tendency to be a workaholic rather than a bastard that ran most of his serious relationships into the ground. Now that he thought about it, the two went hand in hand.

"You're probably right," Drew told her.

He looked down at his watch and did a double take. It was nearly two in the morning. When he glanced toward the window, he saw that the rain outside had slowed to a light drizzle.

London glanced over her shoulder. "It looks as if the rain has finally let up."

Drew couldn't deny the disappointment that swept through him when she stood. But then his brow creased in a frown when, instead of retrieving her shoes and bidding him farewell, she walked over to the bar. She picked out the mini bottle of gin, emptied it into her glass, and downed the contents in one swallow.

Then promptly broke out into a coughing fit.

Drew rushed over to her. "You okay?" He patted her back until she stopped coughing.

"Holy shit," she said. "I haven't done that since college."

"I would suggest you not do it again."

"I think you're right. Thank you."

Drew reached for a clean highball glass and poured himself a finger of bourbon. He probably shouldn't have any more tonight, but he was so keyed up after spending this time with London that he figured he'd need something to relax him once she left.

"You okay now?" he asked her.

"Yeah, sorry about that. I just really needed another drink." She paused, then said, "I'm not drunk enough to have sex with you, so I'm trying to fix that."

He choked on his bourbon. "Excuse me?"

"You heard me. I want sex tonight. And, well, you're here."

He cleared his throat. "Who says I want to have sex with you?"

London rolled her eyes. "Don't think for a minute that you can convince me you've changed *that* much since high school." She took the glass out of his hand and swallowed down his drink. "At one time you would sleep with anything with a pulse."

She reached for the decanter, but Drew stopped her. "First, there won't be any sex happening here if you get drunk. That's not the way I operate. And give me some credit, Dr. Kelley. Anyone I slept with also had to have a personality."

"Mallory Lawrence didn't have a shred of personality."

"It was the tits when it came to Mallory."

"Yeah, I can see that." London nodded. "She *did* have tits for days."

Drew hooked his thumb toward the coffee table, where he'd left his cell phone. "I can call her. I'm sure she'll come over and join us."

"Oh my God. Shut up!" London said. "Just...don't talk anymore. You'll remind me how much I don't like you. Now, are you going to take your clothes off, or what?"

The fact that she'd asked that question with such nonchalance blew his mind. This could not be real life.

But it was. *The* London Kelley was standing in his hotel room, looking like a goddess, and asking—commanding—him to take off his clothes.

"Why me?" Drew asked. Because he had to make sure this was something she really wanted. "You just said you don't like me?"

She hunched her shoulders. "To be honest, after all these years I don't know you well enough to decide whether or not I like you, Drew. But I don't have to like you to fuck you.

"Here's the deal: I haven't had sex in nearly a year. I'm under a ridiculous amount of stress at work, and my friends think ending my drought is the perfect way to relieve some of the stress. They suggested I find a single doctor at the hospital and get laid, but I refuse to have a one-night stand with a coworker. However, I also want to make sure it's with someone I at least semi-trust."

"And you trust me?"

"*Semi*-trust," she reiterated. "You're better than a stranger I pick up at a bar." She cocked her head to the side. "Although, I kinda *did* pick you up at the bar tonight, didn't I? Or you picked me up." She waved that off. "It doesn't matter. The important thing is that after we sleep together, I won't have to worry about awkward run-ins in the hallway at work." She nodded toward his foot. "How's that ankle feeling? You think it will hold up?"

"I don't know what kind of kinky stuff you're into, but my ankle isn't the body part you should be concerned about, Dr. Kelley."

Her brow arched with mild irritation. "Are we doing this or what, Drew?"

Drew couldn't help but think of those long-ago nights

he'd spent in bed, praying his mother didn't come into his room and discover him damn near bruising himself as he self-pleasured his way to sleep with thoughts of London swimming in his head. After all this time he finally had the chance to experience the real thing, and she thought there was a question as to whether he would be interested?

He thought about Monday and what her reaction would be when she discovered that she would, in fact, have to encounter him in the hallways at work. At least on a temporary basis. Members of his team would be at the hospital most of the time, but he would be required to be there for the occasional meeting over these next three to four weeks.

"Uh, London, before we do anything, maybe we should talk about the work I'll be doing while in Austin. You should know that..."

Drew's voice trailed off. He stared at London in awe as she reached behind her head and unhooked the clasp at the base of her neck. She shrugged her shoulders out of the jumpsuit and shimmied her hips, letting the sparkly material glide down her legs and pool onto the floor at her feet. She stood before him in a sheer bra that did nothing to hide her deep brown areolae. The matching panties didn't hide much either.

His pulse pounded as he drank in the sight of her.

"You were saying?" she asked.

He would figure out how to deal with the fallout on Monday.

He clutched her hip and pulled her to him. "You're damn right we're doing this."

4

The effort it took to lift a single eyelid gave London insight into how the rest of her day was likely to progress. On the bright side, there was a delicious ache to muscles she had not used in far too long. She wanted to savor that feeling before the reality of what she'd done sank in.

Too late. *Way* too late. Her mind began to bombard her with screenshots from last night.

Drew Sullivan. She'd given her goodies to Drew fucking Sullivan.

Her archnemesis. Her biggest rival. The boy she'd wished death upon after every single test and quiz she'd taken her senior year of high school. Who would have thought *that* bastard could give her enough orgasms in a single night to make up for her yearlong dry spell?

"Shit," she cursed.

"Good morning to you too."

She cocked one eye open and looked to where he stood, just a few feet from the bed. He wore a pair of slate-gray pajama pants and nothing else. His abs were so chiseled they looked unreal.

But she now knew that every inch of him was real. Decadently real. Amazingly, toe-curlingly real.

London pulled the sheet up over her head. "I can't believe I slept with you last night."

"Technically, you didn't fall asleep until well into the morning."

"Ugh, please shut up, Drew." She lowered the sheet, tucking it under her chin, and raised up on her elbows. "Is that coffee I smell?"

"I had some brought up. Do you want breakfast?"

"No," she said. "What I want is hot coffee in a to-go cup. And then I want you to turn around while I get dressed and out of this room and, hopefully, to not see you again for another fifteen years."

"You sure about that? You went without sex for only one year and look at how thirsty you were last night. I think we should make this a monthly thing. I'd say weekly, but I know how busy you are, saving lives and all that."

And this was why she couldn't allow one night of his acting like a decent human being to erase who he'd been fifteen years ago. This was the real Drew Sullivan.

"I really can't stand you," London said. "I don't care that you have a magic dick, I still cannot stand you."

His sexy grin made her growl.

She tore the covers away, not caring that he wore pajama bottoms while she walked around his room naked, in search of her underwear.

"Your clothes are in there," he said.

She looked to the adjoining room and spotted her jumpsuit and underwear folded neatly over the back of the love seat. Her heels were lined up next to it.

"You touched my panties?" she asked with an incredulous shriek.

His right brow arched. "You *do* remember where my tongue was last night, don't you?"

That was a reminder she did not need.

The worst part of all this was that she had not been drunk. She'd gotten into his bed—well, first on his conference table, and then in his shower, and then straddling the fucker on the sofa—with hardly a buzz going. She had willingly ridden Drew Sullivan's face like he was a champion quarter horse. And if she didn't get the hell out of here right now, she would likely beg him to let her do it again.

He followed her into the living area and walked over to the conference table, where a silver coffee carafe and dozens of documents were arranged in neat stacks. A set of reading glasses sat atop one set of documents.

"You don't have to leave, you know," Drew said. "Unless you have a surgery scheduled at the hospital?"

"I don't schedule surgeries on Sundays," London said as she stepped into her sheer panties.

"Then why are you rushing out?" He walked over to her, stopping a couple of feet away. It was still too close for her peace of mind, so she took several steps back.

"We can grab breakfast." He paused long enough to look at his watch. "Brunch."

London gaped at him. "I'm not having brunch with you, Drew. We don't like each other, remember? What happened here last night was a onetime thing. I appreciate it, because I really, *really* needed it—"

"Yeah, you did," he interrupted.

"I can do without your commentary." She put on her

bra, then unfolded her jumpsuit and stepped into it. London inwardly cringed when she realized she'd have to ask for his help in zipping it up. She turned her back to him. "Can you zip this? Please," she tacked on.

He took so long to move that she thought he wasn't going to help her, but then she felt his hands grasp the zipper pull at the base of her spine. He guided it up her back, his fingers brushing the spot between her shoulder blades before lingering too long at her nape.

"You don't have to leave," he repeated. His breath was warm against her skin, the gentle wisp of it causing goose bumps to pebble up and down her arms.

He was so, *so* wrong. She absolutely had to leave. And *right* now.

She slipped into her shoes, grabbed her keys and her phone, and headed for the door. She turned the door handle, but then paused. When she looked back at Drew, he was still in that same spot near the sofa. Those ridiculously chiseled abs taunted her with promises of an afternoon spent in bed running her hands and tongue along them.

"Umm...thanks for the orgasms and stuff," she said, then wrenched the door open and speed walked to the elevator.

If this were one of those rom-coms she watched on Netflix, he would come racing down the hallway in his bare chest and bare feet and beg for her to return to his room. Cheesy music would play as the numbers on the elevator steadily climbed, reaching a crescendo as it dinged its arrival and waited for her to make her choice.

But Drew didn't come charging out of his luxury suite. He was probably pouring himself another cup of coffee as he reclaimed his seat at the conference table and got back to making his millions, his night with his old high school nemesis already forgotten.

The elevator arrived and London stepped inside the car, forcing herself not to glance down the corridor as she did. She stood against the back wall and closed her eyes. She tried to remember the breathing techniques Taylor had taught during the yoga class she'd taken some weeks ago, but she had fallen asleep in the middle of it because she was so exhausted these days.

Fuck this. She was not losing her breath over Drew freaking Sullivan. She'd gotten exactly what she'd wanted from him—hours of amazing sex—and now she could put him out of her mind and go back to business as usual.

"Stop lying to yourself," London muttered.

She would eventually fall back into her normal flow, but she wasn't going to forget her time spent in Drew's bed anytime soon.

She made her way to the parking garage and her Mini Cooper. Once behind the wheel, she slipped the parking ticket from the cup holder where she'd stashed it after getting it validated by the banquet manager yesterday, then backed out of the parking spot and tore out of the garage.

London set her phone in the cradle attached to the dashboard and group FaceTimed Samiah and Taylor. They came on at the same time.

"Meet me at the Kerbey Lane Cafe near UT's Campus. This is an emergency."

She had an overwhelming urge to drown her shame in pancakes.

She clicked out of the call. She wasn't one to FaceTime and drive, having witnessed the results of distracted driving in surgery more than she wanted to think about. But these were desperate times. She needed her friends.

She also needed to remind herself not to curse her friends out the moment she saw them. This was *their* fault. They were the ones who suggested this random hookup in the first place.

"Samiah and Taylor didn't tell you to screw Drew Sullivan," she said to herself. That was all on her. Well, and on Drew. Who in the hell told him to walk around their reunion looking like he belonged on the cover of that magazine Tabitha had shoved in his face?

London reminded herself that this wasn't the end of the world.

So she'd slept with Drew. Big deal. Now that they were past the awkward morning-after phase, she didn't have to worry about him. He would soon be back in New York gazing out at Central Park while he shaved in the morning, and she would be at the hospital saving lives.

They were two consenting adults who'd spent the night showing each other a good time. What was wrong with that?

"This is fine," London said. "Everything is fine."

Fifteen minutes later, she pulled up to the restaurant and was relieved when she didn't see a crowd of people waiting to get in. All the college kids were probably still sleeping off their partying from the night before. The local chain was an Austin institution, and right now there was nothing she wanted to do more than stuff her face with their blueberry buttermilk pancakes.

She was shown to a booth that overlooked one of UT's many residence halls, but just as she slipped onto the sky-blue vinyl, she realized that her bladder was seconds from bursting. She'd been so eager to get away from Drew, using the bathroom had been the furthest thing from her mind.

When London rounded the corner on the way back from the restroom, she spotted Taylor Powell's maroon-colored box braids piled on top of her head. Both she and Samiah were sitting in the booth.

"There she is," she heard Taylor say. Her forehead creased in a frown as London approached. "Uh, don't you think you're a bit overdressed for pancakes?"

London glanced down at her red sequined jumpsuit. There were still a few spots dotted with chocolate. She looked like a hot-ass mess.

Samiah slid from the booth and enveloped London in a hug. "What's going on?" she asked. "Are you hurt?"

"No, no, it's nothing like that." London disengaged from her hold and gestured for Samiah to take her seat. Then she slid into the booth next to her. She looked across the table at Taylor and frowned. "How did you make it from Georgetown so fast? Were you speeding again?"

"Jamar and I spent the night at my apartment here in town," Taylor answered. Her friend had fallen hard for her new man after first working as his personal fitness coach.

"What's the big emergency?" Samiah asked, getting right down to business, as usual.

Samiah had also taken a swan dive into love's deep end. She and her boyfriend, Daniel, had just celebrated their four-month anniversary. London had rolled her eyes at the pictures Samiah had posted on her Instagram of her apartment crowded with candles and roses, yet she could also admit that she had been the teeniest bit jealous. She'd never been one for over-the-top romantic gestures, but that shit had melted her heart.

"Food first," London said as the server arrived at their table with water glasses and a coffee carafe. They put in their breakfast orders, and London turned her attention to her coffee, ripping the top off five sugar packets. She pointed to Taylor as she added them to her mug.

"I don't need a lecture about refined sugar this morning," she warned.

"Fine," Taylor said. "I'll close my eyes so that I don't have to see you fill your body with the devil's candy."

"I'll tell you when you can open them again."

"Can you tell us why we're here?" Samiah asked, impatience making her voice shrill.

London took a sip of her coffee. It was too sweet for her liking, but she couldn't say anything because she didn't want to hear Taylor's mouth. She set the cup down and folded her hands on the table.

"I did something I'm ashamed of," she said. She looked first to Samiah, then to Taylor, giving them both the stink eye. "I took your advice."

Taylor's mouth screwed up in a frown. "Our advice?" Then her eyes went wide and she squealed. "You got some dick last night!"

The two older women sitting at the table next to theirs released twin scandalized gasps.

"Dammit, Taylor," London hissed. "Why don't you hire a skywriter to plaster that shit all across Austin?"

"But this is a good thing," Taylor said.

"Yes." Samiah nodded. "We all agreed that some stress-relieving sex should be at the top of your priority list. But, based on your reaction this morning, maybe we should have clarified that you needed *good* sex."

"That's the problem," London said. "It was *so* fucking good." She glanced over at their neighbors, who thankfully hadn't heard her.

"I'm not following," Taylor said.

"The sex isn't the issue. It's *who* I had sex with that has me second-guessing my life choices this morning."

"Not Craig!" both Samiah and Taylor screeched.

"No!" London said. "That loser hasn't tried to contact me in months. He's probably somewhere scamming a senior citizen out of her social security money." She cradled her face in her hands. "It was one of my former classmates. I hooked up with him after the reunion last night."

"Ah, okay. That explains why you're still wearing that jumpsuit. So, what's the problem?" Samiah asked. "He isn't married, is he?"

"No, he's single," London said. "He's single. He's gorgeous. And he's worth millions."

"Holy shit! I repeat. I am *not* following," Taylor said. "What's the issue?"

"The issue is that Drew Sullivan has been the bane of my existence since the moment he first walked through the doors of Barbara Jordan High School. And, yes, I know it's been fifteen years, but of all the men who were there last night, I *cannot* believe I ended up in Drew's bed. And I cannot believe how freaking *good* it was." She covered her face again.

"I swear it was the best sex I've had that didn't require batteries. No, scratch that. The best *ever*," London said. "Do you understand how frustrating it is to discover that someone who has been at the top of your shit list for years gives a tongue job like he's trying to win a medal?"

"The Cunnilingus Olympics. Jamar would definitely receive a medal," Taylor said.

The server chose that moment to return to their table. Given the utter shock on her face, it was safe to assume she had overheard Taylor's previous remark. She hung around a tad longer than necessary, adjusting the water glasses, salt and pepper shakers, and ketchup bottle.

"Thank you," London said in her most *you can leave now* voice. Once they were alone again, she said, "You guys just don't get it. I've been in competition with Drew Sullivan since the last semester of our junior year of high school. After what happened last night, he's now winning!"

"Because you're such a prize?" Samiah asked.

"You're fucking right I'm a prize," London said as she attacked her pancakes with a knife and fork. "And this gives him the upper hand."

"Does this Drew know that you still think you two are competitors, or is this just a London thing?" Taylor asked.

"It's probably just a me thing," she admitted. "Okay, it's definitely just a me thing."

London doubted Drew had ever been aware of just how intense their rivalry had been back then. Because, honestly, it wasn't about Drew. From that very first calculus quiz, when he'd scored a perfect A plus to her inferior A minus, he'd become an unwitting player in the dysfunctional crusade she'd been engaged in to gain her dad's attention. Drew Sullivan was nothing more than a symbol, a goalpost by which everything she'd strived to accomplish in high school had been measured.

But it had been easier to put all the blame on Drew than to face her fucked-up relationship with her dad. It was *still* easier to do that.

"It doesn't matter," London said as she stuffed a forkful of syrup-drenched pancakes in her mouth and nearly had another orgasm. These things were amazing. "It doesn't change the fact that giving up my goodies to Drew last night gives him a leg up in this... this..."

"This imaginary contest you've conjured," Samiah finished for her.

"Yeah, something like that."

"Okay, so let me get this straight," Taylor said. "This guy is rich, gorgeous, and can sling tongue like nobody's business. If you asked me, *you're* the one who's winning here."

"She's got a point," Samiah agreed.

She could go along with their reasoning if she were in a different headspace, but all London could think about at the moment was Drew's smug face.

Except he hadn't looked all that smug. He had not made any snide comments or said anything that would make her think he would run and tell everyone that they'd hooked up.

Still, this was Drew Sullivan. Nothing good could ever come from what she'd allowed to happen last night.

Well, other than the multiple orgasms. Those had been pretty damn good.

She reached for her coffee but then thought better of it. Signaling for the server, she called, "Can I have a new cup of coffee? I put too much sugar in this one."

"Hmm," Taylor hummed.

"Yeah, yeah. You told me so," London said. She thought about the warning she'd received from her primary care doc a few weeks ago and suddenly regretted eating that second pancake. "I need to start paying better attention to what I put in my mouth."

"I just want to clarify that you're talking about food," Taylor said. "Because there's actually health benefits to giving a blow job."

"Please, shut up," London pleaded.

Needing to get her mind away from her own issues, she turned the conversation to her two friends. She'd been so busy with last-minute reunion preparations that they'd skipped their usual Friday girls' night out. Samiah excitedly filled them both in on the tech conference where the phone app she'd created was featured in a spotlight for up-and-coming entrepreneurs.

Taylor, on the other hand, lamented about every one of the classes she was taking in her first semester of college. London knew she didn't say it often enough, but she was proud as hell of her. Taylor had recently been diagnosed with a learning disorder, but she didn't allow it to deter her from pursuing her degree to grow her fitness consulting business.

"Just hang in there," London told her. "I can't promise that it'll get easier, but it'll be more interesting once you get past these core requirements and start taking classes in your actual field of study."

"Why can't I just skip the core requirements?"

"Because they are *require*ments," London said. "It's right there in the name."

Pushing her plate away, London leaned back against the booth's soft vinyl and released a contented sigh. She really did feel better, as she knew she would after loading up on carbs and talking to these two. She probably should have skipped the salty, perfectly fried bacon, but how could a comfort meal not include bacon?

The server returned with the bill.

"This one is my treat," London said as she reached for the check. "Thanks for coming to my rescue. I needed you both today."

She got along well enough with her colleagues, but she hadn't realized what she had been missing out on by not having close friends that she could call on whenever she needed them. That was just a small part of what Samiah and Taylor brought to her life.

London glanced on both sides of her seat, then looked around the table. "Wait," she said. She must have left her purse in the car. "I'll be right back."

She slid out of the booth and rushed for the exit, jabbing her Mini's key fob the moment she walked out the door.

"Please be there, please be there," London prayed under her breath. She opened the door and did a quick search of the car, looking underneath both the driver's and passenger's side seats before checking the back. Her heart sank.

"Damn!" London said.

"What now?" Samiah asked as she and Taylor approached.

London closed the driver's side door and slumped against it. "My purse," she said. "It's not here." London closed her eyes tight. "I must have left my clutch in Drew's room."

"I covered breakfast, so don't worry about it," Samiah said.

Just then, London's phone buzzed in her pocket. She pulled it out. It was a text from a number she didn't recognize.

How did you get this number?

The class directory.

London rolled her eyes.

You left something in my room.

"*Fuck!*" London shouted.

The woman who'd just walked past her car covered the ears of the kid walking alongside her.

"Sorry," London called out to her.

But really. Fuck!

"Is that him?" Samiah asked.

"Yes." She sighed. She answered his text.

Leave it at the front desk.

His response was almost instant.

That's not safe. Just come up to my room and pick it up. I'll be here until five.

"Ugh. Why is he so hardheaded?" she groused. She looked to Samiah and Taylor. "I have to go. I have a ton of charts to review, and now I have to drive back downtown to pick up my stupid purse."

They all shared hugs and promised to meet up on Friday.

"There's a restaurant on South Lamar I've been wanting to try," Samiah called as they walked away. "They serve a spicy hibiscus margarita that's supposed to be spectacular!"

"Sounds like a plan," London said. "See you all Friday."

She slipped behind the wheel and made her way back

downtown. Once at the Hilton, she refused to acknowledge her quickening pulse as she stepped inside the lobby and boarded the elevator. She was here to retrieve her clutch. Nothing else.

"Knock on the door. Grab the purse. Leave," she mumbled.

Simple and easy.

Drew must have been waiting for her at the door. The moment she knocked, it opened. He now wore a slate-gray T-shirt to match his lounging pants, but he was still barefoot and much too sexy for words.

London held out her hand. "Can I please have my clutch?"

"You can come in," he said, turning from the door and walking back into the room.

"I don't want to come in," she said. She inwardly cringed at her churlish tone. She didn't mean to sound so rude but couldn't seem to help herself when it came to Drew.

His head fell forward. "Really, London? Don't you think that's a bit harsh, especially after last night?"

"I'm sorry," she said. She was upset with herself. It wasn't fair to take it out on him. After all, Drew had done exactly what she'd asked of him, ending her dry spell in spectacular fashion. "I just...Never mind."

Against her better judgment, she entered the room and closed the door behind her.

Drew turned back around, and London was struck by how good the stubble she hadn't taken the time to notice this morning looked on his strong, square jaw. His T-shirt wasn't tight by any means, but it was just snug enough to highlight the detail of his chiseled chest.

He cleared his throat, and her eyes shot to his.

Shit. Had she really been staring at him? What was *wrong* with her?

She still wanted him. *That's* what was wrong with her.

"My clutch," London said again, her voice catching on the last word.

His eyes never leaving hers, Drew picked up the black clutch from the conference table and sauntered back toward her. London suppressed the urge to meet him halfway. She was not moving a single inch farther into this den of sinful pleasure.

Once he made it to her, he held out the clutch. But before she could retrieve it, he pulled back, holding it just out of her reach.

"As I said earlier, you don't have to leave."

Yes, I do.

But she wasn't going to.

5

Drew stared out the window of the Uber he'd called not long after London fled his hotel room for the second time in less than twenty-four hours. He'd left soon after, moving into the furnished apartment his assistant had rented for the duration of his time in Austin. His clothes were already hanging neatly in the closet, and the fridge was fully stocked.

But he didn't want any of the food Larissa had ordered. One whiff of spicy chipotle from a street vendor triggered a memory that his stomach refused to shake. He only hoped the hole-in-the-wall taco stand on the corner from their old place in Austin was still there.

The scenery transitioned from the skyscrapers of downtown to rows of apartment buildings that had seen better days on the city's east side. He'd spent less than two years here, but the impact this place had on his life was unlike any other. He hated being back here, but it made him appreciate how far he'd come.

"Is this it?" the Uber driver asked.

Drew peered out at the galvanized steel roof and the paint peeling off the dingy wood siding. "Yes, it is."

"You said you wanted me to wait for you, right?" the man asked.

"Yeah, I should only be a few minutes," he said, getting out of the car. As he closed the door, he caught sight of the basketball court across the street. Drew rapped on the driver's window. "You can take off," he said. "I'm going to stick around for a bit."

Drew went into the taco shack and ordered three chorizo and steak street tacos with extra cilantro. These tacos had been his dinner countless nights after practice, when his mom was pulling a second shift and his uncle, Elias, was either out looking for work or hooking up with some girl.

Drew brought his tacos over to the basketball court and took a seat on a bench that probably hadn't been painted since he'd played here fifteen years ago. He mindlessly ate as he watched some teen boys battle in a three-on-three pickup game. How many afternoons had he spent doing the same?

And why did the memories leave such an uneasy feeling in his gut?

It wasn't as if anything traumatic had happened during his time here. He'd excelled in Austin, accomplishing more than any of the teachers or counselors at his previous schools had ever encouraged him to achieve. But there was something about being back here that made his hands clammy and his chest tight.

His attitude toward Texas had undergone several metamorphoses over the years. When his mom had first moved them here during his junior year of high school, he'd been as indifferent to Austin as he'd been to any of the other places where he'd lived. He began warming up to it when he started to make a name for himself at Barbara Jordan High, but Drew had learned from an early age to never let himself to get too attached to any one place. They'd averaged fourteen months tops in all the other cities they'd lived.

There was something about Austin that was different. Something about Texas that changed the game.

His mom had fallen in love with its wide-open spaces. After he left for college, she'd moved to a small town about an hour west of here, in the foothills of the Texas Hill Country. She'd remained in that tranquil little town, with the flower baskets that hung from the streetlights on Main Street and shop owners who knew every customer by name. She told him the only way she would leave would be by hearse.

And that's exactly the way it had happened.

Drew winced.

He wasn't in the right mood to think about his mom right now, not when he had all these other emotions about being back in Austin to contend with.

But thinking about his mom reminded him that he owed his uncle, Elias, a call. His mother's much younger brother had stood in as his pseudo-dad for much of Drew's life, even though only eight years separated them. His uncle had settled in Fort Worth. Like his sister, he had developed an unexplainable love for Texas.

Drew pulled out his phone and clicked into his favorites. His uncle's number was one of only a few saved there.

Elias picked up on the third ring.

"What's up, old man?" Drew said in his usual greeting.

"Hey, nephew! You in Austin yet?" Elias asked.

"Yeah. Believe or not, I'm at the playground near our old place. I would shoot a few hoops if I wasn't wearing my good shoes."

Elias laughed. "What are you doing all the way out there? You feeling nostalgic?"

"For tacos," Drew said. "But I'm about to head back

downtown. The apartment I rented became available earlier than expected, and I need to get settled in before meeting up with the team from Trident later. Say, if you're in the mood for an impromptu vacation, there's a nice suite at the downtown Austin Hilton that's fully paid for until Wednesday."

"I would if I could," Elias said. "Can't afford the days away from the job."

Drew rolled his eyes.

He'd waited until after he'd earned his first ten million before offering to buy a house and provide a stipend to both his mom and uncle so they wouldn't have to work anymore. He'd known they would both turn him down if his net worth were less than eight figures, but had hoped they would take him up on it if they figured he was financially secure.

His net worth was nearing the nine-figure mark, yet Elias still insisted on keeping his job as a mail carrier, claiming that he'd worked too hard to earn his pension and he wasn't letting it go.

"I may drop in on you in a few weeks, though," E said. "Me and a few buddies are driving out to Big Bend later this month for a long-overdue fishing trip. I figured I'd leave a day early and hang out with you in Austin. That is, if you're still here."

"I'll still be here," Drew said.

"I'll believe it when I see it," his uncle said. "But, while you *are* here, I think you need to take a drive out to Hye and go through Doreen's things. You can't leave her house sitting like that forever."

That's exactly what Drew had planned on doing. His mother's home had stood untouched since she passed away last year. He wasn't ready to face it. He wasn't sure if he ever would be.

"I'm going to be pretty busy with the project I'm working on, but I'll try to get out there," Drew said noncommittally.

"Do more than try," his uncle said. "You know Doreen would never want her house to just sit there like some kind of museum. Stop avoiding this."

Drew's phone dinged with a calendar reminder. *Saved by the fucking bell.*

"E, I need to get going."

"Working on a Sunday?"

"It's just a short meeting," he said. Drew wasn't in the mood for his uncle's harassment over his work schedule. "Give me a couple of days' notice before your fishing trip so that I can schedule the time off. Maybe we can hang out for a bit. Come back to this playground and shoot some hoops."

"Oh yeah, your ass is feeling nostalgic. I wouldn't be surprised if you ended up back in Austin permanently," Elias said.

Not a chance in hell.

"I don't know about that," Drew said.

"You should consider it. You told me yourself that New York has never felt like home. You need to plant some roots, Drew."

He was *not* having this conversation right now.

"I have to go. I'll catch up with you later, E."

He ended the call and clicked into his text messages to share the address of the building where he would be staying with Elias. After sending the text, he spotted the one he'd sent to London earlier today, letting her know that she'd left her purse in his hotel room.

Drew closed his eyes and forced himself to take a cleansing breath.

He should give her a heads-up about tomorrow. He was only making it worse by not telling her that he was the one who would assist County's governing board in deciding whether to sell the hospital to a private company.

But instead of writing the text message he knew he damn well should write, Drew switched to the Uber app and ordered a car to come pick him up.

He would deal with London tomorrow.

6

London marched at a brisk clip up the hospital's bright corridor. She dodged a phlebotomist wheeling a cart into a patient's room and made her way to the nurses' station. The square-shaped area—dubbed "The Hub"—sat in the center of the four arms of the pediatric care ward at Travis County Hospital. It was empty, save for this shift's board nurse, Kia Jackson.

"Have you seen my SpongeBob SquarePants stethoscope sleeve?" London asked as she approached the chest-high counter. "I can't find it anywhere."

"Have you checked in a pineapple under the sea?" Kia asked.

"You're a better nurse than comedian," London said to the twentysomething who'd started at County around the same time she had. She gestured at the tray of cookies to Kia's right. "How much for a white chocolate macadamia?"

"Sorry, but those are Carmen's favorites. I love you, Doc, but no one messes with the charge nurse's cookies unless they want to get got."

London looked over both shoulders. "Yeah, well, I'm not afraid of Carmen," she lied, reaching over the counter and snagging a cookie. "If you see my stethoscope sleeve hanging around anywhere, please let me know. It's Jason Milner's favorite. I want to make sure I'm wearing it when he wakes up from his surgery."

The earliest lesson she'd learned about working in the pediatric ward: Do whatever you can to disguise medical equipment and help kids forget they're in a hospital.

"Will do," Kia said. She arched a brow as she looked past London. "You'd better finish that cookie."

A gruff voice called out, "I'm short two CNAs and someone needs to answer for it."

London stuffed the entire half of the cookie in her mouth just as Carmen Francis, the charge nurse who had been at this hospital since Moses was a toddler, came stomping up to the nurses' station.

"It's a good thing I work in a hospital, because I swear these people are trying to give me a heart attack," Carmen said. She wore a barrette with tiny gardenias at the part in her salt-and-pepper 'fro today. London speculated that her various hair ornaments were an attempt to soften her brusqueness, but it didn't work. The woman was terrifying.

London gave both nurses a wave, intending to haul ass before Carmen took an account of the white chocolate macadamia cookies, but the charge nurse stopped her with a terse "Dr. Kelley, one minute."

London prayed she didn't choke on the cookie as she swallowed. She cleared her throat.

"Yes, Carmen?"

Unlike the other doctors on the floor, London had been given permission to call Carmen by her first name. A right earned after London approached the hospital administration on the nurses' behalf regarding understaffing and mandatory overtime. Even the attending physicians addressed her as Nurse Francis or Miss Francis.

What could she say? The nurses loved her.

"Have you heard anything about the meeting happening this morning?" Carmen asked. "Nurses weren't invited. Even the ones who have been here for decades."

"I heard the meeting is about Dr. Myers announcing his retirement," Kia said. "His *forced* retirement. His wife is *demanding* it. And I think we all know why."

Carmen plopped a hand on her hip. "What did I tell you about spreading rumors?"

"But is it a rumor if it's true?" The intercom system buzzed, and a woman's soft voice came through a speaker, asking for a nurse's assistance. Kia pressed a button and replied, "I'll be right there."

As she pushed away from the desk, she said, "The redhead with the freckles that started in accounting last month? You haven't seen her around, have you?" She held up her hands. "I'm just saying."

"Go check on the patient," Carmen said.

The minute Kia was out of earshot, London asked, "Any truth to Dr. Myers and the redhead?"

The charge nurse folded her arms over her ample chest. "Really, Dr. Kelley?"

Her clipped tone had London rushing to apologize, but before she could, Carmen said, "Of course Myers was slipping her the banana, but I doubt that's what this meeting is about. Myers has been doing that kind of thing for years." Carmen leaned in closer. "This is about money."

London nodded. That slipping-the-banana reference had robbed her of speech.

"I'll let you know if I hear anything else," Carmen said in a terse whisper. "You'll do the same?"

"Of course," London said. "You know I've got the nurses' back."

Carmen gave her two solid pats on the shoulder before pivoting on her heel and marching back down the hallway.

London's Apple Watch buzzed with a reminder that rounds would be starting in five minutes.

She rushed to her office, which was basically a broom closet that had been converted into an office. But she was one of only a few residents in this hospital who had been given their own space, so she didn't complain.

She rummaged through the drawer where she kept her various props for making surgical rounds, retrieving a red clown nose; a lapel pin featuring Olaf, the talking snowman from *Frozen*; and her Spider-Man stethoscope sleeve. She attached the pin to her lab coat and stuck the rubber nose in her pocket, then gave her desk a once-over, making sure she had everything she needed just in case she didn't have a chance to come back to her office before this morning's much-speculated-about meeting. It was set to begin at eleven, which meant she needed to get to her rounds if she wanted to attend.

First on the list was Aubrey Charles. London had received the call to assist on the five-year-old's emergency appendectomy last night as she was driving home from Drew's hotel.

Don't think about him.

The one thing she did not need right now was a reminder of Drew Sullivan and the things she'd allowed him and his talented tongue to do to her yesterday. Or a reminder of the things she'd done to him with her own tongue.

Great, now she was thinking about it.

"Glad to see you could join us, Dr. Kelley," London heard the moment she rounded the corner.

Dr. Nigel Malone, the attending on-call for today, stood just outside Aubrey Charles's room. Two first-year residents stood on either side of him, along with one of the registered nurses, Mya Townsend.

"Good morning," London said to the team as a whole. She nodded at the attending. "Dr. Malone."

He returned her nod with a sharp one of his own.

She'd learned when it came to this particular attending physician, it was better to just let his attitude roll off her back. London was convinced Nigel Malone spent his evenings studying TV medical dramas so he could emulate the one doctor who was always a jerk. The man was straight out of central casting.

"You assisted in the surgery last night, so you should run point," Malone said.

"I'm happy to," she answered. She pasted on her *doctors aren't scary* smile and opened the door.

"Good morning," she greeted as she entered the brightly colored room.

Each room on the pediatrics floor had a different theme. There was the Jungle, Under the Sea, the Circus, the Hot-Air Balloon, the Fairy Princess, and the Rodeo. It was something she had pushed for when she first started at County, after reading a study on the effects hospital aesthetics play in the recovery of young children. When the administration had balked at the cost, she'd offered to paint the rooms herself. Thankfully, they had coughed up the funds in the end because her artistic skills left much to be desired.

"How are we feeling?" London asked. She looked to

Aubrey's mother, whose bloodshot eyes and rumpled clothing spoke volumes. "Last night was a bit scary for both you and Mom, wasn't it?" she asked. Aubrey's blond pigtails bounced with her nod.

"I know," London said as she slipped the stethoscope's earpieces in her ears and held the chest piece to the girl's abdomen. "But you have nothing to worry about because you made it through surgery like a champ." She moved the drumhead around, listening for anything abnormal and breathing a sigh of relief when she found nothing.

"All sounds good to me," London said as she slung the stethoscope around her neck. She reached into her pocket. "You're not the only one who's been feeling a bit under the weather. I can't stop blowing my nose." She twisted away and quickly popped on the clown nose. "Any idea what could be wrong?"

The little girl, along with one of the first-years, burst into giggles.

London gasped. "Are you laughing at me?"

Aubrey nodded emphatically. She pointed at London's nose. "Can I have it?"

"Aubrey," Ms. Charles admonished.

"Hey, if anyone can pull off this look, it's you," London said. She looked to the girl's mother for permission, placing the foam nose over Aubrey's after getting the okay. "Oh, yes, honey. This nose was made for you. Now, if you follow the nurse's orders, we may be able to release you by tomorrow morning." She wiggled the nose.

"That soon?" Ms. Charles asked.

"Yes," Dr. Malone answered.

Because of course he had to assert his authority. London suppressed the urge to roll her eyes.

"That wouldn't be the case if Aubrey's appendix had ruptured before we could take it out," London said. "But Mom got you here just in time. High five to Mom." London held her hand up to the girl's mother. She turned to Aubrey. "And to you, because you are a rock star. I'll be back in to check on you this afternoon," she said with a wink.

She turned to leave, but stopped at Ms. Charles's feebly uttered "Uh... Dr. Kelley?"

All five members of the medical staff looked back in unison.

"Yes?" London answered.

Dr. Malone cleared his throat. "Dr. Kelley, we have to continue with rounds."

"Please go ahead," London said. "I'll catch up in a minute."

His thin lips became nearly nonexistent as they pulled into a tight frown, but he only nodded and led the others out of the room.

"I'm sorry," Ms. Charles said, peering nervously at Malone's back.

"No worries at all," London said. "How can I help you?"

"First, I wanted to thank you for everything you did for Aubrey last night. You literally saved her life."

"You saved her by getting her here in time," London countered. "Thank *you* for not trying to diagnose her yourself with Google."

Her cheeks turned crimson. "I did Google her symptoms first," she said. "It's how I knew things were serious." She bit her bottom lip as she shot a quick glance at her daughter. "You're probably way too busy to concern yourself with this, but do you have any idea how much all of this will cost? I make too much to qualify for Medicaid, but my health insurance's deductible is sixty-five hundred dollars."

"That is the last thing you should be worrying about," London said.

"Well, it's all I can think about."

London covered her hand. "The hospital will work with you. I'll talk to someone in accounting, if necessary. Right now, your focus should be on Aubrey and her recovery. And I know it's difficult, but try to get a little sleep. You can't care for Aubrey unless you first take care of yourself."

"That's such a nice way of telling me I have bags under my eyes." The woman laughed.

London squeezed her hand. "You've been through a lot in the past twenty-four hours, but everything will work out."

As she exited the room, London released a string of curse words under her breath. How many worried parents had she comforted over these past five years whose concern about going bankrupt was as virulent as their worry over their sick children? It was unacceptable for a country as wealthy as this one to have any person stressing about hospital bills.

London caught up to the team and continued rounds, visiting three more patients on the main wing and another two in the PICU. She finished just in time for her ten a.m. hernioplasty.

It took longer than usual for the patient to respond to general anesthesia—the one thing she could not control in the operating room—so the surgery ran over by nearly twenty minutes. After leaving instructions with the post-op team, she shucked off her PPE and deposited it in the discard bin for personal protective equipment on her way out the door. She quickly went through her ritualistic post-surgery cleanup and then took off for the first floor, where today's meeting was being held.

London slipped in just as Dr. Coleman started to speak. The room was packed with people from every department, eager to hear news about the fate of the hospital. He began with his usual monologue about the state of public medicine and the important role it played in the well-being of Austin's residents.

So why in the hell were you considering selling this public *hospital to a* private *company?*

The question was on the tip of London's tongue, but she refrained from saying anything just yet. One of her colleagues had bet her that she couldn't get through five minutes of a meeting without playing devil's advocate, so London had made it a personal challenge to wait at least ten minutes before speaking up.

She looked around the room for Aleshia Williams, the head of radiology and her closest confidant here at the hospital. As her gaze roamed over those seated at the oval table in the center of the conference room, she stopped short and squinted in confusion.

It took several seconds to register that she was indeed looking at Drew Sullivan. He stared back at her, his face expressionless except for his eyes, which were piercing. Knowing.

What in the hell was *he* doing here?

"News of a potential sale of the hospital has been the poorest-kept secret in town," Dr. Coleman was saying. "The rumors were never confirmed or denied by anyone on the board, but I can tell you now that, yes, we have been discussing selling the hospital to a private firm. There are a number of factors the board of directors and hospital administration have weighed these past few months, and we've come to a decision."

London held her breath.

"Before we take the next steps, we've decided to bring in consultants to audit our finances and procedures so that we can have a clearer picture of what we're dealing with," Dr. Coleman continued. "And this is the gentleman who will help us get to that clearer picture."

Dr. Coleman turned in his seat and motioned to Drew, who sat a few chairs down from him.

"I would like you all to meet Drew Sullivan. Drew is a partner in Trident Health Management Systems, which specializes in revenue generation, overhauling information technology, and reallocating resources so they are used to the hospital's best advantage."

That son of a bitch.

London started to speak, but a familiar voice beat her to it.

"So, what does this mean regarding the sale of the hospital? Is that off the table?" Aleshia asked from where she stood in the corner of the conference room. She was on the same side of the room as London, which was why she hadn't seen her.

"I want to caution everyone that Trident's involvement doesn't mean a sale is imminent," Dr. Coleman said. "Nor does it mean that it is out of the question. We're still in the assessment stage, and we will be deciding our next steps once Mr. Sullivan and his team complete their work. The board of directors is asking for the staff's support. You may not realize it, but this is a compromise. Half the board voted for an outright sale."

There were murmurs throughout the conference room.

London was so mad she could barely see straight. She crossed her arms over her chest and squeezed them tight in an effort to curb the anxiety pressing against her skin. Her head started to throb at her temples, a sure sign she needed to calm down.

"Trident will be here for the next three to four weeks. Trina Erickson from HR will be contacting many of you over the next few days to schedule an interview time with members of the audit team. We expect full participation and expect honest, unbiased answers from *our* team."

The hint of reprimand London heard in Coleman's voice went down her spine like a cheese grater. If there was one thing she could not abide, it was that paternalistic bullshit. They were professionals and adults, and not a damn one of them needed Coleman to play the role of daddy. She didn't put up with that shit from her own father.

"That's it for now," Dr. Coleman said. "When you run into members of the Trident team around the hospital, give them a warm Texas welcome."

London knew one member of the team that she wanted to run into. With her Mini Cooper.

The ancient relic of a beeper she carried—okay, she would admit they could use help in the technology department—went off, paging her to the PICU, where her hernioplasty had just been wheeled in for recovery. She waited a second, just long enough to catch Drew's attention, and pointed her middle finger at him before leaving the conference room.

7

Drew's leg bobbed nervously underneath the table as he waited for the man next to him to finish opining on the necessity of raising insurance premiums on a yearly basis so that people didn't get too comfortable. Drew wished he could rip into this asshole. How had someone like this even made it to a public hospital's board of directors?

A better question: How had *he* been roped into this conversation?

He'd tried to make a getaway the moment the meeting was over, but Dr. Coleman had pulled him into a discussion with two members of the board. He'd kept his eyes on London long enough to see her flip him her middle finger, and then she was gone.

Blindsiding her like this was a dick move. Even if he hadn't meant to blindside her.

He should have told her that he would be working at County the moment she mentioned the hospital back at the reunion. He'd started to tell her later when they were in his hotel room, but he'd gotten distracted by the sight of her stripping out of that cherry-red jumpsuit.

It was no excuse. He'd had ample opportunity over these

past couple of days to disclose that he was in charge of the company that would be conducting the audit. Would she have been pissed? Yes. *Hell* yes. But he should have been straight with her regardless of the potential backlash.

He needed to find her. He owed her an explanation.

Drew pushed his chair back from the table.

"I appreciate the introduction to Travis County Hospital, gentlemen, but I need to make sure the folks from my team are getting settled into their various spaces around the facility. We have another meeting scheduled tomorrow, at Dr. Coleman's request. I will be able to fill you all in on everything you need to know then."

Remembering tomorrow's meeting reminded Drew that he needed to discuss time allocation with Dr. Coleman. The man had already scheduled three meetings for their first week. Drew planned to curb this practice pretty damn quick. His disdain for useless meetings was well-known throughout Trident and the Meacham Group, the hedge fund where he'd worked prior to starting this venture. If it couldn't be handled via email, it could wait until the weekly office-wide meeting. The *once* weekly office-wide meeting.

Drew stopped at the hospital directory near the information desk, then boarded the elevator and rode it to the third floor. It let him off just outside the nurses' station. He went to the desk only to find it empty.

"Can I help you?"

He turned to find a tall Black woman in blue hospital scrubs marching toward him. The scowl on her face declared that she was too busy to deal with anyone's bullshit.

"Can I help you?" she repeated as she approached.

"Ah, yes, I'm looking for Dr. London Kelley," Drew said.

"She's with a patient." The woman scrutinized the identification badge on his lapel.

Drew stuck his hand out to her. "I don't think we've met. I'm Drew Sullivan with Trident Health Management Systems. We're conducting an audit of the hospital."

Her expression didn't change. Nor did she accept his handshake.

Well, damn. He guessed word had already traveled around the hospital that he was in league with the enemy.

"I'll handle this, Carmen."

Drew twisted around at the sound of London's voice. She marched with the same sense of purpose as the older nurse, but she somehow made it look sexy as hell. It should be a rule that no doctor should look so damn good wearing hospital scrubs.

Drew nodded at the nurse. "Thank you, Carmen."

"That's Nurse Francis," the woman answered. She hitched her chin at London. "She's the only one who gets to call me Carmen."

"I see you're making new friends," London said. She grabbed him by the arm. "This way."

Yeah, she was pissed.

Drew followed her down the opposite hallway. Once they reached the second-to-last door, London opened it and waited for him to enter the tiny room ahead of her. The moment she shut the door, she whaled on him.

"You are a lying son of a bitch, Drew Sullivan."

"I know I should have told you."

"You're fucking right you should have told me," she hissed.

Drew figured the only reason she wasn't screaming at the top of her lungs was that she didn't want her young patients hearing their doctor curse like a sailor.

"You knew damn well that you would be working in *my* hospital, and you said *nothing*!" She plunked her hands on her hips. "What did I tell you Saturday night before we slept together? That I wanted to hook up with someone I wouldn't have to see every day. That was my only rule when it came to this random sex business. According to Dr. Coleman, I'm going to have to see your lying ass every day for the next month!"

Technically, he didn't plan to be at the hospital every single day, but he was pretty sure that wouldn't make a difference to her right now.

There was a knock at the door.

"Come in," London practically growled.

The door opened about six inches. "Umm . . . Dr. Kelley?"

"Yes, come in," she repeated, this time in a calmer voice.

It opened all the way, and a baby-faced blonde wearing green scrubs and a white coat that was shorter than London's stepped into the office. "Sorry to disturb you, Dr. Kelley, but Nurse Beverly in Obstetrics sent me. She wanted to know if you've had a chance to discuss the staffing issue with Dr. Waller?"

London threw her head back and sighed up at the ceiling. "I haven't," she admitted. "Tell her that I'll talk to Waller before the end of the day. I promise."

The other doctor smiled before turning and closing the door behind her.

"Well?" London asked once she and Drew were alone again.

He hooked his thumb toward the door. "You're in pediatric surgery. Why are you handling an issue for Obstetrics instead of someone from that department?"

"Because their nurses don't feel as comfortable with some

of the residents and attendings as they do with me," she said. "And we're not talking about the nurses in Obstetrics right now. You were about to explain why I had to find out you were working at County this morning in front of half the hospital."

"I have no excuse," Drew said, lifting his hands in surrender. He hadn't been straight with her this weekend, but he would do so now. His honesty would likely earn him a black eye, but that's the price he would have to pay. "I should have told you about Trident's new contract with County at the reunion. If not at the reunion, then definitely once we went up to my room. Or when you came back to my room to get your purse on Sunday."

The anger that flashed across her face was so intense that, for a moment, Drew feared for his safety. But being a surgeon, she wouldn't use her hands to hurt him. They were too precious to her profession. She was more likely to deliver a swift kick to his groin.

Lucky for him, London had more restraint than a lot of women he knew.

"You are such an asshole," she said. "I *knew* better than to trust you." She folded her arms across her chest and perched on the edge of the desk. "You know, I called this," she continued. "I figured this was all some elaborate joke for you. A stupid game of one-upmanship so that you can have the upper hand."

"Wait a minute. You think I slept with you as a joke? To try to get the better of you?"

"Don't try to deny it."

"You're way off base here." He shook his head. "You want to believe I'm an asshole for keeping you in the dark about my work at County? Go for it. That's fair. But I would never sleep with you under false pretenses, or as part of some twisted game to gain a competitive edge against you. I'm not *that* much of an asshole."

"So, why didn't you say anything? We talked for hours Saturday night. I must have mentioned the hospital a dozen times. Not once did you think to say, 'Oh, hey, guess what, London? I'll be there on Monday.'"

He had no answer.

"I'm sorry," Drew said, because he *was* sorry for not being totally honest with her. But he would never be sorry for Saturday night. Or Sunday afternoon.

"I messed up and I'm sorry," he said again. She stared at him, her face impassive. "And, obviously, you're not ready to accept my apology at the moment."

"If ever," she stated.

Drew tilted his head back and sighed. "Look, London, I know things may get a bit awkward now that we've seen each other naked, but we don't have to make a big deal out of this. This weekend was something that happened. We both enjoyed it. Now we can move on."

She pointed to her chest. "*I* decide what is or isn't a big deal for me, okay? You don't get to tell me how I should feel about any of this." She looked him up and down. "And I didn't enjoy it *that* much."

"Bullshit," Drew flung out before he could stop himself. He held up both hands. "Fine, you're pissed. And with good reason. But I have marks on my shoulders from you biting the hell out of me when you came. You can lie to yourself if you want to, but I have no problem admitting that was some of the best sex I've ever had. And don't think for a minute that I'll believe it wasn't the same for you."

He propped his hands on his hips and stared at her, challenging her to deny his words. London's chest rose and fell, her nostrils flaring with each breath she took.

"You arrogant bastard," she ground out between clenched teeth. "I can't believe I fucked you while sober."

"Multiple times," Drew shot back. If he was going to be on her shit list from now until eternity, there was no need for him to pull any punches.

But, dammit, that's *not* what he wanted.

He wanted to go back to Sunday afternoon, when she lay in his bed basking in post-orgasmic bliss. If he'd told her about Trident's contract with the hospital then, she would have been upset, but not this upset. Then again, this was London. She may have had this same reaction no matter when he'd told her.

It was irrelevant at this point. He was here to do a job, one that was crucial to this community. He wouldn't allow London's feelings to get in the way of completing the task at hand.

Drew approached every contract with the goal of performing beyond the client's expectations, but when it came to *this* particular contract, he couldn't help but feel more invested than usual. More than 70 percent of Travis County Hospital's patients lived below the poverty line. He'd been in their shoes. Hell, it was only a few years ago that he'd stopped waking up in a cold sweat, fearing everything would come crashing down on him and he'd end up right back in their shoes.

It wasn't hyperbole to assume that some of the people who walked through this hospital's doors would die if County were no longer an option for them. It was his job to make sure it never came to that.

Which meant he and London would have to put their differences aside. She may not like it, but they were on the same team.

"I've apologized," Drew said. "Whether you accept my apology is up to you, but I can't let this, or you, disrupt my work."

"*I'm* a disruption?" She barked out a harsh laugh. "This is *my* hospital. You're the interloper here."

"Dr. Coleman and the rest of the hospital's administration don't see me as an interloper. They brought me here. I suggest you get on board."

For half a breath, Drew was certain she was going to deck him. Instead, she marched to the door. "Get out, Drew. If you see me in the hallway, pretend you don't know me."

Even though he knew she was probably the angriest she had ever been with him, her words still shocked and stung.

As he moved past her, he caught the subtle floral scent he'd consumed while skimming his lips along her neck, and behind her ear, and in the bend of her knee this weekend. A brutal pang of longing spasmed within his chest.

He stopped just after crossing the threshold and turned.

"For what it's worth, I really am sorry I didn't just tell you the truth from the very beginning, London."

"It's Dr. Kelley," she said.

Then she shut the door in his face.

8

London had never been so grateful for an emergency bowel obstruction in all her life.

Two patients had been brought into the ER within the last hour, both needing immediate attention. As much as she hated to see anyone in pain, she'd desperately needed the distraction this case had brought to her day.

Anything to keep her mind off that shady son of a bitch.

Her hand tightened into a fist just at the thought of Drew Sullivan and what he'd done. He could take that pitiful excuse for an apology he'd tried to feed her and choke on it.

The worst thing—the absolute *worst* thing in *all* of this—was that she still wanted that motherfucker!

She'd specifically told him that she didn't want to sleep with someone she would have to see every day. He *knew* he would be working at her hospital and he'd said nothing! It was low-down and she would never forgive him.

She would consider fucking him again, though.

"No, you will not!" London scolded.

She mentally collected all thoughts of Drew and locked them away. She had more important things to focus on, namely the fifteen-year-old who had been on her operating table an hour ago.

The teen girl, who had been brought in by her cheerleading coach after collapsing in pain at a competition, had more scar tissue in her large intestine than London had ever seen in a patient, which meant she'd had multiple procedures done. London had spent the past half hour reviewing records that had been emailed from Driscoll Children's Hospital in Brownsville, where the girl lived. She wanted to have some answers for her parents when they arrived following the five-hour drive up from the border town.

Although London had seen the distress in countless eyes before, she couldn't imagine the anxiety parents faced in this situation. Now that she had operated on their daughter, it was her job to put them at ease and figure out what could be done to prevent these repeated bowel obstructions from occurring.

There was a knock on her door.

"Come in," London said without looking up from the iPad she cradled in her lap.

"Heard you scrubbed in on that interesting bowel obstruction case," Aleshia Williams said as she entered the office. "I just saw the scans that were ordered before surgery. It looks pretty nasty."

"It is, thank goodness." London gasped as she looked up at Aleshia, whose expression was rightly horrified. "That came out the wrong way," London said.

She set the iPad on the desk and rubbed her temples. "It's not that I'm happy this poor girl's intestines are so scarred. It's just been... it's been a damn day." She took a sip of lukewarm water from the refillable water bottle Taylor had bought her. "I needed the distraction of this case."

"I understand. I'm still pretty pissed after this morning's meeting."

If only this morning's meeting were the sole issue fucking up her day right now.

Actually, this morning's meeting *was* at the crux of it all, because it's where she'd discovered that Drew would be working in this hospital.

"I guess we should be grateful that the board has brought in this consulting firm," Aleshia continued. "It would have been a lot worse if they'd decided to just sell the hospital outright."

Any other day, London would have immediately agreed with her. But when she was still damn near ballistic over her confrontation with Drew, if given the choice between the hospital being privately owned or seeing Drew every day, she might just pick option number one.

"Let me know if you need any help with the bowel obstruction case," Aleshia offered.

"Thanks," London said. Once Aleshia left, she returned her attention to the iPad, but then her desk phone rang. "Dr. Kelley," she answered.

London's eyes fell shut as she listened to the person on the other end of the line. Ten minutes later, she was sitting in a chair that had seen better days, opposite Dr. Douglas Renault, the man who had convinced her to transfer to the residency program at County following her first year at a private hospital.

After three minutes of waiting for him to get off the phone, London had decided to take a seat, even though he hadn't given her permission. She and Doug Renault shared a unique relationship. Basically, he allowed her to get away with shit most residents wouldn't even attempt to pull.

She slouched back in her chair and folded her hands over her stomach as Dr. Renault gave her an *I'm almost done* look. A second later, he ended the call.

"Why do I feel as if I've been called to the principal's office?" London asked before he could speak.

"Why are you giving Coleman a hard time?" Renault asked.

"What?" She sat up straight. "I haven't said a thing to Coleman all day." Even though she'd wanted to light into him.

"He said you gave him a look in the meeting this morning."

"Are you kidding me?"

"When you have a reputation for being the squeaky wheel, sometimes you're heard even when you don't speak."

"So, I'm now being called out for the way I *look* at people?"

"We've had this conversation before."

"Yes, we have. And with all due respect, Dr. D—"

"Cut the 'all due respect' crap, London. Give it to me straight."

"Fine," she said. "You want to know the truth? People like Coleman take the joy out of working here."

"Coleman has a hard job to do too. This hospital has been running at a deficit for the past decade—"

"So has this country, but no one is talking about selling it to the highest bidder." Dr. Renault stared at her with a raised brow. "Okay, that was a bad example. Still," London said. "Coleman and his crew have refused to listen to anyone who's tried to provide solutions. There's a group of us who have been working on other paths the hospital can take—myself, Aleshia Williams in Radiology, Lennox Templeton in Ortho, Joslyn—"

Renault held up his hands. "That's all well and good, but I don't know how much of a difference that will make with the board of directors. They're doing what they think is best for the hospital." He pointed at her. "You have a laundry list of projects you want to implement—something most hospitals wouldn't even entertain from a resident."

"It's because my ideas add value to patient care," she said.

"It's because you have more fans on the staff than that NSYNC band, and they all get behind whatever you champion."

"Umm, again, with all due respect, Dr. D, NSYNC hasn't released an album in twenty years. And calling other staff members my fans is a bit...icky."

"How else do you explain it," he said. "Your influence at this hospital is unprecedented, especially for a resident. You had this rock star aura about you because of that solo cholecystectomy when you were a first-year, and it has only gotten stronger." He held up his hands. "I'm not saying it's a bad thing. Just be mindful of it, London. People listen to you. They look up to you."

London would argue that that surgery four years ago had nothing to do with it. People listened to her because she treated everyone with the dignity and respect they deserved, from the nurses, to the security guards, to the custodians.

"And here's another thing you need to be mindful of," Renault continued. "Those ideas you want to implement? They're good, but they cost money. It sounds as if this new consulting firm may give at least one of those programs a fighting chance, so you'd better choose wisely."

London paused for a moment before saying, "What if I decide to go somewhere that doesn't make me choose?"

Renault's brow arched again. "Is that something you've been thinking about?"

If he only knew how frequently other hospitals tried to poach her away from this place.

London had gained a reputation as a first-year resident when the doctor who was performing a gallbladder surgery had a breakdown and quit in the middle of the procedure. She immediately took over in a way that would later be described by members of the surgical team as something you see on TV. It had made news around the medical community, both for the doctor's bizarre mid-surgery departure and her swift action. Doug Renault had lured her to County soon after.

Now that she was nearing the end of her residency here, she received offers on a fairly regular basis from hospitals around the country. She'd glanced at their emails and accepted a few virtual meetings but had never entertained the idea of actually leaving Austin.

Until the most recent inquiry.

One of Chicago's most distinguished hospital systems had been hounding her—that was the only word she could use to describe their constant emails—for the past two months. They'd floated an offer for a surgical fellowship that was so lucrative London had questioned whether the email had a typo. But it wasn't just the money. The prestige that would come with this position would give her the chance to dabble in the speaker circuit. If she *was* interested in filling her bank account, that's where the real money resided.

But the biggest thing the hospital in Chicago had going for it, by far, was Dr. Eveline Mayberry. The legendary surgeon was one of London's biggest idols. She was an idol for every young Black female doctor London knew. She could not just dismiss the opportunity to work with *THE* Eveline Mayberry out of hand, especially with Coleman becoming more hostile by the minute. If not for her patients, and how invested she'd become in their lives, she would give Chicago some serious consideration.

"Look," Renault said. "This hospital is lucky to have you. I know this. Everyone here knows this."

And some resented her for it.

Some, like Frederick Coleman, thought she was too cocky. As a woman, she was expected to be demure and modest, and to allow her male counterparts to take the lead whenever possible. The bastard had actually said that in a staff meeting. As if they were still living in the mid-twentieth century instead of moving at lightning speed toward the middle of the twenty-first.

"I'm at County because I want to be here," London said. "I remain here because I care about my patients, because I know that they're often given the table scraps when it comes to health care. I want to continue fighting for them, but some of the people here aren't making it easy, Dr. Renault."

"Just give them time," he said. "Let's see what this consulting firm will do." He folded his hands on his desk and asked, "Now, what about that other thing?"

London averted her eyes.

"I'm fine," she mumbled.

"Dr. Kelley?"

"I am fine." She enunciated each word carefully. He had a right to meet her statement with skepticism, but she resented it all the same. "I've found all kinds of ways to de-stress lately," London told him, ticking items off on her fingers. "Yoga. Crochet. S—" She almost said *sex*. "Sewing," she lied. "And I have a ton of essential oils a friend recommended I diffuse. My stress level is way down these days."

"That's good to hear. But what about your blood pressure?"

She twisted in her chair and stared at the faded picture of Texas bluebonnets on the wall behind his desk.

"It could be better," London said. "But I'm handling it. You don't have to worry about me."

"Okay," he said. "Stay out of trouble."

"I'll take that under consideration," she said as she pushed herself up from the chair and left the office.

If her mentor wanted to help keep her stress level down, he really should stop bringing up the fact that her blood pressure had moved from "elevated" to "get your ass on a beta-blocker—pronto" in the last month.

It began with what she thought was just a regular tension headache, but when she felt a slight dizziness, she'd taken her BP, just to be on the safe side. She'd stared at the sphygmomanometer in disbelief for a solid three minutes, convinced there must be something wrong with the blood pressure cuff.

The hypertension diagnosis shouldn't have surprised her, yet she hadn't been ready when her general practitioner confirmed the news. It was the ultimate gag gift from her dear father, who hadn't given her so much as an "atta girl, London" in twenty years, yet had passed along his shitty genes and hereditary coronary disease.

Even though her privacy was protected under HIPAA, London had felt obligated to tell Dr. Renault about her diagnosis. Now she wasn't so sure she should have told him anything. He nagged her like a mother hen—emailing her literature on the latest ACE-inhibitors as if she weren't a doctor who could find this information for herself.

London made a mental note to skim the most recent one

he'd sent. She'd bookmarked the website but hadn't had time to look it over.

Hmm...maybe if she told Renault that having Drew's consulting firm here at the hospital only added to her stress, he would make sure London didn't have to deal with him?

Yeah, and then she would have to explain to Renault *why* Drew added to her stress. No, thank you.

By the time she arrived back on her floor, her bowel obstruction patient's parents had arrived. She directed them to the minuscule consulting room, just off the nurses' station. She was able to get the surgeon who had performed their daughter's previous two surgeries in Brownsville on a Zoom call, and together they discussed possible prevention tactics so that they wouldn't find themselves in this same place a year from now.

She was grateful the pediatric surgeon from Driscoll Children's Hospital wasn't super territorial and more concerned about ego than finding the right treatment for the patient. She dealt with those types way too often and made a concerted effort to never become one.

Did she sometimes disagree with another resident's course of treatment? Of course. But as long as it was viable and wouldn't put the patient more in harm's way, London knew how to step back and allow another resident to take the lead. She was arrogant when it came to her work, but she wasn't *that* arrogant.

She was already an hour past the end of her shift by the time she finished with the family from Brownsville. London downloaded the files she wanted to look over tonight from the shared server and packed up her things so she could leave. She didn't want Dr. Renault to catch her here. One of the promises she'd made him was that she wouldn't put in the abundance of extra hours she'd been known for during these past five years.

Of course, she'd also promised that she wouldn't bring so much work home with her either. She doubted her mentor would approve of the number of case files she planned to review tonight.

She locked up her office and made her way to the elevator, hoping but failing to find any more of those cookies from this morning. The nurses had already gone through their shift change, so any leftovers would have already been inhaled by the night shift.

She got off the elevator on the second floor and walked across the enclosed bridge that connected the hospital to the covered parking garage. Her assigned spot was near the entry—a perk she'd earned for being voted Resident of the Year by fellow staff.

London's steps slowed as she reached her parking spot. Drew was standing next to her Mini.

Correction: He was *leaning on* her Mini. One hand was casually stuffed in his pants pocket—the other occupied by the cell phone he was currently scrolling through.

London hit the panic button on the key fob and took no small amount of pleasure from the way he jumped at the shrieking alarm. She quickly hit the off button before hospital security rushed over to see what was going on.

"Get away from my car," she said as she walked up to him.

"Can I please have five minutes to apologize?"

"Oh, so you agree that the bullshit you fed me in my office this morning wasn't a real apology?"

"At the risk of pissing you off even more, don't you think

you're being a bit dramatic about this?" He held up his hands. "Look, I'm not trying to tell you how you should feel. If this is a big deal to you, then fine, it's a big deal. But what happened this weekend shouldn't have an impact on the work we have to do here at the hospital. One is personal, the other is professional."

London closed the distance between them, getting right in his face.

"Don't lecture me on how to keep my personal and professional lives separate, Drew Sullivan. It's a skill I've been forced to use more times than you will ever have to. I wouldn't be able to sleep at night if I wasn't able to block out some of the shit I see here."

"You're right. I'm sorry," he said. "I'm not trying to make comparisons. I can't imagine how hard your job must be. But that's why we need to work together if we're going to help make things better here at County."

He slipped his hands in his pockets, his relaxed pose like something out of an ad campaign for a top-of-the-line suit designer. He'd removed his tie at some point during the day and unbuttoned the top two buttons on the light blue shirt.

Her eyes zeroed in on the tantalizing indentation at the base of his throat. Her mouth now had intimate knowledge of that sexy dip.

She tore her gaze away.

Stay focused.

"Here's what I think we should do—" Drew said.

She cut him off. "I just love how you keep using the word *we* so casually."

"I used *we* because I need us to be on the same team. After only a few hours I recognize how well respected you are around here. I visited various departments today, trying to gain insight into how County's personnel regards the hospital overall. Whenever I asked what people found most favorable, your name came up. If Trident is going to be successful in completing the task we've been handed, we're going to need allies like you, London."

"Ally?" She couldn't help it; she burst out laughing. "Did you miss the part when I said that I am *against* what the administration is doing at the hospital?"

"Did *you* miss the part about how Trident is here to possibly prevent the hospital from being sold?"

"Possibly," she said. "Which means it possibly could still happen."

"Better than definitely," he countered.

London bit her bottom lip.

He had a point. Coleman said that half the hospital's board was ready to put up a FOR SALE sign. London and her colleagues had been trying to read the tea leaves for months, but it was clear now. Drew's company could very well be the only thing standing between County remaining a public hospital or being taken over by some profit-hungry conglomerate.

She would be *such* a fool to trust him after the way he'd kept her in the dark about the real reason he was back in Austin, but could she trust the hospital's top brass?

"*If* I felt the inclination to help you—which I still haven't decided yet," London stressed. "What would it take to change that possibly into a definitely—as it pertains to preventing a sale?"

"There are no guarantees, London. You know that."

She threw up her hands. "Then why should I help you at all? Why should I use my hard-earned capital with the staff to make your job easier when there's still a chance the hospital will be sold to the highest bidder once you're done?"

"Because—"

"Because nothing," she said. "Everyone will think I sold them out." She shook her head. "Sorry, Drew, but I can't do that."

He dropped his head back and groaned. "You are stubborn as hell. Always have been."

"Oh, that will *certainly* help your case," she deadpanned. "Please, pay me more compliments."

"Shit," he cursed.

"I can't believe you thought I would just go along with this, especially after your lack of transparency this weekend," London said. She tipped her head to the side as a thought occurred to her. "Is that what Saturday night was about? Was that your way of softening me up? You thought after spending the night in your bed that I'd be more agreeable when I walked into the conference room and found you sitting next to Coleman?"

He took a step toward her. "Are you forgetting whose idea Saturday night was? Or Sunday afternoon? It was yours, London. *Both* times." His voice dropped in volume, the tone huskier. Sexier. "I didn't have an agenda to get you into my bed because you invited *yourself* there, not the other way around."

"Who's bringing up the personal now?" London asked.

She stared him directly in the face, refusing to back down despite the urge to close her eyes and relive just a few of those sublime moments from this weekend.

He was so close she could feel his heat, smell the subtle spicy scent of his cologne.

"This audit is happening, whether you're for it or not," he

said, his voice unyielding. "Don't make it more difficult than it has to be."

Her eyes landed once again on that sexy dip in his throat, just below his Adam's apple. This time she couldn't escape the memories of the way her tongue had explored that spot this weekend.

"Screw you, Drew Sullivan," London said, the words catching as they skirted past the lump of desire clogging her throat.

"London, please. This is—"

"No, really," she said, slipping her phone from her pocket. She clicked into the folder of travel apps and, in less than a minute, had a room booked. "I quite literally mean screw you—as in I *want* to screw you." She held the phone up to him so he could see the reservation. "There's a Hampton Inn two blocks away. Meet me there."

9

London sat on the edge of the bed, her back to Drew. She could feel his eyes on her as she threaded her arms through her bra straps and hooked the eyelets behind her.

The hotel room's air-conditioning unit kicked on, but London couldn't give it credit for the goose bumps that pebbled along her skin. Those were 100 percent courtesy of the man lounging in the middle of the king-size bed.

She stopped herself from glancing back at him because she just knew she would find an arrogant, self-satisfied smirk on his face. Not that he hadn't earned the right to be conceited when it came to the particular set of skills he'd displayed in the past hour.

"Is this going to be an ongoing occurrence, or was this yet *another* onetime thing?" Drew asked.

London lifted her panties from the nightstand and stepped into them. She stood, pulling them up her legs.

"London?"

Finally, she turned. There wasn't as much conceit as she'd expected, just that normal air of self-assuredness that clung to him at all times.

"London?" he said again.

"What?" she asked with an exasperated sigh.

He arched a brow. "Are you going to answer my question?"

"I don't know, Drew."

"You don't know if you're going to answer the question, or you don't know if you're going to offer me a standing invitation to meet you at the Hampton Inn on Monday afternoons?"

The air conditioner clicked off and, despite the persistent goose bumps that remained on her arms, London walked over to the thermostat to lower it. She pushed her fingers through her naturally coily hair, scraping her nails along her scalp.

"Give me a minute to think about this," she said.

"What's there to think about?"

She didn't answer him, opting instead to walk over to the minifridge and help herself to a bottle of water. Resting her butt against the desk, she gulped down half of it, peering directly into Drew's dark brown eyes as she did so. Her eyes lowered, skimming over the smooth, chiseled planes of his chest and torso.

Didn't this bastard spend most of his day behind a desk? How could he be so cut?

The bedsheet stopped just below the sexy indentions at his waist, where the inguinal ligament and transversus abdominis met.

For goodness' sake, girl, this isn't Anatomy 101.

"How long do you plan to be in Austin?" London asked abruptly.

"Until Trident's work at County is completed."

She took another gulp of water. "And once you're done, you go back to New York?"

"It *is* where I live."

She studied him, taking in the rudimentary Greek letter

branded into his chest, just above his left nipple. The omega symbol. The mark of the fraternity he belonged to. Her dad was also a member, but she wouldn't hold that against Drew.

"I can't believe I'm about to say this." She paused for a moment, then shook her head. "But you are exactly what I've been looking for, Drew Sullivan."

"It took you long enough to figure that out. I've known since high school."

There was nothing she wanted more in this world at the moment than to knock that cocky grin off his face.

"You are *such* an asshole," London said. "However, you're also the perfect hookup partner." She ticked items off on her fingers. "You're temporary, you sling dick like you've taken a master class on it, and there's not a chance in hell of me ever falling for you."

London couldn't be sure if the light in his eyes had actually dimmed a fraction, or if the change was due to his movement as he pushed himself up so that his back was against the headboard. His adjustment caused the sheet to fall even lower, barely covering his lap. She had to clutch the edge of the desk to stop herself from going to him. She wanted to crawl up the bed and plant herself on that lap.

"Why, London," he said in a droll voice, "how could I ever turn down such a romantic proposal?"

"Do I come across as the romantic type?"

He didn't answer. Instead, he folded his arms behind his head, and asked, "Why me?"

"I thought I just went over that," she said. "Believe it or not, you're literally what the doctor ordered, Drew." His brow arched in inquiry, so London decided to explain. "My job—my life in general—has been overly demanding lately.

My mentor at the hospital, Dr. Doug Renault, suggested I find ways to decrease my stress. My two best friends, Samiah and Taylor, believe casually hooking up is the perfect way to accomplish this. I wasn't entirely sure they were right, but based on how relaxed I've been since Saturday night, I have to say that sex with you has done amazing things for my stress level. Much better than crocheting."

He barked out a laugh. "That's one I haven't heard before, but I'll take it."

"You don't have to look so smug," London said.

"I'm not smug, I just have a high level of confidence in my ability to handle this job. Drew Sullivan, stress reliever. At your service, Dr. Kelley."

She dropped her head back and sighed up at the ceiling. "I'm going to regret this."

"I promise you won't."

His voice had dropped an octave, the deep, rich timbre adding to those goose bumps on her arms and thighs.

"If we're going to do this, we can just go over to my place," he said. "The apartment I'm renting is about the same distance from the hospital, and the bed is a lot more comfortable."

"Really?" London asked. "I was just thinking that I need to check what brand this mattress is. It's better than what I have at home."

"You sure you aren't just projecting your feelings for me toward this mattress?"

She cut her eyes at him, and he laughed.

"Joking," he said. "So, how is this going to work?" He held up a hand. "The better question is, how stressed are you? Do you require daily attention? Today *does* make three days in a row that you've had a dose of Drew."

"And just like that, I've changed my mind."

"That was a joke! Riling you up used to be my favorite pastime when we were in school. It's hard to turn it off."

"See, I knew it. Irritating me was like some weird hobby for you."

"I would have lettered in trying to get a rise out of you if they'd offered it as a sport back at Barbara Jordan High. I promise to do better," he said. He patted the bed. "Come on. Let's hammer out the details."

As if she was getting anywhere near him while he was still naked and she was in only her underwear.

Why *was* she still wearing only her underwear?

She reached over and snagged his shirt from where he'd folded it across the back of the room's lone chair. The soft material felt heavenly against her skin. London pulled the two sides across her chest and sat in the chair.

"To answer your previous question, *this* is how this is going to work." She crossed her legs, propped her elbow on her knee, and settled her chin on her fist. "First, nothing, and I mean absolutely, positively *nothing* happens at the hospital. We don't even exchange smiles there, got that?"

"Why must you make everything so difficult?"

"Got that?" London asked again.

"I got it. Only frowns and sneers while at the hospital."

She responded with a firm nod. "Second, this is just sex. I don't want to get to know you any better. I don't need to hear about your hopes and dreams for the future. The only thing I'm interested in is racking up as many orgasms as I can before you leave town. Wham bam, thank you, Drew."

"Have you ever considered writing greeting cards as a side gig? It's a shame to let all that sentimentality go to waste."

London rolled her eyes. "I would add 'no speaking' to the list, but you would never go for that."

Before she knew what he was doing, Drew threw off the sheet and swung his legs off the side of the bed. He stood and started for her, his naked body looking like a vision from some ambitious director's idea of upmarket porn.

She quickly stood, not wanting to be at a disadvantage.

Drew stopped just inches away. His deep brown chest, covered with a light dusting of hair, was close enough for her to feel the heat radiating from it.

"These are the terms that *you* will agree to," Drew said. "We meet at my place whenever you're feeling stressed and need to work off some steam on my much more comfortable bed. However, at least once a week, we meet up for dinner or even just coffee. Outside of the hospital, of course. I agree about keeping the personal and professional separate."

"I'm not dating you, Drew."

"I'm not dating you either. That's not what I'm suggesting."

"Going out for dinner? What is that if not a date?"

He shrugged. "Two people don't have to date in order to go to dinner. Think of it as hanging out with a former classmate and friend."

"I'm not your friend."

"And I won't be some faceless dick you screw and forget about. Despite what you may have thought about me all this time, I actually *do* have some standards, and one of them is not being used." His brow hitched. "So? What's it going to be?"

London stared him down, refusing to so much as blink as she considered his terms. The tension between them pulsed like a heartbeat, the steady thump escalating with each second that passed.

She blinked first.

"Fine, you son of a bitch." She latched on to his shoulders and pulled him to her. Drew caught her by the waist and lifted her up, setting her on the desk.

"For the record, I still don't like you," London said.

"But you don't have to like me to fuck me." He threw her words from Saturday night back at her.

"You got that right," she said, wrapping her arms around his head and linking her wrists at the base of his neck. She tilted her head to the side, giving him better access to the spot underneath her jaw where his tongue was currently engaged in all kinds of delicious pursuits.

London squeezed her thighs tight against his hips. This insatiable need she had for him was, without a doubt, the most surprising and frustrating thing to come out of that stupid class reunion. But she could not deny how greedy she was for the pleasure he unleashed on her.

He reached over for his suit jacket and pulled an unopened three pack of condoms from the inside pocket, identical to the one on the nightstand that was down two condoms.

"You brought backup?" London asked.

"I didn't reach this level of success in life by being unprepared, Dr. Kelley."

"You're such a cocky bastard," she grumbled as she unhooked her bra. She nodded at the foil packet. "Get that thing on."

He opened one of the condoms and quickly rolled the latex over his erection, then hooked his thumbs onto the waistband of her panties and tugged them off.

London hoisted herself slightly off the desk and thrust her hips toward him, pleasure seizing her limbs as he entered her.

He was the perfect fucking girth. Because why wouldn't her sworn enemy be the perfect fucking girth!

She tried to block out the fact that this was Drew, but something unexplainable denied her that ability. He was too... *there.* With every drive of his hips, every pull of his mouth on her nipples, he forced her to recognize that he was the source of all the blissful sensations overwhelming her.

He lifted her from the desk and carried her back to the bed, following her down to the mattress. London thrust her hips upward, meeting him as he plunged deep. He hooked his arm under her right knee and lifted it high, forcing her legs to spread farther apart as he drove himself into her over and over again.

She spiraled, the intense pleasure shooting through her limbs, making them seize with anticipation of the mind-blowing orgasm she'd already come to expect from him. It took only a few more pumps of his hips before she erupted with the most breathtakingly exquisite sensations she'd experienced since... since...

Since the last time Drew Sullivan had unleashed his magic dick on her.

He buried his face against her neck as he continued to pummel her with thrust after thrust, until his body went stiff and then shuddered violently against her. He shook with the force of his own orgasm.

"Fuck," Drew whispered against her skin.

"I concur," London said.

He let go of her leg and she wrapped both around him, keeping his weight pressed against her.

Over these past few months London had felt as if she'd made

one remarkably bad choice after another. From accepting that first date with Craig Johnson to the numerous run-ins she'd had with Dr. Coleman. But there was one thing she was sure about: Concocting a hookup plan with Drew Sullivan was one of her smartest moves in ages.

10

At the sound of the doorbell, Drew pushed away from the small conference table and went out to answer his apartment door. He accepted the tray of breakfast sandwiches from the delivery guy and handed him a twenty.

"Um, you already tipped me in the app," the guy said.

"Oh." Drew tried to think up an excuse to avoid having to admit that he had no idea how the food delivery app worked. His assistant, Larissa, always did the ordering. "Yeah, I know. This is just an extra bonus for bringing these up here instead of making me come down to the lobby."

Drew closed the door with his foot and retreated into the apartment. He and his team had a long day ahead of them. Not only did they need to discuss their first week of observations at Travis County Hospital, but they'd already been thrown a major curveball: A decrease in area population meant the hospital wouldn't be receiving as much funding from the state this year. So now they had to brainstorm an initial set of cuts that could be made.

"I ordered some brain fuel," he said as he returned to the collaboration room.

Five heads popped up from where his team stood huddled

over the laptop of project manager Samantha Gomez. Their pensive expressions immediately got Drew's guard up.

"Does someone want to tell me what's going on, or is this something I should see for myself?" he asked.

Wordlessly, Samantha spun the laptop to face him and pushed it toward the center of the table.

Drew set down the tray and reached for his reading glasses that he was just vain enough to despise. Even with the glasses, he had to lean in close to the screen to read it.

When he did, his blood ran cold.

Bryce Dowell Named Partner
at the Meacham Group.

Drew fought to keep his face expressionless, but he knew his colleagues would see right through any attempt to hide his feelings. All but one of them had followed him from Meacham when he and his partners, B. J. Clark and Melissa Edwards, left to form Trident.

Drew closed the laptop and pushed it back toward Samantha. "Fuck Bryce and the rest of them," he said.

"Fucking right," Josh Hall said with a fist pump.

Trident's director of planning and business development had been at the Meacham Group for three years already before Drew joined the hedge fund, and had remained in the same position the entire time. Like Drew, Josh knew what it was like to be screwed over by the boys in the corner offices.

"What's going on back at that other firm in New York isn't our concern," Drew said. "Remember what Trident is about. Our work has a purpose. And one hundred percent of our focus must remain on Travis County Hospital." He slapped the table. "Get some food in you, then we meet back here in fifteen to hash out what we've learned about the hospital operations so far."

As the rest of the team fanned out, Drew reclaimed the chair at the head of the table and pulled up Google on his phone. He typed "Bryce Dowell" and "the Meacham Group" into the search bar. The article Samantha had been reading was the second hit, right behind the one about Bryce single-handedly reinventing one of the nation's largest fast-food chains that had been on the brink of bankruptcy.

The same account Drew had brought to Meacham *and* done most of the work on.

Just the sight of the top search result irritated him. He clicked on the second article and scanned the story. It was the typical rundown of Bryce's educational background, his years at Meacham, and, of course, his being lauded as a rising star because of the account he'd stolen from Drew.

What pissed him off more than anything was that Meacham's chief investment officer knew that Drew was the one who put in the work to lure that client to Meacham, and he'd said nothing. It hadn't just pissed him off, it had hurt. He'd given so much of himself to the firm, and everyone just shrugged it off.

Bryce came from old money. His father and grandfather had both been prominent bankers, and the prestige a Dowell brought to the hedge fund was worth more to them than the years of hustling and the billions—fucking *billions*—of dollars Drew had brought in.

He should have left Meacham long before he did. Sure, he'd walked out of those glass doors with nearly a hundred million dollars in investments and cash, but he'd also left with a mountain of regret. Because he'd given Meacham something worth far more than the money he'd earned with them: his time. Time that should've been spent with his mother.

Precious time he would never get back.

Drew sucked in a deep breath and pushed away from the table. He went into the kitchen, grabbed a bottle of water from the refrigerator, and swallowed down half of it.

He refused to give energy to these dark thoughts—not with the important work facing him right now. To a certain extent, his mother was the reason he was here now, helping hospitals like County. If he'd known about her cancer in time, he could have brought in the best doctors in the world to treat her, but a person's bank balance shouldn't determine whether they lived or died.

And there came a time when a person needed to be known for more than just their ability to acquire wealth. He didn't want that to be his sole legacy.

Drew could never make up for those priceless moments he'd lost with his mom, but he would do what he could to ensure others had more time with their loved ones, regardless of their ability to pay.

To accomplish that at County, he had to get the people working there to buy into the changes that would have to be made. That's why he needed London to get on board. She had more clout with the staff than doctors who had been there for decades.

Drew finished his water on his way back to the makeshift conference room. As the team reassembled around the table, he unbuttoned his shirt at the wrists and rolled up his cuffs.

"I don't have to reiterate the significance of the job that's been put before us. I'm sure you all saw it at various times this week. Travis County Hospital serves a special purpose for many in this area. It's vital that this community has a reliable source for their health care.

"Understand that there will be major pushback if privatization is even whispered about, but don't allow those voices to knock you off track. Our goal is to find the best answer to this hospital's financial and management issues." Drew paused for a moment. He knew his next words would leave a foul taste in his mouth, but they needed to be said. "If our data findings suggest that County should no longer be publicly run, then that's what we recommend. But we can't get ahead of ourselves. We need to keep our biases out of this and go into this assessment with eyes wide open," he added as much for himself as for the team.

He flipped over several of the pages he'd printed earlier. "I've already noticed a lot of fat that can be trimmed. Starting with discarding medical supplies. I questioned a nurse about why she was throwing out several boxes of sutures, and was told that they restock every six months, regardless of the expiration date on the items. But when I searched the policy and procedures manual, I saw nothing stating there should be a six-month overhaul of the surgical supplies.

"After investigating a bit further, I discovered the practice has been passed down by word of mouth over the years. No one knows when it started—it's just part of the culture. Those sutures cost over four hundred dollars a box, and I personally saw her throw out at least seven of them. When you're running at an eight-figure deficit, that doesn't seem like a lot, but it adds up."

"It's so wasteful," Samantha said. "Who did you say was doing this?"

"It doesn't matter *who*," Drew pointed out. "We're not here to blame any one person in particular. We're focused on the *system* that created the mindset that it's okay to toss out thousands of dollars of medical supplies simply because someone said to do it years ago."

Heads nodded around the table, and for the next two hours, the team methodically went through a list of obvious evidence of wastefulness. As they tallied up the expenditures, Drew's earlier anger over news about Bryce Dowell's partnership faded.

Not being made partner at the Meacham Group had made leaving that much easier. And he had no desire to go back.

What he was doing now saved lives. He and his team brought struggling health-care facilities back from the brink. If the small, rural hospital in his mother's hometown had hired a company like Trident to help it run more efficiently, maybe it would have been able to afford more advanced technology that could have caught her cancer earlier. Maybe she would still be here.

He had not been able to save his own mother, but the work he was doing now could possibly save someone else's. That would always mean more to him than a partnership.

11

Pressing together the Velcro seams of the new SpongeBob stethoscope sleeve she'd just received from her favorite Etsy shop, London made her way to the Under the Sea room. Jason Milner wasn't on her patient list today, but the ten-year-old was being discharged, and London couldn't let him leave without saying goodbye.

The gut-wrenching thing was that she would probably see him again in a few months. He had been born with a congenital heart defect that required multiple surgeries.

She tapped her knuckles on the door twice before entering.

"Hello there," London greeted Jason and his parents. "I heard someone is going home today."

When he saw her, Jason's smile grew as bright as the Austin skyline. London was continually amazed by his ability to maintain such a positive outlook after everything he'd been through in his short life.

Just as she made it to the ten-year-old's bedside, there was another knock on the door and Kia Jackson walked in.

"Dr. Kelley? Can I see you outside?"

"Sure, one minute," London said. She turned to Jason and

gave him a hug. "Sorry I can't stay longer, buddy. Now, I don't want to see you here for a while, you hear me?"

He nodded.

"Dr. Kelley." The underlying hint of distress in Kia's voice immediately set London on edge.

She gave Jason's shoulder a squeeze before leaving the room. "What's going on?" she asked the minute she and the nurse were in the hallway.

"You're needed in the ER."

"I'm not on call."

"It's your father," Kia said. "He was brought in an hour ago."

"Shit." London took off down the corridor. She bypassed the elevators, opting instead for the stairs. She released a string of curse words as she made her way down the two flights, the fear in her stomach knotting tighter with each step she took.

Her father had been in her hospital for an hour already, and she was just finding out?

She spotted Xander Caldwell the moment she exited the stairwell. Doug Renault had recruited the senior resident the same year he'd brought London to County.

"Xander." London caught him on the arm. "You have a patient that was brought in an hour ago. Black male. Late fifties. Bald with a goatee. Very fit."

"Yes. Mr. Kelley." His eyes widened. "Is he—"

She nodded. "My dad."

"Wow. I didn't put two and two together." He pointed to his face. "You have his eyes."

"I know," London said. "How is he? Where is he?"

"First, don't get too alarmed," he said. "It was just a TIA."

"Thank goodness," London said, her shoulders wilting in relief. No one campaigned for a transient ischemic attack, but if you were going to have a stroke, that's the kind you wanted.

"He's in Exam 3," Xander said.

London thanked him before crossing over to the exam room. She found Kenneth Kelley sitting upright on the exam table, dressed in khakis and a polo shirt. He held his phone out about eight inches from his face and was laughing at whoever was on the other end of the video call.

"I had a stroke and two bogeys, and still whipped your tail today," he said.

Golf? The man was talking about fucking golf?

Why was she surprised?

"Hello, Dad," London said as she walked to his bedside.

He looked past the phone, his brow wrinkling with subtle irritation. "I'll catch up with you later, Percy," he said before disconnecting the call and setting the phone in his lap.

"Hello, London," he said.

She motioned to the phone. "You had time to call your golf buddies, but didn't have time to call your own daughter to let her know you were in the ER of the hospital where she works?"

"You're a pediatrician. What could you have done for me?"

The strained tension that consistently hovered between her and her dad surged. London fought against it, biting down on her lower lip to stop herself from lashing out. Instead, she peered at the patient monitor, reading his vitals.

Once she was certain she could speak without initiating World War III, she asked, "How are you feeling?"

"Like someone who could have finished his round of golf," Kenneth answered.

"You had a stroke."

"The other doctor said it was just a ministroke. I'm fine." He grunted. "Percy only called the ambulance because I was three shots ahead of him, and he knows I play the back nine at the club better than he does."

London rolled her eyes. "A ministroke is still a stroke. TIAs are a warning sign that something more catastrophic may happen if you don't take your doctor's orders seriously."

Thoughts of the pancakes and bacon she'd had at Kerbey Lane the other day immediately popped into her head, but London mentally batted them away. This was about her dad's health scare, not her own.

"April said that you were placed on a new statin," London continued. "Have you been taking it?"

"It appears I need to have a talk with my wife. I know you're a doctor and all, but that doesn't mean she has to share information about my health with you."

"She didn't share it with me, she shared it with my mom. So maybe tell your current wife not to share your health information with your ex-wife."

The unconventional friendship between her mother and stepmother was baffling, but London had stopped trying to understand it years ago.

"And even though I am nothing more than a lowly pediatric surgeon, I know what happens to adults when they don't take the medications they've been prescribed. High cholesterol and high blood pressure can lead to serious issues."

Shit. Was she talking to her dad or herself here?

Just then, the door opened and Xander Caldwell walked in.

"Ah, you found him," he said to London. To her dad he said, "You should have mentioned you were Dr. Kelley's father. Not that the family of hospital royalty gets preferential treatment or anything, but it would have been good to know," he said with a wink. He held up his tablet. "I assume it's okay if Dr. Kelley remains in the room as we go over your CT scan?"

London thought for a moment that Kenneth would answer no, but he nodded.

The CT scan confirmed a transient ischemic attack. She listened as Xander listed the litany of things her father should do to prevent further TIAs, and realized how many of them she wasn't practicing herself. Limit sodium and alcohol intake. Reduce stress. Exercise regularly.

Could she count what she and Drew had spent the week doing in bed as exercise? The sex was vigorous, but probably not physically exerting enough to prevent a stroke.

"It's still your call, but I don't think it's necessary to go through with the transfer to St. David's," Xander was saying.

"Transfer?" London whipped her head around. "Why was that even discussed for a TIA? He's not being admitted, is he?"

The doctor shook his head. "No, but he requested it."

She looked to her dad. "Why?"

But she didn't need an answer. She already knew. His bougie ass thought he was too good for a state-run hospital.

"Let me guess, you tried to pay the EMTs to bring you to another hospital, but County was closer." London released a derisive snort before she could stop herself. "Don't worry, both Xander and I went to school with some of the doctors at St. David's. The only difference between us is that their scrubs aren't as threadbare."

"I'm more familiar with the care at St. David's," her dad stated.

"Uh-huh," London said.

"Can I cancel the transfer?" Xander asked.

"Yes," London said.

"Umm . . . Mr. Kelley?" Xander asked. "Sorry, Dr. Kelley, but this is the patient's call."

"If you think it is unnecessary, I will go along with that, Dr. Caldwell," Kenneth said.

Xander nodded. "I'll have the nurses start on your discharge forms." Then he left the exam room.

"You are nothing if not true to form," London said.

"I can say the same about you," Kenneth replied. "The check I wrote you still hasn't been cashed."

And it wouldn't be. It would remain right where she'd stashed it, in the junk drawer in her kitchen.

During a rare visit to her house a couple of months ago, Kenneth noticed her neighbor's newly added porte cochere and decided London's Hyde Park bungalow needed one, as well. He'd written her a check on the spot for twenty thousand dollars to cover the cost.

Writing a check was his answer to everything.

London had no illusions that his offer had anything to do with wanting to make sure she didn't get drenched while running from her car to her house. He wanted to be able to show his golf buddies the porte cochere he'd given to his daughter, to puff out his chest at his law firm's office parties while his associates oohed and aahed at his generosity.

"I already told you that I don't want or need any additions to my house," London said. "And if I did, I can cover the cost myself." Before he could launch a rebuttal, she asked, "Is April coming to get you?"

"You don't have to worry about me. I can get home."

"Dad," London said.

"She'll be here soon. She's picking the kids up from school."

It figured that her stepmom was out taking care of London's three younger siblings while Kenneth, if he hadn't been in the ER, would have been playing the back nine at his country club. It was disappointing—but not surprising—to see that some things never changed.

"Tell her that I'm sorry I missed her, but I can't stick around."

It was Friday, and she was already running late for her dinner with Taylor and Samiah.

London leaned over to give him a kiss on the cheek, but he had already turned his attention back to his phone. She'd been dismissed.

That's what she got for presuming they could have something that even came close to a normal father-daughter relationship. She didn't even say goodbye as she left the room.

Forty-five minutes later, London was turning down Gibson Street in South Austin.

She made the sign of the cross before she parallel parked her Mini between two monster trucks, next to Odd Duck, the restaurant Samiah had chosen for this week's girls' night out. She got out of the car and checked the front and rear bumpers. She still had two inches to spare on each side.

"Not bad." She pointed up at the sky. "Good looking out."

As she walked past the restaurant's wall of windows, she caught sight of Samiah and Taylor sitting at a table. She maneuvered around the pockets of people waiting to get inside, muttering, "Excuse me," about a dozen times before she finally reached the entrance. It was just like Samiah to pick the place where all of Austin wanted to spend their Friday night.

It wasn't until a couple of weeks ago that both London and Taylor had realized that Samiah always seemed to choose the place for their weekly gathering. But then they both conceded that neither of them wanted to go through the hassle of seeking out happy hours around the city. Besides, other than that fondue place a couple of months ago—no one needs to eat *that* much cheese—Samiah picked some real winners.

"My friends are already seated," London told the woman standing at the hostess desk.

She strode across the stained concrete floor, holding her hands up in apology as she approached the table. Samiah and Taylor were used to her showing up late due to her unpredictable work schedule. Still, London felt bad about always making them wait.

Not that they ever actually waited to get started. The table was crowded with colorful frozen drinks and an array of fragrant dishes.

"Sorry I'm late," London said, taking the seat opposite Samiah and snatching a roasted carrot from one of the plates before she even set her purse down. "It turns out this is the week for emergency appendectomies. I swear the eight-year-olds in Austin have a pact going or something." She considered mentioning her dad's showing up in the ER, but talking about his health scare could easily lead to a conversation about her own health. She wasn't up for a lecture from Taylor.

Instead, she picked up the menu and scanned the cocktails. "So, how was everyone's week?"

When neither spoke, London lowered her menu to find them both staring at her with odd looks.

"What?" she asked.

"Exactly how much sex have you been getting lately?" Taylor asked.

"*Excuse* me?" London asked with a shocked laugh.

"You're glowing, honey," Samiah said. "I mean, you are

practically effervescent. There is only one thing I can think of that puts *that* look on a woman's face."

"You cannot tell just by looking at me," London said.

"Oh, really?" Taylor held her phone up and snapped a picture, then turned the screen so that it faced London.

She leaned forward and squinted at the image. "I'll be damned," London muttered. She had to admit that she looked well and thoroughly fucked, in a totally good way.

"Told ya," Samiah said with a grin. She rested her chin in her upturned palm and asked, "Is it the former classmate?"

"It is," London confirmed. "It's been kind of a daily thing since the reunion last weekend."

"Daily? Damn, girl," Taylor said.

"Well, you did have quite a long dry spell," Samiah pointed out. "I don't blame you for making up for lost time. But I thought this guy was from out of town? Is he hanging around Austin because he can't drag himself away from you?"

London was about to respond when the server arrived to take her drink order. She gestured to the pale pink slushy cocktail in front of Samiah. "What's that one?"

"That's our spicy hibiscus margarita," the server said. "It's a fan favorite."

"It's the sole reason I wanted to come to this place, and it alone makes the drive across the Congress Avenue Bridge worth it," Samiah said.

"Sounds good to me," London said. "Can I also get the Wagyu burger—medium rare? Wait." She held up a hand. "Umm... actually, change that to grilled salmon and a house salad with balsamic dressing on the side."

"No problem," the server said before collecting London's menu.

"I had a big lunch," London offered in an attempt to stave off inquires from her friends, but Taylor seemed more interested in talking about Drew than London's dinner choices.

"So," Taylor said. "How do you spend the entire week shagging a guy you hate? That doesn't seem like you."

"Yeah, where did you even find the time?" Samiah asked. "I thought you had a bunch of surgeries scheduled this week."

"The fact that Drew is working at the hospital helps with logistics," London said.

"Working at the hospital?" Samiah asked with a frown. "Is he a doctor?"

"Wait." London held up her hands. "I just realized I haven't spoken to either of you since we met up at Kerbey Lane on Sunday."

"No, you've been too busy getting it on with your old classmate," Taylor said.

"That's just the half of it," London said. She snagged another carrot from Samiah's plate. "We have *so* much to talk about, ladies."

"Start with the part about him working at the hospital," Samiah said. "I'm confused."

London spotted the server approaching with her drink and waved her over.

"Perfect timing. I need a little alcohol in me before I dive into this story." Eating broiled fish instead of the burger she was craving would have to be good enough for tonight, because she would not deprive herself of alcohol. She took a sip of her margarita. "Oh, this *is* good. Too bad I arrived so late. I won't have time to get a second." She set the glass down and folded her hands on the table. "Who's ready to hear about how my luck is absolute shit these days?"

She started with how she fell back into bed with Drew last Sunday afternoon when she returned to his hotel for her purse. Then she told them about the shock she received when she walked into the meeting on Monday to find him sitting at the table next to Dr. Coleman.

"Can you believe that? My past nemesis and current nemesis sitting elbow to elbow. I swear I heard the theme music from *The Twilight Zone* playing in the background."

"That is the stuff of nightmares," Samiah said.

Taylor made a *speed it up* motion with her hand. "I have a long drive back home. Get to the part where you two start going at it like rabbits."

"We are not going at it like rabbits," London said. She tipped her head to the side. "Okay, maybe we are, but that's beside the point." She hiked her shoulders up to her ears. "I can't explain what's happening here. I've hardly thought about this man since high school, and the few times I *did* think about him in the last fifteen years, it was never in a positive light. Yet I'm probably going to text him once I get back to my car and ask if I can stop by his place on my way home to bone. It makes zero sense."

"It makes *all* the sense." Taylor laughed. "It's like Samiah said, you're making up for lost time. You deserve this, girl." She picked up her phone and swiped across the screen. "What's his name again? I'm going to Google him. I need to see what Magic Mike looks like."

"His name is Drew," London said. "And you don't need to bother with Google. I can show you." She pulled up Tabitha Rawlings's Facebook page and scrolled back to her pictures from last Saturday. The girl was not subtle at all. Drew was in just about every single snapshot she'd taken.

Obsessed much?

London found one that showed a full-on face view. *Have mercy.* She had to stop herself from licking her lips before turning the phone to Taylor and Samiah.

"Whoa," Samiah said.

"My God," Taylor said. "You weren't kidding, were you? And he's rich too? Not that it matters, but it also doesn't hurt."

London pulled her phone back and glanced at the picture one more time before setting the phone facedown on the table.

"It doesn't matter. I own my house outright and am totally satisfied driving a Tinker Bell car, as my mom calls it," she said. "I could not care less about Drew's money. I only wish I felt the same way about his pipe-laying skills." She shook her head, taking another sip of her drink. "It's been a week and I still can't believe that of all the hospital management consulting firms in the entire world, it's Drew's firm that is working at County."

"Well, it's not totally unbelievable," Samiah said. "There can't be all that many firms that specialize in this type of work, right? And he *does* have a local tie." She shrugged. "When you think about it, the odds are pretty high that his firm would be the one working with your hospital, especially if his firm has a good reputation."

"You and your logic are raining on my pity parade," London said.

"What's there to pity?" Taylor asked. "This sounds like exactly what you've been looking for. I know you wanted to find a fuck buddy you wouldn't have to see at the hospital every day, but it sounds as if this Drew won't be there permanently, right?"

"No, he won't be," London answered. "Another three weeks or so."

"Okay, that is *beyond* perfect!"

"Exactly," Samiah said, tipping her margarita glass at Taylor. She looked to London. "You may think you've had bad luck lately, but that glow indicates otherwise. It looks to me as if you're one of the luckiest women in Austin."

"The problem is, I don't *want* to want Drew Sullivan," London said. "I swear, I would be shitting rainbows and unicorns if this was *anyone* else—"

"Except Craig," Taylor said.

"Never that creep. But Drew isn't all that far from Craig when it comes to men I'd consider being in a real relationship with."

Even as she said the words, London knew they weren't true. He did not belong near the same category as Craig Johnson, and it wasn't fair to put him there. She didn't know Drew well enough to decide whether she would consider being in a relationship with him. It had been a single week since they'd reconnected, and there hadn't been much talking going on in the time they *had* spent together so far.

Much of her antipathy toward him was rooted in a grudge she'd been holding on to since high school. A grudge that, if she were being honest, didn't have as much to do with Drew as it had to do with how Drew's emergence as an academic rival had dulled London's ability to shine bright enough to draw her father's attention. Being number one in her class had given her dad something to brag about to the men in his golfing circle. *My daughter is almost best* didn't have quite the same panache.

Maybe she should work on disassociating Drew from her

messed-up issues with her dad. It wasn't fair that she'd held something that wasn't even his fault against him all this time.

Then again, he would be gone soon. Why did it matter?

She wasn't looking to start a relationship with Drew. What they had going right now suited her needs just fine. He'd been at the hospital for a week, but she rarely saw him there, which was precisely how she wanted it. Once her shift was over, she drove the few blocks to his rented apartment with the ridiculously comfortable bed and spent several hours getting thoroughly fucked. Then she went home. Why couldn't she be satisfied with that?

She *was* satisfied. As long as things remained exactly as they were, she would get her fill of Drew Sullivan and then happily bid him farewell once he was done with his work at County.

12

Drew sat in the exact chair he'd occupied at this time last Monday when he and the Trident team were introduced to hospital staff. In the week that followed, their team faced some skepticism, but for the most part Drew gathered that the people working at Travis County Hospital didn't care whether their paychecks came from the state or a private entity. As long as the paychecks continued and their work conditions remained the same or improved, they were happy.

At least that was the consensus of *most* of the staff.

There was a small but vocal contingent, led by the woman who had been in his bed every single night this week, that was adamantly opposed to the hospital being taken over by the private sector. They were also highly suspicious of anything the hospital's administration endorsed. With good reason. Drew had encountered several stories of the administration reneging on promises they'd made in the past. It only made his job harder.

He never brought up the audit when he and London were away from the hospital, respecting her request to keep their personal and professional lives separate. But their professional encounters were about to become a lot more frequent.

Drew nervously tapped his pen against the edge of the table as he waited for the hospital personnel who had been selected to work more closely with Trident's team to file out of the room. They'd chosen people from every area of the workforce, from janitorial staff and paraprofessionals, to nurse practitioners, phlebotomists, and surgeons. The plan was to have these well-respected staff members become ambassadors for the cost-cutting measures Trident would eventually recommend implementing.

London had missed the meeting, having been called in for an emergency hernia repair just prior to its start. It worked out perfectly as far as Drew was concerned. He'd suggested from the very beginning that they meet with her privately. He understood how influence worked; if London had been in the meeting with the rest of the staff, everyone would have waited for her reaction before deciding how they felt about Trident's proposal.

London didn't seem to recognize just how much power she wielded with the staff. It went deeper than normal admiration. She wasn't afraid to buck the system on behalf of her colleagues and had earned their devotion in return.

London's obliviousness to the clout she had here at the hospital was both surprising and refreshing, given the Texas-size ego she'd had fifteen years ago. She would walk into a room just knowing she was the smartest person there.

The thing is, when it came to London, she had the chops to back up all that arrogance. Because she usually *was* the smartest person in the room. He'd told her at the reunion that she owed him for pushing her to do better when they were in high school, but it was the other way around. That big, beautiful brain of hers had fascinated him. He'd done all he could to impress her, busting his ass in every single subject his senior year to keep up with her.

Instead of being impressed, she'd labeled him a threat.

It never failed. She inevitably took the inverse position of what he was shooting for. Case in point, engaging in these impersonal, unemotional hookup sessions after work instead of taking the time to reconnect in a more meaningful way. He didn't expect her to share her deepest, darkest secrets with him, but her ability to remain so detached after the hours they'd spent in bed this week had begun to grate on his nerves.

Although, despite her declaration that she wanted only sex from him and nothing more, Drew had persuaded her to at least have a drink and talk for a bit before they got undressed in the evenings. But it was mostly casual conversations about things happening in the world around them, nothing too personal. He'd learned that she hated discussing politics, even with people who shared her political views. And that she hadn't seen a movie in a movie theater since the first *Black Panther*.

He'd also discovered she didn't keep in touch with any of their former high school classmates, even though she'd remained in Austin. He hadn't kept up with many of them because he'd known them only a short time, having transferred to Barbara Jordan High halfway through his junior year, but London had gone to school with most of their classmates for the entire four years.

She talked more about the two friends she'd met because of the guy who'd been dating all three of them. It was as if she were closer to people she'd known only a few months than those she'd gone through four years of high school with.

Maybe he should recruit her two friends to help convince her to work with Trident's team. He was willing to try anything.

Drew had no doubt that if news of Dr. Kelley sanctioning their audit hit the hospital grapevine, others would hop on board.

First, he had to ensure that she *was* on board. And having Frederick Coleman in the room probably wouldn't help his case. Drew had heard rumors about the tension between the administrator and London. There was no love lost there.

"Dr. Coleman," he said, striving for an air of perplexed concern. "I have a question about Dr. Kelley."

"Ah, yes," Coleman said. "The superstar darling of the pediatric unit."

If the patronizing undertone of Coleman's words hadn't told him enough, the snide lift to the man's lips sure had.

"She does seem to be well-liked among hospital personnel," Drew said.

"She's a bit too unorthodox for my taste—and too mouthy—but the staff listens to her. That's why Doug—Dr. Renault—wants her on this team. I don't think you've had the chance to meet Doug yet, have you?"

Drew shook his head.

"If you ask me, Doug is the one responsible for Dr. Kelley thinking she's the best thing that ever happened to this hospital. He wined and dined her to get her to join our residency program, and now she thinks she walks on water."

Drew was stunned that a man in Frederick Coleman's position would discuss another colleague in such terms, and to someone he barely knew. If a member of his staff ever did something like that, Drew would immediately escort them out the door.

He still wasn't clear on what the beef between London and Dr. Coleman was about, but he would be on her side even if he wasn't having sex with her.

Shit. It just occurred to him that if she *did* join his team, she may decide to end their little post-workday escapades altogether. Maybe she would see it as a conflict of interest, even though they both had the same goal—saving County.

The door to the conference room opened and a tall, slim Black man with a bald head and a white goatee walked in. London followed right behind him. They were both in their blue hospital scrubs and white coats.

"Ah, Doug. Glad you could make it." Dr. Coleman gestured to the older man. "Dr. Douglas Renault, this is Drew Sullivan from Trident Health Management Systems. He's the head of the consulting team."

"Happy to finally meet you," Dr. Renault said. "I was out much of last week in Sonoma, walking my youngest down the aisle."

"That's right," Coleman said. "How did that go?"

"It was the wedding of her dreams," Renault said. "That's all that matters." He looked at his watch. "I have a consult in another twenty minutes, so why don't we get down to business."

London had taken a seat next to Renault. Drew followed her eyes as she took in the room's occupants. He noticed the barest hint of confusion, but she played it off well.

"Drew, why don't you take the lead here," Frederick Coleman said.

Of course, Coleman would have Drew run point at this meeting. For all the man's bravado, Drew suspected Coleman didn't enjoy going toe to toe with London. Lucky for him, Drew did. There came a point back in high school when he relished their confrontations—especially once he realized that she was never going to see him as anything but her academic rival. These days, he had more pleasurable things to do with her than locking horns.

But this was the job he had been hired to do. He couldn't allow his and London's relationship—he used that term in the loosest way imaginable—to get in the way of it.

"Earlier this morning, I presented the results of Trident's initial assessment to the hospital's board of directors and the executive committee," Drew began.

"We did that Zoom thing," Coleman interjected. "That's how we were able to get everyone in the meeting even though they weren't physically here."

You gotta be kidding me. Drew wouldn't be surprised if they eventually uncovered that Frederick Coleman was the number one reason behind County's archaic technology. They'd had to strong-arm him into using Zoom for the meeting, and now he was touting it as some type of marvel.

He acknowledged Coleman with a tight smile before continuing. "The good news is that Trident is confident that with the right strategies in place, this hospital will be able to remain a publicly funded health-care resource for the people of Travis County."

London's mouth fell open for a moment before she quickly shut it. "That... that's great," she said.

If this were anyone else, Drew would have been disappointed in that subdued reaction. From London, it felt as if he'd hit gold.

He hated to take any of the shine off the news he'd just imparted, but also knew he needed to be straight with her.

"However, in order to achieve this, we must implement a number of cost-cutting measures," Drew continued. "We've pinpointed several key areas of County's overall operations that we believe should be addressed as quickly as possible. To do this, we will need buy-in from all hospital personnel." He listed them on his fingers. "Medical staff, clerical, cafeteria workers, everyone.

"One thing we've found in doing this work is that personnel tend to listen to fellow colleagues they know and trust a lot more than they listen to a bunch of suits brought in." He tried to gauge London's reaction. Her face remained impassive. "The best way to achieve buy-in is to employ ambassadors." He picked up the document with the names. "Members of the administration have come up with a list of people who they feel will be the best to help champion these ideas."

"Ah, and you see me as one of these ambassadors?" London asked.

"Yes, we do. People listen to you, London," Dr. Renault said. "They'll get behind this if they see that you're on board. But if you dismiss the work that Trident is doing, there are many on this staff who will do the same without even taking the time to hear them out."

She folded her hands and smiled serenely at Dr. Coleman. "Hmm... I wonder why that is."

"Because you're loud and cause a ruckus every other week," Dr. Coleman said.

"With all due respect, Dr. Coleman, the fact that I'm vocal is only one reason the staff here listens to me," London said. "I also speak *to* them and not *at* them. And questioning hospital administration when I encounter something that is problematic is not causing a ruckus, it's advocating for my patients."

Coleman pushed up from the table. "I can't deal with this. I have things to do."

London sat at the table with a bored look on her face as Dr.

Coleman made a production out of gathering the three-ring binder, leather portfolio, and the dozens of other materials he'd brought in with him—all of which could be electronically stored if the man weren't still living in 1982.

"You and Dr. Coleman need to figure out how to work together," Dr. Renault said the moment the other doctor left the room.

"It's been five years. I'm not sure it's going to happen."

"London." The man rubbed the spot between his eyes. He looked across the table at Drew. "Can you give us a minute?"

"No, let him stay. And forget about Coleman for now. Tell me more about this ambassadorship? What exactly would it entail?"

"Basically, Trident will work with the hospital's administration to come up with a list of viable budget cuts. As an ambassador, you'll sell our ideas for cutting costs to the staff," Drew answered.

"Oh!" Her brows arched. "Is that all!" She turned to her mentor. "So, Mr. Sullivan hasn't been around long enough to know how adamantly opposed I am to the majority of the cost-cutting ideas the hospital administration has proposed this past year, but you have, Dr. Renault. I can't imagine you would have me champion something that I have been fighting against. I would look like a total hypocrite."

"You would look like someone who is willing to put aside her differences for what's best for this hospital's bottom line," Renault said.

"This hospital's bottom line is not my main concern. My concern is for my patients. The budget cuts that have been proposed in the past have not been in the patients' best interests."

"It's a luxury for you to be able to focus all your energy on your patients, Dr. Kelley, but there isn't a money tree growing outside. This hospital has to make some tough choices," Renault said.

"Will these 'ambassadors,'" she said, making air quotes, "have any input in what gets in the budget and what doesn't, or are we expected to just smile and regurgitate whatever the administration tells us to say?"

Drew chose his words carefully. "Trident's charge is to conduct an assessment and make recommendations. What's done with that is ultimately up to County's board of directors."

"Of which half were ready to sell the hospital. This board has also agreed on budget cuts in the past that would take needed services away from young mothers."

Doug Renault held up his hands. "Look, London, the board of directors know how lucky Travis County Hospital is to have a resident of your caliber on staff. But having a rising star surgeon in our pediatric ward only gets us so far. Trident was brought in to try to save this hospital, and we need voices like yours to impart the seriousness of this situation to the others on staff. Now, can you please just hear Mr. Sullivan out?"

Just as she leveled her gaze at Drew, her beeper went off. She glanced at it.

"I'm needed in the ER," she said, pushing back from the table. She spoke directly to Drew. "Hopefully, I can grab a bite to eat in my office at some point today. I'll try to find you later."

Drew made sure she didn't have to seek him out. He spent the afternoon on the pediatric floor, interviewing nurses and support staff. Conducting on-site interviews didn't fall under a managing partner's typical duties—in fact, he and his two partners tried to refrain from getting too much into the weeds. But Samantha had flown back to New York this morning for a family emergency, leaving them one person short. Drew knew how to roll up his sleeves and do the day-to-day work when necessary.

He'd just finished a discussion with Nurse Francis, the scary-as-hell charge nurse who just didn't seem to have the personality for working in pediatrics, when he spotted London walking through the doors of the surgical rooms. She looked exhausted as she walked up to the nurses' station.

"Please tell me some grateful parent sent a tray of cookies, or brownies, or something unhealthy today," she said.

The other nurse, Kia, shook her head as she pointed to a cellophane-wrapped fruit basket.

"Maybe the strawberries are sweet," she told London.

London's shoulders slumped and she gave Kia a thumbs-down. "It's probably a sign that I should lay off the sweets, but I need sugary carbs after this last surgery. I'll take my chances with something from the vending machine." She finally acknowledged Drew. "Are you ready for the ambush?"

"It's not an ambush," he said, following her down the hallway toward her office. "And I can have my assistant order something from Uber Eats if you don't have lunch."

She glanced at him over her shoulder. "Your assistant? Do you mean to tell me you can't be bothered to order your own Uber Eats, Drew?"

He didn't want to admit that he didn't know how to use the app because it would make him feel too much like Dr. Coleman, the techno dinosaur.

"Do you need lunch?" he asked her.

She shook her head as they entered her office. She sat behind the desk and opened a drawer, taking out two packets of peanut butter crackers.

"I have backup. I just wanted something sweet and unhealthy as a reward for getting through a six-hour surgery on an MVA patient with multiple traumas. That's multiple vehicle accident," she clarified. She opened the crackers and stuffed a whole one in her mouth, making a *get on with it* gesture with her hand as she chewed.

"First, this is not an ambush," Drew started. "I won't try to coerce you into doing something you're opposed to doing, London. Dr. Renault believes you would be an asset to this committee, and I'm betting he's right. But you've been clear about where you stand in regards to Trident's work, and I have to respect that. All I'm asking is that you don't purposely sabotage what we're doing."

She picked up another cracker, taking a daintier bite. She chewed slowly, looking directly at him the entire time. Drew didn't understand how she could be so sexy and intimidating and aloof all at the same time. The combination turned him the fuck on, even when he didn't want to be turned on.

"Tell me, Drew," she said as she dusted crumbs from her fingers. "Do you believe I'm the type of person who would sink so low as to *purposely* sabotage Trident's work? Do you think I have that kind of time and energy? And, even if I did, that I could be so conniving?"

Now that he thought about it, he could see why she would take offense to his statement.

"I'm sorry." He held up his hands. "Maybe *purposely* wasn't the correct word here. No, I do not think you would intentionally undermine the assessment process, but many on the staff will get their cue from you. If they sense you're against our recommendations, then they will be too."

London folded her hands on her desk. "Earlier, I asked if ambassadors would have any say in these recommendations we're being asked to push to the rest of the staff, but I never got a clear answer."

"We value the input of everyone on staff," Drew said.

"You can value my input and still toss it in the trash. I've seen this before, Drew. Coleman and his cronies on the board have proposed cuts to everything that will actually improve patient care. I won't allow myself to be used as some rah-rah cheerleader for their bullshit."

"It's not like that, London. Trident's work is independent of the board and the administration."

"You may think that, but I know how these people operate," she said.

Drew pinched the bridge of his nose. What would it take to convince her that this was different? "Why are you still being so damn difficult after the week we've had together?"

"And why do you think this past week would change anything?" she asked. "Do I have to remind you that what goes on in this hospital has nothing to do with the other thing we're doing?" She leaned forward, and in a low-pitched voice, said, "As much as I appreciate the work you put in last night, it doesn't mean I'm going to all of a sudden play nice today. I'm still against what the hospital's administration is trying to do here, and I see you as an extension of that."

There could not possibly be a more stubborn person on the face of this earth, but Drew knew better than to allow those words to move past his lips.

After talking to the nurses on this floor today, Drew had no doubts that London could sway them and a bunch of others at this hospital to do whatever she said. She had just that much influence over the staff. They respected her, even though she was still a resident and one of the youngest surgeons here.

When he'd followed her into this office ten minutes ago, he'd resigned himself to the fact that London wouldn't budge on this. But being reminded of her passion for her patients gave Drew the motivation he needed to try one more time to convince her to help him.

"You're against what we're doing, even after hearing from Dr. Renault how dire things are?" Drew asked. "We're not talking hypotheticals here, London. Financially, this hospital is on life support. With crap health insurance. After just one week of examining operations, I can tell you that things are *not* good. I need you to help me save this hospital. Too many people are counting on County to allow it to go under."

Drew could swear he saw the switch flip in her head. The stubborn defiance that had dominated her expression softened into pensive concern, her brows drawing together as she absently flicked at the empty wrapper from her crackers.

"I'll think about what you said." She gestured to the door. "I need to finish my lunch and take a twenty-minute power nap before my next consult."

It took every bit of restraint Drew had in him to rise from the chair and start for the door. He was close to convincing her. His instincts, honed by years of closing deals others declared impossible, told him to go for the kill.

But London wasn't a deal for him to close. He needed to step back and give her time to think. And pray that she came to the right decision on her own.

13

No matter how hard she tried, London couldn't seem to shake the uneasy feeling that had settled in her gut after her conversation with Drew. She knew junk food wouldn't help the situation; it would, in fact, get her in a shitload of trouble if Doug Renault happened to catch her inhaling a Twinkie. Never mind the fact that it wasn't good for her triglycerides. But that still didn't stop her from going in search of something sticky and sweet and obscenely unhealthy.

She took the stairs down to the first floor—that counted as exercise, right?—and made her way to the collection of vending machines near the ER's waiting room, where they stocked the *really* good stuff. A group of nutritionists had sent around a petition last year, demanding an overhaul of the types of snacks offered. The forceful pushback from the rest of the hospital personnel had put a stop to that crusade pretty damn quick.

London browsed the array of cookies, potato chips, chocolate bars, and other processed junk, but nothing really excited her. Until her eyes landed on the devil's food cupcakes.

"Yeah, baby," she said, pressing the numbers for the cupcakes. The steel coil stopped moving just as the package reached the edge of the row.

"Oh, no you don't," London groused.

She tried to shake it, but it had been bolted to the floor some months ago following an altercation between brawling brothers-in-law that ended with them both pinned underneath one of the vending machines.

"Dammit."

This day was further proof of why Monday had such a bad reputation. The fucker had earned it.

London fished out another buck fifty and inserted it into the machine. Both packages tumbled to the tray below. Of course.

Though tempted, she knew if she brought them up to her office, she would have both packs eaten within the hour. Her nightly workouts with Drew last week had burned off more calories than anything she'd done in the past year, but she didn't need four cupcakes.

Okay, so she didn't need any cupcakes, but she convinced herself that one wouldn't hurt.

She walked down the corridor to the employees' lounge. Unlike on the upper floors, where the lounge was about the size of two broom closets tied together, the main floor's was big enough for several tables and chairs, a couch that had probably been bought during Clinton's first term, and a Ping-Pong table that was always in use. It looked like an Ortho versus Oncology tournament today.

Aleshia Williams walked up to her, stirring a cup of muddy-looking coffee.

"Becca Duhon said that she saw you in a conference room with Coleman, Renault, and the fine-as-hell guy who's running that consulting team from New York," she said. "What's up?"

"Can a person even sneeze around this place without it being breaking news?" London asked.

"No. So, what's going on?" Aleshia asked.

"Can you believe they asked me to be an 'ambassador' for this project?" London said. "The freaking nerve of them—especially Coleman." She shook her head. "I told Drew that I would think about it, but there is no way I'm working with them."

"Drew?" Aleshia asked.

"Uh, Drew Sullivan. He's the fine-as-hell guy you mentioned who's over the team from Trident. We went to high school together," London explained as she mentally chastised herself for the slipup. She knew better than to refer to him in such informal terms while here at the hospital. "Coleman and Renault tried to feed me some bullshit line about my influence over the hospital's staff and how it would go a long way in convincing personnel to buy into this assessment they're trying to sell us."

"They aren't wrong," Aleshia said.

"Except I don't want the staff to blindly go along with this," London said. "You know as well as I do that this can all end with the hospital being sold."

"But if you're one of their ambassadors, you can be our eyes and ears on the inside."

"So a spy?"

Aleshia hunched her shoulders. "That's one way to look at it. At least you would be able to give us a heads-up if the administration decides to go the privatization route. Hey, do you have a few minutes to sit?" Aleshia tilted her head toward an unoccupied table. "I've been on my feet way too much today. I don't know how you get through those marathon surgeries."

"Energy drinks and salsa music," London said as she followed her. She grabbed a couple of napkins from the coffee station before sitting in the chair next to Aleshia. She opened her cupcakes and offered one of them to her coworker. "Not the healthiest lunch I've had, but it'll have to do today."

Aleshia shook her head. "They look good, but if this is all you're having for lunch, you should eat them both."

London reached into the pocket of her lab coat for the other pack of cupcakes and tossed them on the table. "Don't make me eat this junk food alone."

"Bless you, woman," Aleshia said, ripping the package open. She bit into a cupcake and moaned. "Worth the extra time on the treadmill." Wiping cream filling from the corner of her mouth, she continued, "Back to this ambassador thing. Wouldn't it be better to know exactly what this group from Trident is telling the administration than to have Coleman and the board of directors tell us after it's too late to do anything about it? You can keep an eye on what's happening and be a voice for the opposition."

"You mean cause a ruckus," London said. "Apparently it's my specialty."

She would never admit to it, but Coleman's words had stung. What hurt even more was that Doug Renault hadn't pushed back on her behalf. There was a fine line between being an advocate and being a troublemaker, and she thought she'd been traveling on the right side of it.

Aleshia playfully bumped her with her knee. "Hey, causing a ruckus isn't always a bad thing. Those are the people who get shit done."

London laughed, but Aleshia's words had only caused that uneasy feeling in her stomach to grow.

Is that how the people at this hospital viewed her? As some kind of instigator who thrived on stirring up trouble? That was *never* her intention. It wasn't the kind of reputation she wanted. What if she decided to give the hospital in Chicago a closer look? What if the absolute worst happened and County closed entirely, forcing her to have to move elsewhere? Would being labeled a firebrand who routinely bucked the administration be enough of a deterrent to hurt her chances of getting on at another hospital?

London folded the remaining cupcake in a napkin, her appetite suddenly nonexistent. She stood.

"I need to get back up to the third floor," she said. "I'll let you know what I decide about the committee."

"No pressure." Aleshia raised her hands. "Just remember that your powers of persuasion are strong, Dr. Kelley. You can steer those people from New York in the right direction if you sense they are heading in the wrong one." She held up the empty cupcake wrapper. "Thanks for the extra treadmill time."

London managed to conjure up a smile as she waved goodbye.

She returned to the pediatrics ward and realized that she was looking forward to losing herself in the mountain of charts waiting for her. Just more evidence that this Monday needed to chill the hell out. London entered her office and stopped short at the surprising yet welcome scent in the air. She caught sight of a brown paper bag with a receipt stapled to it on her desk.

Frowning, she walked over to the desk and unfurled the top of the bag. The delicious aroma that wafted up from it awakened her appetite with renewed gusto. She reached inside and pulled out a translucent bag with a perfectly fried egg roll.

"Oh, thank you, food fairy," she said before biting into it.

That's when she noticed the grease-stained handwritten note that had been stuck to the bottom of the bag.

> *Didn't know what you were in the mood for, but everyone loves Chinese food. —Drew*

"That son of a bitch," London whispered, her heart melting like butter underneath a July sun.

She slumped into her chair and stared at the note, taking another bite from her egg roll as she studied his bold, crisp handwriting.

She had not been prepared for the sweet side of Drew Sullivan. She wasn't sure she wanted sweetness from him. Satisfying, enthusiastic sex she could handle. Heartwarming gestures that hinted at affection or concern?

No. That was more than she expected or wanted from this arrangement between them.

"Why did you have to go and complicate things with Chinese food?" London muttered. Her stomach rumbled and, she couldn't be certain, but she was pretty sure it told her to shut up and eat.

She removed the plastic lid on the takeout container and nearly started to weep as steam lifted up from the chicken lo mein. But as much as her body appreciated the sustenance, that anxious feeling persisted in her gut.

London set the container down and narrowed her eyes at it. Had he bought this because he knew she was hungry, or was there an ulterior motive? Was this his way of buttering her up?

"I don't know if I can trust you, Drew," she murmured.

He'd made a good argument for her working with Trident this morning, but how did she know it wasn't all an act? How could she be sure he had the best interests of the *entire* hospital at heart, and not just the accounting department's? How could she be sure he would look at every aspect of this facility, and not simply run numbers through some spreadsheet and decide that County should cut its losses?

There was no way for her to know for certain, but Aleshia was right: There was one thing she *could* do that would give her a better vantage point.

She picked up her phone and sent a text to Doug Renault.

I'll be one of your ambassadors.

14

Drew walked over to the eighty-inch LCD screen that had been brought in for today's meeting. He had Larissa rent it after discovering Travis County Hospital was still using the pull-down projection screens whenever someone had to give a presentation. In the grand scheme of things, updating the AV equipment didn't even crack the top twenty on the hospital's necessities list, but he was ready to donate his own money if that's what needed to be done to bring them up to the current century.

"Is everything ready?" Drew asked Samantha Gomez.

"It is." She looked at her phone. "We've got about twenty minutes, so we can just give everyone a chance to trickle in. Those are mine!" she called, looking past Drew's right shoulder. "I ordered a couple dozen cupcakes. I figured a little late afternoon treat would put everyone in a good mood."

"Works for me," Drew said.

Hell, he would buy them all steak dinners if that's what it would take to convince them to support Trident's efforts here at County. If he had his way, he would move this meeting completely off hospital grounds, to somewhere with more space. This room wasn't much bigger than the collaboration room at his apartment.

He'd finally gotten the full story on why they couldn't utilize the largest conference room here at the hospital. According to the custodian he'd spoken to this morning, the main conference room was pulling double duty as storage after a busted pipe took out one of the storage rooms on the second floor several months ago. No move had been made yet to repair it. Trident had only been here a week, yet even that tiny glimpse into how this hospital was managed was enough to show Drew how it had gotten into such a pile of shit.

He didn't want to get too far into the weeds when it came to this job—that's what their project manager was there for—but Drew also knew there was too much work to be done here for him to return to the sidelines. He would pull back if his team asked him to do so, but he'd already resigned himself to being more hands-on.

He walked over to a cardboard coffee carrier delivered from a local shop—another thing Drew had insisted upon after tasting the hospital coffee. He filled his cup from the spigot and added a packet of sweetener, then turned just in time to see London walk through the door.

His body experienced that now-familiar jolt he always felt upon seeing her.

Last night was the first time since their class reunion that she hadn't spent at least a few hours in his bed. It was scary to think that he'd gotten so used to having her there after just over a week, but he could still feel the disappointment that had assaulted him when she'd responded to his on your way? text with a pulled into surgery response. A few hours later, she'd texted that the surgery was over but she was too exhausted to do anything except sleep.

Drew had offered up his bed, strictly for sleeping purposes.

He was only a couple of minutes from the hospital, and it just made sense for her to spend the night.

But she was already home by the time she'd read his text. And her follow-up response made it clear that her thoughts hadn't changed regarding the boundaries they'd set. When it came to his bed, there was only one activity she wanted to engage in while there, and it wasn't sleeping.

Drew had spent the rest of the night in a state of frustrated restlessness. It wasn't that he had a problem with being London Kelley's boy toy for the next few weeks. He'd gone into this former-high-school-classmates-with-benefits arrangement with his eyes wide open.

He wanted the sex, but he also wanted more. What that more was, he wasn't sure yet. He hadn't taken the time to define it. But after last night, maybe *more* was her being comfortable enough with him to crash at his apartment following a three-hour emergency surgery at the end of her shift. That didn't seem all that outrageous.

She walked up to him and nodded at his cup. "That coffee doesn't look like motor oil. Please tell me there's more."

He moved to the side so that she could see the coffee setup on the table. "Help yourself."

"Is this a perk to working with Trident?"

"This is a perk to being anywhere that I am," Drew said. "I'm not particularly picky about my coffee, but it must at least be drinkable. So, yes, there will be coffee brought in whenever this group meets."

She sniffed the steaming coffee before taking a sip. She closed her eyes and released a satisfied sigh. "Maybe I won't regret this after all."

Drew chuckled. "I'll be honest, I was surprised when I got

word from Dr. Coleman that you would be joining us. After yesterday's *non*-ambush, I was pretty sure you would turn down the invitation."

She shrugged as she took another sip of coffee. "I had a change of heart."

"Brought about by?"

"By the thought of this hospital potentially closing altogether. I've always been afraid of it being sold to a private corporation, but state-run hospitals get shut down all the time."

"That won't happen," Drew said. "Trident will make sure of that. It's why we're here." He paused, debating whether to continue with his thought. London had made it clear that she was against privatization. Drew didn't want them to start off on the wrong foot by bringing it up before their first official meeting even started.

Then again, he needed to be completely transparent with her, especially after not being straightforward about his working at County.

"We're going to do everything in our power to make sure County remains in operation, but you need to understand that a takeover by a private corporation is still on the table, London. It may be the only solution." He put his hands up. "I don't know yet. None of us do. That's why we're here."

"And I'm here to make sure we explore every possible avenue," she replied. "I'm also here to make sure that your recommendations aren't just a regurgitated list of the budget cuts Coleman and his cronies tried to shove down our throats last year."

Drew took a sip of his now slightly cooled coffee before massaging the bridge of his nose. "How hard are you planning to make my life? I just want an estimate so that I can have my assistant adjust the amount of ibuprofen she adds to the shopping list."

"First, of all, I am not here to be difficult," she said. "And second, you're in a hospital. Just ask one of the nurses for some. You don't have to get your assistant to buy ibuprofen."

"Actually, I do. One of the recommendations Trident will be making is that raiding of the supply closet for personal use must be curbed. Immediately."

She laughed as if she thought he were joking. When Drew didn't join her, her eyes widened with surprised amusement. "Wow. You come out swinging with those types of changes and you'll be at the very top of everyone's shit list, Mr. Sullivan."

"That's okay. Being seen as the bad guy isn't new to me. The hospital is losing too much money. When you have hundreds of employees who think it's no big deal to grab a box of latex gloves or bandages from the supply closet to bring home, it ends up costing the hospital tens of thousands of dollars per year."

"I'm not saying you don't have a point." She raised a hand in concession. "I'm just saying it's a good thing you bring your own coffee. Because once it's revealed that you're behind these changes, someone would probably spit in it if you bought coffee from the cafeteria."

"Thanks for the warning," he said with a laugh. He checked his watch. They still had about ten minutes before the meeting would begin. "What about you?" Drew asked. "Do *you* plan to spit in my coffee? Metaphorically, of course."

"Spitting is nasty," she said. "I have access to substances that would cause you a lot more pain."

His brow arched.

"I'm joking," she said. "Again, I'm not here to be difficult. However, I will not be silent if I disagree with something.

And I do have a habit of playing devil's advocate." She shrugged. "I can't help myself. I like to pose questions. I've seen how they can spark new ideas."

Drew perched on the edge of the uncomfortable conference table and set his coffee next to him. Folding his arms across his chest, he said, "You don't have to tell me about your penchant for playing devil's advocate. I once sat in a classroom and listened to you argue about the patriarchal themes of Homer's work with Mr. Brown. The man could hardly utter a word by the time you were done with him."

A rueful grin curled up one corner of her mouth. "He tried to get me transferred to Mrs. Cornwall's English lit class after that."

Drew laughed. "You're kidding?"

She shook her head. "Not kidding. He said that my strong attitude was a disruption."

"You made some good arguments. The fact that women are literally given out as prizes in *The Iliad* is pretty messed up."

"Goodness, that was so long ago. How do you even remember that?"

Drew's gaze swept over her face. Softly, he murmured, "How could I forget?"

She stopped in the act of lifting her coffee cup to her mouth, her expression nonplussed.

"Drew, it's two o'clock." They both startled at Samantha's interruption. "Time to get this show on the road."

"Yes, of course," Drew said. He motioned for London to sit in the open chair, but then he walked to the rear of the room and stood against the wall. He was confident in his project manager's ability to lead the meeting.

As Samantha began her presentation, Drew observed the

eight people the hospital administration had put forward as the best ambassadors for the project. They would be tasked with providing Trident's team better insight into the day-to-day operations at County, but also assisting in encouraging the rest of the staff to participate in the analysis.

At least, that was the plan. How well Trident's plan was received and executed would depend a lot on how things went in today's kickoff meeting.

Drew's anxiety level had decreased exponentially by the time Samantha concluded her presentation. He'd gauged the reactions in the room through every bullet point, and it was exactly what he'd expected from the hospital's employees: curiosity, concern, and just a touch of dismay.

It shocked him how clueless most people were about the financial health of their workplace. There was no doubt they had heard the rumors floating around, but Drew could tell by the disturbed looks on their faces that this was the first time they'd understood how dire the situation was here at County.

Samantha brought the meeting to a close and informed everyone that she would be setting up a private Slack channel where they could all communicate. She then had to explain what Slack was to the two members of the team who were obviously Dr. Coleman's contemporaries.

He went over to Samantha. "Good job," Drew said. "Everyone has their marching orders, so we shouldn't have to meet until Friday, right?"

She saluted him. "Aye, Captain."

Drew made his way around the room, introducing himself to everyone they'd brought in to work with Trident. By the time he arrived back to where London had been sitting, the chair was empty. He left the conference room and took off down the hallway. He caught up with her at the elevator.

She glanced over at him. "Did I leave something in the conference room?" she asked, her voice droll.

"Unfortunately, it would appear you brought that attitude along with you."

She kept her head facing the elevator, but Drew caught the smile playing at the corner of her mouth.

"Have your feelings about what Trident is doing changed at all after getting a closer look at what we're up against?" he asked.

"Not yet."

The elevator dinged with its arrival. She boarded it. He followed.

"Don't you have anything better to do?" she asked him, her eyes on the numbers above the door.

"Better than convincing this hospital's most influential staff member that we need her to be on our side? No, I don't think so."

"Hmm," she murmured. "Tell me, how much money is the hospital shelling out for you to spend your time harassing me?"

Such a smart-ass.

"Trident's fees will show up in next year's audit," he said. He leaned over just as the door opened on the third floor, and said in a lowered voice, "And this isn't harassment. It's aggressive campaigning."

She shook her head, that grin still on her lips. Drew walked in step with her as they made their way to her office.

"I literally have fifteen minutes to catch my breath before I have to make my afternoon rounds," she said. She yawned as she sat behind her desk. "I was hoping to catch a quick cat nap, but I guess that's not possible because of you and your aggressive campaigning."

"You wouldn't be so tired if you had come over to my place last night," Drew told her.

She laughed. "I'm pretty sure I would be even more exhausted if I'd done that."

"To sleep," he reminded her, sitting in the chair across from her desk.

"Do you really think I would've spent my time at your place sleeping?"

"Yes, because that's all I was offering you last night. However, tonight I'm also offering dinner."

"Haven't we had this discussion? All I want from you—"

"Yeah, I already know what you want from me, London. But I think we need to redefine this imaginary line that you're not willing to cross."

She hunched her shoulders and shook her head. "I don't think we do. I'm pretty damn happy with things the way they are."

Drew sat back in his chair and crossed his ankle over his knee. He rubbed his thumb back and forth over his chin as he stared at her.

"What if I'm not?" he asked.

Her brows nearly touched her hairline. "Really? You seemed pretty damn happy Sunday night."

"What if being pretty damn happy isn't enough for me?"

She released a sigh. "Drew, don't mess this up."

"It's dinner, London. A simple meal between fr—"

"Two people engaged in a mutually satisfying sexual arrangement," she finished.

"Would it really kill you to think of yourself as my friend?"

"We're not friends."

"I want us to be friends."

"Ugh. Please stop." She dragged her hands down her face. "I want a nap."

"London."

"Drew, I can't just tell myself that we're friends after spending the past fifteen years hating you."

"You've spent the past fifteen years hating the *idea* of me. And after spending the past week sleeping with me, I think we've moved to at least a base level of friendship. I'm not saying we spend the night doing each other's hair and watching rom-coms, but dinner seems reasonable."

She burst out laughing. A genuine laugh this time. It felt as if Drew had scored his biggest win since he'd arrived in Austin.

"So?" he asked.

"I can't have dinner with you tonight," she said.

"Why?"

"Because I'm having dinner with my mom and stepmom tonight."

He wanted to believe her. Honestly, she had no reason to lie to him. It wasn't as if she would try to spare his feelings.

"What about tomorrow night?"

She sat back in her chair and folded her hands over her stomach, regarding him with cool but intense scrutiny.

"Maybe. If my schedule allows it," she finally answered. "But even if I do agree to have dinner with you, I am still not your friend, Drew Sullivan."

He grinned. "Yet."

15

"Come on, come on, come on," London muttered under her breath as she glanced in her rearview mirror, looking for an opening so that she could move into the right lane. Austin traffic was always a bitch, but evening rush hour was a special kind of pain in the ass.

That's what she got for canceling on her mother and stepmom for the past month. Their weekends were now all booked up—because they both had more interesting lives than she did—and a weeknight was the best either could do. London had come close to suggesting they just skip their monthly dinner altogether, but she was in no mood for the backlash that would cause. She heard enough shrieks of "you work too hard" and "we never see you" already; the last thing she needed to give The Mothers was more ammunition for their argument that she was a workaholic.

Besides, she was intrigued by the sense of urgency she'd gleaned from their multiple text messages today, reminding her at least a half-dozen times about tonight's dinner. She'd inquired about her dad, wondering if he'd had another TIA, but April had assured her that Kenneth was doing fine.

She quickly took the exit for Bluff Springs, grateful to get out of the traffic snarl. But one quick glance around as she pulled up to an intersection reminded her that she was now smack dab in the middle of Suburban Hell.

Someone could offer her a million dollars for the Craftsman-style bungalow she owned in Hyde Park—in fact, multiple people *had* offered her well over a million for it—but there was no way London would leave her charming little neighborhood. Not if this tan-colored, strip mall–laden existence was the alternative.

Her mother adored the cookie-cutter house she'd bought several years ago in a planned development just south of the city. And despite the fact that London would get lost if she didn't know the house number—because there were only three home designs in the development, and they repeated over and over again—she was happy that her mom was happy. Having London's stepmother, April, nearby also helped.

She always got strange looks whenever she told people that her mother, Janette, and her father's current wife were best friends.

No, they didn't grow up together. No, April didn't steal London's dad from her mother. Kenneth Kelley had gone through three wives between the time her parents divorced and his latest—and, hopefully, please, God, last—marriage. Her mother and April had hit it off from the very beginning, despite April's being ten years younger. And her ex-husband's new wife.

Her family was strange. There was no other way to describe them.

London pulled into the parking lot of the chain restaurant—another aspect of suburban life she could do without—and spotted her mom and stepmom walking up to the restaurant entrance. She blew her horn to get their attention, and pointed to an empty parking spot a few yards away.

Of course, a Prius swooped into the spot before she could get it. Because that's just how her luck rolled these days.

She circled the steakhouse a couple of times before finding a spot, then quickly made it inside to where her mother and April were waiting. Hugs were dispensed, and the obligatory "skipping meals again?" and "are you getting enough sleep?" questions were asked.

London answered with yes and no, because why lie?

She gestured for them to go ahead of her as they were ushered to a table, but moments after they were seated and served glasses of water, she noticed something was off. The Mothers both had pensive looks on their faces.

"What?" she asked, setting her menu on the table.

Her mother looked to April. "Do you want to tell her?"

Panic immediately seized the air in London's lungs. "What's going on?" she asked. "You said Kenneth is doing okay, so who's sick? Is it you?" she directed at April. "You?" she turned to her mother.

"No one's sick. It's not anything like that," her mom said.

"Then what? You know I don't play this vague, guessing-game shit. Somebody tell me what's going on."

"It's Nina," her stepmom said. "She's not sick, but she is having... issues."

Nina was her fourteen-year-old half sister, the oldest of her dad and April's three children. Koko, the youngest of the girls, and Miles, her dad's only son and his true pride and joy, were eleven and eight. All three were named after Kenneth Kelley's favorite musicians, Nina Simone, Koko Taylor, and Miles Davis. London was forever grateful that her own mother had pushed back against naming her after Muddy Waters.

"What types of issues is she having?" London asked, finally able to breathe again now that she knew no one was on their deathbed. She took a sip of her water.

"I caught her taking nude photos of herself yesterday," April blurted.

London choked on the water. "What?"

"You heard me. And not just topless, but full-on nudes! Front and back!"

"Oh, God," London groaned. She set her elbows on the table and started to massage her temples. "Please tell me she didn't text them to anyone."

"April was able to stop her before she could," her mother said.

"And I stood there and made sure she deleted them from her phone," April added. "I watched her as she did it."

"Did she delete them from the deleted files?" London asked. They both stared at her like she'd just flown in from Mars. *Wonderful.* London took another drink from the cup of water, hoping against hope that it had magically turned into vodka.

"Just a little tip," she said. "When you delete pictures and videos from your phone, they go into a deleted files folder where they're still available for thirty days."

"Oh, I didn't know that," April said. She frowned. "I need to make sure some pictures Kenneth and I took—"

"Stop right there." London held her hand up. "Do not even *attempt* to finish that statement." She sucked in a deep breath and slowly blew it out. She made a mental note to contact Taylor about those stress-relieving yoga techniques.

"Back to Nina," London said. "Why was she taking nudes?

Does she have a boyfriend? Did he pressure her into taking the pictures? And did you tell her how easily those can get out and fuc—freaking ruin her life!"

Dammit! She would have hoped that Nina knew better than to do something like this!

"I don't think she has a boyfriend," April said. "I think she likes this boy, and she took the pictures because she's trying to get his attention. The two of them are in the marching band together. He's a drummer, of course."

"I thought he played saxophone?" Janette asked.

"No, it's definitely the drums."

"That is not the important thing here!" London said.

"Hmm," her mother said. "As two women who were both married to a musician, let me tell you, it matters, honey."

"It does." April nodded.

London had never wanted to flip a table more than she wanted to at this very second.

"Fine," she said. "This saxophonist or drummer kid, did he pressure Nina into taking the photos? And are you sure this is the first time she's done this? Or that she hasn't tried to do it again?"

Damn, how could April even be sure of that? Nina could have taken a bunch of nudes ten minutes after her mom made her delete the ones she'd caught her taking. Those pictures could be making the rounds on the cell phones of horny little marching band members as they sat here ordering dinner. Or, worse, already plastered all over the Internet.

"I don't know," April said, her voice trembling. "We got into a big fight over it. I wanted to take her phone away, but then I thought, what if there's a school shooting or she gets into an accident? How would I get in touch with her?"

London pressed her fingers hard against her temples. She didn't have any kids because she didn't want to deal with this kind of shit. Yet, here she was, dealing with this kind of shit.

And where was Kenneth in all of this? Had April even bothered to tell him? Would he have left the golf course, or practice with the seventies cover band he played with on the weekends, or whatever the hell he was into these days to see about his daughter?

The server finally showed up to take their meal order, placing a basket of hot bread in the center of the table and running through a list of dinner promotions. London told him she was good with just the bread, but one look from The Mothers had her adding a side salad and an order of shrimp scampi, which looked to be the least threatening items for someone who was prehypertensive.

Of course, their current conversation was doing more to send her blood pressure through the roof than anything on this menu could ever do.

"I'm assuming you want me to talk to Nina?" she asked once the server was gone.

"Yes, please," April said. "She looks up to you so much more than you realize, London. She'll listen to you."

London wasn't so sure about that. The fact is, she didn't see her younger siblings very often. It wasn't something she was proud of, and she constantly promised herself that she would try to do a better job at being a big sister, but with her schedule and *their* schedule, which was nearly as hectic as hers with all their extracurricular activities, months could go by before she saw Nina, Koko, and Miles.

The only reason she saw April as much as she did was that she usually tagged along when London and her mom got together for their monthly—okay, every other month these days—dinner.

"I just don't know what to do about any of this," April said. "Nina and I have always had such a good relationship, but lately it's as if I'm enemy number one."

"She's fourteen and you're her mother," Janette said as she picked up a roll. "Believe me, you *are* enemy number one. I speak from experience. And it will only get worse."

"I was not that bad," London insisted. She looked to April. "I'll be honest, I'm not even sure how to approach Nina without biting her head off. She should *know* better."

"She's fourteen!" Janette reiterated. "She's a walking hormone who is trying to impress a boy. You don't want to hear the kinds of things I did to get boys to notice me when I was that age."

"No, I do not," London said. "I never want to hear about that. *Ever.*" Her mother rolled her eyes at her. "I'll talk to her," London said. "And I'll try to impart just how awful life could get for her if those pictures were to fall into the wrong hands."

Fall into the wrong hands? Her sister had nearly delivered them with a fucking bow into the wrong hands. Because a fourteen-year-old boy's hands were *always* the wrong hands. London's heart started to pound with panic just at the thought of what could have happened if April hadn't caught her in the act.

Oh, God. The breadth of this horrible situation suddenly hit her. April had caught her. In. The. Act!

How humiliating must it have been for Nina to have her mother walk in on her taking full-frontal nude photos? London would cringe into eternity if something like that had ever happened to her at that age—or any age.

And now they wanted her to talk to Nina?

But how could she say no?

"What about Saturday?" London asked. "Maybe I can take her to the mall or bowling alley or wherever teenagers like to hang out." It's not as if she knew. She hadn't hung out with other teenagers even back when she *was* a teenager.

April reached across the table and covered London's hand. "Thank you so much, honey. I hope you can get through to her."

London just hoped she made it through the conversation without her head literally exploding.

After dinner, her mom invited her to come over to the house for pound cake. Even though Janette lived only five minutes away and pound cake sounded divine, London declined. She also declined her mother's leftover flatbread pizza, while making a promise that she would not skip any more meals.

By the time she was in her car and heading back to the freeway, London's nerves were completely shot, and she was in desperate need of a way to unwind. As she waited at a red light, she picked up her phone and texted Drew.

> Want company?

His response was almost instant.

> You never have to ask that question. Get over here.

She cursed the stupid smile that formed on her lips, but it refused to go away. They still weren't friends, but maybe she could move him into the frenemy category.

16

Drew divided his attention between his computer and the door to his apartment. His body had been humming with anticipation ever since he received London's text. But he needed to finish typing up his notes on the request for proposal one of their managing partners sent for review before he could focus on tonight's activities. The RFPs from a chain of urgent care clinics based out of Kansas City had come in earlier this week, and if Trident was chosen to evaluate their management system and come up with best practices, it would be their largest project yet.

And further confirmation that leaving the Meacham Group had been the right move. Although, the fact that he no longer chewed antacids like candy was all the confirmation Drew needed to know that leaving his old hedge fund had been the best—the *only*—choice. Whoever said money can't buy you peace of mind knew what the hell they were talking about.

The knock on the door came just as he hit send on his email to Melissa, the partner taking the lead on the urgent care project. Drew closed his laptop and set it aside before quickly making his way to the door.

He opened it, prepared to trade barbs with London, per

their usual twisted brand of foreplay. But that changed the moment he took in her expression.

He stepped out of the way so that she could enter the apartment.

"It doesn't look like you're here for what I thought," Drew said.

"I am very much here for the reason you think I am," she said. "I've had a rough evening. Mindless, blow-my-back-out sex is exactly what I need right now."

"I can deliver that," Drew said. "But if I'm being honest, I'm not sure you can handle it just yet. Not based on what I see here."

She laughed. "You can just come out and tell me I look like shit, Drew."

"You don't." She looked amazing, as always. But it was blatantly obvious that something was troubling her. The fact that she went to his kitchen instead of the living room or straight to the bedroom solidified it. Drew followed her, stopping at the fridge to get her a bottle of water before continuing to where she rested her backside against the kitchen counter.

"Thanks," she said, taking the bottle from him. "I wish I could have something stronger, but I still have to drive home."

"Or..."

"I'm not spending the night."

"I have a fully stocked bar. It could be at your disposal."

"Stop trying to tempt me," she said. She dropped her head back and stared up at the ceiling, releasing an exhausted, frustrated breath.

"What's wrong, London?"

"I'm a shitty big sister," she said.

Drew's head snapped back. "You have a sibling?"

She nodded, uncapping her water and taking a sip. "Two sisters and a brother. All much younger than me. I'm mistaken for their mother whenever I bring them somewhere." She tipped her head to the side. "I wonder if that's subconsciously why I *don't* spend as much time with them as I should."

"If you don't mind some unsolicited advice, try not to psychoanalyze yourself when you're in this kind of mood. Nothing good can come of it."

Her lips curved with a teasingly inquisitive smile. "You sound as if you speak from experience."

"You don't know the half of it, Dr. Kelley." He walked over to the built-in wine rack and chose a bottle of Shiraz. "I'm assuming these are your dad's kids?"

Another nod. "Yeah," she said, focused on his movements as he uncorked the wine. "My dad went through half of Austin's female population before finally settling on one of the loveliest people you will ever meet. I honestly like his wife more than I like him." She shook her head, as if knocking herself out of a daze. "I don't know why I'm telling you any of this. I didn't come here to talk about my family. I came here for sex."

"You'll still get the sex," Drew said. "But it's obvious you need to talk about whatever is bothering you."

And the fact that she was talking to *him* about it made Drew happier than he thought possible. He slipped two wine-glasses from the stainless steel rack and filled them a third of the way.

"I told you I can't drink," London said.

"You'll be here long enough for the effects of one glass of wine to wear off." He handed her a glass. "Or, you can just spend the night and drink the rest of the bottle."

Her smile broadened. "You just don't know when to quit, do you?"

"Nope," he answered. "Admit it, London. I'm growing on you."

"Like an annoying weed," she said with a snort.

He laughed. This was the kind of connection and ease he'd been craving with her. But Drew wasn't letting her off this quickly. Her smile didn't reach her eyes, which were still clouded with worry.

"So, why do you think you're a shitty big sister?" he asked. He angled his head toward the living room, gesturing for her to follow him. Drew grabbed the wine bottle, but he wouldn't push her to have any more if she really didn't want any.

She settled on the sofa with one leg folded underneath her. The way her dark jeans stretched across her inner thigh made him instantly hard.

Goddamn, the things this woman did to him!

Resting her elbow on the back of the sofa, she cradled the side of her head in her upturned palm. Drew itched to reach over and drag his fingers through those thick coils. He knew how soft they would feel against his skin.

"I'm not winning any Big Sister of the Year awards because I can't tell you the last time I saw my sisters and brother. Halloween, maybe?" she said, taking a sip of wine. "I cleaned out the candy aisle at CVS and plied them with enough guilt chocolate to last a year. But Nina wasn't even there at the time. She was at a Halloween party."

"Nina is the oldest?" he asked.

She nodded. "And she's...gotten herself into a bit of trouble." She gulped down even more wine. "My stepmom, April, walked in on her taking nude selfies."

"Oh, shit." Drew said. "How old?"

"Fourteen."

He released a low whistle as he shook his head. "I can't imagine being that age with the technology available these days. I think back to high school and I'm grateful that the iPhone wasn't released until the summer after we graduated."

London's brows creased, a frown pulling at the corners of her mouth. "Are we really that old?"

"Yep. My uncle Elias bought me one my freshman year at Howard. I thought I was hot shit because of that phone, but never once considered using it to send nudes of myself to anyone. Or ask someone for nudes. Now it's commonplace."

"I'm just hoping April really did stop her in time. I've heard too many horror stories of what can happen when a girl sends pics to one guy and, the next thing you know, he's sent them to half the school." She gripped her curly hair tight. "It only takes seconds to become the girl everyone is talking about, and for all the wrong reasons."

"Technology," Drew reiterated. "It makes it so easy to turn one stupid mistake into a disaster that can follow you around forever."

"I still can't believe Nina would be so irresponsible. Even at fourteen, I never would have done something like this."

"I didn't know you when you were fourteen, but at sixteen you were more mature than some adults I know. Don't compare your sister or any other teenager to the kind of kid you were at that age."

"You're right," she said. "I have to remember that when I see her." She sent him a pained look. "I told The Mothers I would talk to her."

"The Mothers?"

"My mom and my stepmom. They're sort of best friends. Don't ask," she said, draining the rest of the wine from her glass. She eyed the bottle he'd set on the coffee table, but then she shook her head. "Nope. Not falling for it."

Drew shrugged off his disappointment as he finished his own glass. Before he could lower it from his mouth, London lifted the wine stem from his fingers and set both his glass and hers on the coffee table. Then she crossed her left leg over both of his legs and straddled his lap.

Drew's hands immediately sought her waist. He held her with a firm grip, his thumbs slipping underneath the hem of her clingy black top.

London locked her wrists behind his head. "I didn't come here for wine or to talk about my family," she said. "I came here to, well, come. And I would like to come over and over again. You up for making that happen, Mr. Sullivan?"

"I'll repeat what I texted you, Dr. Kelley. You never have to ask that question."

She attacked him with a brutal kiss, her mouth eager and demanding as she plunged her tongue past his lips with punishing force. Drew pulled her shirt over her head and made quick work of getting rid of her jeans. He would give anything for just a few minutes to take in the sight of her body, but all he got was a glimpse of the lacy pastel peach panties and bra against her rich brown skin before London had taken both off.

She helped him with his clothes, working on his pants while he unbuttoned his shirt. In minutes they were both naked with London once again straddling his thighs. She grabbed a condom from the drawer of the table next to the sofa—they'd learned over the past week to store condoms in every corner of the apartment—and ripped open the foil packet. Drew helped her roll it over his erection, and then she moved his hand out of the way so that she could grip his dick and guide it inside.

They cried out with matching groans as she planted herself on top of him. Her head fell back, exposing the slope of her neck to his mouth as her hips undulated against him. Drew captured her waist again, his fingers sinking into her flesh. He attempted to take control of her movements but soon relented, letting her set the pace.

"How are you... so fucking... good at this," London said between gasps.

"Practice," Drew replied.

She released a breathless laugh. "If you keep in touch with any of your other practice chicks, tell them I said thanks."

Drew dipped his head and captured one of her nipples between his lips, just to shut her up. It did the trick. She clasped her arms around his head, holding him in place as she continued to ride him. She began to pump harder, but Drew slowed them down. He wasn't ready for this to end just yet. He knew from experience that the moment she found her release, she would be out of here.

Instead, he pulled out and lifted her off his lap. Standing, he turned her around, taking both her hands and placing them on the back of the couch. Then he grabbed hold of his dick and eased into her from behind.

London let out a cry, her hips bucking as she pushed against him, meeting his forward thrusts. He palmed her stomach with one hand and gripped her hair with the other. The sight of her back arching was so damn erotic he nearly came, but still he held off.

He spun London around again and lifted her into his arms. She wrapped her legs around his waist and pointed to the bedroom.

"In there," she said.

"You're so bossy," Drew said.

"And you don't mind it one bit."

"Hell no, I don't," he replied, carrying her into his bedroom.

Once in bed, they went through another two condoms before finally collapsing in a heap of twisted sheets and tangled limbs. Drew rolled off her and onto his side. He listened for the moment when she would climb out of bed and get dressed. She never waited more than a few minutes after they were done to gather her things and leave him with that strange mix of blissful satisfaction and frustration.

Yet, every time he worked up the resolve to tell her that this sex-only arrangement was no longer enough for him, something stopped him. It wasn't just *some*thing that stopped him. He didn't want to risk her leaving his bed and never coming back. The pleasure he derived from the hours spent exploring her body far outweighed any disappointment he endured once she went home.

Drew froze when he realized that at least five minutes had passed and London hadn't left the bed. He pushed himself up on his elbow and looked over at her. She lay staring up at the ceiling with her hands clasped over her stomach. The sheet had fallen just far enough down her body so that one taut nipple peeked out over the edge of it.

And just like that, he started getting hard again. But the look on her face told him that sex was no longer on her mind.

"What's wrong?" Drew asked.

She glanced at him, then back at the ceiling. "I'm regretting not eating the pound cake."

Not what he'd expected to hear. "London, what are you talking about?"

"My mom offered me pound cake after dinner. I'm sorry I didn't take her up on it. Don't get me wrong, the sex was fantastic, but pound cake is pound cake."

Drew shrugged. "Yeah, I get it. It's hard to compete with cake." He nudged his head toward the door. "I have a couple of those fancy cupcakes left over from today's meeting."

She tore the sheet off her and scrambled out of the bed. A couple of minutes later, she returned carrying a pink-and-brown box. She climbed back into bed and sat up with her back against the headboard and the box of cupcakes on her lap.

Even though he'd spent over a week seeing this body in varying stages of nakedness, Drew struggled to maintain his composure at the sight of all that smooth, flawless skin. He still wasn't convinced that this wasn't a dream, because in what version of real life did he find himself in bed watching a naked London Kelley lick icing from a cupcake?

She held up a yellow one topped with white frosting and sparkling sugar. "It's not my mom's pound cake, but it'll do."

She took a huge bite, leaving a smear on her cheek. Drew used it as an opportunity to taste her, tenderly kissing the sweet frosting from her skin.

She edged her head back and stared at him, her gaze roving over his face. Their eyes locked moments before she leaned forward and claimed his mouth with a soft, tentative caress of her lips.

The fiery, demanding kisses they'd previously shared had

been fueled by lust and need, but this felt different. It felt like it *meant* something, like more than just another element of the physical act they'd been engaging in over the past week and a half.

The lack of heat and hunger added to his sense that things were changing between them, that her feelings were shifting. The cautious, thoughtful exploration of her tongue as she gently traced a path along the seam of his lips filled Drew with a hope he was almost afraid to let materialize.

She moved the cupcakes to the bedside table and brought both her hands up to cradle his face, kissing him deeper as she did so. They changed position, with Drew sitting up against the headboard and London flush against his chest.

But when she reached over for the box of condoms, Drew stopped her. He shook his head.

"Not yet," he said. "I just want to kiss you."

He held his breath as an array of emotions flashed across her face: confusion, suspicion, and finally acceptance. He welcomed the flood of relief that flowed through him as she yielded to his kiss. He slowed them down, keeping the pressure light, giving her the chance to pull away.

She didn't. Neither did she push for more. They remained in that safe, intimate, unhurried place, leisurely exploring each other's mouths with sweet, tender kisses. The kind of kisses that couldn't be disregarded as detached, heat-of-the-moment acts of passion. There was something more here, something intensely personal.

Something undeniable.

This was no longer just two people hooking up; this was two people on the precipice of something deeper, something more profound than casual sex.

"Don't think I don't know what you're doing, Drew Sullivan," London whispered against his lips.

"Kissing you?" he asked.

She pulled just far enough back to look at him. "I'm still not your friend," she said, but the relaxed humor in her voice belied her declaration.

"I think you are." Drew shifted his hips, stroking her inner thigh with his dick. London released a moan and pulled her bottom lip between her teeth.

"It doesn't matter if you're ready to accept it or not," Drew murmured as he went in for another kiss. "We're friends."

17

Noooooo!"

Taylor and Samiah's matching mortified shrieks made London feel marginally better about her own reaction to the situation with Nina.

"Unfortunately, yes," she told them as she angled her computer monitor down a bit. The glare from her office's fluorescent light made it look as if Taylor had a glowing sword growing out of her forehead.

"Do either of you want to trade places with me this weekend?" London asked. "I promised my stepmom I would talk to Nina on Saturday, and I'm afraid I won't be as magnanimous or calm as I probably should be in this situation."

"You couldn't pay me to trade places with you," Samiah said. "But try not to be too hard on her." She held up a hand. "I'm not saying you shouldn't put the fear of God in her, but remember how it is to be fourteen and seeking attention from a boy you like."

"Don't even get me started," Taylor said. "We would be here all day if I had to list all the regrets of fourteen-year-old Taylor. Your little sister is still too young to grasp just how close she came to getting herself into a shitload of trouble with those pics."

"I know," London said with a sigh. "Drew said the same thing. But it's—"

"Drew?" Taylor and Samiah both exclaimed.

"So, you've already talked to Drew about this?" Samiah asked.

"I—" London started, then stopped.

It suddenly occurred to her how odd it was that she had gone to Drew first instead of Taylor and Samiah. For the past six months, ever since she'd met them, she had immediately called on these two whenever she needed to talk through something.

"Huh." Taylor sucked her teeth. "See what happens when you start getting some dick? You just toss your friends aside like yesterday's trash."

"Oh, shut up," London said with a laugh.

Samiah shrugged. "Hey, I can't say I blame you. He's giving you something that neither of us can."

"Um, hello!" London waved at the computer's camera. "Remember who you're talking to here. I am not replacing my friends with a man—especially one who is temporary. Once the Orgasm Train pulls out of the station, I will be right back to blowing up both your phones and begging you to join me for margaritas."

"Oh, speaking of, I have to miss the two Friday get-togethers," Samiah said. "Trendsetters has a gala this Friday and I'm flying up to Philly to meet Daniel's parents next Friday."

"Whoa, that's huge," Taylor said.

"Why is it a big deal? Jamar has met your parents," Samiah pointed out.

"Yeah, but we were just pretending to date at the time,"

Taylor said. She scrunched up the side of her mouth. "Well, we were *sorta* pretend dating. The sex we had in the guest room at my parents' house was very, *very* real."

"See, two weeks ago, I would have been pissed at you for bragging about that," London said. "Now?" She hunched her shoulders. "Doesn't even bother me."

"You have been a lot calmer now that you're getting some," Taylor agreed. "But, look, even if Samiah can't be there, do you want to still get together? Actually, I'm not asking, I'm straight up saying that I *need* to see you, London. This stupid math class is kicking my ass and your brain is the only thing that will help me get through it."

"Absolutely!" London said.

"I just remembered that I promised Jamar I'd come to this thing at the high school where he'll be coaching this coming Friday, but does next Friday work?"

"Sure. Come over to my house. We'll order in some Thai and I can take a look at your assignments."

"You're a bit too excited about doing her math homework, and I find that very disturbing," Samiah said.

"Nobody asked you." Taylor stuck her tongue out. "I need to get out of here. My creative writing class starts in like twenty minutes, and huge surprise here, but I actually *like* this one."

"Really?" London asked. "So the coping techniques you've been using for your learning disorder have been helpful?"

"Seems that way," Taylor said. "It also helps that I'm writing manga, which I love. And that my story is totally kick-ass. I'm thinking I just may become a famous writer in my spare time."

"This coming from someone who hated the thought

of anything to do with school just a couple of months ago," Samiah said.

"Don't get it twisted. I still hate everything else about school," Taylor said. She stood, and a framed, poster-size photo of her boyfriend, Jamar, wearing nothing but a football helmet over his groin area hung on the wall behind her.

"Holy shit!" London said.

"Where the hell are you?" Samiah screeched.

Taylor turned to the picture. "I'm in the pool house, or my she shed, as Jamar calls it. I'm redecorating."

"What exactly did you have to promise that man in order to get him to pose for that picture?" Samiah asked.

"You don't want to know, but it was worth it," Taylor said. "Talk to you two later."

She disconnected from the video call, and Samiah's face instantly took up the entire screen.

"I'll deny it if you ever say anything, but I'm regretting not taking a screenshot of that picture while Taylor was still on the phone," Samiah said.

"You and me both." London slung her stethoscope around her neck. She had rounds in another five minutes. "So, are you nervous about meeting Daniel's parents?"

"Not as nervous as I was when I didn't get my period this week, but yeah, there's some nerves."

"Bitch, what?"

"Don't worry, it finally came and I took a pregnancy test just to be sure, but if I ever considered questioning whether I was ready for kids, I have my answer," Samiah said. "Shit, the guy they've put in my old position is texting me again. I swear, I'm doing both damn jobs. Good luck with Nina," Samiah said. "Remember, don't go all London on her."

"It's hard for me not to take that as an insult."

"It was meant to be one," Samiah said, sending her an overly sweet smile.

"Bitch," London laughed before ending the call.

She was still smiling as she gathered a collection of toys and sugar-free candy to dispense during rounds, but she couldn't help but think about what she would have felt if she'd faced what Samiah had this week.

Pure, unadulterated panic.

For someone who worked with kids every day, she couldn't accurately describe her terror at the thought of having one of her own.

London had found herself in that situation exactly one time in her life, during her sophomore year of college. The ten minutes between when she'd peed on that little stick and when the single line had appeared were some of the most fretful moments of her life. She knew a bunch of women who had raised kids on their own—her own mother for one, because even when Kenneth had still technically been her husband, he'd never been there in any meaningful way—but it was something London had never wanted for herself. She had devoted her life to helping other people's kids, which suited her just fine.

That incident back in college had been enough to scare her into being overly cautious when it came to protecting herself against pregnancy. She tracked her cycle religiously and made sure she didn't come within five feet of sperm when she was ovulating. Not that she'd had that to worry about this past year.

Shit, you do now!

She pulled up the ovulation forecast app on her phone and checked the calendar.

Good. She still had at least a few more nights of worry-free fucking before she had to put the kibosh on sexy times with Drew for a couple of days. She was already regretting the lost time. They might have to double up some nights to make up for it.

As much as London hated to admit it, she would miss him when he went back to New York.

"You'll miss the sex," she murmured.

Fine, so maybe she would miss him too. Just a little.

That admission was so much harder than she expected, which said a lot about how this casual hookup arrangement had gotten completely out of hand.

Last night, wrapped up in Drew Sullivan's arms post-orgasm, she'd felt zero desire to leave his bed. Even after she had left, she'd considered turning back around up until the moment she put the key in the lock at her own house just after midnight.

She'd gone from just hooking up with a guy she hardly knew to being totally dick-whipped in a matter of days.

No, she wasn't just dick-whipped. That she could handle. London was starting to... like him. She actually liked talking with Drew Sullivan. He listened and didn't try to mansplain or offer suggestions on how to fix her issues.

"Goodness, you cannot fall for him," London said, hoping to God that she wasn't already there.

She put Drew out of her mind and turned her focus to the eight patients currently occupying beds on the surgical floor. As she left her office, London spotted Aleshia marching down the corridor. The other doctor grabbed her by the hand and pulled London back inside.

"What's going on?" London asked.

"That's my question," Aleshia said. "Is the rumor about the new telehealth system true?"

"Where did you hear about that?" Trident had only discussed it with the group of ambassadors an hour ago.

"Where I heard about it isn't important—except for the fact that it didn't come from you. You're supposed to be my spy on the inside, remember?"

"I'm not spying," London said. "And, to answer your question, yes, one of the changes Trident will likely propose is utilizing telehealth to cut back on in-person care delivery."

"I knew it." Aleshia folded her arms over her chest. "So, did you share with the folks at Trident why practicing medicine via smartphone is not the best move for this hospital?"

"Initially," London said. She had never been one to shy away from technology, but she adamantly opposed the impersonal nature of telehealth.

Until Drew hit her with the cold hard facts.

He shared statistics from over a dozen hospitals Trident had worked with this past year, and the results didn't lie. Increasing virtual visits had no adverse effects on patient care and lowered operating cost substantially.

"What do you mean by *initially*?" Aleshia asked.

"I've seen the numbers," London said. "Not only will it save County millions over the next five years, but surveys from patients who have switched to majority telehealth visits show that they're just as happy with their care. And it saves them time. Think about the people we serve and how many of them have to catch several city buses to get here or take time off from work."

"I hadn't thought about that," Aleshia said.

"Neither had I, and if I'm being honest, I'm a bit ashamed," London admitted. "In all this time, I never really looked at telehealth from the patient's perspective—at least in the way it would make life easier for them. We both pushed back against it because we believe face-to-face is better, but is it up to us to make that choice for our patients?"

Aleshia released a sigh. "Fine. I get what you're saying." She turned and London followed her out of the office. "Just don't let Trident get rid of the slushie machine in the cafeteria," her friend added. "I understand budget cuts are necessary, but let's not go too wild."

"I promise to fight for your slushie machine, even if I have to chain myself to it," London said.

"It's why I love you," Aleshia said.

London's laughter trailed off as she continued down the hallway, her mind returning to the debate she'd had with Drew and his team over implementing a more robust telehealth program at County. London's argument had been based on her gut and emotions. Trident's was based on logic and substantiated data.

She prided herself on putting her patients' well-being above everything, but how often did she make decisions for them based on what she believed was best without considering how those decisions would affect other aspects of their lives?

The thought left a sour taste in her mouth.

She would find time for a little soul-searching later. Right now, she needed to focus on the kids due to have surgery soon.

She walked into the room of her first patient, Ahmad Jefferson, and found him playing a spirited game of trash can basketball with Drew. So much for her focus.

"And what exactly is going on here?" London asked as she walked over to the whiteboard to the right of the mounted television.

"Give us two minutes, Dr. K," the fifteen-year-old cancer

patient told her. Towing the IV standing behind him, he did a half-spin move and skirted around Drew's left side on his way to dunking the balled-up wad of paper into the wastebasket, which had been hung up on a second, out-of-service IV stand.

London folded her arms across her chest and leaned against the wall, watching them go at each other.

She could tell Drew was taking it easy on his opponent when it came to the physical game, but he pulled no punches when it came to the trash-talking. As she watched them, she wondered where Drew stood when it came to kids. Did he have any interest in eventually starting a family, or did his job take up too much of his time?

Why are you even thinking about this?

Drew Sullivan's procreation plans were of absolutely no concern to her.

"All right." London clapped her hands. "That's enough, LeBron and Steph."

Ahmad looked at her with wide eyes. "What do you know about LeBron James and Steph Curry?"

"I know enough," London said, taking hold of Ahmad's IV stand and guiding it back to the bed. She stood by as he climbed in, smiling at his Marvel Comics pajama bottoms.

"Are you ready for next week's surgery?" London asked.

He nodded. "Not sure my mom is, but she's coming around."

The fifteen-year-old had undergone eight surgeries in the last three years. London had been there for seven of them. She'd witnessed the toll it had taken on his family, how frightened his parents were every time their son was wheeled into the operating room. She could not fathom what it was like to wait helplessly while a team of strangers took a scalpel to your child.

"Don't worry about your mom," London told him. "I'll put her mind at ease as much as possible before the surgery. Will she and your dad be here later today?"

"After they get off work," he said.

"I'll try to drop back in. Meanwhile, no more basketball for you. Your body needs rest."

"That's okay. I was tired of kicking his ass anyway," Ahmad said.

"Sir," London said in a chastising tone.

"His butt."

"Hey, I let you win," Drew said. "Do you think I brought my A game to a kid with cancer?"

"Don't even try it, dude. You were huffing and puffing like a chain-smoker by the second game," Ahmad said.

"That was acting. I wanted you to think you were getting to me." Drew looked over at London. "That's a lie. He was kicking my ass—butt," he amended.

She burst out laughing. "No more basketball for *either* of you."

"Thanks for the game," Drew said, holding his fist out to Ahmad. The fifteen-year-old bumped it with his own fist, then picked up his cell phone. And, just like that, both London and Drew had been dismissed.

"Hey," Drew said once they were out of Ahmad's room. "I hope that was okay. You know, the little pickup basketball game."

"It's fine. As long as he doesn't overexert himself. It's actually good for him—anything to take his mind off the fact that he's facing another long surgery next week."

"He seems like a good kid." Drew glanced up and down the corridor, then at his watch. "Can we go to your office for a few minutes? Well, more like twenty minutes."

London narrowed her eyes at him. "You remember what I said about doing"—she looked around them and lowered her voice to a whisper—"those things here at the hospital."

He leaned toward her and whispered back, "Get your mind out of the gutter, Dr. Kelley. This has nothing to do with *those things*." Drew laughed. "No, really, it's about an outpatient program here at County. I want your take on how effective you think it's been this past year."

Okay, so maybe she was a little disappointed he had work on his mind instead of…*things*. Which was ridiculous because they were following her rules when it came to this line between the personal and professional.

"I have evening rounds in like one minute," London said. "But I should be done in about forty-five. Maybe an hour."

"Will that be the end of your shift?"

"If nothing comes through the ER between now and then."

"In that case, I'll wait for you. And, if I'm doing my math correctly"—he looked at his watch again—"you'll be done just in time for me to take you to dinner at an actual restaurant. Like *friends*. Isn't that something?"

She rolled her eyes. "You just don't know when to quit," she said as she started toward the next patient's room. She couldn't hold back her grin at the sound of Drew's laughter behind her.

18

"This is not what I had in mind when I said I wanted to take you out for dinner," Drew said as he walked side by side with London along the greenbelt that flanked the Colorado River.

"Too bad. This is what I felt like eating." She took a huge bite out of the giant pretzel he'd bought her from a street vendor.

When her shift ended a half hour ago, they quickly left the hospital before she could get roped into an emergency. But she'd thwarted Drew's plans of wining and dining her at one of Austin's legendary restaurants by claiming she wasn't all that hungry. She decided she needed a walk to clear her head, thus their current early evening stroll.

She held the pretzel out to him. "Want some? It's good."

He shook his head. "Enjoy your carnival food. I plan to have a real dinner once I get back to my place. You know, like an adult."

"Whatever," she laughed, rolling her eyes. She took another bite of her pretzel, leaving a trace of mustard at the corner of her mouth.

Drew considered kissing the mustard off her face as he'd done with the cupcake frosting last night, but then thought better of it. They were in public, not the privacy of his bedroom. Depending on her mood, she would either punch him in the eye or rip his clothes off and mount him in the middle of the park. There seemed to be no in-between when it came to London.

Not wanting to risk injury or an indecent exposure arrest, Drew caught her by the elbow and said, "You do eat with your whole face, don't you?" He swiped the mustard away with his thumb.

"I'm around kids all day," she said. "I guess they've rubbed off on me."

Her eyes followed his thumb as he licked the mustard off it. He let his tongue linger a bit longer than necessary just to mess with her.

"Ready to go back to my place?" Drew asked.

"I thought you were going to have dinner like an adult?" she asked.

"We can order in. Dinner in bed. That could be very adult."

She pulled her bottom lip between her teeth, her eyes still on his mouth. "I'll stick to my pretzel. For now," she added.

They continued along the walkway, hugging the right side to give the bike riders access to the path.

"So, what's the outpatient program you wanted to talk to me about?" London asked.

"I didn't think we could talk about it now that we're no longer at the hospital."

"Of course we can."

"Wait, so how does this 'no mixing business with pleasure' thing work? Does it not go both ways?"

She shook her head. "No hanky-panky at the hospital, but we can have hospital talk after hours," she clarified.

"For future reference, I prefer *sexy shenanigans* to *hanky-panky*."

"Noted." She stuffed the last of her pretzel into her mouth and walked over to a trash can to throw away the wrapper. When she returned to him, she made a *get on with it* motion with her hand. "So, this program?"

"Yeah, it's this thing that Dr. Coleman—"

"Hold up." She held up a hand. "Just to let you know, if it's something to do with Coleman, I probably hate it."

"What's the deal between you two?"

"Frederick Coleman has not liked me from the moment I stepped into that hospital."

"What did you say to him, London?"

She gasped. "Why do *I* have to be the bad guy here?"

"Because, as someone who has been on the receiving end of that razor-sharp tongue of yours, I know the damage it can cause."

She stopped walking and folded her arms across her chest. "Since when do you have a problem with what I do to you with my tongue?"

"Okay, I like your tongue much better now, but when we were in high school, I had a very different perception," Drew said. He was as tempted to kiss that smug smirk off her lips as he'd been with the mustard. "Are you going to give me the dirt on your feud with Coleman, or what?"

"If it's a feud, then it is one-sided," London said. "I try my best not to spend any of my precious energy on that man. And, to be honest, I'm still not sure why he doesn't like me." She shrugged. "Well, other than him being a misogynist who thinks men should be doctors and women should be nurses."

"No shit?" Drew asked.

"No shit," she answered. She let out an exhausted breath. "Actually, I *do* know what his issue is with me. He doesn't like the 'hype' surrounding me."

"You're too much of a badass for him?"

"It would seem so. It's not as if I make a habit of touting my accomplishments—okay, that's a bit of a stretch. Even I can admit that I'm the queen of the humblebrag, but I'm working on myself. Anyway, there are not many residents with a CV as decorated as mine." She shrugged. "I'm an overachiever, what can I say?"

"You think you have to tell *me* you're an overachiever? As if I didn't have a front-row seat to watching you twist yourself into knots over test scores."

"If you think it was bad in high school, it's nothing compared to how obsessed I became about grades in college and med school," she said. "But the *real* hype started after an incident that happened back when I was a first-year resident, during my general surgery rotation. The patient's gallbladder had erupted, and the attending had just removed it, and then he quit."

"What do you mean he quit?"

"He quit. Right there in the middle of the surgery. He said, 'I'm done,' put down the number eleven blade, and walked out of the operating room."

"What the fuck? Who does that?"

"Those may have been my exact words. It's one of the few details I can't recall from that day," London said. "I just remember taking over. After getting past the shock of what had just happened, several of the nurses ran to get another surgeon to help, but by the time that surgeon arrived, I was in the zone. She allowed me to complete the procedure." She flicked imaginary dust off her shoulders. "And that's how the legend was born."

"Damn, London. That's pretty badass. No, that's *totally* badass. You've earned the right to brag."

"Well, if you ask Coleman, what I did that day wasn't a huge deal."

"So he's a hater," Drew stated.

"A big one. The fact that I'm a woman only irritates him more. I wasn't being hyperbolic when I said the thing about him believing that women should only be nurses and not strive to be physicians. He's actually said those words. I haven't heard them directly, but several of my colleagues have."

"And no one has brought it up to Human Resources?"

"The thing you need to know about Coleman is that he's been at County since they laid the first bricks on the building. No one questions him because he's such a legend. And when someone *does* question him, she's labeled a troublemaker.

"I'm never disrespectful to his face," she continued. "I understand that I'm a resident and he's been at this for decades. But I won't just sit there and take shit either. Or remain quiet when I see something I don't agree with."

"You shouldn't," Drew said. "I think if more people had questioned some of the decisions that have been made at County, the hospital wouldn't be in the position it's in now. Which brings me to this program."

Drew gestured to the knee-high rock wall that lined this portion of the walking path. He waited for London to take a seat before continuing. "Now, I know geriatrics isn't your wheelhouse."

"The exact opposite of my wheelhouse," she pointed out.

"Yeah, but I still want your opinion. It's about the Seniors Clinic that's attached to outpatient care services."

"That's still in operation? I thought County disbanded it after the city built that new Council on Aging facility last year."

"*That's* the reason for the sudden drop-off." Drew snapped his fingers. "I couldn't figure it out. It looks as if the number of patients using it has steadily declined over the years, but there was a significant drop about fifteen months ago, and no explanation for it."

"From what I hear, Coleman was pissed because that Seniors Clinic was a feather in his cap," London said. "Now he can't tout the success of the program to the hospital's board of directors."

"Yeah, but the hospital is still putting a good portion of its budget into a clinic that no one is using."

She looked over at him, a furious scowl on her face. "Are you kidding me?"

Drew held his hands up. "Don't blame the messenger. Trident's chief auditor discovered it this morning. It raised a huge red flag for him. When I looked a little deeper, it just didn't seem to make any sense."

"I can't believe it," she said. "I have been begging for the past year for a sensory room on the pediatric floor, and Coleman has shot me down, citing the budget. Yet he's spending funds on a clinic no one uses?"

Drew raised his hands again. He didn't have an answer for her. Instead, he asked, "What's a sensory room?"

Her anger remained palpable. Drew could tell that she was struggling to get it under control.

"It's a room to help calm kids—particularly my ASD patients, those who have autism spectrum disorder," she explained. "Being in a hospital is scary for all kids, but the loud noises and those bright fluorescent lights—hell, even the ID bracelets we have to put on their wrists—can be intolerable for a child with sensory issues. I want to design a room for our unit with special lighting, weighted vests and blankets, and other things that help calm patients with autism.

"Even the patients without autism would benefit. There have been studies that show that just a few hours in a sensory room prior to surgery can have a big impact on kids. It's like you playing basketball with Ahmad earlier today. It gives them a sense of normalcy and makes them forget they're in a hospital and about to undergo this frightening procedure."

"Have you looked into how much it would cost?" She leveled him with a droll look. "Stupid question," Drew said. "Of course you, of all people, have done your homework."

"I have it budgeted down to the cost of the multiple textured rugs for the floor," she said. "It would run well over a hundred grand for the room I *really* want, but I'm willing to settle for something on a much smaller scale. It can be done for about forty thousand."

Drew wouldn't dare tell her how much had been spent on that defunct clinic this past year. Given the state of the hospital's financial health at the moment, and the amount of items on the priority list, he wasn't sure Trident would find an extra hundred thousand for her room.

Of course...

"I can give the hospital the money for it."

She started shaking her head before he could finish. "No. It's not as simple as just throwing money at it," she said. "That's my dad's answer for everything." The derision in her voice told Drew all he needed to know about that.

"Besides," she continued. "It will take more than just

money for the sensory room to be a success. It takes an ongoing commitment from the hospital. There are new therapies being discovered all the time, and the room would need to be updated every few years."

He could make sure there was enough to cover upkeep well into the future, but Drew had a feeling she would shoot that down as well.

"Don't give up hope just yet," he said.

"I haven't, but I know it's an extreme long shot," she said.

"It is." He shrugged. "But it may not be as out of reach as you're thinking."

Her eyes narrowed in suspicion, but then they widened with hopeful excitement. "Are you saying there's space for my sensory room in the budget?"

"Slow down, Dr. Kelley. I can't guarantee anything. That's not in my job description." Drew stretched his legs out in front of him and crossed his ankles. "But, as you know, one of the key outcomes of the work Trident is doing will be the recommendations we make about which programs should be slashed and which would add value to County. The team will need to perform a deeper assessment, but it sounds as if this sensory room deserves a place on the recommendation list."

Her mouth dropped open and that hope in her eyes turned to excitement.

"This is probably against the rules, but I so want to give you a blow job right now."

He threw his head back and laughed. "That is definitely a violation of the hospital's code of ethical conduct for contract employees, and against Texas law, if I'm not mistaken."

"Yeah, you're probably right."

"You can always give me a blow job just because you like doing it."

"I *do* like it." There was a tinge of wonder in her voice. She looked over at him, shaking her head in disbelief. "Did you imagine back in high school that would ever be the case?"

"Not in a million years," Drew answered honestly. Had he hoped for and dreamed about it? Every fucking night for his entire senior year and several years beyond.

Yet, for some reason, Drew held himself back from admitting it. He wasn't sure why he couldn't bring himself to tell her how infatuated he'd been with her all those years ago. Maybe because it still hurt to know it had been so one-sided.

Drew heard the faint sounds of a guitar being strummed from somewhere in the distance. He tipped his head in order to hear it better.

"Did you hurt your neck playing basketball with Ahmad?" London asked.

"No." He held up his hand and listened for a moment longer. "Albert King. 'Born Under a Bad Sign.' I knew that bridge sounded familiar." He smiled. "If there's one thing Austin has going for it, it's being the live music capital of the world."

"That is just one of the things this town has going for it," she said. "Funny enough, it's the one thing about Austin that I don't pay much attention to. I'm not a huge concert fan."

"But there are so many. There's a blues festival in Zilker Park next weekend that I was thinking about going to."

"Please don't tell me you're a fan of blues."

"Yeah. A huge one. What's wrong with blues?"

"Oh, Drew. Drew. Drew." She heaved out a dramatic sigh. "If I was afraid for even a second that I was catching feelings for you, that admission would be enough to quash them."

She laughed, but Drew had a hard time finding any humor in her words. They'd been together nearly every evening for going on two weeks. She hadn't caught even a *few* feelings in that time?

"Why do you say that?" he asked.

"Well, first there's the whole hating-you-for-most-of-my-life thing. Granted, I haven't been entirely fair to you on that front—"

"Not fair at all," he interjected.

She shrugged. "Yes, I know. I'm working on it. But that's not the only reason." She gestured in the area of his chest. "That Omega symbol branded into your pec? My dad belongs to that fraternity. And now I find out you love blues music too."

"Again, what's the problem with blues?"

"All three of my siblings are named after blues musicians, because that's just how big a fan Kenneth Kelley is of the genre. He's been playing with a local cover band for years. Which means, Drew Sullivan, you're basically my dad." She leaned forward and pretended to hurl. "If the sex wasn't so good, I would break off this thing we have going right this instant."

Well, fuck. He should just go ahead and tell her how obsessed he'd been with her back in high school. Her reaction couldn't make him feel any worse.

"Why do you look so sad?" she asked with a laugh.

"In the span of five minutes I went from being the guy you like giving blow jobs to, to the guy who reminds you of your dad. I want to throw myself in that river over there."

She laughed even harder.

"Come on," she said, rising from her perch on the rock wall and tugging at his arm. "There's only one way for me to make this up to you."

They continued east on the walking trail, but after a few steps, Drew stopped.

"What's wrong?" she asked.

He hooked his thumb back over his shoulder. "My apartment is that way. Unless we have different ideas about how you can make up for comparing me to your dad?"

"I guess there's more than one way to make it up to you," she said. "We can do both. But, for now, let's go find out where that music is coming from."

19

They came upon the band exactly where London expected to find them, performing in the small semicircular plaza where Colorado and Cesar Chavez Streets met. The open space butted up to the river, providing a gorgeous view of downtown Austin's south shore. A faint breeze blew off the water. It was cool, but not too cold. Still, London was glad she'd grabbed her knit cardigan from her office before leaving the hospital.

A sizable crowd had gathered to enjoy the band. This was Austin, after all. The music lovers in this city didn't wait for the weekend to have their fun.

She and Drew stood several feet back, away from the crowd. Drew leaned against the railing that surrounded the plaza, his arms folded across his chest, one foot tapping in time to Double Trouble's "Love Struck Baby."

"I'll be honest," London said. "I never pegged you as a Stevie Ray Vaughn fan."

He peered over at her, his arched brow suggesting that he was impressed. "So, you know blues music, you just don't like it?"

"You don't have to know blues to know Stevie Ray Vaughn. There's a statue of him just across the river there," she said.

"But, yes, I do know music. I was in our high school marching band, after all."

"You were not."

"Excuse me," London said, heavy on the affront. "I played clarinet from the ninth grade to the middle of my junior year, thank you very much."

Drew's mouth dropped open. "Are you telling me I missed seeing you in that bright orange band uniform by a matter of months?"

"That's right." She nodded. "I looked pretty damn sharp in that uniform. Especially with those shiny spats over my boots and that Mohawk-looking plume down the center of the helmet."

"Name your price," Drew said. "I will pay anything to see you in that uniform again."

She burst out laughing. "Or you can just find an old yearbook and see it for free. I'm sure there's a bunch of them floating around. There was probably one at the reunion."

"I don't want a picture," he said. "The real thing, London. I need to see the real thing."

"Well, that's too bad, because I don't think that uniform is getting past these hips. I was never able to get rid of the Freshmen Fifteen, and med school added another ten on top of that, at least."

"Your hips and everything else about that body is perfect."

A delightful flutter swept through her belly, and she cursed herself for having such a foolish reaction to his remark. A little flattery from a casual sex partner was *not* supposed to set off butterflies. Besides, she didn't need his compliments to be fine with her body. She loved her curves, slight as they were.

"Speaking of adding on pounds, I don't think you're going

to make your adult dinner," London said. She pointed in the direction of several food trucks that were parked across the street. "That's probably your best bet."

"Do you have something against sitting in a proper restaurant and eating with real utensils?" Drew asked.

"I'm trying to help you out here," she said. "I'm still full from that pretzel, so I wasn't planning on having dinner with you anyway."

"You weren't planning on having dinner with me because you think it will mean we're going steady or something."

"Going steady?" She laughed. "Have you been watching sitcoms from the fifties? It wasn't called 'going steady' even when we were in school."

"I don't care what you call it. Sharing a meal doesn't have to be a big deal," Drew said.

"If it's not a big deal, why are you so pressed about the fact that I won't have dinner with you?"

"Because I want to sit across the table from you and talk like—"

"Like two people on a date," she said.

"Fine. Yes. I want to go on a real date with you, London. One hour. Two," he quickly amended. "Two hours at a *real* restaurant. We can talk, we can eat, we can drink wine, and just be like a normal couple—that isn't really a couple," he added.

"I'll consider it, but not tonight. It's too late to get a reservation anywhere good, and if I'm going to agree to have dinner with you, I want five-star dining, Mr. Sullivan."

"I don't believe in anything less, Dr. Kelley. And why can't we go tonight?"

"Because you have so many options just steps away." She took him by the hand and started for the crosswalk. "Austin's food truck scene is unlike any in the country. You'll find more gourmet meals here than you'll find in restaurants."

They crossed to the other side of Cesar Chavez and began browsing the menus of the five trucks lining the street.

"What do you feel like?" Drew asked.

"I had the pretzel. I'm good."

"You cannot convince me you're full after eating just a pretzel. It was big, but it wasn't that big." He glanced over at her. "You don't have to fit into your old band uniform anymore, remember?"

No, she didn't, but London doubted any of those trucks offered dishes that a cardiologist would approve of, especially after that carb-loaded pretzel. And the cupcakes earlier in the week. And the breakfast taco she'd picked up on the way to work yesterday. She would *have* to make better choices the rest of the week.

They chose a truck selling kebabs and other Middle Eastern fare. London ordered the falafel basket with tzatziki, and Drew got a lamb kebab wrapped in a pita that was about the size of his head. Once they crossed the street again, they happened upon a bench that had just been vacated. It was far enough from where the band was playing for them to hear the music without giving London a headache.

She gestured to Drew's kebab. "No way are you eating all of that."

"Wanna bet?" he said, taking a huge bite. He closed his eyes as he chewed, then swallowed. "I will never turn my nose up at a food truck again."

"Again? So that means you have in the past?"

"I've never eaten food from one of these trucks before," he admitted.

"Goodness." London looked toward the sky as if searching for answers. "You have your assistant ordering your groceries and you turn your nose up at street food?"

"Not all street food. I did have tacos from the taco shack in my old neighborhood last week. But it was the first time I've eaten like that in about a decade."

"Tell me, Drew, when did you become so pretentious? Was it after the first million, or the first ten million?"

"Nah." He shook his head. "I was pretty down to earth until my net worth reached about fifty mil." He glanced over at her. "I'm kidding."

"Hey, I'm not hating on you. Apparently you're good at your job, and you're compensated well for it. It's not the same as saving the lives of sick children, but you know?" She shrugged. "I guess hedge fund managers serve a purpose too."

"Well, I'm no longer a hedge fund manager, and the work I'm doing now helps to save hospitals. So, technically, I *am* helping to save the lives of sick children."

"Nah-uh," London said. "Not the same."

"I'll give you that one, Dr. Kelley." He chuckled. "When it comes to the most noble professions, you're winning." He took a sip of the citrus-flavored soda he'd bought from the truck. "I do like what I'm doing these days with Trident. It feels as if we're really making a difference in people's lives. Not that I wasn't before," he quickly added. "Pulling a company back from the brink of insolvency and saving thousands of jobs is something to be proud of, but working to keep hospitals running... It just seems as if the impact is more tangible, if that makes sense."

"I get that," London said. She twisted on the bench so she could face him. "What steered you in this direction? I can't imagine what it would take to leave a job making the kind of money you were making. I mean, seriously, you were able to buy an apartment with a bathroom that overlooks Central Park."

He narrowed his eyes as he chewed the bite he'd just taken out of his kebab. London burst out laughing. She would never get tired of needling him about this.

"When do you have time off from the hospital?" he asked.

"I'm not sure," she said. "Why?"

"Because the next time you have a day off, we're flying up to New York and you're going to see that view from my bathroom for yourself. That'll shut you up."

His suggestion tempted her so much more than it should have. London considered for a moment what it would be like to let Drew whisk her away to New York. To leave behind this drama with Nina, and with Coleman, and with the hospital in Chicago that was flooding her inbox with inquiries about that fellowship.

If she could have just a day without all of these issues weighing her down.

She couldn't even remember the last time she'd taken a vacation. She was supposed to go to the Texas Hill Country with Samiah and Taylor a couple of months ago, but that fell through. What did it say about the state of her work-life balance that she couldn't manage to get two hours away from this place?

"I may eventually take you up on that," London heard herself say.

Drew's head jerked back, his eyes bulging with shock. "No shit?" he asked.

"Maybe," she said. "It won't be anytime soon. I'm nearing

the end of my residency and have a ton of decisions to make. And then I'll have to oversee the creation of that sensory room that *will* make its way into the budget, right?"

"We haven't agreed on the exact terms of that deal just yet," he said.

"True. The only thing we agreed to is no blow jobs."

"We did?" He looked over at her with sheer panic in his eyes.

"Yes." She nodded. "You'll still get them, just not in exchange for a sensory room."

He slapped a hand to his chest. "Thank God."

She laughed and was once again struck by how odd it was to find herself having such a good time with this man she'd detested for so long. A hollow sensation blossomed in her chest when she realized he would be gone in a couple of weeks.

London pitched those thoughts out of her head. The benefit to casually hooking up was that life went on without any baggage or regrets once the sex was over. This was still just a fling for her.

That dull feeling in her chest intensified.

"You never answered my question," she said as she dipped her last falafel in the tzatziki. "Why did you leave your old company to start Trident?"

"My mom," he said. "She got sick a few years back. Cancer. She passed away last year."

"I'm sorry," London said softly.

"Thanks." He balled up the empty wrapper from his food and rolled the wad of foil between his palms. "She lived in a town about an hour and a half west of here."

"I didn't realize she'd remained in Texas."

He nodded. "Despite my many attempts to bring her up to New York, she refused to leave this state. I found out too late that the small, rural hospital where she began her cancer treatments was both underfunded and mismanaged."

"Those two things tend to go together."

"Yes, which is unfortunate for those who have no choice but to use those hospitals. My mom did have a choice, of course. I could have sent her to any hospital in the country—in the world." He shook his head. "She kept me in the dark, not wanting to worry me. I didn't even know she had cancer until nearly a year after the initial diagnosis."

"Why are parents like this? It's like pulling teeth to get anything out of my mother, especially related to her health. And don't even get me started on my dad."

"I've discovered that the span of time between when you go from being the child to the adult in the relationship is amazingly short," Drew said. "You can't imagine how stubborn my mom was, especially toward the end." He huffed out a laugh that wasn't really a laugh, more like a sigh. "I'd give anything if I could deal with that stubbornness again for just a little while longer."

She reached out and gave his arm a squeeze.

"Anyway, once I *did* find out just how serious her condition was, I relocated her to Houston for treatment, but her cancer was aggressive and too far gone by then." He shrugged one shoulder. "During that time, I realized that not everyone can afford world-class treatment at one of the premier cancer centers in the world, and that money should never be the thing that makes the difference between life or death."

"So you left a job that paid millions because you want to live in a world where anyone can get the medical treatment they deserve, despite their tax bracket?"

"In a nutshell," he answered.

London found his idealism breathtakingly sweet.

"Well, damn," she said with a teasing smile. "You sure as hell can't play the villain in my story anymore, not after hearing this."

"I was never the villain you made me out to be," he said.

"No," London said softly. "I guess you weren't."

All of a sudden, he sat up straight. Then he stood.

"We have to dance."

"What? No." London slapped at the hand he held out to her.

"No, really. They're playing 'Uptown Blues.' Jimmie Lunceford. You have to dance when you hear this song, London. It's the rule."

"I'm not dancing with you in the middle of the sidewalk. We'll look like fools."

He motioned to the other couples swaying in slow circles around them.

"And they all look like fools," London pointed out.

"Then we'll be in good company."

He took her empty container and tossed it in the trash, then grabbed both her hands and pulled her toward where the others were dancing. London did her level best to pretend she wasn't having a good time, but then the bastard dipped her, and how could she resist smiling after that?

Drew pulled her against him and rocked to the bluesy music.

"I think this means we really are going steady," he said against her ear.

She laughed. "Why can't you be satisfied with copious amount of no-strings-attached sex?"

"I had enough of that in my twenties. A few strings aren't so bad."

"I don't even want to imagine what you were like in your

twenties," London said. "Wealthy, cocky, and looking the way you look?" One brow arched as he twirled her. "Oh, don't give me that," London said with a laugh. "You know you're gorgeous and always have been."

"Always have been?" This time his brows nearly reached his hairline.

"Every girl in school was after you, Drew."

"Except for my co-valedictorian."

"Maybe because she was too busy trying to keep up her grades," London pointed out. "And because the plain Janes at Barbara Jordan High didn't get many second glances." She spun around again. "But, that's okay, because I know I look damn good now."

"Is this more of that humblebragging you were talking about?" Drew asked.

"Admitting that I was a plain Jane back in high school? No, that's just accepting the truth."

"Wait." His forehead furrowed. "You thought you were plain in high school?"

She shrugged. "I wasn't into makeup or any of that other stuff. My focus was on getting into my top pick undergrad program. Being popular and getting attention from guys never mattered that much to me." She paused. "Okay, maybe it did a little. I lost my virginity to Malik Perry because he always kept a seat open for me on the bus after band practice." Her mouth fell open. "And he played the snare drum! Fucking drummers. There *is* something to that shit."

"London."

She stopped short at the odd, awed look on Drew's face. "What?"

"I'm trying to figure out if you're being serious right now," he said. He stopped dancing and guided her to the edge of the plaza where they'd first stopped to listen to the band. "*Were* you being serious a minute ago?" Drew asked.

"About?"

"London, how can you..." He looked up at the dusky sky and released a tired laugh. "Do you not realize that you drove me out of my mind when we were in high school?"

"Well, yeah. And I told you why. It's because I was so upset that you gave me so much competition when I'd had the top spot in the class locked in since freshman year."

"No. I mean, you drove me out of my mind because I was so infatuated with you that I could barely breathe when I was around you. The main reason I worked so hard is because I saw how smart you were and thought it would impress you. And, then, when I realized that you really did hate me and it wasn't just some ploy to get me to like you, well, then I did it to piss you off."

London's thoughts scrambled as she tried to determine whether she'd heard him correctly. Based on the way he was staring at her, she had. Which made absolutely *no* sense. There was no way Drew Sullivan was into her back in high school.

"But you could get any girl in our class, Drew. You probably could have convinced a couple of the teachers to sleep with you if you'd tried."

"Yet the one girl I wanted more than anyone told Mr. Bailey that she would rather staple her fingers together than partner with me for the science fair," he said.

"You're kinda blowing my mind right now," London said. "I had no clue."

"Would it have mattered if you did?" Drew asked.

She thought for a moment, then answered honestly. "I don't

know. The truth is, I really did hate you so much back then that I can't imagine what I would have done if I knew you liked me. You *liked* me?" London asked, unable to hide the incredulity from her voice. "*Liked* me, liked me?"

"Fantasized about you every single night *liked* you," he answered.

"Holy shit," she whispered. She stared at him in disbelief, completely floored by his revelation. "Well, if it's any consolation, you're getting much better than Malik Perry got. I learned a few things in college."

He grinned. "Why don't we go back to my apartment so you can show me?"

20

No matter how hard he tried, Drew couldn't get his heart rate to slow down. It hammered against his rib cage, reminding him of that time he drank six shots of espresso while cramming for a final. Evidently he didn't need caffeine to get this effect; all it took was unintentionally admitting to London how he'd felt about her all those years ago.

Why was he obsessing over this? Fifteen years had passed. They'd both gone on to build successful careers and live separate, fulfilling lives. It shouldn't make one bit of difference that he'd finally owned up to the fact that his teenage self had been in love with her.

So why did his damn heart still feel like a tambourine inside his chest?

The Uber that Drew had insisted they take back to his apartment pulled up in front of the entrance. A line of people wrapped around the building, no doubt waiting to get into the noodle restaurant on the ground floor. Drew didn't understand the hype, but apparently some celebrity had talked about it on Instagram or TikTok. That was all it took for an unknown commodity to become a household name these days.

"Maybe next time we should just come back to your place and

order some of these noodles," London said as they walked past the line. "Although we probably wouldn't eat until midnight."

"As a resident, I have a direct line to the building's concierge." He waited for several people to clear the door before he and London entered the building. "I can have food from any restaurant on the property delivered right up to my apartment and bypass the long lines and wait time."

"Hmm," she murmured, sounding impressed. She leaned closer and whispered into his ear, "You. Me. Noodles. Naked. That sounds like a date."

"That is not a date," Drew said. "That *will* happen, but it would not count as a date."

"Does a date with Drew Sullivan end with us getting naked?"

"Hell yeah," he said.

"That's what matters. Let's go and do that now."

Her playful, teasing tone eased the anxiety he'd been grappling with. London wasn't acting any differently after what he'd let slip a little while ago, so he could stop stressing about it. Of course, he now had to grapple with the fact that she knew how he'd felt about her back in high school and it apparently hadn't changed anything for her.

They turned the corner, and Drew's footsteps halted at the sight of his uncle Elias standing in front of the building directory.

"E?" he called.

Elias spun around, his eyes bright with his smile. Drew's joy upon seeing him in the flesh was visceral. He rushed over and brought him in for a hug.

"What's up! It's good to see you, man!" Drew said, clamping him on the back.

"You too." Elias tightened his arms around him before letting go. "You're looking good." He pointed at the directory. "But you didn't tell me you were living in a shopping mall."

"It's called a mixed-use building," Drew said.

"It's a mall," Elias returned.

Drew chuckled as he gestured to London. "E, this is London Kelley. We...uh...went to high school together. London, this is my uncle Elias, although he likes to tell people he's my brother."

"Because no one believes I'm old enough to be his uncle," Elias said. He extended his hand to her. "You're the one who's the doctor, right?"

"I am," London said, clearly surprised. So was Drew.

"Doreen mentioned you a few times over the years," his uncle continued. "She would call you that pretty girl who was just as smart as my nephew here."

Elias looked pointedly between London and Drew. His brow dipped slightly before his eyes widened with sudden awareness.

"Uh, you know, I was going to bunk on your couch for the night, but maybe that hotel across the street would be better," Elias said. "They have a rooftop bar and pool situation that's worth checking out."

"No. No, don't," London said. "I was on my way to pick up my car from the hospital so that I can head home."

"No, you weren't."

"Yes, I was," she stated more firmly. "I'll see you tomorrow."

Damn. He knew there was no way his night could continue on the path it had been headed prior to finding Elias waiting for him, but still. *Damn.*

Drew took out his phone. "I'll call you an Uber."

"Put that phone away. The hospital is only three blocks from here," she said.

"But it's almost nine o'clock."

"I'm a big girl, Drew. I can handle a short walk by myself, even after dark." She held her hand out to Elias again. "It was lovely to meet you. Although we probably *did* meet back when Drew and I were in high school."

"I still remember the speech you gave at graduation."

London beamed. "That was a pretty memorable speech, if I do say so myself."

"Legendary." Elias smiled.

Drew looked between the two of them. Was his uncle flirting with his . . . his hookup partner?

"If you won't let me call you an Uber, you can at least let me walk you to the hospital," Drew said. He looked to his uncle. "I'll text you the code to get into my place, E. It's on the twenty-second floor. Apartment 2209."

"Would you quit this chivalry nonsense," London said. "I'll be fine. Enjoy your time here, Elias."

And then she turned and walked back the way they came. Drew couldn't tear his gaze away from her. Even after she'd rounded the line of customers and exited through the building's double doors, his eyes remained focused in that direction, as if she would change her mind and come running back. He would put Elias up in a hotel suite for the night, and he and London could pick up where their plans had left off.

"Shit, man, why didn't you say something?" Elias said, smacking Drew in the chest.

"Me?" Drew said. "Why didn't you text before you left Dallas?"

"It's called a surprise," Elias said. "But if you had told me you were going to be otherwise occupied in the evenings, I would have known better than to just show up unannounced."

"Well, you did say you would be stopping by on your way to your camping trip," Drew said. "I just didn't remember it was this week."

"Because the trip was originally planned for *next* week, but there was some kind of mix-up and they offered me and my friends a bigger cabin if we agreed to come a week early. But I could have gone straight to Big Bend if I knew I'd be interrupting... well, that." He hooked a thumb back toward where London had gone. "Damn, Drew. Even *I* would tell me to get the hell outta here if I were you."

Drew chuckled, shaking his head. "You don't want to know how close I came to doing that."

"You should at least go make sure she's okay. You keep looking back for her."

"I should," Drew said. He sent London a quick text, telling her that he was on his way. But she responded just as quickly, letting him know that she was already at the crosswalk across from the hospital's parking garage.

"Too late," he said, putting his phone away. He picked up the duffel bag at Elias's feet and wrapped his other arm around his uncle's shoulders. "Now that you've fucked up my plans for the night, let's get drunk."

They took the elevator up to the twenty-second floor.

"I'm not sure if you knew this when you mentioned it downstairs, but you actually *do* have to sleep on the couch," Drew told him as he deposited the duffel on the coffee table. "Trident is using the spare bedroom as a conference room."

"You want me to show you where I'll be sleeping over the next few days?" Elias asked. "You could put me in the bathtub and this place would still feel like the Ritz compared to those cabins." He walked over to the expanse of windows and let out a low whistle. "It's unfair for one man to have such a great view all to himself." His uncle looked at him over his shoulder. "You *are* living here alone, right?"

"Technically," Drew answered.

Elias turned around fully and crossed his arms over his chest, waiting for further explanation. He wasn't getting anything more.

"Don't ask," Drew said. "And don't try to make it into something it isn't. London and I reconnected at our class reunion a couple of weeks ago, and she happens to work at Travis County Hospital, where Trident is working. We've just been hanging out."

He skipped the part about their being naked most of the time they hung out, because his uncle didn't need to know that. Of course, Elias likely already expected it, given his reaction to seeing Drew and London together.

He went over to the refrigerator and grabbed two bottles of a local IPA he'd picked up from the gastropub downstairs. He brought the beer over to where Elias still stood, looking out the window.

"What the hell is this?" his uncle asked when Drew handed him a bottle.

"Try it before you turn your nose up at it. There's more to life than Budweiser."

"Yeah, it's called Bud Light." He took a swig from the bottle and grimaced. He swallowed and took another sip. He looked at Drew out of the corner of his eye. "Whatever," he muttered as he tipped the bottle back again.

Chuckling, Drew took a sip from his own bottle before he

motioned at the window. "You know, there are some pretty nice condos in Deep Ellum where you could have a view like this all the time. Just say the word and my real estate guy would have you moved in."

"No thanks. I'll stick to my little hovel in North Dallas. Move me to Deep Ellum and the next thing you know I'll be drinking weak shit like this every day."

Drew could only shake his head. They both knew that he would offer to buy Elias a new house, because he always offered to buy his uncle a new house. They also both knew that E would turn him down, because he always turned him down.

Drew figured if his uncle was ever in true financial need, he would push his pride to the side long enough to come to him. Maybe.

They walked over to the couch and plopped down, simultaneously stretching their legs out and crossing their ankles on the coffee table on either side of the duffel bag.

"You gonna admit that you and the pretty doctor are doing more than just hanging out?" Elias asked.

"Nope," Drew said.

"That's fair." His uncle nodded. "Not my business anyway." He took a long pull on the so-called *weak* beer. "How's the work you're doing here in Austin going?"

"We're trying to save a state-run hospital that is so far in the red that it would have been shut down years ago if it wasn't publicly funded."

"In other words, you have your work cut out for you," Elias guessed.

"Yeah." Drew sighed. "We've got maybe another week of the audit, which means the hard part is about to start." Drew looked over at him. "We have to make recommendations about what should be cut from the budget. Do you continue to fund the in-house lab, the nursery for employees' kids, the nutrition program? Not all of them will survive." Drew tipped his bottle back. "I don't even want to think about it right now."

"Well, I have something you probably want to think about even less," Elias said.

Drew closed his eyes. "Don't start."

"You can't put this off any longer, Drew. You're here in Texas for the first time in a year. And you're less than two hours away from Hye."

He looked over at his uncle. "It's not as if I'm on vacation, E. I'm working."

"Are you saying you can't afford to take a single weekend off to go box up your mom's house? You don't even have to put the stuff in boxes. The Realtor left color-coded stickers. Green for keep, yellow for donate, red for trash. She'll take care of everything, but she needs some guidance."

Drew released a deep groan as he leaned forward and rested his elbows on his thighs. He cradled his head, roughly massaging his scalp. He flinched as Elias's hand gripped his shoulder and gave it a squeeze.

"I know this isn't easy, Drew. Nothing about this process has been easy. But it has to be done."

"Why?" he asked, looking back at his uncle. "I own her house. Why can't I just leave it as it is?"

"Because you know damn well that isn't what Doreen wanted. She left instructions—"

"For it to be used as a transitional home for domestic violence victims. I know," Drew said.

Because she had been one.

Drew knew hardly anything about his dad, and his mother never talked about him, but Elias had remembered enough to give Drew some insight into just how awful that motherfucker had been. Elias had been eight years old when Drew was born, and was being raised by his older sister after their parents had been killed in a house fire.

Over the years, his uncle had shared bits and pieces of the terror Drew's mother had escaped the night she'd packed up her little brother and her newborn baby and left her abusive boyfriend. She'd found her way to a shelter for domestic violence survivors—the Clubhouse, as his mom had nicknamed it for Elias's sake.

After eight months, Drew's mom was offered a home in a safe neighborhood that cost next to nothing in rent. It allowed her to afford childcare while working and going to school. That transitional home, as Drew later learned it was called, had been the key to his mother's being able to break free and build a new life for him and Elias.

As of today, Drew had funded more than a thousand transitional homes around the country. He'd hired a Realtor whose sole purpose was to coordinate the purchase and renovation of foreclosed homes that could be donated to area shelters as transitional housing.

But Drew also knew that Elias was right. He could buy a million homes around the country, and his mother would still be upset at the thought of her house sitting unused when it could provide shelter for a family escaping the same kind of abuse her own family had faced all those years ago.

Drew dragged his palms down his face.

"Let me talk things over with my team," he said to his

uncle. "If I'm going to be absent for a few days, the lull between audit mode and recommendation mode is probably the best time for that to happen." He looked back at Elias again. "I can't believe I wasted my good beer on you."

"See, I would have thought you'd be more upset about that pretty doctor leaving early for the night than about the beer."

Drew shut his eyes. "Don't remind me. I just might make you sleep in the bathtub."

Elias threw his head back and laughed. Drew had no choice but to join in.

21

London nervously shifted from one foot to the other as she waited to order burrito bowls for Koko and Nina. Miles had inhaled the corn dog she'd bought him from one of the other food court restaurants while standing in line next to her. He'd eaten it from the side, as one ate an ear of corn, instead of from the top like a person from planet Earth.

As they stood here, London tried to think of something to say to her little brother, but it would appear she lost the ability to communicate with children if they weren't in hospital gowns. Not that it mattered. Miles talked enough for the both of them.

Unlike his sisters, who'd rattled off the litany of items they wanted in their bowls and then headed to the accessories store, Miles hadn't left London's side from the moment they arrived at the shopping center. He'd asked her no less than two dozen questions—everything from her favorite color to what kind of mileage she got with her Mini Cooper. The kid really needed to hang out with someone other than his dad.

Maybe if his big sister were around more...

Thing is, she wasn't supposed to be with Miles today either. London had meant for this to be her outing with

Nina so they could discuss the nude selfies, but as she backed out of the driveway at April and Kenneth's, a minivan pulled up alongside her, and Koko and Miles jumped out. They begged to come along. There would be no nude selfie talk today.

"So, how is baseball going?" London asked, figuring that was at least one thing she knew Miles enjoyed.

He shrugged. "It's okay. I haven't hit a home run yet, but Dad said there's more to life than hitting home runs."

"He did? Well, that's true," London said. And both surprising and refreshing to hear. Maybe Kenneth was starting to mellow out in his old age.

She snorted. Her dad would go apeshit if he heard her refer to him as old.

"Just remember that having fun is the most important thing," London told him.

"Did you have fun when you played baseball?"

"I never played baseball."

"Basketball?"

She shook her head.

"Well, what do you do to have fun? And why do you wear your hair that way? And don't you think you should wear more rings? Dad always buys Mom new rings because he says that girls like them. Why don't you have a husband?"

"Can I help you?" the girl behind the counter asked.

"Thank God," London said. She pointed. "Let's get Nina and Koko's lunch. And then maybe we can all get ice cream for dessert."

By the time London finished ordering the burrito bowls, Miles had moved on to questions about cows and milk and why ice cream doesn't taste like grass if that's all cows eat.

London gave him a bullshit answer because who had the time to explain that process, but it was still better than tackling the husband question.

"Did you two find something you liked?" London asked as Koko and Nina approached.

"Just this." Koko held up a tie-dyed headband.

Nina rolled her eyes. "She has like fifty thousand headbands already."

"And you have fifty thousand pairs of earrings," Koko countered. She grabbed her burrito bowl and sat at the table London indicated. "She bought big hoop earrings that she knows Dad won't let her wear," Koko said.

Nina shrugged. "He won't see them." She sat across from Koko. "Besides, I didn't buy them, my big sister did. Thank you, London."

Great, now she would get accused of buying contraband.

"Just make sure Kenneth doesn't see them," London told her.

"Why do you call Dad by his first name?" Miles asked.

"I . . . uh . . ."

How could she explain to her younger brother that she'd started calling their dad by his given name to piss him off? It was probably better to just stop doing so in front of Miles.

"I would hear my mom do it all the time, and I guess it just rubbed off," London lied.

Miles rubbed his hands together, a mischievous grin lighting up his face. "I should call him *honey* the way Mom does."

"Please don't." London laughed. Between Nina's earrings and Miles's new name for Kenneth, she would be lucky if she was ever permitted to take these kids anywhere again. She'd better check Koko's pockets for cigarettes before they left this mall.

Although she couldn't see her middle sister doing anything that would get her in trouble. Of the three, Koko reminded London most of herself. If only for her acerbic tongue. The one-liners she hurled at Nina were so good, London had made a mental note so she could use them on Samiah and Taylor.

Why was she just discovering that she liked hanging out with her siblings? Despite Miles and his endless, sometimes inappropriate questions, and Nina with her stank teenage attitude, London had enjoyed herself.

She worked with other people's children all day long, but when it came to these three, London realized that she'd hardly gotten the chance to know them. She didn't have to be the much older sister who saw her siblings only on holidays or their birthdays. She could be the sister who carted them to the mall on the weekends, and who FaceTimed during the week to check in on them.

She *had* to do better when it came to these three.

London pushed her own burrito bowl away as a heavy weight sank to the pit of her stomach. She'd missed so much of their childhood, and now that she'd decided to finally be the big sister she should have been all along, there was the possibility of her leaving Texas for her fellowship. She felt like shit.

"I've had a great time today," London said. "I think we should do it more often. How about each of you getting your own day out with your big sister, where we each do something really special?"

"Can you take me to the BTS concert next month?" Koko asked.

"Uh, sure," London said.

"It's sold out," Nina said with another eye roll.

"Oh. Well, maybe we can stop by the record store and buy their newest CD? Wait, is there a record store in this mall? There used to be one," London said.

"No one uses CDs anymore," Nina said.

"I do," London said. "I prefer to own the music I buy, but we'll stream BTS and have a dance party," She looked at Nina. "But I think Nina's day should be first since she's the oldest. What do you say we go somewhere next weekend? Just the two of us."

Nina shrugged. "Sure."

Oh, she could not wait to get this one alone. They would talk about more than just the nude selfies.

They finished up their lunch and spent another hour walking around the mall. London had to stop herself from checking in with the hospital at least a dozen times, which said more about her than she cared to think about.

When they arrived back at April and Kenneth's, her stepmom gave London a curious, questioning look. London imperceptibly shook her head. No, they hadn't discussed the photos.

"I'll see you next weekend?" she said to Nina. London looked to April. "I've promised each of the kids that they'll get their own special day. I'm going to find something really fun for me and Nina to do next weekend."

"Oh, that sounds great!" April said. "Yes, you should."

London hugged the three kids before leaving. She felt only slightly guilty for not asking about Kenneth after his TIA scare, but if there was something wrong, April would have told her. She'd designated the rest of the day her "self-care day," and talking with her father was the opposite of self-care.

An hour later, London was in her favorite chair adding a few rows to the stroller blanket she'd been crocheting for Samiah's four-month-old niece, when her phone chimed with a text.

Looking for company?

She grinned. Sorry, not tonight. I'm practicing self-care.

We can practice self-care together.

"Yeah, right." She knew exactly what kind of self-care he had in mind.

The only self-care I've planned for is crocheting and a bubble bath.

Three dots appeared as Drew typed a response. Perfect. You crochet a washcloth and I'll use it to scrub your back.

London burst out laughing. She switched from the messaging app to the phone and called him.

"I am an excellent back scrubber," Drew said by way of greeting.

"I have no doubts that you are, but you're forgetting one thing," London said. "We are not friends, and you coming over to my house is a bit more...friendly than I'm comfortable with."

He sighed. "Come on, London. It won't hurt you to invite an *acquaintance* into your home, especially one who can give you multiple orgasms."

A shot of heat rippled through her. London put it on ice.

"Sorry, but it's the wrong time of the month for orgasms," she said.

"Well, I can rub your back or do whatever you need me to do," he said. "Let me come over." The earnest plea in his voice had her rethinking the hard-and-fast rule she'd set for herself.

London pulled her bottom lip between her teeth, debating the wisdom of taking this next step. Having him over shouldn't be a big deal, but it felt that way. There was something too intimate about it, too... beyond friendly. It would push them out of hookup-partner territory and into something she wasn't sure she was ready to explore.

Yes, you are, the voice in her head countered.

Tamping down the butterflies that had taken flight in her belly, London said, "I'll text you my address."

She heard Drew's car pull up twenty minutes later. London set the yarn on the coffee table and fluffed her coils as she made her way to the door. The heat shot through her again at the sight of him. He'd traded in his usual suit for khaki slacks and a wheat-colored sweater that looked so soft London immediately wanted to curl into it.

He held out a bag.

"Dark chocolate and chamomile tea. The woman behind the counter at CVS said both were essential."

"Dammit, Drew," London said, taking the bag from him. Did he not understand how hookup partners worked?

"You don't like dark chocolate?" he asked.

She loved dark chocolate. She didn't like his being so sweet. It made it that much harder to resist these feelings she'd been trying to resist.

"Get in here," London said, taking him by the hand. That's when she noticed that his other hand held a briefcase. "Are you planning on working?" she asked him.

"I figured I could work while you crochet," he said, his eyes roaming the entryway. "This is nice. Unexpected as hell, but nice." He pointed to the baroque curio cabinet she'd found at an antiques shop back when she first bought her house. "This doesn't seem like your style."

"Well, I guess I'm just full of surprises," she said.

She led him into the living room and couldn't deny her own surprise when he opened the briefcase and took out a sheaf of documents. He was serious about working tonight?

Drew looked up at her. "You want me to make you a cup of the tea?" he asked.

She shook her head. "I can do it. Do you . . . uh . . . want a cup?"

"Nah, I'm good," he said, returning to his documents.

She made herself some tea and settled in with her crocheting. London wasn't sure she was comfortable with just how, well, comfortable this felt. But after a while, she relaxed and allowed herself to enjoy Drew's quiet companionship. He asked her a question about County's on-site pharmacy and explained that some hospitals had opted to shutter theirs due to cost, but then he promised not to ask anything else work related.

After an hour had passed and London had finished the interior square of her blanket, she rolled up the yarn and set her project aside.

"You ready for that bubble bath?" Drew asked.

She motioned to his briefcase. "Do you have a change of clothes in there?"

"Why would I need a change of clothes? I'm not getting in the bath with you."

"Are you not even going to try to get in my pants tonight, Drew Sullivan?"

He shook his head. "Nope."

"I think I may be offended," she said.

"That wasn't my intent."

She knew what his intent was. He wanted to prove that there was more to what they had going on than just sex. It scared her to think he was right.

Determined to refute that thought, London walked over to where he sat on her couch and climbed onto his lap. Drew's hands immediately clutched her waist. She crossed her wrists behind his head and went in for a kiss, plunging her tongue inside his warm mouth. The effect on her body was instant, her nipples tightening to sharp points as desire blossomed between her legs. She ground herself against his pelvis, smiling as she felt him growing hard beneath her.

"It won't work," Drew spoke against her lips.

"You wanna bet?" London asked.

He gripped her waist tighter, then lifted her off him.

"What the hell, Drew?" she asked as she bounced onto the couch.

He stood and straightened his clothes. It was hard to ignore the telltale bulge that remained behind his zipper.

"I'll run you a bubble bath, massage your back, and feed you chocolate, but I'm not getting naked."

London arched a brow. "Who's being stubborn now?"

"I have my moments," he said. "Only when warranted." Drew leaned down and planted the sweetest kiss against her lips. "What's your answer? Am I running you a bath, or should I get back to work?"

She pointed toward the hallway. "Second door on the right. There's peony-scented bubble bath underneath the sink."

He winked and kissed her again, this time on the tip of

her nose. "Give me ten minutes." He picked up the fat pillar candle she kept on her coffee table. "We can use this to create a soothing atmosphere. I hear that helps with cramps too."

"Drew?" London called. He turned. "I like my water extra hot. Scalding."

"I expected nothing less from you, she-devil."

London burst out laughing. Once alone in the living room, she dropped her head back against the couch and sighed up at the ceiling. She would continue to deny it until she turned blue in the face, but one thing was becoming clearer by the second. She was totally falling for her hookup partner.

22

"London, are you even listening to me?"

London sat up in her chair and looked over at her phone, which she'd propped against a stained coffee mug on her desk. Her mother glowered at her on the screen, that telltale V creasing the center of her forehead.

"Remember when you used to tell me to stop scowling, or my face would stay that way?" London asked her. "Now I understand what you were talking about."

"Dammit." Janette started massaging her forehead. "I've been meaning to schedule a Botox treatment. A regular facial isn't doing shit for me anymore."

"You look fine, Mom. Now, what were you saying? Because, you're right, I wasn't listening. I have a complicated surgery on my schedule today and I've got a list of important things I need to take care of before it starts," she said as she scrolled through pages of locally dyed yarn from a shop just east of Austin.

Her idea of what was important probably differed from her mom's, but whatever.

Besides, this wasn't just yarn shopping, it was technically research for the outing her mom and April had insisted she have with Nina.

London had been at a loss trying to figure out where she and her sister should go for that conversation she was already dreading more than just about anything she'd dreaded in her life. She'd stalked Nina's Instagram page, which was a shitty way to have to get to know your own sister, but that's where she found herself.

London had learned that Nina wasn't just into wearing jewelry; she liked making it, specifically charm bangles. She'd even sold a few pieces.

She'd decided she would take Nina shopping for jewelry-making supplies, and in the process of seeking out stores, had discovered an entire craft village in a small town about a half hour away. Now her biggest issue was limiting the amount of money she spent on hand-dyed yarn from one of the village's cute yarn shops. Even though her nightly rendezvous with Drew these past few weeks had stolen much of her crocheting time, she was still buying up yarn like sheep were about to go on strike.

She put several skeins of dyed wool in her cart—only to remind herself to check them out once she could look at them in person—then minimized the page and turned her attention to the phone.

"I'm sorry," London said again. "Now, what were you saying? Something about Renaldo? And nothing that will make me want to find mind bleach, please! I'm still your daughter, and I don't need to hear about your sex life."

Lord knows her mother had no problem sharing.

Granted, it had been much harder to listen to Janette go on and on about the younger man she was dating—he was forty-eight to her sixty—before London started hooking up with Drew. Still, she didn't need to know the details.

"I was trying to tell you that we broke up," her mother said. "Renaldo was too much of a homebody for me. He thought a drive down to San Antonio counted as a vacation."

London would think the same.

"I tried to convince April to come with me to Vegas for the weekend," her mother continued. "But with Nina going on her little trip to Houston and Kenneth having some conference or something, she's stuck at home with Miles and Koko."

"Excuse me?" London picked up the phone and brought it closer to her face. "Where is Nina going this weekend?"

"To Houston," her mother said. Her eyes grew wide. "April didn't tell you? Their band made the finals of some competition."

"She's letting her go on a trip with the marching band? The same marching band with the drummer Nina tried to send nudes to? What the fuck!"

Janette held her hands up. "I thought the same thing, but she's not my child. Now, if that had been *you*, your butt would have been banished to your room for a month. But they don't raise kids that way anymore."

As footloose and fancy-free as her mother was these days, she'd had no qualms about being strict when it came to her only daughter. Of course, London hadn't given her mom a reason to be strict back when she was Nina's age.

She dropped her head into her palm. She should be buying her sister condoms instead of jewelry-making supplies.

"Well, I guess my weekend just opened up," she said.

"Wanna go to Vegas?" her mom asked. London stared wordlessly at her. "Fine." Janette rolled her eyes. "I need to find a more spontaneous group of friends. And younger. You people make me feel old."

"You would tire out a bunch of middle schoolers," London told her.

An alert popped up on her phone, reminding her to eat before today's surgery. The fact that her phone had to tell her when to have lunch said so much about the current state of her life.

And, of course, she hadn't thought to bring any lunch from home. Nor did she have time to go to the cafeteria for their rubber chicken and clumpy mashed potato special.

"I need to go, Mom. If you *do* go to Vegas, try not to marry a stranger at some chapel on the Strip, okay?"

"I make no promises," Janette said before ending the call.

She would totally come back with a husband. Or, at the very least, a new, younger boyfriend.

Shit, maybe she *should* join her mom in Vegas, now that she wouldn't be visiting the craft village. She'd probably spend less money at a casino than she would at the yarn shops.

She didn't need Vegas or a yarn shop to have a good time. She had friends.

Except Samiah was on her way to Philadelphia to meet Daniel's family, and Taylor had texted last night, canceling their plans for Thai food and math homework in exchange for a cookout at Jamar's parents' home near Houston.

"Thank goodness for Drew," London muttered.

She sat up straight. It was hard to believe those four words had even crossed her lips. What kind of upside-down reality was she living in?

The kind where she was actually looking forward to seeing Drew Sullivan at the end of the day.

The most surprising part? The sex wasn't the only reason she looked forward to seeing him. Sex had become more like dessert at the end of a good meal—the icing on a cake layered with thoughtful conversation, unbearably silly jokes, and the kind of teasing, lighthearted flirting a girl could become addicted to.

She was comparing time with Drew Sullivan to *cake*! She truly was living in the Upside Down.

London opened her bottom desk drawer and stared at her stash of snacks: a bag of salted peanuts, Funyuns, and two fun-size Kit Kat bars.

Was there any wonder why she was prehypertensive? She sighed and closed the drawer.

She quickly made her way down to the cafeteria and grabbed a premade spinach, feta, and grilled chicken salad, then spent ten minutes that she really couldn't spare answering questions about the audit from the cafeteria's cashier. London had been tasked with educating the nurses and fellow surgical residents about Trident's role at County, but it seemed as if everyone came to her with their inquiries.

She brought the salad back to her office and scarfed it down while simultaneously reviewing the last of the charts she needed to tend to before Ahmad's surgery. Then she texted the anesthesiologist, Dr. Samuels, to let him know she would be meeting the rest of the surgical team in the prep room so they could have one final walk-through of today's surgery.

His response to her text had the same dip London had seen on Janette forming in the middle of her own forehead.

She reread his text. "Change of plans?"

She locked up her office and hustled to the other side of the wing, down the corridor to where the patients' rooms were located. She arrived at Ahmad's room to find his parents and Dr. Peter Foster from Oncology standing around Ahmad's bed. The pensive look on the fifteen-year-old's face sent a trickle of unease down London's spine.

What in the hell was Peter Foster even doing in here? The hematology-oncology resident had been working at County for only about four months, and as far as she knew, had nothing to do with Ahmad's care.

"Good morning, Dr. Foster." She nodded curtly. "How are you, Sarah? Charles?" she directed to Ahmad's parents in a friendlier tone. Then she turned to the teen. "Are we ready for today?"

Ahmad looked apologetic. And scared. "Um, I—"

"Mr. and Mrs. Jefferson have elected not to go through with the surgery," Dr. Foster said.

London's head swung around, her eyes wide. She was able to stop the *what the fuck* from flying from her mouth just in time.

"Really?" she said instead. "When did this come about? And why? We've discussed Ahmad's condition and—"

"Dr. Foster explained that another surgery isn't the best course of action right now," Sarah said. "Apparently there's a clinical trial that Ahmad may be eligible to participate in that would be better for his type of cancer. And less invasive than surgery."

"And less risky," Charles Jefferson added. "Ahmad has gone through so many surgeries already."

London had to concentrate on taking slow, deep breaths without it looking as though she was trying to concentrate on taking slow, deep breaths.

"I understand your hesitancy," London said. "As you know, there are always risks with surgeries, but we have done everything we can to mitigate those risks. And as much as I respect my colleague here, I have to disagree with his assessment regarding the clinical trial. There's an inherent risk just by the nature of it being a trial."

In coordinated movements that were so synchronized it seemed scary, Sarah and Charles Jefferson looked at each other before looking to their son and then to Dr. Foster and then to London.

"I think we'll take our chances with the trial for now," Sarah said. "We can always revisit the idea of surgery, right?"

"His tumor can grow," London pointed out.

"Or it can shrink with the treatment he'll receive as part of the trial," Dr. Foster said.

London avoided glancing at him because she knew she would go completely apeshit if she saw his face, which would not be a good look in front of a patient and his parents.

She smiled at the Jeffersons and sent Ahmad an *it'll be okay* wink before turning and saying, "Dr. Foster, can I have a minute?"

His overly bored expression as he followed her out of the hospital room sent London's rage into the stratosphere. She did her best to maintain her calm as she marched down the hallway. She dipped into the unoccupied jungle-themed room. The moment Peter Foster closed the door behind him, she whirled around and went in.

"What the hell do you think you're doing?" London yelled, so angry she could barely form the words.

"You do not have ownership over a patient," he countered.

"I have been part of Ahmad Jefferson's care for the past three years. How dare you even talk to his parents without consulting me or the attending surgeon on this case, let alone suggest they cancel his surgery!"

A dull pain began to pound at the base of her skull.

"It didn't take much convincing for them to change their minds, which should tell you that they don't want their son going through another surgery. The problem with you surgeons is that you don't consider an alternative treatment. You think slicing into someone is the only way to go. And from what I've heard about you, you're more arrogant than most."

This motherfucker...

"Don't ever try to pull something like this again," London said.

She swayed slightly as a wave of dizziness slammed into her.

"Dr. Kelley?"

Foster reached for her, but London slapped his hand away.

"Stay away from me and stay away from my patients," she told him. "Go peddle your clinical trials to some...one..."

London felt herself tipping over but could do nothing to stop the fall. Peter Foster caught her before she tumbled to the floor. She tried to right herself but couldn't seem to do it. Her limbs were rubbery, her balance completely off.

"Dr. Kelley!"

She heard Foster's voice coming from what seemed like yards away, even though he was right next to her, propping her up. The monkeys painted on the walls looked as if they were really swinging from the tree limbs. London blinked hard.

Foster walked her over to the hospital bed. She sat, but she refused his offer to help her lie down.

"I'm okay," she said.

She was not. Her vision was clearing, and Foster's words no longer sounded as if he were speaking to her from the bottom of the ocean, but she wasn't sure she could honestly categorize how she felt as being okay.

Kia Jackson rushed into the room, with an entourage following in her wake. London didn't even try to avoid their fussing.

Twenty minutes after that mortifying episode, which was made even more cringeworthy because it happened in front of a fellow resident she'd just cursed out, London found herself sitting across from Doug Renault. As someone who had never been called to the principal's office a day in her life, it felt as if she'd been so twice in the last few weeks.

Dr. Renault had spent the past five minutes relaying Foster's version of what happened.

"I appreciate his helping me," London said. "But if he thinks I'm going to apologize, he can kiss my...shoes," she finished. Because she *would* curb her language in front of Dr. Renault.

"I don't care about Peter Foster," Renault said. "Poaching surgical patients for his clinical trial is underhanded."

"Exactly!" London said. "He shou—"

"Stop." His voice was sharp. "We're not talking about what Peter did right now. And the only patient I want to discuss at the moment is you."

"I'm not a patient."

"But you will be one soon if you don't get things under control, London. Your BP was elevated. Way elevated."

"It's called stress! A fellow colleague just convinced one of my longtime patients to go against my plan of care. It would be a surprise if my blood pressure had *not* gone through the roof."

"You know it's more than just stress," he said.

Yes, she did. It was hereditary. And she knew she needed to get a handle on it before it turned into something even more serious. The last thing she needed was to stroke out in the middle of surgery.

"I'm putting you on leave," Doug said.

"You're what!" She rose halfway out of her chair, but the harsh glare her normally calm supervisor shot her way had London rethinking her next move. "Dr. Renault, please. I don't have time to go on leave. I'm at the end of my final year of residency. Are you trying to sabotage my career or something?"

He tapped his pen against his desk.

"Vacation then," he replied after several intense moments. "As of tonight, you're on vacation for the next week. I'll reassign whichever surgeries cannot be postponed. This isn't up for debate, London. You're going to Cardiology to get checked out, then you're going on vacation."

The urge to stomp her foot like a petulant child was so strong that London couldn't believe she was able to fight the impulse. But, honestly, how could she argue? She'd almost passed out.

She sat back in her chair and reluctantly nodded. "Okay," she said. She chuckled at the genuine surprise on Doug Renault's face. "Did you think I would argue?" she asked.

"For at least the next half hour."

"No." She shook her head. "You're right."

When was the last time she'd truly taken time to just... exist? To engage in the smallest amount of self-care?

The closest she came to doing something solely for her own enjoyment was her Friday night outings with Samiah and Taylor, and her crocheting. Yet, she'd canceled on her friends twice in the last few months, and she usually allowed herself to crochet only when there was a new lecture on surgical technique she could listen to. And even then, she felt guilty, as if she should be doing something more productive.

Why was it so hard for her to give herself a fucking break? When had her life become this never-ending grind?

Had she started buying into her own hype? Believing she was this superwoman who could do it all without ever slowing down? She'd spent the past five years pulling eighty-hour workweeks while covering shifts for fellow residents. Add planning a class reunion on top of that, researching surgical fellowships around the country, and now this ambassadorship she'd been roped into doing. Was it any wonder she'd nearly passed out today?

She could blame Kenneth and his shitty genes all she wanted to, but London knew that played only a small part. She needed to do a better job of taking care of herself, both physically and mentally.

She needed some *me* time.

"You're right," London said again. "Life has been . . . it's been pretty wild lately. I can use a few days away from this hospital, even if it's just to veg out on my couch and watch Netflix."

"I'm almost disappointed that I won't have the chance to plead my case," Dr. Renault said. "I had some good arguments locked and loaded."

"Use them on someone else." London slapped her hands on the armrests and pushed herself up. "I'm officially on vacation." She paused. "Okay, I do have a few charts I need to finish up before I can leave."

"We also need to go over the surgeries you have scheduled for next week." Doug looked at his watch. "If we can get it done in the next hour, your vacation can start at noon."

She nodded. "Deal."

23

Drew massaged his temple as he listened to B. J. Clark on the other end of the line. He could always tell how upset B. J. was by the speed of his voice. It's when the Oregonian in him came out.

His partner was speaking so fast Drew could barely catch the words, which did not bode well for Trident.

"Do I need to come up to New York?" Drew asked.

B. J.'s deep sigh came through the phone. "I think we can handle this remotely. But you, me, and Melissa need to get on this, and fast. I've set up a meeting for tonight. We have to do this on Tokyo time."

"Yeah, I agree," Drew said. He tried to hide his annoyance, but *fuck*!

This would make two nights in a row that he wouldn't be able to spend time with London. How had he become so addicted to having her near that two nights away gave rise to such agony?

"We need to strategize before the call," B. J. pointed out.

"Melissa is meeting with the contact in Kansas City right now, but let's conference as soon as she's done. We are not losing this account to Meacham," Drew said.

"Damn right we aren't," B. J. said. "I'll fly to Tokyo myself if I have to."

"We'll do our best to convince them to go with Trident without anyone having to go wheels up. But keep your passport handy—just in case."

Drew disconnected the call with B. J. and immediately went in search of London. He'd heard mumblings through the hospital grapevine about some incident that happened earlier between her and another doctor. He figured it was Coleman, but he didn't bother to seek out more info. He wanted to hear it directly from her.

Drew knocked on her door and was relieved to hear her call for him to come in from the other side.

"Hey," Drew greeted. She looked past her computer monitor and smiled.

Goodness.

It still struck him as unbelievable that London Kelley directed smiles like that his way. It was a smile straight out of his adolescent dreams.

"I heard you had yourself a morning," Drew said as he closed the door behind him.

"Nothing but gossips around here." She rolled her eyes. "Last I heard, I had to be hooked up to an IV."

His footsteps halted after two steps. "An IV? I thought you got into a fistfight with Frederick Coleman? Why would you need an IV?"

"The gossip is worse than I thought." She motioned for him to sit down. "Give me just a minute," she said, returning to her computer. She finished up whatever she had been working on, then rolled her chair a few inches to the right and folded her hands on her desk. "First, it wasn't Frederick Coleman, it was another resident, Peter Foster from Oncology. And it wasn't a fistfight that took me out, it was a dizzy spell. Nearly put me on my ass right there in the Jungle Room."

Drew's chest instantly grew tight. "Are you okay?"

"I feel fine," London said. She glanced to the side, then back at him. "My blood pressure was slightly elevated."

"Stress?" he asked.

"Definitely a factor," she answered. "And hypertension runs in the family on my dad's side." She pushed her fingers through her thick hair. "I'm being forced to take a short leave."

"Can they force you to take time off?"

"It was strongly suggested and... well, it's probably for the best. Doesn't mean I won't lose my mind, but it's starting to feel like I'm halfway there already. How much worse can it get, right?"

In all the time he'd known her, Drew had never seen London so off balance. She was self-assured to a fault. He usually found that confidence sexy as hell, but this touch of uncertainty didn't look bad on her. It made her seem more approachable—more human.

"How long is this forced leave?" he asked.

"A week," she answered.

"A week? You're complaining about a week off?"

"Drew, I honestly don't think I've taken an entire week off since my first year of medical school. But my supervisor has warned me that I'm going to burn myself out if I don't slow down."

"He's right," Drew said. "I've been there. It's not pretty."

Her brows arched. "How bad was it?"

"Bad," Drew answered. "It's not fair to compare our jobs because you literally have people's lives in your hands, but it can be damn stressful when you're dealing with people's livelihoods too. One misstep on my part, one bad decision, and tens of thousands of people can be out of a job, have their retirement accounts go to shit, or lose everything they own."

"Yeah, I'd say that's stressful. What did you do when the burnout hit?"

"I powered through it, which I do not recommend," Drew said. "If you're going to take some time off, then do it and be smart about it."

A thought occurred to him. He'd promised Elias that he would drive to the Hill Country to go through his mom's things. Drew had planned to head out early tomorrow morning, but he was more than willing to postpone it by a day. He knew London was taking her little sister somewhere tomorrow so they could discuss the nude-selfies incident, but maybe he could convince her to join him once she returned.

"When does your leave start?" Drew asked.

"Noon." She looked up at him. "I'm not flying to New York to see Central Park from your bathroom."

Drew laughed and shook his head. "That would have been my suggestion if my partner had asked me to fly up there today," he said. "Thankfully, I think B. J. will be able to handle this current issue Trident is dealing with without my having to leave Texas. However, I *am* going out of town for a couple of days."

"When?"

It was possible that his mind's capacity for wishful thinking had reached epic levels, but Drew could swear he'd noted a touch of despondency in her single-word question.

"This weekend," he answered. "I need to see about my mom's house. It's been sitting empty for the past year, and my uncle thinks it's time I go there and figure out what I want to keep and what needs to be donated." He hunched his shoulders. "I've been putting it off for obvious reasons."

"It's tough to see things that remind you of her?"

She didn't know the half of it.

"Something like that," Drew answered. He sat back in his chair. "Anyway, there's some really nice wineries on the way there, along with a few day spas. If you're going to take some time off to unwind, maybe we could make use of both?"

The smile that slowly formed on her lips was hesitant at first, as if she still wasn't sure she could trust him. It killed him that she continued to hold back, that she couldn't have just a little more faith in these feelings he knew damn well she was starting to feel for him.

She lifted a pen with a bright yellow sunflower attached to it and tapped it on the desk. Studying him with an arched brow, she said, "Are you threatening me with a good time, Drew Sullivan?"

"I don't make threats, Dr. Kelley. I make promises."

She pulled her bottom lip between her teeth and allowed her eyes to travel the length of him. "When were you planning to leave?"

Drew reined in the urge to pump his fist in the air, though he did allow himself a moment to release the breath he'd been holding.

"Saturday morning," he answered. "But we can put it off until late afternoon or evening. I know you have your outing with your little sister tomorrow."

"Actually, I don't," she said. "Believe it or not, she's on a band trip with the same boy she was going to send the nudes to."

"What?" Drew's head reared back. "Just how long has it

been since your dad and stepmom were teenagers? They have to know better than that."

"Don't get me started." London shook her head as she tossed down the sunflower pen. "I've decided to keep my opinions to myself. I'll eventually talk to Nina." She set her elbow on the desk and rested her chin in her upturned palm. "I'm not sure about going away with you for the weekend, though."

"Two words: couples massage."

She rolled her eyes, a bemused smirk tugging at the corners of her mouth. "You are just determined to make me admit that we're friends, aren't you?"

"Friends? When was the last time you had a couples massage with a friend?"

"Oh, so we've moved past just being friends?"

Drew leaned back in his chair and folded his hands over his stomach. He projected an air of nonchalance, but inside sat a knotted ball of anxiety. He may have pushed too far. She could decide right here, right now that she wasn't interested in going beyond what they already had. She could decide that the sex was good while it lasted, but a weekend getaway implied more than she was willing to commit to, and she'd rather just cut things off completely than continue moving in the direction he obviously wanted to take them.

He could laugh it off. He'd made a career of finessing himself out of prickly situations, of salvaging the unsalvageable. He could go through the motions of pretending it was only a bluff, a way to ruffle her feathers. He could.

But he wouldn't.

"Yes," Drew finally answered. "Does that scare you to think of us in those terms?"

She stared at him for a heartbeat before asking softly, "What terms, Drew? What exactly are we doing here?"

He rubbed his fingers over his lips, contemplating her question and a subsequent answer that wouldn't send this suddenly consequential discussion careening into a guardrail.

The truth was, he wasn't sure how to define them. In his opinion, they'd moved past the random hookup stage after that Sunday afternoon when she'd come back to his hotel room to retrieve her bag. He'd had a couple of friends-with-benefits relationships over the past fifteen years, but this felt different. Deeper. In the span of just a few weeks, he'd formed a more intense connection with London than with any former girlfriend.

Did that say something about her, or about how resistant he'd been over the years to put himself out there? Maybe it was both.

"I don't know," Drew answered honestly. "Maybe this weekend away will make exactly what this is a bit clearer."

"Or maybe it will become clear when you finish this job at County and go back to New York," she said.

"That won't have the effect you think it will," Drew said. "Trident owns a private jet. And if it's in use, I can charter a flight to Austin every single week if I have to. Or you can fly to New York on your days off. It's only a few hours."

"It's even closer from Chicago," she murmured.

Drew frowned. "Chicago?"

She shook her head. "Forget I said that."

"No, what did you mean?"

She looked past his shoulder, toward the door. "I'll tell you about it later. On the drive to the winery."

He couldn't hold back his triumphant grin, even though he

knew she'd probably give him shit about being cocky. Drew pushed himself up from the chair and flattened his palms on her desk.

Leaning forward, he whispered against her lips, "I'll see you in the morning."

"The morning?" She jerked her head back before his lips could connect with her mouth. "Not tonight?"

Drew grimaced. "Yeah, sorry. I forgot to mention this earlier, but I have what promises to be a long conference call with my two partners tonight."

"So, no sexy shenanigans for the second night in a row? You're killing me, Sullivan."

"I will make it up to you this weekend," Drew promised. He leaned closer, seeking permission.

She met him halfway, gracing his lips with a sweet, quick kiss. "You'd better."

24

London studied the smorgasbord before her on Samiah's glass-topped coffee table, unsure where to even begin. There were three types of Thai fried noodles, coconut curry chicken, some kind of spicy shrimp that was so fragrant London was certain the people down the hallway could smell it, and an array of vegetable side dishes. Not to mention the chicken satay and spring rolls, because appetizers were always necessary.

"Do you think you ordered enough, or should we just call and empty out what's left of the restaurant?" London asked.

Samiah lifted a heaping forkful of pad see ew onto her plate. "Everything looked so good, I just ordered it all." She shrugged. "I figured I can eat the leftovers all weekend while I tweak my Just Friends app." She pointed her fork at Taylor. "Thanks for the feedback. I incorporated a drop-down menu on the suggestions page, along with a place for users to provide open-ended responses."

"Do I get credit in the app for this?" Taylor asked as she added edamame to her plate. "Like the credits at the end of a movie?"

"No," Samiah answered.

"I should have negotiated that before I gave you my feedback." She returned to her favorite crossed-legged position on the floor next to the coffee table. "It kinda sucks that you have to spend the weekend working instead of in Philly, but knowing you, you would have probably carved out time to fiddle with that app no matter what."

"When will Daniel be back?" London asked.

"He said on Monday, but I know that can change," Samiah answered.

It turned out that everyone's plans had changed in the span of a few hours. Just as London had wrapped up her meeting with Doug Renault, where they'd reassigned or rescheduled her surgeries for next week, she'd gotten a group text from Samiah, letting them know that her and Daniel's trip to Philly was postponed due to a work emergency.

Daniel, as a federal agent who could be pulled into an assignment at a moment's notice, had a job that forced Samiah to be flexible. Of course, Samiah's promotion at Trendsetters, the software firm where she'd climbed the ranks in record time, could be just as demanding. Those two made for a good pair.

Taylor had responded to Samiah's text with news that she and Jamar were going to wait until tomorrow morning to make the three-hour drive to Houston.

And, just like that, their Friday girls' night out was back on. Although they'd opted to order in instead of dealing with a crowded restaurant or bar. The music festival taking place this weekend had brought a slew of people into the city.

"Have you and Nina had 'the talk' yet?" Taylor directed at London.

She shook her head. "That's what our trip to the mall was supposed to be about, but Koko and Miles tagging along kinda changed the plans. I didn't want to discuss it in front of them, you know?"

"Maybe you should have," Taylor said. "It's never too young to teach kids to not do stupid shit over the Internet."

"You're probably right," London said. "I was going to bring Nina to this craft village tomorrow, but my stepmom sent her on a band trip instead. With the boy."

Taylor and Samiah both responded exactly as London knew they would. She listened to them screech for a solid five minutes about April's misguided parenting decisions.

"It's as if they just forget what it was like to be that age," Taylor said. "I refuse to be so clueless when I have my own kids." She held up a hand. "That was just me making a declaration. I'm not pregnant, so don't jump down my throat. I'd never get pregnant for a guy I've only been dating a few months."

Samiah's eyes flew to London's. London responded with an imperceptible head shake. She hadn't said anything about Samiah's brush with babydom.

"There's a birthday party for Miles next weekend," London said. "I'm going to steal Nina away for a bit. Maybe we'll go for a drive and talk." She ladled curry over a scoop of white rice and, as casually as possible, said, "But now that I won't be hanging with Nina, I'm going away with Drew this weekend."

The room went completely silent. Even the air conditioner cut off. She glanced up to find Taylor and Samiah both looking at her with intense, confused stares.

"What?" London asked. "Don't try to make this into a *thing*, okay? We're still just hooking up."

More silence.

"It's not a big deal," London stressed. "We're just going to a winery, and a spa, and to his late mother's house so he can decide what to do with her belongings."

"Um, do you know how fuck buddies work?" Taylor asked. "They don't go to wineries together or help each other go through a dead parent's belongings."

"Unless—" Samiah started, then she shook her head. "No, I can't think up a scenario where fuck buddies would visit a winery. And going to his mother's house? That's pretty damn personal, if you ask me. You probably need to redefine whatever it is that's going on between you two, because it's more than just hooking up, chick."

"I know." London groaned. "How did things get out of hand so quickly? This was supposed to be simple!" She set down her plate and cradled her head in her hands. "I am *not* falling for him. That much I'm sure of." She blew out a breath. "Okay, maybe just a little."

Taylor and Samiah wore matching expressions—brows arched and bullshit meters on full blast.

"I will not own up to more than that, and neither of you can make me," London said. "Look, the sex is amazing—like *beyond* amazing—and I'll admit that Drew is funnier than I would have ever given him credit for. I swear he wasn't like this in high school."

"It's called becoming an adult," Samiah said.

"Which I usually am, except when I'm around him, he makes me feel like the kind of giddy teenager I hated even back when I *was* a teenager. And, for some strange reason, I find myself sharing stuff with him that I would never share with previous boyfriends."

London slapped her hands over her mouth.

Samiah gasped and pointed at her. "You called him your boyfriend!"

"That was a mistake!"

"Nope. Too late to take it back," she said in a singsong voice. "You, London Kelley, are blushing, and it's the most adorable thing I've seen in my life!" Taylor clapped like a trained seal. "Look how cute you are!"

"I hate both of you right now," London said.

"But you really like Drew," Samiah said, her voice still dialed to annoying.

"I do." London sighed. She dropped her head against the back of the couch. "Fuck. What is wrong with me?"

"I've been trying to figure that out since you told us you weren't looking for anything serious with him, even though he's funny, rich, and gives good dick," Taylor said. "Why do you insist on keeping this casual again?"

If she got into the complicated emotions surrounding her feelings for Drew and how they were weirdly tied to her dad, both Samiah and Taylor would *really* think she'd lost it. But she couldn't just write those feelings off either. They were too close to the center of this absurd push-and-pull thing she had going when it came to Drew.

London sat up straight and cleared her throat. "This is a no-judgment zone, right? Well, slight judgment is allowed because Lord knows if either of you were to share what I'm about to, I would judge the hell out of you."

"This sounds juicy." Taylor planted her elbows on the coffee table and set her chin on her fists. "Go on."

London rolled her eyes. She could not believe she was about to admit to this, but if she couldn't share her twisted teenage thought processes with her two best friends, who could she share them with?

"I will start by saying that I know how warped this is," she began. "As someone who prides herself on being sensible and pragmatic, it baffles me that this has remained an issue all this time, but it has." She clenched her fists, then flattened her palms on her thighs. "It's hard for me to let go of my animosity toward Drew because I blame him for the strained relationship I have with my dad."

Samiah frowned. "Is this about to go in a direction that will have me tweeting to Iyanla to come and fix your life?"

"Definitely." London nodded.

"I am so confused," Taylor said. "What? How?"

"You know what?" London said. "Why don't we just forget I said anything?"

"Hell no," Taylor said. "You both know about my daddy issues. Share, honey." She made a *come to Mama* gesture with her hands. "Just let it out."

London would give anything to put this toothpaste back in the tube. She now recalled exactly why she wasn't a sharer, because she didn't like having people all up in her damn business.

Fine time to remember that.

She reached over for the lemongrass and Thai basil cocktail Samiah had made for tonight's meal and took a sip. She directed her attention to Taylor.

"So, you know how all this time you thought your dad wasn't proud of your accomplishments, when, in fact, he was?" London asked her. "For me, it's the opposite. No matter how hard I work and how much I achieve, I can never seem to make my dad proud."

"Sorry, but you will not convince me that Austin's hotshot, superstar pediatric surgeon isn't the apple of her father's eye."

"You would think, wouldn't you?" She shook her head. "But, no, I'm definitely not the apple of my dad's eye. Or, if I am, he sure as hell hasn't said anything to me."

"What does this have to do with Drew?" Samiah asked.

London gulped more of her cocktail. She needed all the courage she could muster to get through this, and would gladly take it in liquor form.

"I busted my ass throughout high school to get good grades," she said. "The only time my dad paid any attention to me was when he could brag on my accomplishments to his colleagues at his law firm. He wouldn't even mention it to me. I had to hear about it from his secretary, Manda, who would tell me how Dad told everyone in the office about some award I received, or my straight-As report card, or whatever. I was so starved for his attention that I would email her with the most transparent excuses my little teenage brain could come up with, just to see if my dad had talked about me at work that day."

London could feel the disgust building in her throat but managed to swallow it down.

"That's...heartbreaking," Samiah said.

"It's pathetic is what it is," London said. "And I will totally own up to being pathetic back then. That was life as Kenneth Kelley's daughter. I clamored for any morsel of attention I could get from him, and if that meant being the best of the class, then I was willing to do whatever it took to maintain that 4.0 GPA.

"All was going great. I was sitting comfortably at the very top of my class, and then along came Drew Sullivan. Suddenly, life wasn't so simple." She huffed out a humorless laugh as she took another sip of her drink. "What really gnawed at me was how easy things seemed to come for him. He had everything. He was the cutest boy in school by a mile. He got stellar grades. He immediately joined the basketball team and became the star player. I *hated* him," London said. "And then when graduation came around and I found out that I would have to share the valedictorian spot with him?"

"Uh-oh," Taylor said.

"It was supposed to be my crowning achievement. The one thing that would make it so that I would never have to wonder if my dad was proud of me. But who wants to brag about their child being 'co' anything? Not Kenneth Kelley."

"Drew stole your thunder," Samiah said.

"Yep." London lowered her voice, even though they were alone in Samiah's condo. "I will admit this only to the two of you, but for a millisecond I contemplated poisoning that son of a bitch."

"You did not!" Taylor laughed.

"I swear I did." London held her hand to the sky. "Picture me standing in the chemistry lab with the key to the cabinet that contained all the deadliest chemicals. Ya girl almost ended up as the star of an episode of *Dateline*."

Taylor and Samiah burst out laughing.

"That's really not fair to Drew," Samiah said. "You do realize that, don't you?"

"Of course I do," London said. "But it's stunning just how difficult it was for me to shake those feelings from all those years ago."

"Don't hate me for saying this," Taylor said. "But your dad sounds like a bit of an asshole."

"He's a major asshole," London said. "Believe me, I've only scratched the surface. He's arrogant, a chauvinist, and a philanderer, and the bastard is the reason why I've been placed on leave from the hospital for the next week."

"Hold up. Record scratch," Samiah said. "On leave?"

Shit.

This was rapidly turning into an unwelcome therapy session. London hadn't shared this much about herself since that time she was forced to go to confession prior to making her First Communion in the second grade.

"I didn't want to say anything because I know how you two can blow stuff out of proportion, but I'm borderline hypertensive."

She gave them an abbreviated version of the incident at the hospital that day, and explained how Dr. Renault had ordered her to take some time off.

Samiah reached over and grabbed the drink from her hand.

"Hey!" London said.

"Take the food too," Taylor said. "It's salty. That's not good for people with high blood pressure."

"Don't touch my spring rolls," London warned. "Look, I'm fine. I said that I am *borderline*. I haven't been diagnosed with anything, and I won't be." She released a deep breath. "I'm going to learn how to relax. I'm going to schedule time off. I'm going to do what I need to do to take care of myself."

"You should journal," Samiah said. "It's relaxing. And it'll give you an outlet to work through your daddy issues."

"I no longer have daddy issues," London pointed out. "I am well and truly over trying to please Kenneth Kelley."

"Are you sure?" Taylor looked unconvinced.

"Yes," London assured her. "My mom forgave him for treating her like shit years ago, but I've decided it's just better for me to maintain my distance."

Although she was sure to see him at Miles's birthday party, because when it came to his son, her dad never missed a thing.

It was yet another reason to steal some time away with Nina while down in Bluff Springs next Saturday.

London reached for her drink, but Samiah held it farther out of her reach. Instead, she picked up the one Samiah had left unguarded on the table and downed the remainder of it in one large gulp.

Samiah gasped. "You sneaky bitch. I can't believe people trust you with their children."

"I love you too," London said. She pushed up from the sofa and grabbed her purse. "I have a weekend getaway that I need to pack for. I'll see you ladies next Friday?"

"Unless I'm in Philly," Samiah said.

"Bring back some wine!" Taylor called. "And have fun!"

London waved on her way out the door. "I plan to do both."

25

Drew parked at the curb in front of the quaint, powder-blue bungalow with a gabled roof, white decorative beams, and matching white window shutters. It was dark when he'd last come here, so this was his first good look at London's home. The right side featured a porch with green vines growing along the railing. Neat flower beds with perfectly trimmed hedges lined either side of the stone steps that led up to the front door.

It surprised the hell out of him.

He'd first pictured London living in a high-rise condo with sleek lines and ultramodern furnishings, like the corporate apartment he'd rented, only nicer. When he found out that she owned a single-family home, he'd expected lots of steel, stucco, and glass. Something with an open-concept floor plan and not a window shutter in sight.

This was...cute. It was cozy and welcoming and so unlike anything he'd expected from no-nonsense London Kelley. The woman continued to be a fascinating conundrum, and Drew was enjoying every aspect of peeling back her layers and learning more about her.

He wanted more of that this weekend. He'd decided this

trip to the Hill Country would be his best opportunity to convince London to see him as something other than a temporary hookup partner. He still wasn't sure how to properly define what they were—something between being friends with benefits and an official couple.

They were much closer to being the latter, and it was his goal to continue steering them in that direction.

Drew slid from behind the wheel of the black Porsche Cayenne he'd rented for the weekend. It had taken a minute to acclimate himself to being behind the wheel, it having been over a year since he'd driven a car. He used a car service to take him where he had to go in New York.

He walked up to the short wooden gate just as a postal worker arrived carrying a collection of envelopes and glossy mailers. The man tipped his wide-brimmed hat to Drew.

"Good morning," Drew said, following him up the stone-paver walkway to the porch.

London opened the front door before either of them could knock.

"Hey!" she directed at Drew. She reached out a hand to the mailman and smiled. "Thank you."

Another delivery van pulled up to the curb as the mailman started down the steps.

"You're popular this morning," Drew said.

"I wasn't all that popular in high school. I'm making up for lost time," she answered. She accepted this second package with a curious frown. "I don't remember ordering anything, but who knows. I probably did." She gestured for Drew to follow her inside as she tore into the padded yellow envelope.

Drew entered the house and was once again surprised by

the homey feel of it. The flowered patterns, the cool blues and yellows and soft peach colors, the warm oak furniture—it was hard to reconcile this coziness with the woman he knew.

Yet another reminder that he didn't know her as well as he wanted to.

Drew turned at the sound of London's laugh. She held up a journal of some type, again in a flowered pattern, along with stickers, glittery pens, and rolls of colorful tape.

He lifted a brow in question. "Not something you ordered?"

"No. It's a self-care journal," she explained. "My friend Samiah had this overnighted because she thinks it will help me to decompress."

Drew shrugged. "From what I hear, journaling does help some people. To me, it just seems like more work."

"I'll indulge her once I return home," she said. She stuffed everything back in the padded envelope and placed it on the oak console table in the entryway, next to her mail. Then she lifted a set of keys from a ceramic dish along with her purse.

"Okay, Mr. Sullivan. Take me to the Hill Country. I'm ready to drink all the wine." She motioned to a camel-colored duffel with leather straps that sat next to the door. "You mind bringing that to the car for me while I lock up?"

She told him that she was going to take one last glance around to make sure she'd turned off everything. Drew waited at the passenger-side door for her, opening it as she made her way down the front steps.

"Nice car," she said as she slid in.

He stowed her bag with his on the back seat, then got in on his side and pulled his seat belt across his chest.

"Maybe I'll consider one like this when my Mini gives out on me," London said.

"You know, between your Mini Cooper and this house, I realize that you really *are* full of surprises."

"What's wrong with my house?"

"Nothing's wrong with it. It's just not what I expected. You have chintz wallpaper," he said, putting the car in drive. "I pegged you as more of a sleek-gray-and-black-with-splotches-of-red kind of person."

"You sound like someone who watches way too much HGTV in your spare time." She laughed. "And you never got the chance to see my bedroom last week. Red velvet walls. Whips. Chains."

Drew slammed on the brakes and immediately put the car in reverse. London burst out laughing and covered his hand on the gearshift.

"I'm joking," she said.

"Don't put that visual in my head if you don't plan on making the fantasy a reality, London."

"That's a fantasy of yours?"

He looked at her as if she'd lost every single bit of her mind. "The Dominatrix Doctor? Fuck yeah."

Laughing again, she nudged his hand, which was still covered with her own. "Take me to that winery. There's a glass of Cabernet with my name on it."

There were well over three dozen wineries between Austin and the small town of Hye, Texas, where his mom had lived out the last ten years of her life, but Drew had chosen the one in Dripping Springs because of its spectacular views. They headed south on I-35 and then west on highway 290, toward the foothills of the Texas Hill Country.

"Do you know the last time I was outside of the greater Austin area?" London asked.

"When?" Drew asked.

"No, I'm asking you. It's been so long since I've traveled outside the city that I can't even remember." She released a satisfied sigh as she nestled her head against the soft leather headrest. "Thanks for inviting me, Drew. I needed this."

"Thanks for accepting the invitation," he said. "And, yeah, you did need this. I could tell."

"I should bring Dr. Renault a bottle of wine as a thank-you gift. If he hadn't forced me to take the week off, I'd be prepping for a tonsillectomy right now."

"No, you would have been taking your sister out for that all-important talk."

She shook her head. "That was supposed to happen this afternoon. I still had the surgery scheduled for this morning."

"Damn, London. Do you do anything besides work?"

"I do," she said defensively. "I get together with two of my girlfriends every Friday night for drinks and girl talk. And I have my crocheting," she added.

"I forgot about that," Drew laughed. "Maybe because you haven't offered to crochet anything for me yet. What's a man gotta do to get a beanie?"

She gave his arm a playful tap. "You make fun of my crochet and then demand a beanie? I think not."

There was amusement in her voice, but when Drew glanced over, he caught a hint of uneasiness tightening the edges of her mouth.

"What's wrong?" he asked.

"Huh?" She shook her head. "Nothing. It's just...six months ago, I didn't have either of those things," she admitted. "My crocheting. My friends, Taylor and Samiah. It's only been six months since I found them. Before that, I didn't take any time off. Craig Johnson—the asshole I thought I'd bring to the reunion—was the first guy to pop up on the dating app I joined. I was too busy to take the time to swipe through to anyone else."

London huffed out a small laugh. "The morning after I met Taylor and Samiah, we came up with this idea—our boyfriend project—where we were going to work on goals that each of us had pushed off to the side. Samiah used her time to develop a phone app. Taylor worked on building her fitness brand and is now on her way to getting a college degree. You want to know what my goal was? To find a hobby. That's how the crocheting came about."

"You had to actively search for a hobby? Like, just a regular hobby?" Drew asked as he swerved into the left lane to pass a semi.

"It sounds even more pathetic when you say it out loud, but yeah, I did."

"So you had no interests outside of the hospital?"

Her shoulders hiked up to her ears. "I'm in the final year of my residency. Where am I supposed to find the time to have interests outside of the hospital?"

Drew could tell by how quickly she'd unleashed that excuse that she used it for everything. He had to admit it was a good line. There was only a select group of people on this earth who could end their workday saying they gave parents decades more time with their children.

Yet...

"You know, London. As a doctor, it's easy to convince yourself that being a workaholic is noble—necessary even. But you can't allow your job to cannibalize all of your time."

She rested her head against the headrest again and tilted

her chin up to the sky. Sucking in a deep breath, she said, "I'm learning. This weekend will be a major lesson in how to let go of my work duties and just relax." She lolled her head toward him and scrunched up the side of her mouth. "Don't let me work on the charts I brought along with me."

"My God, woman." Drew shook his head. "You need this wine tour and massage even more than I thought."

"Are we really going for massages?" she asked. "I'm not sure how I feel about that."

Drew glanced over at her and frowned. "What do you have against massages?"

"A stranger's hands all over me? Not my usual thing." She leveled him with a stare. "You were not a total stranger the night of the reunion, so shut up. And what happened that night wasn't usual for me either."

Drew laughed. "I'd offer to give you the massage if you're opposed to a stranger touching you, but I highly recommend letting the professionals handle it. At least the first one. I can take over tonight."

"You sound like a pro," she said with a laugh. "Just how many massages have you had?"

"I don't know. I haven't kept count. But I try to get one every week."

Her mouth dropped open. "Are you serious?"

"Stressful career, remember? Massages reduce stress."

"For a workaholic, it sure sounds like you treat yourself to a lot of *me* time," she said, making finger quotes.

"I didn't always," Drew admitted. "And I learned the hard way what can happen when you don't take the time to slow down and...well...live."

"The burnout you mentioned?"

Among other things. But he wasn't ready to talk about his mom and the regrets over time lost with her that were carved into his very soul. It was going to be hard enough to step into her house tomorrow. Drew wanted to steer clear of any of those thoughts until avoidance was no longer an option.

"I made a promise to myself that I would take the time to stop and smell the roses, because roses aren't always guaranteed in this life, and neither is time," Drew said. "As you will discover later this afternoon, having a trained professional's hands massage the kinks out of your muscles is one of life's true pleasures."

"This is after wine, right? I have a feeling I'll need to get myself liquored up so that I don't freak out."

"I'll be right there with you," he said. "It's a couples massage, remember?"

"A threesome," she murmured. "I figured you were into that kind of stuff."

His shoulders shook with his laugh.

As they continued toward the winery, Drew found himself wishing it were a little closer to spring. In a couple of months the highway would be flanked by millions of Texas bluebonnets. Drew had usually tried to time his occasional visits to his mom so that he'd be in San Antonio during wildflower season. He smiled, thinking of how he would pull onto the side of the road and pick a few bluebonnets and yellow daisies for her.

A familiar ache settled in his chest. He should have prepared himself for this. Even though he'd vowed not to let these memories take up space in his head until tomorrow, he should have known better than to think he could travel this road and not be pummeled by a cascade of mixed emotions.

Why hadn't he brought his mother more flowers while she was still alive? Why hadn't he visited her more often? The unmitigated arrogance in assuming that he would always have time with her still took Drew's breath away. There was not a single thing on this earth that was promised. It was a brutal lesson, but a lesson learned nonetheless.

His phone's navigation app indicated that their destination was three miles away. Though highway 290 wasn't nearly as clogged as the city's roadways, traffic had thickened the closer they approached the turnoff to the winery.

"Oh!" London pointed straight ahead. "It's the party bus. My girlfriends and I were supposed to take one of those wine tours. They bring you to about a half-dozen wineries, and you don't have to worry about not getting drunk because you don't have to drive back. It's perfect."

"Well, I never get drunk, so you don't have to worry about that," Drew said.

She shifted slightly in her seat, turning to look at him. "I noticed that you never have more than two glasses of wine. And, don't take this the wrong way, but your pour is pretty stingy, so it's more like one and a half glasses."

"I thrive on being in control," he answered with a shrug. "The more alcohol I consume, the less in control I feel. So I tend to back off after a drink or two."

At least that was part of it. The truth was that he trusted the science behind alcoholism and heredity, and he was determined to never turn out like the man who'd sired him. Elias had shared stories of how scary Drew's biological dad was when he drank, how he would sit at the kitchen table and consume beer after beer after beer until he either passed out or unleashed his drunken fury on Drew's mother.

Even as his hand tightened on the steering wheel, Drew banished those thoughts from his head. He wouldn't allow that faceless bastard to ruin his weekend with London.

"If you want to drink more than usual, you're more than welcome," Drew said. "It sounds as if you can use it."

"I'll enjoy myself, but I promise not to get too wild."

"Go for it," Drew said. "You've earned it."

Five minutes later, they turned in to the gravel parking lot in front of a limestone building.

"I already know I'm going to like this," London said. They got out and met at the front of the car.

"I booked a tour at this one because the views are amazing, and they allow you to wander through the groves on your own."

London peered at him through narrowed eyes. "You didn't bring me out here to live out some kind of kinky vineyard fantasy, did you?"

"Now that you mention it, that sounds like a good way to spend an afternoon." He took her by the hand and leaned over to whisper in her ear. "We can save the kinky stuff for later. For now, let's go find that glass of Cabernet that has your name on it."

26

Rays of sunlight cut through the bistro's bougainvillea-covered pergola, casting a blanket of welcoming warmth over London's face and arms. She held the ruby-red blend at eye level and swirled it around the blown crystal before tipping the glass to her lips.

"This is divine," she said, releasing a satisfied sigh as the burst of smoky fruit flavor hit her tongue. She motioned to the expanse of rolling hills that lay before them, with their rows of grapevines stretching into the horizon. "And this view. If I pretend hard enough, I can believe we're sitting in a vineyard in Tuscany instead of Texas."

"We can go to Tuscany too," Drew said.

The lack of teasing in his voice caused London to quickly look over at him to make sure he wasn't serious.

As if he knew what she was thinking, he said, "Just say the word and we can be on our way to a villa in Arezzo, or on the coast in Cinque Terre. If you think this is nice, just wait until you see the Italian Riviera."

He winked, and it set off a delicious tingle low in her belly.

Oh, for goodness' sake.

She was too old for this shit. Tingles were for teens

like Nina, experiencing their first brush of attraction. Or for Taylor and Samiah, who'd been bitten by the love bugs that were everywhere these days, sinking their sneaky teeth into unsuspecting asses all over Texas. Tingles were not for busy pediatric surgeons in their final year of residency and who already had a surplus of hassles piling onto their plates.

But there was no other way to describe the sensations Drew sparked within her with a simple, silly wink. Those were definitely tingles and she was unquestionably smitten.

Fine, so maybe she was more than just smitten.

London wondered what he would say if she took him up on his offer.

You'd better not!

Agreeing to a weekend in the Texas Hill Country was one thing. Flying to Italy together was something entirely different. It would catapult this...this...whatever *this* was between them into a realm she didn't have the bandwidth to even think about right now.

"Just knowing that I can get a little taste of Tuscany so close to home is good enough for me," she told him.

No doubt about it, that was disappointment she saw sweep across his face. He *had* been serious. He was ready to whisk her off to Europe.

And she'd turned him down.

Who turned down a free trip to Italy that promised amazing scenery, fantastic food and wine, and an abundance of toe-curling orgasms? No wonder her mother thought she was a dud. Janette would be ready to disown her if she knew what London had just done.

"Well, maybe we can explore some of the other wineries

in the area while I'm still in Texas," Drew said. "There are dozens more to see."

"Now *that* we can do," she said, tilting her glass toward him before taking another sip of the rich, slightly spicy wine. "Those other wineries had better bring it," London said. "This one will be hard to beat."

Their early afternoon visit had begun with a tour of the wine-making facility. The guide, whose enthusiasm about the varietals offered reminded London of an overzealous cheerleader trying too hard to make the varsity squad, explained the wine-making process as they walked among the large stainless steel vats and oak wine barrels. She and Drew were taken to the bottling room, where they watched the bottles whiz by on a conveyor belt before being filled by the automatic dispensers.

London tried hard not to lose her mind when they made it to the aging room. She'd looked upon the thousands of racked wine bottles with the same wonder as a kid visiting Willy Wonka's Chocolate Factory.

They were then shown to the tasting room, where they sampled flights of wine, from sweet, crisp whites to deep, earthy reds. Drew suggested they pause their tour and have a light lunch in the bistro instead of heading straight to the vineyards, a plan London had quickly seconded. There was only so much she could expect of the protein bar she'd eaten while packing her clothes this morning.

They'd spent the past half hour grazing on an antipasto platter of meats, cheeses, and olives, along with a goat cheese and grape pizza that was to die for. Between the scrumptious lunch and gorgeous view, it felt as if she'd found a tiny slice of heaven right here in the heart of Texas.

Drew had skipped a glass of wine with lunch, choosing mineral water while London sipped on her Malbec-Syrah blend. As she studied his sun-dappled profile, she realized that she would have no problem enjoying afternoons like this for a long time to come. It still blew her mind to think it, yet she couldn't deny what had become more than obvious.

She'd fallen hard for Drew fucking Sullivan.

If this wasn't the most warped twist of fate...

She considered the string of events that had led her to where she now found herself, sitting at a table enjoying a relaxed, cozy lunch with her former high school nemesis. London couldn't help but think about how easily things could have gone in a different direction.

What if she had done a better job avoiding Drew at their class reunion? Or, what if either of them had skipped the reunion altogether? There was no way she would've found herself in Drew's bed if their first encounter had been that Monday morning meeting where Trident was introduced to the hospital staff.

Now her most pressing question—one she would eventually have to face, no matter how much she wanted to put it off—was what was she going to do about this when his work at County was done?

Wait. What in the hell was she thinking? This situation with Drew was *not* her most pressing issue. She was on the brink of making a decision that could potentially affect her entire career: remaining at Travis County Hospital once her residency was done, or accepting that fellowship in Chicago and working with her idol. Or maybe following through on one of the other half-dozen fellowships she had been offered.

That was a more pressing issue.

Impressing upon her baby sister the dangers of sending nude photos of herself to boys she wanted to date was a more pressing issue.

Getting a handle on her hypertension so that she didn't stroke out in the middle of a surgery was a more pressing issue.

When she thought about it, the answer to the Drew Sullivan question should be the easiest out of everything she was currently juggling. He'd already laid it out. A quick flight up to New York for her, or down to Texas for him. Even quicker trips if she landed in Chicago. She could spend her weekends being thoroughly fucked against the wall of his shower while looking out at Central Park. What was tough about *that* decision?

A server came to their table to remove the remnants of their lunch.

"Can I get you anything else?" the woman asked.

London shook her head. "I think I should take a break from the wine for now."

"That's a blasphemous thing to say at a winery, but I understand," the server said with a smile. "But maybe you can try some of the grapes. They're best when you pick them from the vine."

"That sounds like a plan," Drew said, pushing back his chair. He held a hand out to London. "Are you ready for your stroll through the vineyard, Dr. Kelley?"

She placed her hand in his. "Lead the way, Mr. Sullivan."

They remained hand in hand as they traveled down the covered walkway that led to the vineyard. Another woman dressed in a maroon polo shirt with the winery's logo embroidered onto the breast pocket greeted them as they approached the entrance to the fields. She held up a sign with a QR code and instructed them to scan it on their phones in order to download a guide that would explain each type of grape and which wines they were used to produce.

As she and Drew started down the row of Petit Verdot grapes, London tipped her face skyward, relishing the feel of the sun on her skin.

Drew stopped walking.

"What's wrong?" London asked at the sight of his curious expression.

"You look like a painting," he said. There was a hint of awe in his voice, layered with a trace of tenderness that set off another round of those tingles low in her belly.

London closed her eyes and tilted her head back again. "*Avid Wine Drinker in a Vineyard*," she said with a laugh.

"You think I'm joking?"

When she looked back at Drew, he held his phone out to her, showing her the photo he'd snapped. London's mouth opened as she stared at the screen. Surrounded by the green leaves that had not been affected by the mild Texas winter, and with the sun's rays bronzing her skin, it did indeed make for a stunning image.

"Would it weird you out if I got this printed in a poster size?" Drew asked.

"Yes," London answered.

He huffed out an amused grunt as he slipped his phone in his pocket. "I may still do it. How would you ever find out?"

"I don't know," she said, recapturing his hand and continuing their stroll. "Maybe I *will* visit that fancy New York apartment of yours one day."

She'd said it teasingly, but immediately sensed a change in the air. There was an undercurrent of seriousness to Drew's tone as he said, "My door will be open for you, London. Just tell me when you're ready to walk through it."

She fought the urge to answer with a wiseass response, recognizing that the instinct had no place here. He'd issued a serious invitation, and it deserved equally serious deliberation.

"The thought of doing that doesn't unnerve me as much as it did just a couple of weeks ago," she answered honestly.

The smile that slowly stretched across his face couldn't be described as anything other than pure, unadulterated pleasure.

"I'll make sure Trident's Bombardier is fueled up and at the ready," he said.

He moved a ringlet of her hair behind her ear and leaned forward, pressing a delicate kiss on her lips. London closed her eyes and gave herself permission to experience all the emotions she'd previously shied away from—fully succumbing to feelings that could no longer be brushed off as simple lust. The depth and breadth of her yearning for Drew should scare her, but all she sensed was contentment as his skillful mouth both teased and tormented her.

He was unhurried, his tongue making slow, thoughtful passes along her lips before gently pushing its way inside. He tasted better than any of the wine she'd sampled today, sweet and spicy and addicting.

London was stunned at how bereft she felt after he finally released her from his kiss. Even though her heart was gradually coming to terms with it, her mind still fought to accept that she could be falling in love with Drew Sullivan.

Because that's what was happening every second that she was with him. She was slowly, joyously tumbling in love with this man.

Another winery employee walked down the row they were

on, greeting them with a quiet "excuse me" and grinning as he moved past them.

"I think we've put on enough of a show," London murmured.

Drew leaned over and whispered against her ear, "This is just a preview. Wait until tonight."

Tingles. Persistent-ass tingles. They raced through her stomach and lower at an accelerated rate.

Drew entwined their fingers as they continued along the slight trough that had been made by the thousands of footsteps that traveled through this vineyard.

"I've been meaning to ask you about that jet you mentioned," London said.

"Yes, the seats are heated and there is a fully stocked wet bar," Drew replied.

"That was not my question." She laughed. "But both are good to know. Actually, I wondered why you don't have one of your own. The other day you said that you could either use Trident's or charter one."

Drew slapped a hand to his chest. "You think less of me because I don't own a private jet, don't you? That breaks my heart, Dr. Kelley."

She nudged him with her shoulder. "Stop it," she said. "It does surprise me, though. Is it just a rumor among the class of 2007 that you're worth over a hundred million, or is it true?" She winced. "Ugh. I can't believe I just asked that. That's so tacky." She paused. "But I still want to know."

Drew's head flew back with his laugh.

"To answer both of your questions, yes, I am worth about one hundred million dollars. That isn't all liquid, of course," he quickly pointed out. "But I've done well over the past ten years."

"I'd say the hell so," London said. "I honestly thought it was just your fans hyping you up."

"My fans?"

"Please," London said. "Our entire class treated you like a rock star from the day you arrived at Barbara Jordan High."

"Not true," he said. "It was only after I made that game-winning shot against Anderson High that I attained rock star status."

"Whatever." She rolled her eyes. "At least you've now earned your spot on that pedestal everyone put you on." She gave his hand a slight squeeze. "Your mother must have been so proud of you."

"No one needs to put me up on any pedestals. As for my mom." He shrugged. "The money didn't faze her at all. You'll see what I mean by that when we go to her house tomorrow. She was just fine living a simple life out in the country."

"I'm not a country girl, by any means," London said. "But I could definitely use a bit more simplicity in my life right now." She bumped his shoulder again. "So, what about the plane? Why are you mooching off your company when it comes to how you fly?"

He laughed again. "Honestly, it just isn't a sensible purchase."

"Even for someone with your kind of money?"

"A hundred million won't last forever if you don't spend it wisely," he said. "Between the cost of the jet itself, the maintenance, the fuel? It doesn't make financial sense, especially when Trident's jet is just fine." A sheepish grin tilted up the corners of his lips. "I guess my mom and uncle's frugality has rubbed off on me a bit."

"Your uncle too?"

He nodded. "I offer to buy him a condo in downtown Dallas at least once a month. And at least once a month, he tells me that he's just fine in his little two-bedroom, wood-frame house in a working-class neighborhood north of the city. Neither my mom nor Elias expected anything from me—shit, most times I have to fight E over who's going to pick up the check when we go out to dinner."

"You don't have to worry about fighting me," London said. "You're more than welcome to always pick up the check."

"Does that mean you're finally going to let me take you to dinner?"

She pointed back toward the bistro. "Hey, we just had lunch."

"Not the same," Drew said. "We're going out for dinner when we get back to Austin. A real dinner, at a place with cloth napkins and dishes neither of us can pronounce."

Now it was her turn to laugh.

"Something tells me that you'll be just fine going to a place where we actually know what we're eating," she said. "You're refreshingly down to earth for someone with your kind of money."

"Money shouldn't change anyone," Drew said. "Don't get me wrong, there are some things that I will gladly pay to have done for me—"

"Like grocery shopping."

"Definitely. I haven't seen the inside of a grocery store in years. But I also won't forget my humble beginnings. Even if I do reach the point where I decide to buy my own jet, I won't forget what it was like to hitchhike from Alabama to Arkansas as a five-year-old with my mom and uncle."

It was becoming harder for London to reconcile the cocky,

most popular boy in school she absolutely despised with the kind, thoughtful man walking alongside her. She was slowly coming to the realization that she'd known hardly anything about Drew. She hadn't taken the time to get to know him. Once she learned that he'd arrived with an academic record that would put her chances at being the top student at risk, she'd made her own assumptions and decided he was the enemy.

She'd been so unfair to him.

"I'm sorry," London said.

He shook his head. "Don't be. The hitchhiking wasn't that bad. My mom and uncle would tell me that we were going on a fun adventure."

"No, not about that," London said. "Although I am sorry you had to endure so much while you were growing up. It couldn't have been easy, no matter how fun your mom tried to make it for you."

She stopped walking and turned to face him. "I'm sorry for hating you all these years when you gave me no reason to. Not that you cared how I felt about you all this time, but I'm sorry that I lost out on fifteen years of being your friend. And maybe?" She shrugged her shoulders. "I don't know. Maybe something more."

"Don't," he said. He cupped her jaw in his hand. "Don't think that it wouldn't have made a difference to me. London, I would have given anything to have had you as a friend all these years. And to have been *more* than friends?" He shook his head. "The list of things that I wouldn't have done to make that happen is so short it's barely detectable."

He brought his other hand up to her face and held her steady as he looked into her eyes with an intense stare. "The last fifteen years are over and done. I want to focus on the next fifteen. And the fifteen after that. And the fifteen after that. I'm not asking for more than you're ready to give, London. I'm just asking that you'll be open to giving me more than just your body. We don't have to figure it out yet, but can we both agree that this is more than just a casual hookup?"

"It became more than just a casual hookup when you convinced me to dance with you on the sidewalk," she said. She tipped her head up and pressed a quick kiss to his lips, then whispered, "I think this means we're going steady."

"Finally," Drew said. "Only took fifteen years."

27

Typically, when Drew climbed onto a massage therapist's table, he was prepared to feel his most relaxed. That was the point of the experience.

But his typical massage didn't involve lying two feet away from a seminude London Kelley emitting low, sexy little sounds every five minutes. Her satisfied moans accounted for the excited current that continued to streak through Drew's veins and wouldn't allow for his body to loosen up—despite the massage therapist's skillful hands. How could he relax when all he wanted was to banish both of the day spa's employees from the room and strip London out of the single piece of clothing she wore? He could not be thinking about her pair of barely there silky underwear right now if he didn't want this massage to get hella awkward, hella quick.

He concentrated on reciting nursery rhymes in his head in an effort to hoist his mind out of the filthy gutter where it was currently stuck. He'd booked a room at the boutique hotel attached to the day spa, so he'd have the chance to get down and dirty with London soon enough.

He would have *many* chances, if their discussion back at the vineyard was any indication. Somehow he'd finally managed to win over the girl of his dreams.

Drew thought about all that time he'd spent—well into his early twenties—considering what it would have been like if London had shown him even a hint of the attention he'd sought from her in high school. If she'd smiled at him instead of always rolling her eyes, or worse, ignoring him altogether. If she had been his friend instead of his foe. He wouldn't have been totally satisfied with being only friends, but he would have gladly taken it if that's all she'd offered him back then.

But she wanted more than friendship now. She wanted more than just a few hours in his bed in the evenings. He didn't know what she envisioned that *more* to be, but when the time was right, Drew was all too ready to share his opinions.

He wouldn't allow himself to think too far ahead. But at least he could breathe a little easier, knowing that their time together wouldn't end when Trident wrapped up its work at County.

The massage therapist drove the heels of her hands up Drew's spine, then around his shoulder blades, ending with a delicate pat down the length of his arms.

"There you go," she spoke in a soft voice. "Take your time getting up."

London's massage therapist did the same, and a minute later, both were gone from the room.

London released a long, contented sigh. "I will never question you again, Drew Sullivan."

Her words were slurred, but he knew she wasn't drunk. She hadn't had any wine since lunch. That was total relaxation he heard in her voice.

"I take it you enjoyed your first massage?" Drew asked.

"I'm not sure I'm even awake. Am I awake?" she asked.

"Semi-awake," he said. "You know, with the amount of stress you carry on your shoulders, a massage should be part of your weekly decompression routine."

"I first have to create a decompression routine. When I do, a weekly massage will be at the top of the list," she said. "They won't allow us to sleep here, will they? Because I could totally fall asleep right now."

"As nice as it is here, our hotel room is even better." Drew pushed himself up from the massage table, with London reluctantly following. It took considerable effort to remain on his side of the room while they both dressed. Knowing he would be alone with her in their hotel room within the hour was the only thing that kept him away from her.

They were greeted on the other side of the door with fruit-infused water and bags filled with complimentary miniature bottles of the products that had been used during their massages. And now all he could think about was using these on London later.

The boutique hotel wasn't the kind of place with online check-in service, so they had to go the old-school route and visit the front desk. They were handed yet another gift bag, this one with peach-and-lavender-scented soaps and candles, and other items representing the Texas Hill Country. The woman at the front desk started to tell them about things to do in the area, but Drew cut her off in the nicest way possible.

"We're only here for the night," he said. "Thanks for your help." Then he took London by the hand and started for the hotel's elevator.

By the time they arrived at their suite, the anticipation that had been building in Drew's blood since the moment London undressed for her massage had reached cataclysmic levels. He dropped the two gift bags on the table next to the door and shoved his fingers in London's curls. He backed up against the door and pulled her to him, shoving his tongue past her lips and drowning in how good she tasted.

They both worked in a hurry, stripping each other of their clothes while attempting to keep their mouths connected. They fell onto the bed with London ending up on top. Drew shut his eyes tight and hissed as her short nails dug into his chest.

Fuck. He loved it when she did that.

He willingly gave her free rein to do whatever she wanted to him, knowing it would be a thousand times better than anything his mind could conjure.

She straddled his lap and ran her hands along his torso.

"Shit," she said, stopping mid-stroke.

Drew's eyes popped open. "What's wrong?"

"Condom."

Holy shit. How had they forgotten that?

She climbed off him and got out of bed. She looked around. "Wait. Where are our bags?"

"Bell services still has them," Drew said. He'd left the bags with the luggage service before their massages. "They were supposed to bring them up after we checked in."

Had he replaced the condom he'd taken from his wallet the first time they were together? He hadn't bothered to check because the only place they had sex was in his apartment, which was fully stocked.

As if on cue, there was a knock at the door. "Bell services."

Thank God.

"One minute," Drew called. In a lowered voice he told London to go into the bathroom.

He pulled the top sheet from the bed and wrapped it around his waist. Where was his jacket? He found it on the floor and pulled his wallet from the inside breast pocket. He got a twenty for the bellhop and opened the door just wide enough to poke his head through and slip the guy the cash.

"You can leave those outside the door," Drew said.

The guy looked at him strangely, but then dropped the bags, took his money, and left. Drew peered up and down the hallway before opening the door wider and quickly pulling both duffel bags inside. When he turned around, London was standing near the bathroom door, a towel wrapped around her.

"This is like a scene out of a sappy rom-com," London said.

Drew let go of the sheet he held around his waist. "I don't watch many sappy rom-coms. How dirty do they get?"

"Ours will be very dirty," she said, dropping her towel. She nodded at the duffel. "You can grab some condoms from the front zippered pocket of my bag."

"I brought my own," Drew said.

"Are they strawberry flavored?"

Drew unzipped the front compartment of her overnight bag and pulled out the red-and-black condom packets, then directed her to get on the bed. He climbed in beside her and indulged himself, delighting in every inch of her perfect body. He sucked her nipples between his lips before trailing his tongue down her torso, and along her right hip.

"Hey, where are you going?" She grabbed hold of his head and tried to direct him between her legs, but Drew resisted.

He looked up at her. "Stop being so bossy."

"Don't tease me, Drew."

He nipped her thigh, and the mewl she released nearly did him in. Knowing he would make it worth her while was the only thing that kept him on the original path he'd chosen. He continued down her body, relishing the softness of her skin, the way it felt against his lips.

Drew made his way to her feet before starting the return journey. He kissed his way along her inner thighs, peppering her with whispery-soft pecks and gentle bites. A shudder rushed through him as he reached the apex of her legs. He splayed his fingers on her thighs and pushed her legs open before dipping his head low and flattening his tongue against her.

London lifted her hips up to meet him. She grabbed hold of either side of his head and ground herself against his face, releasing desperate, passion-filled cries that echoed around the room.

Drew was torn between keeping his head right where it was and lifting it so that he could look at her. He'd never understood the appeal of making a sex tape until this very moment. He would give anything to see the expression on her face as he sucked on her clit.

He tucked his hands underneath her, clutching her ass and holding her steady as he worked his tongue inside, licking and nipping and sucking until her entire body shook and a scream tore from deep in her throat. Her response was like a drug, addicting and enticing him to seek more and more and more. He could spend the rest of his life right here and never want for anything else.

Once the shudders from the first of many orgasms he planned to give her tonight had subsided, Drew grabbed a condom and quickly rolled it on. He gently turned London onto her stomach and wrapped one arm around her waist. He lifted her lower half until she was facedown and ass up, and then he wedged himself between her thighs. With his free hand he grabbed hold of his dick and guided it inside her.

London's hands gripped the sheets on either side of her head. She pushed her ass back hard against his pelvis, meeting him thrust for thrust.

"Harder," she said, the word coming out on a soft cry.

Drew enthusiastically obliged, grasping her hips and driving into her with so much force that he was already preparing to cover the cost of the bed they were bound to break.

Why in the fuck weren't they recording this?

But as he flattened his palm against the small of her back, Drew knew that a recording wasn't necessary. Every delicious moment of this would be seared into his brain. Tipping his head back, he pounded into London over and over again, until they both erupted in twin cries of pleasure that ricocheted off the walls.

She collapsed onto the bed, and he quickly followed. He rolled off her, not wanting to crowd her. He trailed his fingertips along her bare shoulder, still marveling at its softness. She smelled like the mint-and-lavender-scented oil the massage therapist had rubbed into her skin. But she smelled like something else. Like him.

Smelling himself on her sent a powerful surge of lust rushing through his veins, but Drew managed to tamp it down. His days with London no longer had a limit. He could slow things down, take his time. They would figure out the logistics later. Right now, he just wanted to exist in this place where everything was perfect.

He moved her thick curls out of the way and buried his face against the curve of her neck. She purred, the low moan sending a signal straight to his dick. He'd likened her to a drug, but it was more than just the way she responded to him that was addicting. Everything about their time together was habit-forming. He wanted more of her. He wanted it all.

"I'm usually one to let bygones be bygones, but it's hard not to be at least a little upset that you kept us both from experiencing this for fifteen years," Drew said.

"We're more than making up for lost time," she returned with a laugh.

"You think so? I say we're just getting started." He kissed her neck and brought his hand up to cup her breast, moving his palm in slow circles against her nipple until it pebbled against his skin.

Her body's reaction elicited a matching response from him, making for an enthralling cycle of erotic sensations that Drew never wanted to end.

She gasped, then said, "I'll never forgive myself for hating you so much in high school."

"You know," he said as he pressed a kiss against her shoulder blade. "You never told me exactly *why* you hated me so much."

"Yes, I did. It told you it's because you invaded my territory."

"That can't be the only reason, London."

"Why not?"

"Because some perceived threat to your designation as the smartest kid in class wasn't enough to bring about the kind of vitriol you used to hurl my way."

"Shows how much you know," she said with a snort. "It was

imperative that I remain the number one student in class, and you messed it all up."

"If you'd told me that back then, I would have gladly flunked all my finals for you," Drew said.

She looked at him over her shoulder, a huge smile spread across her face. "You're lying."

"Not at all," he said. "Especially if I could have gotten something in return for my sacrifice."

She smacked his arm. "I would not have given you *that*." She paused. "Okay, so it's possible I would have."

Drew burst out laughing. "Being valedictorian was not that serious, London."

"Actually, it was," she said. Her voice no longer held any of the previous amusement.

Drew gently nudged her, encouraging her to turn around. She did, flipping onto her back and staring up at him.

"Why?" he asked.

"I told you that too. Because it was the only way to get my dad to acknowledge I even existed." Her sad smile broke his heart. "I've spent way too much of my life desperately seeking my dad's approval. I've come to the realization that I'll never get it, and, even better, that I don't need it. But back then?" She huffed out a laugh that didn't hold an ounce of humor. "Pleasing my dad meant everything. It makes me physically ill to think of how much I clamored for any little drop of attention I could get from him, any indication that he was proud of me."

"London, you were an A student. How could your dad *not* be proud of you?"

She turned over fully and brought her elbow up so that she could rest her head in her upturned palm. Drew tried not to notice what that did to her breasts.

"I'll give you an example of what it was like to grow up as Kenneth Kelley's daughter," she said. "When you graduate from medical school and start your first year of residency, there's a ceremony that takes place called the White Coat Ceremony. It's exactly what it sounds like, an event where med students are officially given their white coats, signifying that they've completed the required coursework to become medical professionals. It's not as big a deal as graduation, of course, but it's still pretty special.

"A number of my fellow med school classmates were from out of state, and their families made the trip to Austin to attend the ceremony, some coming from as far as Seattle and even British Columbia." She looked at him. "Want to know where my dad was the day of my White Coat Ceremony?"

Drew nodded, but part of him really didn't want to know.

"My little brother's baseball game," she said.

He frowned. "Your little brother had to be pretty young, right?

"Miles was four years old. This was Tee Ball, just a regular game."

"Damn, London."

"Before Miles was born, Kenneth was just your typical uninvolved parent. He figured that as long as he provided financially, his obligations were covered. However, once he finally got the son he'd always wanted..." She shook her head. "The only thing I regret is trying as hard as I did for as long as I did to have some kind of relationship with him.

"The only reason I have one now is because my mom encouraged it, and because of my younger siblings. Still, it's superficial, at best. My days of trying to be anything to him are long over."

"And *he's* the reason you hated me?" Drew asked. "Meaning, if you'd come to this conclusion back when we were in high school, there's a possibility you wouldn't have treated me like a pariah?"

"Sorry." She shrugged. "Kenneth really does ruin everything."

"He doesn't deserve you as a daughter," Drew said. He leaned over and captured her mouth in a deep kiss. "What's his dream car?" he asked.

London pulled back. "What?"

"Your dad? What's his dream car?"

"I have absolutely no idea. Why does that matter?"

"Because I want to buy one for you just to fuck with him. Can you imagine how jealous he would be to see you riding around in a Bentley or a Maybach?"

She burst out laughing. "No, thanks. Throwing money around to show off is exactly the kind of thing my dad does," she said. "That being said, your idea is next-level petty and I love it."

You. I love *you*.

So, so close.

But he didn't want to hear those words from London unless she really meant them. Whether or not that would ever happen was something he refused to dwell on, especially when they had only one night in this hotel and he had such a tough job ahead of him tomorrow.

Instead of sharing words of love, he'd show her what their world could be like if only she gave them a shot at forever.

28

Drew's anxiety began to ramp up the moment they drove past the old post office with the WELCOME TO HISTORIC HYE sign painted on the brick facade. It had been a year since he'd come here. If not for Elias running the biggest guilt trip on him, Drew would have gone the rest of his life avoiding this picture-perfect town that had captured his mother's heart.

It's not that he had anything against Hye. In truth, he was grateful to this tiny town and the tiny number of people who lived here. It was quaint and safe and had provided his mother with the kind of peaceful existence she'd dreamed of after years of running from one place to the next. The residents had embraced her as one of their own, and Drew had reciprocated in kind, becoming a silent benefactor to Hye and several of the small towns that dotted this stretch of highway 290.

He'd anonymously funded the science lab at the high school, bought new computers for the local library, provided a new roof for the veterans' home, and paid off the mortgages of more than a dozen struggling families. He'd given to just about everything in this area.

Except the local hospital.

Drew tightened his hands on the steering wheel. His

biggest regret would forever be the lack of attention he'd paid to the local hospital, naively believing that it was adequately managed.

Because of that hospital, just saying the word Hye left a bad taste in his mouth. It was difficult for him to disassociate the town from the place where his mother had first sought treatment for the cancer that she'd kept from him. It was hard for him not to blame their lack of resources for being a contributing cause to her dying at fifty-three years old. After everything she'd endured because of his father, she had deserved to live a long and happy life.

As he turned onto the road that would take him to his mother's house, the turmoil in his gut had Drew on the verge of losing the light breakfast he'd shared with London before leaving the hotel this morning. If it had been at all possible, he would have gladly paid Larissa to come to Texas and take care of this for him. But Elias was right; this was a task that only Drew could perform. How could he allow someone else to decide which of his mother's possessions he wanted to keep?

There had been countless times over the past few months that Drew had picked up the phone to call the Realtor and tell her to just box everything up and put it in storage. Maybe if he gave himself another year or two, he could eventually bring himself to go through her things. But it would be pushing off the inevitable, and in his heart, Drew knew that a thousand years wouldn't be enough time to heal the wounds he suffered. Or to assuage the guilt he felt when he thought about his mother's final months.

He pulled the Cayenne up to the yellow house with moss-green shutters and felt his heart lurch.

"How adorable," London said. "I love a carriage-style house."

She was out before Drew had the chance to open his door. He took his time leaving the safety of the car. London met him at the front bumper and grabbed hold of his hand.

"Are you okay?" she asked.

He nodded. "I'm good."

"It's okay for you not to be okay," she said. "In fact, I would expect you to not be okay."

"I'll never be one hundred percent okay when it comes to facing the fact that she's gone," Drew said honestly. "But I need to do this." He squeezed her hand.

"Is this your first time returning to her home since she passed?"

He nodded again.

She wrapped her arms around him, and Drew's immediately closed around her. He melted into her hug, clinging to the meaning behind it and drawing in every single ounce of comfort she offered.

"Thanks for coming with me," he whispered against her ear. "I promise this won't take long."

"We have the whole day, Drew. Take however long you need."

He reluctantly released her, and she took hold of his hand once again. Together, they traveled up the walkway. Drew fished the single flat key from his wallet and prepared for the assault on his emotions when he walked through the door.

It was worse than he'd imagined.

The house still smelled like his mom, a combination of Bath & Body Works Cucumber Melon scent and whatever type of hairspray she used. It had been over a year; there was no way those scents still lingered in this house. Yet, just being here evoked memories that clutched Drew's throat in a vise grip.

He let out a slow breath and steeled himself against the pain.

"Can I just say that I adore your mother's sense of style?" London said as she looked around the living room.

As he took in the decor, Drew realized how similar the pieces were to what he'd noticed in London's house yesterday.

"If you see anything you want, just let me know," he said. "I won't be taking any of the furniture. It will all stay here or be donated. Except for the vanity in her bedroom. I don't even know what I'm going to do with it, but I remember how excited she was the day she bought that thing. It was the first piece of furniture she bought from a real furniture store, and not from a thrift shop or secondhand store."

London squeezed his fingers. "Maybe you can put it in your bathroom. I hear it has an amazing view," she said in a teasing voice.

Drew appreciated her attempt to bring some levity into the space. She always knew exactly what he needed.

He spotted a ziplock bag with colored Post-it notes and Sharpie markers, just as Elias had told him he'd find. There was a handwritten note inside, letting him know which color meant keep, donate, or toss.

Most of this would be donated, because knowing his mother, she'd already tossed anything that was in unusable shape. Not having many possessions for much of her life had taught her to take care of the little she did have, even when her son could buy her anything she could ever want.

"Wow," London said as she browsed the pictures on the wall above the rolltop desk. "Someone was very proud of you."

Drew came up behind her, perusing the framed photos of him from high school, college, and grad school. He hadn't bothered to attend the graduation ceremony when he received his MBA—he was too busy working—but his mom had made him take pictures in his cap, gown, and honors stole at one of the last remaining Sears Portrait Studios.

"You know how you said you did everything to make your dad proud?" Drew asked. "It was the same between me and my mom. Except she had no problem showing me just how proud she was. She attended every basketball game and every debate match."

"I remember," London said. She looked back over her shoulder at him. "Did I ever tell you about the time she tried to hook us up?"

Drew's head snapped back. "What? When?"

"The senior awards banquet. She was right behind me in the buffet line, and she spent the entire time trying to convince me that you would be the perfect boyfriend. She said smart people like the two of us should be together because we could match wits with each other."

He barked out a laugh. "She never told me that, but it definitely sounds like something my mom would do. What did you say?"

"That I would rather eat dirt than go on a date with her son," she answered.

Drew slapped a hand to his chest. "The daggers, London. The way you sling them deserves a medal."

"I'll admit that I was harsh, but if you'll recall, you'd just won the award for Student of the Year. Let's just say that I was a bit salty when it came to you."

He chuckled. "I guess Mom was lucky that's all you said to her."

"But that wasn't all she said to me," London said. "She told me that she wouldn't be surprised if I changed my mind one day. Prophetic, don't you think?" London grabbed his hands and brought them up to her lips. She pressed a gentle kiss to the backs of his fingers. "I can only hope that she's smiling down on us now."

A thick, weighty knot of emotion formed in Drew's throat. He fought the urge to drop to one knee and propose marriage. She would laugh it off as a joke, but he was as serious about his feelings for her as he had ever been about anything in this life or the next.

He was fucking in love with London Kelley.

It wasn't the infatuation he'd felt back in high school. This was true and bone deep, and it wasn't going away. Drew felt it with his entire being. Even when he eventually went back to New York, the love he felt for London would remain with him. Even if she couldn't give him everything he wanted, he hoped she was willing to give him time to nurture what was blossoming between them. That would be enough.

For now.

"I know she is," Drew finally answered. He leaned over and pressed a kiss against her soft lips.

"Okay, it's time to stop stalling," London said. "Give me those sticky notes. You talk, I'll write."

She followed him from room to room, commenting on his mother's style and the items he chose to keep. There wasn't much. Mostly things he knew his mother had cherished, like the headband with a flower made out of mother-of-pearl stones—a gift from her own mother—and the afghan she'd knitted years ago in the Barbara Jordan High School colors of orange and blue.

"Wait, your mom was a yarn lover too?" London asked

when they stepped into the bright yellow craft room. The right side of the room was made up of dozens of cubbies to house all her yarn. There were no less than five hundred skeins, all arranged by color.

"My mom started knitting when she found out she was pregnant with me," Drew said. He walked over to the closet where she kept a supply of baby blankets. "Baby blankets were her specialty. She would send them to hospitals, and women's shelters, and she always kept a few on hand for gifts."

"The craftsmanship is breathtaking." London ran her hand along the blankets. "I'm sorry I didn't get to know her better."

"She would have loved you. Despite how badly you treated her son," he added with just enough humor in his tone to show her that he was only teasing.

But when she looked up at him, her face was void of amusement. "What type of cancer was it?" she asked in a soft voice.

"Abdominal," Drew answered.

"Was it pancreatic? Gastric?"

"Primary..."

"Primary peritoneal," she finished for him. She winced. "It's rare. And it can be aggressive."

"It is and it was," Drew said. He took a couple of steps back and perched against his mom's craft table. "It all happened pretty quickly. The fact that she kept it from me for months didn't help. I could have gotten her better care earlier if I'd known she was sick." Drew shook his head as disgust welled up in his throat. "No. I'm putting the blame on her, when it belongs here." He pointed to his chest.

London dropped her head back and sighed up at the ceiling. "I'm going to regret asking this question, because I just *know* your answer is going to piss me off." She leveled him with an irritated look. "Why are *you* to blame for your mother's cancer?"

"I don't blame myself for her cancer. I know I'm not the reason she got sick. But if I had been here, if I'd visited more often and paid attention to more than just my work, I would've known something was wrong. I was too caught up in my own bullshit to even notice that she wasn't herself when we had our Sunday phone calls."

His words hung heavy in the stagnant air. Several long, excruciating moments drifted by before London said, "Have you gotten it all off your chest, or is there more?"

"For a physician, you can be just a little too blunt, you know that?"

"First of all, I'm a surgeon, and we're notorious for not having the best bedside manner. I, however, have an excellent bedside manner when it comes to my patients." She held her hands up. "And I apologize for being blunt, because I get it, Drew. I do. I'm the queen of holding stuff in until I just erupt and spread my word vomit all over the place."

"That's graphic," he said. "Is that what I just did?"

"Pretty much," she said. "And I would tell you that nothing about your mother's illness was your fault, but based on your tone it's obvious that you've already convinced yourself that you're the world's worst son."

"Pretty much," he said, echoing her words.

London closed the distance between them and covered his cheeks with her palms.

"You are not," she said. "You have a demanding career, and you were a thousand miles away."

She was trying to soothe him, and she was doing a damn

good job. But he didn't deserve coddling—not even London's somewhat bristly brand of it.

"I purposely stayed away, even though I knew I should have visited more often. By the time I found out about her cancer, it was too late."

"You purposely didn't visit your mother? Did you two get into a fight or something?"

"No, nothing like that. Never that." He hunched his shoulder. "I hated Texas and didn't like coming here."

She narrowed her eyes at him. "What do you have against Texas? Texas is great—at least Austin is."

Drew shook his head. He started to speak, then stopped, because he honestly wasn't sure how to explain something that had never made much sense to him.

"I was jealous of it. It borders on absurd, but that's the only way I can describe my aversion to this place."

"You were jealous of a state?" she asked slowly, a fair amount of disbelief in her voice.

"Yeah." He laughed, but none of this was funny. "Did you know I went to fourteen different schools before we moved to Austin?" London's eyes went wide. Drew nodded. "Fourteen schools, from kindergarten through the eleventh grade. Five different states, nine different cities." He opened his legs a bit wider to make room for her.

"That's a lot of change for a kid to go through," she said, stepping into the space he'd created.

"It was, but no matter where we were, I knew that I was the central thing in my mom's world. Those places we lived in, they were just locations. Nothing special. It was no big deal for her to pick up and leave, because as long as she had me, she had everything she needed.

"And then we landed in Texas." He gnawed on the inside of his lip for a moment. "I don't know what it was about this place that she found so enchanting, but it captured a piece of her heart unlike anything I'd ever seen. I don't like to think that I was so selfish that I didn't want to share my mom with anyone, even a place—"

"But didn't she raise your uncle? You shared her with him, didn't you?"

"She did, which is why E and I are more like brothers than uncle and nephew."

"Yet you were upset that your mom finally found a place that she loved enough to put down roots?"

"I told you it didn't make sense," Drew said. "What makes it even worse is that it was the perfect time for her to settle down. I was finishing high school and heading off to college. Why *wouldn't* I want her to finally settle down in a place she loved?"

London folded her arms across her chest and tipped her head to the side. "I only did one psych rotation, and it was very early in my residency, so you can take this with a grain of salt. Actually, it's probably best that you take it with a grain of salt, because that psych rotation was the only time I doubted myself as a doctor."

"But..." Drew asked, because that *but* hung in the air like the scent of microwave popcorn a half hour after it's been popped.

"But is it possible you were upset *because* she was finally settling down? Because after so much upheaval—after being uprooted time and time again—she finally chose to settle down just as you were leaving?"

Drew would be lying if he said he hadn't thought the same. He blew out a breath and shrugged. "Who knows? I'm too much of a coward to see a therapist because I'm afraid everything I've suspected about myself will turn out to be true. But it makes sense that I would resent that she decided to stay in Texas after moving so many times. The one thing I *do* know is that I allowed this aversion I have to the state to keep me away. I'd fly my mom and Elias up to New York, but I could have visited more."

"So, what are you doing here now, Drew? You avoided coming here for so long, yet you're working the account at County? You have partners in your firm who could have taken on this job, don't you?"

Damn, she was quick. Then again, this *was* London Kelley, one of the smartest people he'd ever known.

"I'm here because I want to make sure County can provide the best care possible to the people who rely on it," he said. "I guess you can say it has become my mission. One of the reasons I left my hedge fund was to focus on helping hospitals in rural areas and underserved communities operate at their best.

"Even though I could afford to send her anywhere in the world for treatment, my mom used the small hospital that served this area for her normal checkups. I mean, why wouldn't she? It's not as if you go see a specialist if there's nothing wrong. But because of the type of cancer she had, the scan of her stomach lining required more sensitive equipment than what was available, and months went by before they diagnosed it. Who knows what could have happened if they'd discovered the cancer earlier?"

"I'm sorry, Drew, but if it was aggressive, it wouldn't have made much difference," London said.

"That's what her doctors said, but I could have brought in specialists. I would have paid for—"

"An acute case of primary peritoneal cancer doesn't care how much money you have in the bank. Telling yourself that you could have done something to prolong her life, when in actuality there was nothing that you could have done, is unnecessary torture." She captured his hands again and gave them a firm squeeze. "Don't do this to yourself. Your mother loved you. She was proud of you. And by all accounts, she was extremely happy with her life in this adorable little house, and adorable little town. Find the blessings in that, and throw the rest of that shit away.

"Just so you know, I'm mentally jotting this down so that I can repeat it to myself, because that was some grade A advice I just gave you."

He laughed in spite of himself.

"Yes, it was." He pressed a kiss to her lips. "And since you're mentally jotting down good advice, add what I told you earlier about massages to that list."

She rolled her eyes. "Fine, I will. But not every week."

"No, London. Every week. If not the massage, then find some way to decompress that's just for you every single week. I think about how my mom was quick to grab Robitussin and ginger ale whenever Elias or I so much as sneezed, but when she was sick, she just pushed through it. Who knows how long she wrote off her pain as just a stomachache."

London trailed her fingers along a green-and-white baby blanket. "You're probably right. I see it at the hospital all the time. Women, in general, but mothers, in particular, focus so much on taking care of their family that they ignore their own health."

"I'm sure it's the same for hardworking pediatric surgeons."

"You know, it's not so much the massage, or the crocheting,

or taking walks in the park next to the hospital that's the problem," London said. "It's knowing that there are other things I should be doing. My Friday night get-togethers with Taylor and Samiah are supposed to be about taking *me* time, but often I'm sitting there thinking of charts I should be working on, or my patients waiting for surgery, or the dozen other things that are more important than me sipping on a margarita and talking about Taylor's latest antics."

Drew walked up to her and cradled her face in his palms. "You can't be everything to everybody, and you can't do everything, London. And you can*not* feel guilty about taking time for yourself. If there is nothing else you take away from this weekend, let that be it. You deserve to have a life outside of that hospital, away from your responsibilities. Promise me you will take time for yourself. I learned the hard way that time is the most precious commodity on this earth, and once it's gone, it's gone."

"I promise," she whispered.

Drew kissed her again. Partly because kissing her was one of his favorite things to do, and partly because if his lips were pressed against hers, then the words *I love you* were less likely to come out of his mouth.

He still wasn't sure whether she was ready to hear those words from him just yet. And the last thing he wanted to do was mess this up.

He'd been patient all these years, what was a little bit longer?

29

London bobbed her head to the Backstreet Boys playing over the craft store's sound system as her eyes roamed the display wall filled with glittery beads, metal charms, and fake gemstones. She could only hope she appeared calm and collected on the outside, because on the inside her nerves were a tangled mess. She didn't have Koko and Miles as a buffer this time. There was nothing getting in the way of the all-important nude selfies talk.

"How about these?" Nina asked.

London peered over at the string of jade-colored stones her sister held up to her ears.

"I like them," she answered. "What about pairing them with these amber ones?"

"Nah." Nina shook her head. "Those are way too old-fashioned."

"Sorry, I guess I'm a dinosaur," London muttered underneath her breath.

"Look for something sparkly. I think these fuchsia teardrops would be better. Don't you?"

It wasn't exactly London's taste, but then again, she wasn't her little sister's target audience when it came to her jewelry making.

"You know your clientele best," London said. "Pick out the ones you think will appeal the most to them."

She checked the time on her phone and reasoned that they would have to head back to Kenneth and April's soon. Her mom, stepmom, and Koko were all back at the house decorating for Miles's Marvel Comics–themed birthday party. Kenneth had taken her little brother to the batting cages, because hitting several buckets of baseballs into a giant net was exactly how a nine-year-old wanted to spend his birthday. London decided that she deserved extra birthday cake for managing to keep her eye roll to herself when Kenneth carted the poor child out of the house.

Fine, she was going to eat extra birthday cake, no matter what. But at least she now deserved it.

The moment her dad and Miles were gone, Janette suggested London and Nina drive over to the big-box hobby store to buy a piñata for the party. Her mom had followed up the suggestion with a series of rapid winks that had London wondering if maybe she had an eyelash stuck in her eye before realizing Janette was trying to subtly send her a message. As if that woman had ever been subtle a day in her life.

London had set out with Nina, determined to finally discuss the incident with the nude photos. She'd made at least a dozen attempts to bring it up over the past forty-five minutes and had chickened out each time.

She was beyond frustrated with this uncharacteristic lack of gumption. London prided herself on being forthright—beating around the bush was for people with too much time on their hands. But when it came to this particular conversation, she'd danced around the subject so much her feet hurt. Her usual bluntness just didn't seem like the best tactic.

Or maybe it was? Maybe a frank, candid talk about the repercussions Nina could have faced if she'd sent out those photos was exactly what her little sister needed to hear.

London debated waiting until they were back in the car to bring it up, but the house was only a few minutes away. This discussion warranted more than five minutes.

She looked up and down the aisle. They seemed to be the only two people interested in making jewelry today.

"So," London started. "Oh! This is cute!" She picked up a miniature pewter owl, then cursed herself for stalling as she set it back on the shelf.

Just say it!

"So, I...umm...heard about your little photography incident."

"Huh?" Nina's forehead furrowed in confusion.

Great, she really was *going to make her say it.*

London mimed snapping a photo. "You. Buck naked. Your mom walking in."

"Ugh." Nina rolled her eyes. "I should have known she'd tell you. Go on and laugh. Call me names. Whatever."

"She didn't tell me to make fun of you, Nina. She told me because she was concerned. I'm concerned too. This isn't something to joke about. It's serious."

Nina folded her arms across her chest. "I really don't want to talk about it."

"Look, chick, this isn't fun for me either, but I told April that we *would* talk about it, so here we are."

"I didn't send the pictures! Mom made me delete them—

and yes, I deleted them from the deleted files folder too. They're gone. What else is there to talk about?"

London didn't know which irritated her more, the flippant tone or the eye rolling. Both had her on the verge of losing it. But she wasn't about to end up in another viral YouTube video, this time for being a parent who goes off on her kid in the middle of a freaking store. Especially when it wasn't even her kid.

When Nina turned and started walking down the aisle, London caught her by the shoulder and went around her so that they faced each other.

"What if April hadn't walked in on you?" London asked. "Would you have sent those pictures? It's obvious you haven't grasped just how...how *dangerous* it could have been for you if you'd sent those photos out, Nina! What would you have done if this boy had sent them to his friends, and then if they'd sent them to *their* friends?"

She shrugged. "Maybe that's what I wanted."

London's head snapped back. "Excuse me?"

Another shrug. "I would be the girl everybody's talking about around school."

London's mouth fell open. She stood there in stunned silence, completely gobsmacked. "Are you out of your fuc—ever-loving mind?" she asked when she was finally able to pick her jaw up off the floor.

"I am not out of my fucking mind," Nina retorted. "You wouldn't understand what it's like to be invisible, because you went viral and had millions of people watching your video."

"I went viral because the guy I was dating was cheating on me," London said. "That's not the kind of attention anyone wants. It's not as if I'm Instagram famous or anything."

"Nobody goes on Instagram anymore," Nina said.

"TikTok then," she said.

"You're always on the news too."

"I've been on the news twice," London said. She thought about it. "Three times."

"Stop rubbing it in. We all know you're the perfect fucking daughter."

"Okay, one more *fuck* out of you, and things are gonna get ugly," London snapped.

Of course, another shopper picked that exact moment to turn down the jewelry aisle. The woman quickly backed away.

London leaned in closer and lowered her voice. "And what do you mean by the perfect daughter?"

Her sister leveled her with a look of brass and sass that would have made London proud if said look weren't directed at her. Now it just pissed her off even more.

Folding her arms over her chest once again, Nina did a remarkably accurate impression of Kenneth Kelley's deep baritone. "'London got straight As all through high school. London was the class president. Why can't you join the debate team like London did? London graduated valedictorian. If you don't pull your grades up, how will you follow in her footsteps?' I constantly have to hear about how I don't measure up to you."

The nerve of that son of a bitch! After the way he'd ignored her for her entire fucking life, he had the audacity to pull this kind of shit!

London needed a minute to collect herself. She blew out a calming breath and lessened the death grip she had on the piñata she'd picked out for the party. She would not get into a discussion about her issues with Kenneth in the middle of a craft store. And it wasn't her place to badmouth their father to Nina, no matter how much that bastard deserved it.

"It is completely inappropriate for Kenneth to make comparisons between the two of us," she said. "It pisses me off to no end. And you can trust that I *will* be speaking to him about it, but—"

"No!" Nina shrieked.

"Yes," London said. She held up her free hand. "Don't worry. I won't mention that you told me anything. I'll tell him Janette overheard him or something."

The relief that flooded her little sister's face revealed just how concerned she was about Kenneth's opinion of her.

Was it possible...?

London approached this as delicately as she could. "Nina," she started. "Did you take those photos to get Kenneth's attention?"

Her sister's eyes widened with horror. "You think I would send my own dad nudes? That's so gross."

"I didn't mean that you were going to send *him* the pictures," London said.

How in the hell had they ended up having this conversation in the middle of the jewelry-making aisle? Oh, right. Because she'd started the conversation here.

"Look, I know what it's like to jump through a thousand hoops in the hopes of getting just a little bit of Kenneth's attention."

"That is *not* what I was doing," Nina muttered. "I don't even care what Dad thinks." She flicked the huge hoop earring on her right ear. "He hates when I wear these big earrings, but I'm still wearing them."

London wasn't buying her defiance act.

"Are you sure you don't care what he thinks?" she asked Nina. "Because if you wanted him to take notice of you, having those pictures get out and cause a stir around school would certainly accomplish it, especially if it made him look bad in front of his colleagues. If that *is* your goal, there are a million better ways to go about it, Nina. That is not the kind of attention you want."

"You are reaching," her sister said. "Nudes are not as big a deal as they were back when you were in school."

London wasn't about to tell her that nudes going viral wasn't even a thing back when she was in school. She felt old enough around her little sister.

She was done dancing around this.

"Here's the deal," London said. "Once you turn eighteen, you are free to splash your coochie all across the Internet. It's yours, do what you want with it. But at fourteen, this"—she held the piñata shaped like Captain America's shield up to Nina's crotch—"needs to remain behind the shield."

"Seriously?" her sister drawled.

"I was going for dramatic effect," London said. "Look, I'm not here to lecture you—although, I now realize this entire conversation has been one huge lecture. I just don't want you to get hurt. And if you're doing these things in hopes of getting your dad's attention, please don't. Take advice from someone who spent way too much of her life seeking his approval. It isn't worth it, Nina."

London knew she was overstepping, but she couldn't stand by and watch Kenneth put yet another daughter through the emotional turmoil he'd put her through. She would protect Nina and Koko.

"You know that you can always come to me, right?" London said.

Nina nodded. "When you're not working," she said. "But you're always working."

It was true. And if she took that fellowship in Chicago, moments like these, which were already few and far between, would become nonexistent. She could promise to fly her younger siblings up to Chicago for fun weekends in the big city, but she wasn't in the habit of making promises she knew she wouldn't keep. She barely made time for them now, and she lived only twenty minutes away.

For someone who'd asked Santa Claus for a little brother or sister back when she was in kindergarten, she'd sure turned into a poor excuse for a big sister. She had to do better, whether she stuck around Austin or moved to parts yet unknown.

"You can come to me," London repeated. "If I'm in surgery, I'll call as soon as I'm done. That's a promise." One she was determined to keep.

London wrapped an arm around Nina's shoulder. "Now that my chances of being the supercool older sister are shot to hell, what do you say we go back to the house and fill this piñata with candy?"

"You still have a chance to be a cool older sister," Nina said. "I get my driver's license in two years, and your Mini Cooper just happens to be in my favorite color."

"Hands off the car, chick," London warned.

Nina laughed. Then she tucked her hands into her back pockets and rocked on the balls of her feet. "Actually, there is one other thing."

London's heart began to beat faster. She hadn't expected the requests to start this soon. "What is it?" she asked.

"I made the junior varsity volleyball team. Mom was able to come to the first two matches, but now she has to take Koko to her math tutor on Saturdays. And, well, Dad said that he finds girls' volleyball boring."

"What an asshole," London groused.

Nina's eyes widened with shock.

Okay, so calling their dad an asshole in front of his impressionable younger daughter was probably out of bounds, too, but London didn't give a shit.

"Text me the schedule for the volleyball matches. I'll make as many as I can," London said. She would also talk to April about tutoring Koko. There was no need for Koko to see a math tutor when her older sister had never met a math problem she didn't love.

By the time she and Nina arrived back at the house, London was certain she'd gotten her anger under control. But the moment she spotted Kenneth's black Mercedes-Benz in the driveway, her jaw clenched.

She pushed her Mini's door open with more force than necessary, and yanked the bags from the back seat. She caught herself marching toward the front door and forced her feet to slow down. This was neither the time nor the place for a confrontation. She should at least wait until Miles's birthday party was over.

"Oh, good! Y'all are back," April said as soon as London and Nina entered the house.

London headed straight for her father. "I need to talk to you," she said. "Now." She started for the hallway that led to the bedrooms, not bothering to check to see whether he was behind her.

She went into Koko's room. The bright pink walls plastered

with K-pop boy bands should have lifted London's mood, but not even the cuties from BTS and Got7 could break through her haze of fury.

The minute her dad entered the room, she whirled on him.

"How fucking dare you!" London said.

"Hey, watch your language, young lady!"

"Don't pull that paternal bullshit with me. You don't get to pick and choose when you want to play father. Not anymore."

"You need to watch your tone, London."

"And you need to stop using *my* accomplishments to denigrate my little sister. How *dare* you!"

Kenneth folded his arms across his chest. That superior look on his face grated the last of London's nerves.

"Nina doesn't apply herself," he said. "You should take my comparing her to you as a compliment."

"The *nerve* of you," London gasped. "When was the last time you complimented *me* about anything? The only time you care about what I do is when you can use it to make yourself look good to your friends." She shook her head. "I can't believe I wasted so much energy on you. I've spent my life just trying to get on your radar. But you know what? I'm done. I no longer care whether you're proud of me. I no longer care what you think. Period. But I will not stand by while you manipulate my sisters the way you did me."

"You are not going to speak to me this way in my own home," Kenneth said.

"Actually, I will," London said.

Don't! her mind screamed, but the last thing London wanted to do right now was listen to the reasonable part of her conscience.

"I've never told you this because you are my father, and at one time I *thought* that granted you at least a bit of respect, but you don't deserve any respect. You are a chauvinistic, sexist asshole. You treat your daughters like they're shit on the bottom of your shoe." She pointed toward the door. "I don't understand how you convinced those two intelligent women out there to even give you the time of day. Because you bring home a big paycheck? Because you play in some stupid cover band?

"And you know what else? I don't understand what kind of twisted psychology goes on in that brain of yours where you think showing your daughters any kind of affection or even just . . . just simple regard . . . makes you less of a man. It's sick. *You're* sick. And you are no longer worth my time.

"Oh, and thanks for the hypertension. Because you may not have given me any attention, but you did give me your shitty genes."

"Are you finished?" Kenneth enunciated the words slowly. Coldly.

Fuck you was on the tip of her tongue, but apparently somewhere in her heart, she had a modicum of self-preservation.

Instead, London raised her hands in an *I'm done* gesture.

"You will not disrespect me in my home," he said. "I want you to leave."

London didn't say another word. She simply turned and walked out of the room.

"Where's Miles?" she asked when she entered the family room, where April was stuffing the piñata with candy.

"Right here!" her baby brother said, coming up behind London.

London turned and did her best to smile. "Honey, I hate to miss your party, but I have to go."

"But I thought—" Janette started. The look London shot her way shut down whatever she was about to say.

London reached into her purse and pulled out the birthday card with a hundred-dollar bill tucked inside. "I promise to make it up to you," she whispered into his ear as she leaned over for a kiss.

London felt her dad's presence as he walked into the room. She ignored him.

"Have fun at the party," she said to the room in general.

Then she walked out the door.

30

London left the party on autopilot, getting into her car and driving straight to Drew's apartment. She sat behind the wheel of her Mini and sent him a text.

> I'm outside. Bad, bad day. Can I come up?

He was waiting for her in the lobby of the building when she walked through the sliding glass doors. She walked straight into his waiting embrace, both stunned and relieved at how at home she felt in his arms.

But she shouldn't feel stunned anymore. Over these past few weeks Drew had proven to be a steady, calming presence in her world.

"How does a party for a nine-year-old put you in this kind of mood?" Drew asked.

London lifted her head and looked up at him. "I called my dad an asshole to his face. I need a drink."

"I think you need several drinks. Let's go."

They walked wordlessly to the elevator. Drew held her hand in a firm, comforting grip as they rode up, but he didn't press her for details. She appreciated that innate sense of his; it was as if he knew without her saying that she needed some time before she could speak about what happened.

He let her into the apartment and headed straight for the kitchen. London looked on as he slipped one of the wines they brought back from the Hill Country last weekend from the wine rack. He grabbed a couple of wine stems and poured two glasses of the Malbec, then directed her to follow him to the couch. They sat, and London immediately settled her back against his chest. Once again, a rush of contentment flowed through her.

Who would have thought that Drew Sullivan's arms would become her happy place?

"Do you want to talk about it?" he asked after several minutes passed.

Three weeks ago, she would have answered that by draining her wineglass, stripping her clothes off, and mounting him. She still wanted the intense orgasms he excelled at providing, but that could wait. What she craved most right now was that quiet, understanding way he had of listening without trying to fix everything.

She started with the conversation she had with Nina about the photos. Drew's eyebrows nearly met his hairline when she shared her little sister's flippant response to her question about what would happen if the photos had been widely shared.

"So she *wanted* her nudes floating all around school?"

"I honestly don't know if she was telling the truth or just being a bratty teen," London said as she sipped her wine. "And, although she denied it, I honestly think that stunt was more about getting my dad's attention than anything else." She shrugged. "In a way, I get it. Even bad attention is better than none at all." She shoved her fingers into her curls and massaged the side of her head. "I just hate that he's doing this to her. It's exactly what he did to me—ignored me to the point where I obsessed over any bit of attention I could get from him. It's like some sick game he has going."

She took another sip of her wine, then placed her glass on the table. "I definitely got his attention today. The look on his face when I went off on him is permanently imprinted in my mind."

"I'm jealous," Drew said.

She looked at him over her shoulder. "Jealous? Of what?"

"Do you know what I would give to be able to call my dad an asshole to his face?"

London sent him a sad smile. "That puts things into perspective," she said. "I guess you think I should be grateful that I at least have my dad in my life, huh?"

"Nope." Drew shook his head. "A shitty dad is as bad as an absent one. And if you called him an asshole to his face, it's because he deserved it."

"I haven't gotten to the part that *really* makes him the asshole of the year." She told him about how her dad had been using her accomplishments to shame Nina. "It just pisses me off so much that in all the time I was in school he couldn't be bothered to say, 'Nice job, London,' yet he uses me to make Nina feel bad about herself. I mean, who does that?"

"A narcissist," Drew answered.

London paused. "Wow," she said after a moment. "I'd never considered that, but he is the textbook definition of a narcissist," London agreed. "Everything in this world revolves around him. He uses us for what we can do for him, has zero empathy, and you will never find a more self-important human being on the face of this earth. And you want to know what's truly bizarre? People flock to him. They always have."

"Narcissists can be charismatic. Couple that with him being a successful attorney and musician, and yeah, I get it. He's what you *thought* I was in high school."

"That's exactly what I thought," London said. "I'm so sorry."

"As long as you no longer think of me that way, I consider it water under the bridge."

He was far more forgiving than she was. She held on to a grudge like a drowning woman holding on to a life raft.

"I wish I were as wrong about Kenneth as I was about you," London said. "It hurts to know that he will never be the father that I needed him to be—for Nina and Koko's sake. It no longer matters to me, because I'm done with him, Drew. I'm just done."

He tightened the arm that he'd curved around her middle. "I'm sorry he couldn't be the father you needed too," he said softly against her temple. Several quiet moments passed before he added, "But I think I have something that may make up for your bad day."

"I'm way ahead of you," London said. "Let me finish my wine first, and then we can go in the bedroom. I have pineapple-flavored condoms this time."

"That isn't what I was referring to, but I approve of that plan. Highly approve." He took the glass from her and twisted her around so that she could face him. "There's a doctor out of Seattle, Susan Hemingway. Do you know who she is?"

"Of course. She's a rock star," London said. "She's a pioneer in MSE therapy—that's multisensory environment therapy. Why?"

"Because she happens to be in Austin," Drew said.

London's head snapped back. "How do you know that?"

"Those details aren't important," he said. "What *is*

important is that she's taking some time out from the meetings she's holding with one of the tech companies here so that she can meet with *you* at County when you return from your mandatory vacation on Monday. You're going to give her a tour of the pediatric floor, and she's going to consult on the new sensory room."

London felt her mouth take on an O shape in slow motion. She covered her chest with her hand.

"Drew," she whispered. "How did you...? What did you say to get her to agree to this?"

"I told you I would make this happen for you," he said.

London refused to call what she was feeling love. Love *did not* happen this quickly. But this was, by far, the closest thing she'd ever felt to love.

She was ready to fall in love with Drew Sullivan. Not because of the things he did for her, but why he did them. He knew what this sensory room meant to her. That he would go the extra mile of securing a meeting with the authority on the subject meant everything.

London clamped his cheeks in her hands and pressed her lips to his.

"I don't know what to say," she said. "And coming from me, that's huge."

"Don't I know it," Drew said with a laugh. But then he sobered, his face taking on a serious expression. "There are a lot of tough decisions that have to be made at County, but your sensory room isn't one of them. You've worked hard for it and you deserve to see it come to fruition. Your patients deserve it."

Yet, if she went with the fellowship in Chicago, she wouldn't be there when it was all done.

A heaviness settled deep in her bones. She'd spent the past several months mulling over what to do post-residency. She'd even made up one of Samiah's notorious pros-and-cons lists. Both were pretty equal on paper, but when she added weight to each item, the con side was winning.

And that was before she added this newest factor to the mix. If Drew managed to convince the hospital board of directors to green-light the sensory room, she could just throw the entire list in the trash. There was no way any of the pros for moving to Chicago could win out.

She brushed her thumb along his strong jawline, slight shivers running down her spine at the sensation of his stubble against her skin.

"Thank you," London said. "I never allowed myself to consider that you would make this happen. I'm just so used to being let down and having to do things on my own."

"I'm a man of my word, London." He brushed her hair back from her face and cupped her cheek in his palm. "If I make a promise to you, know that I will keep it."

31

Drew followed a few feet behind the two doctors, listening intently as London gave Susan Hemingway a detailed account of what she hoped to accomplish with the sensory room. It was obvious based on the other doctor's reaction that London had done her homework, which didn't surprise him in the least.

What *did* surprise him was how awestruck London seemed by Dr. Hemingway.

Normally, London Kelley's confidence was an entity unto itself—the kind that came with knowing that you were the smartest person in the room. It was refreshing to see her engaged in this little display of hero worship. She wanted to impress the doctor from Seattle, and Drew had no doubts she had.

Exuberance radiated from her as she described her plan of action, rattling off idea after idea. Drew was mesmerized. He could tell by her enthusiasm that her passion for this sensory room didn't come from a place of ego—even though completing a project as ambitious as this one would be a huge feather in the cap of any surgical resident.

But it wasn't about that for London. She wasn't doing this because it would look good on her résumé. This was

100 percent about doing what she thought was best for her patients.

Everything she did at this hospital was for her patients, even if it ruffled the feathers of some of the most powerful people here. London didn't back down from the fight, she brought it.

He'd had no choice but to fall hard for her. How could he not?

Drew did his best to keep a running tally of expenses in his head as London outlined her vision. It would take about fifty grand to design the space to her compromised specifications, but that was more than doable, especially because they wouldn't have to build anything from the ground up. Her plan was to repurpose this underutilized room on the pediatric floor.

Drew was now convinced that the only reason it hadn't been approved by the hospital's administration yet was that Frederick Coleman had personally vetoed the idea. The amount of evidence-based research London had to back up her efforts to customize this room made it a no-brainer.

She ushered them to an area that was currently being used to house decommissioned medical equipment. "And this space is what I call the 'Feel Good' spot. There will be numerous textures used on surfaces throughout the room, but I also want to create a corner that specifically addresses tactile sensory issues," London explained. "It will include weighted vests and blankets. I've even run across weighted stuffed animals and other toys."

"Those are popular with kids," Dr. Hemingway said. "Combining the tactile features with the proper auditory and visual components will go a long way in making this space a calm environment for both patients and their parents before surgery. What measures are you all taking now for patients with sensory issues?"

"We provide teddy bears for the kids to hold on their way to the operating room. It's so ridiculously inadequate," London said. "We can and *should* be doing so much more. I've been pushing for County to create this sensory room for several years now." She looked over at Drew and smiled. "I am so grateful that it is finally being seriously considered."

It would be foolish to read anything more into that look she directed at him, but he wanted her love too much not to see it reflected in her eyes. There was more than just gratitude there. Even if she wasn't ready to say the words, Drew felt them. He felt her love every time she peeled back another layer of herself and allowed him to get closer. This was no longer one-sided. It was real.

All three of them turned at the sound of the door opening. Frederick Coleman walked into the room.

"Here she is," the chief of surgery said. His jovial expression threw Drew off for a moment.

"Fred?" Dr. Hemingway's face beamed with recognition. "I forgot you were in Austin. Is this your hospital?"

"Yes, it is," Dr. Coleman said.

London looked from one doctor to another. "I'm always astounded at just how small the medical world can be," she said. "I guess introductions aren't necessary."

"Susan and I were residents at Cedars-Sinai in Los Angeles many moons ago," Coleman said.

"I was chief resident at the time," Dr. Hemingway said. Drew wanted to high-five her.

"A very good one," Coleman said, though his smile was

tighter than before. London was right. The man had an issue with women in authority, and now they knew where it stemmed from.

"I thought it was just a rumor when I heard that you were at the hospital," Coleman continued. "What brings you to Travis County?"

She gestured to London. "I came to speak with Dr. Kelley regarding the new sensory room you all will be adding here at County. I must say, Fred, I am impressed, especially with Dr. Kelley here. You have a fine pediatric surgeon on your hands. Count yourself lucky that we've already filled all of our fellowships in Seattle, or I would be giving her the hardest sell of my life to try to lure her away."

"Yes, Dr. Kelley is very special indeed," Coleman said. Drew could measure the enthusiasm in his voice using a thimble.

For London's part, she didn't so much as flinch. Drew now realized it was because she'd spent so much time dealing with a father who had the same chauvinistic mindset. Coleman was child's play for her.

Still, Drew felt he needed to set the record straight.

"I'm the one who contacted Dr. Hemingway on Dr. Kelley's behalf," Drew said. "I know there is still a lot for the board and hospital administration to discuss as Trident wraps up its audit, but when I learned that Dr. Hemingway was in Austin, I didn't want to pass up the chance for her to tour County's pediatric ward. I'm jumping the gun here, but I can tell you that the sensory room will be at the very top of Trident's list of recommendations when it comes to additions to the hospital."

"That *is* jumping the gun," Coleman said. "But I applaud you for taking the initiative. We've looked into Dr. Kelley's little project on multiple occasions, but if Trident believes it will benefit the hospital, we may reconsider."

Drew wasn't sure how London managed to hold it together. He was pissed on her behalf. She'd done her homework on this and had more research to back it up than should have been warranted. Yet Coleman was only willing to consider it now that Trident had put it on the table? This guy really was an asshole.

Coleman turned to Dr. Hemingway. "Let me know if you'll be around for lunch, Susan. I'd love to catch up."

"So would I," she said. "I'll find you once I'm done speaking with Dr. Kelley. I assume your office is whichever is the largest in the hospital?"

"You assume correctly," Coleman answered with a laugh. "I'll see you after you're done here." He gave London a pointed look as he exited the room, but she barely paid him notice. Her entire focus was once again on gleaning every drop of information she could from Dr. Hemingway.

By the time they were done, London had secured an invitation to tour the sensory room the other doctor had created at her hospital in Seattle, along with a pledge from Dr. Hemingway to return to County on a subsequent trip to Austin.

"Feel free to pick my brain whenever you need to," the doctor said. "I wasn't joking when I told Frederick that I'm tempted to poach you. County is lucky to have you in their residency program."

"I'm so grateful to the hospital and the physicians here. They've taught me so much, and it has been a true honor to serve the people of my hometown," London said. "I'll always treasure my time here."

Drew's forehead dipped with his frown. There was something odd about both her tone and phrasing.

He took Dr. Hemingway's proffered hand and thanked her for coming, then followed them both out of the room.

London's office was across from it. She pulled Drew inside, closed the door behind them, and pinned him against it. The kiss she laid on him was long, slow, and deep, and if they weren't at this hospital right now, Drew had zero doubts that they would be naked in two minutes flat. It took every ounce of restraint to keep his hand from going to his necktie and ripping it off.

"That was phenomenal," London said. "Did you see how excited she was when I mentioned the bubble wall?"

Drew could barely recall his own name when she pressed her body against his like this, but he nodded anyway.

"I've been struggling with an extremely important decision," she said. "You pretty much made it for me by bringing Dr. Hemingway here today."

"What decision?" Drew asked.

"Whether to remain at County," she answered.

"You considered leaving?"

She held on to his hand as she backed up to her desk and perched against it.

"Remember when I mentioned Chicago?" she asked. He nodded. "I'm coming to the end of my residency. I have offers from hospitals around the country, including a fellowship in one of the most competitive pediatric cardiothoracic surgery programs in the world—that's the one in Chicago. But if we can make this MSE room happen here at County, I just can't see myself abandoning it. I want to see it through."

She cradled his face in her palms. "Thanks for going out

of your way to make this meeting happen and for making my decision so much easier than I anticipated."

"I made a phone call, London. I didn't—"

"That's more than I can normally count on. Don't you understand, Drew? I could never rely on the few men in my life that I *should* have been able to count on to have my back." She squeezed his hands and brought them to her lips. The firm kiss she pressed against the backs of his fingers conveyed even more than her words had. "Thank you," she said again. "Thank you for staying true to your word."

32

The aroma of fried cheese, spicy tomato, blistered peppers, and whatever else Samiah had ordered from their favorite Spanish restaurant's tapas menu permeated her friend's condo. Thank goodness it did, because London had just burned the zucchini that was supposed to be used in place of lasagna noodles in the dish Taylor was teaching her to make.

"What did you do?" Taylor snatched the spatula from London and scraped the charred vegetables from the pan. "You're the only person I know who can burn food so badly that it sticks to the bottom of a nonstick skillet."

"And this is why I ordered tapas," Samiah said. "I still get nightmares from the grilled cheese you made me months ago."

"Ha ha," London deadpanned. "I know the Mediterranean diet is the best for me, but I'm not sure this will work if I have to make the dishes, Taylor. Cooking is the one thing I do not excel at, which is why I don't do it."

"You'll learn!" Taylor said. "The recipes are super simple. You just need some practice."

"Well, can she please practice in her own kitchen? I happen to like mine and don't want it going up in flames," Samiah said. She turned to London. "And remember, it's not just your diet you need to worry about. You still need to do more to reduce stress."

London pointed to the top of her head. "Doctor here. I know all of this."

Samiah pointed to her own head. "Doctor's friend here. I know you know this, but I don't see you practicing it. Have you been journaling?"

"The journal is in my purse."

"Anything written in it?"

"I plead the Fifth." London held up both hands. "I promise to journal and try at least one recipe a week from that book," she said, gesturing to the cookbook Taylor had brought with her tonight. She picked up the lid for the jar of sun-dried tomatoes that had been spared from joining her ruined veggie lasagna. "Can we please just eat? I'll stick to the shrimp and the peppers tonight. Both are pretty healthy."

"Fine," Taylor said, "But I want reports on your meals. And if I have to cook for you, I can do that. I just want you to be healthy."

London's heart jumped to her throat. She set the jar on the counter, walked over to Taylor, and pulled her into a hug. "That is one of the nicest things anyone has ever said to me. Thank you."

"Aww, I love us," Samiah said. She wrapped her arms around both of them.

After a few seconds, London shook Samiah off. "Okay, let go. You know I hate this mushy stuff."

"I could have used another minute or two, but whatever," Taylor said. "Let's eat."

London wiped away the evidence of her ruined dish from the counter, and the three of them went into the living room.

They sat around Samiah's coffee table, where the dozen or so tapas were spread out.

"Okay, woman, what's up with this emergency girls' night?" Taylor asked. "Is Daniel putting a ring on it or what?"

Samiah's head snapped back as she loaded a helping of garlic-butter shrimp onto her plate. "What? No," she said.

"No?" London sat up straight. "Why else would you bring us here on a Tuesday night if not to announce your engagement?"

"Girl, Daniel just moved in like a second ago. We haven't even agreed on what to do about his ridiculous CD collection—he has to put some of that shit in storage," Samiah said in a lowered voice. "Besides, I would have just texted if that was the case." She picked up her phone, swiped across the screen, and turned it so that it faced them both. "The Just Friends app is officially in the App Store. *That's* the reason we're celebrating tonight."

It wasn't the news London had expected, but that was her own fault. Knowing Samiah, she totally should have predicted this would be related to her career.

"Congratulations," London said. She clinked Samiah's glass of sangria with her own. Her friends had agreed the sangria was okay because it contained fruit. "To hard work paying off."

"Amen!" Samiah said. "This app kicked my ass, but it was so worth all the effort."

"There it is!" Taylor swayed back and forth from where she sat on the floor, next to the coffee table. She held her phone aloft. "Taylor'd Conditioning's 'Lost in the Woods' Survival Experience is front and center. Is there some kind of rewards program for the vendor that brings the most people to the app?" she asked Samiah.

"No, but that's not a bad idea. I may add it later."

The door to the bedroom opened, and Daniel walked out. He wore a starched white button-down shirt and blue tie. His bottom half sported ratty basketball shorts and bare feet.

"Evening, ladies," he said. "Don't pay me any attention. Just grabbing a bottle of water before my meeting."

"A shirt and tie instead of a hoodie?" Taylor remarked. "Will the head of the FBI be on this call or what?"

Daniel's eyes shot to Samiah. She held up her hands. "Don't look at me. I didn't say anything."

"Holy shit, you *are* talking to the head of the FBI tonight?" Taylor screeched. "You totally need to put on pants for that, dude. C'mon."

"I'm fine as long as I don't stand up," he said. He walked over and planted a kiss on Samiah's forehead while simultaneously filching an aioli-covered patata brava from her plate. "My meeting with an ordinary fellow government employee who shall not be named will probably run a couple of hours."

"We'll try to keep the noise down," Samiah told him.

He waved that off. "Don't worry about it. My microphone will be muted throughout most of the meeting and I'll have on headphones." He gestured at London and Taylor. "Good night, ladies."

"Tell the FBI director I said hello," Taylor called to his retreating back.

"Is Dimples really going to be on a call with the head of the FBI?" London asked once Daniel had closed the door to the second bedroom. It had been converted into a home office that looked more like the cockpit of a fighter jet with all the computer equipment his job required.

Samiah drew her fingers across her lips and motioned as if she were throwing away the key.

"That means yes," London and Taylor said to each other.

"Remind me never to say anything incriminating while I'm in your house," Taylor said. "This place is probably bugged."

"I don't think undercover agents bug their own homes," London said. "But you still keep the incriminating stuff to yourself. No one is bailing you out of jail again."

Taylor stuck her tongue out at her, but it was all in good fun.

"Oh! Oh! Oh!" Taylor flapped her hands like a bird flapping its wings. "I have got to tell you guys about this chick who went full-on Karen in my humanities class today."

As Taylor began an animated recounting of her entitled classmate's tantrum over her grade, London's thoughts meandered to the impromptu Zoom meeting she'd had just before coming to Samiah's tonight. She had vowed to get out of the habit of checking her email after leaving the hospital—one concession she'd made in her effort to develop a better work-life balance and practice better self-care. But checking her work email was as automatic as cringing when she encountered a pickle on her hamburger—it was just something she did.

And once she saw the email from the director of the fellowship program at the hospital in Chicago, she had to read it. Of course, once she read the email she *didn't* have to accept his invitation to a quick chat over Zoom. But she had.

And she had nearly lost her damn mind at the incentives the three doctors on the other end of the call had lobbed her way.

It was nice to be wanted—okay, so it was better than just nice. It was a full-on ego hand job—but there was a difference between having your ego stroked and having the red carpet laid out for you in mind-blowing fashion.

London had sat behind the wheel of her car, Googling the typical extras fellowship programs used to lure highly sought-after candidates. She could find none that came close to what she'd been offered. The salary was so lucrative that most surgical residents would FedEx their acceptance letter via same-day delivery, but there was so much more. She would get to work with a team of cardiothoracic surgeons headed up by Dr. Eveline Mayberry while they crafted a new study in pediatric heart surgery. It was groundbreaking work, and she would be at the forefront.

Just when she thought her decision to remain in Austin had already been made.

London fought the urge to physically rub her stomach. The ache had settled there the minute the meeting concluded, and nothing she did was able to abate it.

"Hold on," Taylor said. "What's up with you?"

It took London a second to realize Taylor's question was directed at her. "Huh?"

"I just said that I was thinking of adding an interpretive dance class for NFL players to my list of workout classes and you didn't make a snide comment."

"I thought you were talking about the Karen from your humanities class?"

"I moved on from the Karen like five minutes ago," Taylor said. "I knew you weren't paying attention, Ms. Rude Butt. What's going on with you?"

"First, tell me you are *not* serious about that dance class."

"Of course not. *Maybe* not. It was a joke, but you didn't respond, which makes me nervous."

"Same," Samiah said. "You've been unusually quiet tonight. I don't trust it."

"I'm fine," she said with a sigh. London pitched her head back and stared up at the ceiling. "I just have a lot on my mind."

"Work, family, or the fuck buddy?" Taylor asked.

She scrunched up one side of her mouth. "Honestly, all three."

"Oh, shit." Samiah added more sangria to London's glass, using a big wooden spoon to scoop fruit out of the glass pitcher. "Which one do you need to start with?"

"They're all intertwined in a way," London said. She ate a chunk of wine-soaked apple, then repositioned herself on the sofa, tucking one leg underneath her and bending her other knee so that she could rest her cheek against it.

"I guess the easiest to explain is Drew," she started. "He has moved far past fuck-buddy status."

"Has he now?" Taylor asked with a smug lift of her eyebrows.

"I am not in love with him, so don't even go there," London said. Yet, the moment the words left her mouth, she felt as if her nose would sprout a branch like Pinocchio. She groaned, tapping her forehead against her knee. "This is ridiculous. It's way too early to even contemplate being in love with him, but what the hell do you call it when the thought of not seeing someone every day makes your chest hurt?" She pressed a fist between her breasts. "And I'm not talking figuratively here. It literally hurts when I think about him going back to New York."

"Oooh." Samiah winced. "You got it bad, girl." She hitched her head at Taylor. "You know that blend of uplifting essential oils she gave us? I start diffusing it two days before he leaves for an assignment," she said, pointing to Daniel's office. "And I still wait around for his text messages and phone calls like I don't have other shit to do with my day."

"What's up with that?" London asked. "A simple 'how are you?' text from Drew has me smiling like a damn fool."

"You are *so* in love," Taylor said. "It's adorable."

"Shut up." London squeezed her eyes shut. "It just seems so dramatic. And extremely inconvenient. I have too much on my plate right now."

"When does Drew leave for New York?"

"Trident is wrapping up their work. He hasn't said anything yet, but I doubt he'll be in Austin by this time next week. But this is about more than just Drew," she said.

She looked at her two friends. These women who she'd met only six months ago, who were already like sisters to her. She wouldn't be leaving just her family—she would be leaving them.

"I got a job offer," London said.

"What! Congratulations!" Samiah screeched.

"Yes! Girl, gimme some!" Taylor held her hand up for a high five.

"In Chicago," London finished.

Taylor dropped her hand. "Chicago?"

Her words had sucked all the air out of the room, replacing it with a pregnant silence that hovered over them until Samiah finally said, "Umm . . . okay. Wow."

"Are you taking it?" Taylor asked.

"I don't know." London hunched her shoulders. "I would be a fool not to. This is one of the most competitive fellowships in the country, and I would work with some of the top doctors in my field, including one of the first Black women doctors to ever perform open-heart surgery on an infant. She's a pioneer in the field of pediatric surgery and my idol. I can't even describe how amazing this would be for my career."

"Why is it even a question?" Samiah said. "Go!"

"But she has a house here," Taylor said. "And friends."

"Her house isn't going anywhere if she doesn't want to sell, and this isn't the Dark Ages. We can have our girls' night from anywhere in the world. That's what FaceTime and Zoom are for."

"It's not that simple," London said.

"But your residency is coming to an end, so you're not obligated to remain at Travis County Hospital, right?"

"No, but it feels as if I'm abandoning them."

"Exactly," Taylor said. "Stop pushing her to leave."

"Stop pushing her to stay just because you don't want to lose your friend. I'm here," Samiah said sympathetically. She directed her attention back to London. "This is *not* you. You are more practical than this. If this job in Chicago is the best move for your career, you have to do it."

"Okay, so maybe it *is* that simple," London said.

She'd wrestled with this decision for months now. But at the heart of every argument she'd made and every pros and cons list she'd concocted was this one truth that Samiah had laid out so succinctly. This was the best move for her career.

She thought about her patients, many of whom she'd seen multiple times in the past five years. She thought about the MSE room she'd fought for, and how much it would hurt to leave just as it was finally being created.

She thought about Nina, and how much her little sister needed her. Koko and Miles too. She remembered visiting April in the hospital the day Miles was born, and they'd just celebrated his ninth birthday. She'd already missed so many moments of their childhoods; if she moved to Chicago, she would miss so much more.

"I still have some time before I have to give them an answer," London said.

She had a week. One week.

Today's impromptu Zoom meeting was basically a shit-or-get-off-the-pot warning. This was the thick of "match season," that time of the year when residents either were matched with fellowships for further training in their specialties or moved on to full-time positions in hospitals and clinics around the country. The hospital in Chicago couldn't hold her spot forever. She wasn't *that* damn special.

They deserved an answer from her.

It was time for her to figure out what it would be.

33

Drew clicked through the half-dozen stock market apps on his phone as he sat on a bench along the greenbelt that lined Waller Creek, waiting for London to arrive. Even the cars whizzing past on nearby I-35 couldn't detract from the tranquility provided by this little oasis in the heart of the city.

After learning about the marathon heart surgery London had today, Drew decided a little decompression time was in order. He'd asked Larissa to order a picnic lunch to be delivered to this small park near the hospital. Fortunately for him, his assistant never did anything half-assed.

When he arrived at the meeting spot, he found a trio of women setting up a tent made out of gold-painted bamboo and gossamer drapes. Inside were mountains of pillows and plush cushions along with a four-foot-long table that sat about ten inches off the ground. In addition to the china place settings on the table, there were several vases of fresh flowers, scented candles, and sparkling white grape juice chilling in a silver champagne bucket. Drew had no idea when luxury picnics had become a thing, but count on Larissa to be on top of it.

A chef stood next to a portable cooking table a few yards

away, waiting to prepare lobster crepes to go along with the salad and chilled lobster bisque that already awaited them inside the tent.

"What's all this?"

He whipped around to find London walking up to the bench. Drew stood so he could greet her.

"Your lunch."

Her mouth hung open in utter astonishment as she stared at the picnic setup. A speechless London was a rare sight.

"This is...breathtaking," she said. She held up a brown paper bag. "But am I supposed to just ditch the PB&J I brought from home?"

"Definitely." He laughed, taking the bag from her. "Save it for later. For now, we feast on lobster," he said as he kissed her.

Just a few weeks ago she would have shied away from that tiny public display of affection. Now, she welcomed his PDAs—sometimes she even initiated them.

Drew still alternated between disbelief and outright euphoria when he thought about how far they'd come since he approached her at their class reunion. Whoever said lust couldn't turn into love didn't know what the hell they were talking about.

He guided London to the tent, holding her hand as she lowered herself onto one of the cushions. Her awed smile as she took in the furnishings and flowers made Drew mentally tack on an extra five thousand dollars to Larissa's already sizable yearly bonus.

London lifted a carnation from the bouquet at the center of the table and brought it to her nose. Even dressed in surgical scrubs and her white lab coat, she looked as if she were posing for a portrait by one of the world's most renowned artists.

She was fucking art.

She was everything. The energy and power she exuded captivated him. Her dedication and drive compelled him to want to do better. Her sensuality and that way she had of unabashedly stating what she wanted in no uncertain terms made him want to give her everything she demanded and more.

But first, Drew had to know if she wanted the same from him. His time at Travis County Hospital was quickly coming to an end, and while he wouldn't press her for a declaration of love, he had to let her know where he stood. He just had to work up the nerve to tell her.

The amusing irony of his current situation wasn't lost on him. He'd stared down some of the most powerful executives in the world without flinching, yet the thought of telling this woman he'd loved since she was a girl how he felt about her made his hands tremble.

He would tell her, but he would wait until after he'd fed her. He signaled to the chef to start their crepes.

"How did the surgery go?" Drew asked as he served them bisque from the crystal flask that sat atop a bed of crushed ice.

"The surgery was...eventful," she said. "The patient coded on the table."

"Damn, London. Did everything turn out okay?"

"He's in the ICU and likely to recover, but this is the third time in two years that I've operated on this particular patient, and he gets frailer with each surgery. There's just so much an eleven-year-old's body can take." She set the carnation next to her place setting, then looked to him. The despondency in her deep brown eyes pinched his heart. "The toughest part of this job is knowing that, eventually, you're going to lose some of them."

She projected this air of detachment when it came to the surgeries she performed, but Drew had expected from early on that it was a coping mechanism. Approaching her job with a certain level of remoteness allowed her to focus on the task at hand and not the mass of emotions undoubtedly attached to each case.

He leaned over and traced a finger along her cheek.

"I'm sure the patient's family appreciates every second he has on this earth. You're the reason he's had more time with his family. Remember to take credit for the wins. You deserve that much."

She nodded but remained silent. Drew saw the way her throat worked as she swallowed hard.

"You don't have to be strong with me, London." He continued to brush his thumb over her smooth skin, keeping his touch light. "Everyone needs to let go sometimes. Allow yourself to feel whatever you need to feel. I'm here to absorb it."

Her eyes fell shut and she leaned into his hand. Her lips trembled as a single tear fell from the corner of her eye. "It can be so overwhelming," she whispered.

"I honestly don't know how you do it." He brushed the tear from her cheek.

"I don't know how the *parents* do it. I'm just doing my job, but those parents continue to go through this day after day after day. For so many of them, their child's illness becomes their entire life." She opened her eyes. "I'm blown away by their strength. Having kids is not for the weak."

Drew tipped his head to the side. He waited a beat before asking, "Do you want kids?"

She vehemently shook her head. "I never have, and I am not ashamed to admit it."

"You shouldn't be," he said. "I've never had the desire to have kids either."

He stopped there, but he didn't have to put voice to the rest of his statement for it to have an impact. This was yet another example of how perfect they were for each other.

"Lobster crepes?"

They both startled at the chef's intrusion.

"Thank you," Drew said, taking the plates from the man.

"This looks and smells amazing," London said. "My PB&J didn't stand a chance."

"I have to give the credit to my assistant, Larissa," Drew admitted. "My initial expectation when I asked her to set up a picnic was a blanket on the ground with some meat, cheese, and fruit for us to share."

"That would have been nice too," London said. She sent him a wry smile. "You'd better watch out. I can get used to this, Mr. Sullivan."

He deliberately chose to disregard the amusement in her voice when he answered her.

"I want you to get used to it," he said.

"Picnics in the park with you?"

"Every weekend," he said. "And maybe even during the week. All the time."

Her fork arrested on the way to her mouth. "What are you saying, Drew?"

"You've done something that I never thought would happen," he said. "You made me fall in love with Texas. Well, maybe I'm not in love with Texas per se." He sucked in a breath before continuing. "But I am in love with you, London."

He felt as if all the air escaped his lungs as he watched

London's expression change from surprise, to what was possibly joy, but then to unmistakable apprehension.

She set her fork on her plate. "No, Drew. It's too soon."

He shook his head. "Not for me."

"This thing between us... it..."

"It's real," Drew said. "I've been in love before, London. I know what it feels like. And what I feel when I'm with you is so far beyond anything I've experienced in the past. I'm not ready to let that go."

"So you'll uproot your entire life?"

"You say that as if it would be difficult. I'm based in New York, but I can work from anywhere. I'm willing to move back here if it means I get to be with you."

"I'm leaving," she blurted.

Drew's head snapped back. "What?"

"Shit," she released with a sigh. She dragged her palms down her face, then gripped the back of her head. "It's a possibility," she said. "Remember that extremely competitive pediatric cardiothoracic surgery program in Chicago I mentioned the other day? They're pulling out the big guns in their effort to recruit me."

Drew sat back. "This sounds serious."

"It has done wonders for my ego—not that my ego was suffering," she said with a short laugh. "I'm starting to think that hypertension isn't the only thing my dad passed down to me. The line between being proud of your own accomplishments and being a narcissist is thin."

"You are not a narcissist," he said.

"What makes you so sure?"

"I was a hedge fund manager. I'm pretty sure if you research the profession with the most narcissists, that would be at the top of the list. You, on the other hand, were driven to overexcel because of your dad, and in the process became this badass surgeon hospitals around the country are willing to fight for."

She shrugged. "Maybe you're right. And these hospitals *are* putting up a fight. This offer out of Chicago is unlike anything I've heard of for a fellowship. I would have the chance to work with some of the top pediatric heart surgeons in the country, and the salary is so generous that it would allow me to pay off a huge chunk of my med school loan debt."

It was on the tip of his tongue to offer to pay off her student loans, but Drew already knew what her answer would be. And that wasn't what she wanted from him. She'd demonstrated in so many ways that she didn't care about his money. It made him love her even more.

"That actually makes it easier for me," Drew said. A confused frown creased her forehead. "I already have an apartment in Chicago," he said. "In a high-rise on Lakeshore Drive, overlooking Lake Michigan."

"That's almost as impressive as the one overlooking Central Park," she said.

"Almost." He chuckled, but then he sobered. "Is this what you really want? This job in Chicago?"

"It is, hands down, the best move for my career," she answered.

"But is it what you *want*?"

"It's not that simple, Drew." She hunched her shoulders. "I have to consider what makes the most sense for my future. Although, now that I think about it, what's best for my career has never been the top deciding factor."

She fiddled with the petals of the flower she'd lifted

from the centerpiece earlier. When she spoke, a trace of that unapologetic self-assurance he'd come to love had entered her voice.

"I could have had my pick of residencies when I finished medical school," she started. "Honestly, I was more aggressively recruited for residency programs than for these fellowships. You should look me up online. Some of the articles written about me back then really made me look like a rock star."

"I've read some of them," Drew said. "You *are* a rock star. County is lucky you chose to do your residency here. The more prestigious institutions would all love to have had you."

"I began my residency at one of those more prestigious private hospitals, but when Doug Renault contacted me about joining him at County, I didn't hesitate. It was a calling. I needed to be here."

"Do you still feel that way?"

"I do." She nodded. "Not only because of my patients, but I feel a bit possessive about the sensory room after fighting so hard for it. I don't want to leave it in someone else's hands." She blew out a breath. "More than anything else, I want to be the big sister that my siblings need me to be. This incident with Nina really put things in perspective. I can do better when it comes to those kids. I *should* do better."

"It sounds as if you've made your decision."

"I just...I don't know." She massaged her brow. "Feeling this discombobulated is completely foreign to me, and I do not like it one bit. I pride myself on having my shit together at all times, but not these days. And now I have this thing with my dad to contend with."

Drew frowned. "I thought you were done with your dad?"

"So did I." She swirled her spoon around in the cold bisque, but didn't sample it. "April texted me while I was in surgery. She said that Kenneth wants to meet with me, to talk things over." She hunched her shoulders. "Maybe me calling him an asshole to his face affected him more than I first thought." She finally took a spoonful of the bisque. "Oh, yeah, I can definitely get used to this. This is delicious."

She alternated between the crepe and the soup. After taking a sip of sparkling grape juice from the champagne glass, she asked, "Are you really willing to move back to Austin just to be with me?"

"You ask that as if it isn't reason enough. It is, London."

An unhurried smile slowly made its way across her lips. "Liking you is a lot more enjoyable than not liking you," she said.

Drew swallowed past the lump that lingered in his throat before asking, "How do you feel about loving me?"

Her pause was agonizingly long, but then her smile broadened. "It doesn't feel nearly as scary as I thought it would," she finally answered.

The intense, vibrant emotions that crashed into him left him breathless. Drew braced his hands on the table and leaned over it, then captured her lips in a slow, deep, decadent kiss.

"I've been in love with the idea of you for more than a decade," he whispered against her lips. "But now, after getting to know the *real* you, to say I'm in love feels inadequate. I'm not sure what the words are for how I feel, I just know it's a feeling I never want to lose."

34

Drew blew across his steaming cup of black coffee before taking a sip. He felt a breeze whiz past his head as Samantha Gomez's pacing increased. She and the rest of the team had been camped out in his apartment since seven this morning. They'd entered the phase of an audit when everything feels out of sorts yet as if it is all coming together at the same time. There was no getting around the intensity of this point in the process.

Yet his mind repeatedly wandered to the condo listings his Realtor had forwarded him last night. All he could think about was finding a place to live that would keep him as close as possible to London.

Focus.

He could not allow any distractions to knock him off his game, even one as tempting as London. He and his team had poured hundreds of hours into examining Travis County Hospital's finances and operations. Now they were barreling toward the finish line and praying for no stumbling blocks during this final stretch. He owed them his full attention.

"Who's running the numbers on the recommended equipment purchases for the ortho lab?" Samantha asked.

Drew reached for his iPad and pulled up the spreadsheet he'd received via email this morning. He held it aloft.

"Here you go," he said.

Samantha took the iPad from his hand and continued her pacing.

"Calm down," Drew said over his shoulder. "You always get like this toward the end of a project, but there's no need to worry, Sam. The numbers tell the story, and the story is a good one."

"I know that we've done good work here," she said. "But I can't help being nervous. It's just my nature, okay? I keep waiting for the other shoe to drop."

"Stop inviting trouble." Drew caught her arm, putting a halt to her frenetic pacing. "This team has worked its ass off for the past month. Travis County Hospital was on the verge of being sold, and with the recommendations we're making, not only will they be able to function as the low-cost health-care provider this area needs, but they'll be able to provide even better services for the entire community. That's something to be proud of."

If even one family could be spared the heartache of losing a loved one due to a late diagnosis or inadequate care, his hard work here would have been worth it. It would be a small tribute to his mother's legacy. If he could save someone else from a similar fate, her dying so young wouldn't be in vain.

"What the fuck!"

All eyes turned to Josh Hall, who stared intently at his computer with a look of horrified astonishment.

"Oh goodness," Samantha said. "Is it the other shoe dropping?"

"More like the other Timberland boot," he said. "And it's dropping right on our necks."

Drew pushed back from the table. "What's the matter?" he asked as he rounded Josh's seat and looked at his laptop.

Josh set two copies of the document to print before closing out the dialog box, and then he pointed at the text on the screen.

"Stevens v. Travis County Hospital. Specifically, Dr. Frederick Coleman and Travis County Hospital." He lifted the documents from the printer bed, handing one to Drew and the other to Sam. "From what I can gather, the hospital settled a malpractice suit with the widower of Abigail Stevens, who died while under Dr. Coleman's care two years ago. There have been a few legal hang-ups, but the payment is coming due to the tune of nearly five million dollars."

"What!" Drew flipped through the pages.

"Oh, God," Samantha said. "This is why I'm always so afraid to hope. I'd rather set myself up for disappointment, because it always comes."

Drew skimmed the court document, trepidation amassing in his gut. This was more than just bad. This was catastrophic. Based on Trident's calculations, the most the hospital could absorb, even with malpractice insurance paying the lion's share, was a half million. And that was cutting it extremely close.

"But we've been in constant communication with Legal," Drew said. "Why would they keep this from us!"

"Because it makes Coleman look bad," Josh said. "He probably ordered that everything be kept under wraps, even away from other hospital administrators. This is the type of stuff that you hide from as many people as possible if you want to maintain your position of power."

"I could tell that guy was a prick from the first day we arrived," Samantha said.

"I don't care that he's a prick," Drew said. "I care that the powers that be in this hospital intentionally misled us. They had to have known that Trident could not conduct a clean audit without this information."

"None of this is our fault," Josh pointed out. "Our contract states that clients are to disclose all known financial obligations, both current and future. We can't be held liable if they intentionally kept this from us."

Drew wasn't worried about Trident's liability. They'd run the most complete audit possible based on the information provided to them. His concern was grounded in what this new detail meant for the recommendations his team had compiled for the hospital's board of directors. One recommendation in particular.

Samantha put voice to his worrisome thoughts.

"This blows up everything," she said, tossing the document onto the table and resuming her pacing. "We were already working on a razor-thin margin. A malpractice payout also means allocating more money toward insurance for the next fiscal year. Say goodbye to the new employee day care center. There's no way County can fund that now."

"The list of things County can no longer fund is longer than the list of what they can," Josh said. "We'll have to reassess every single dollar now."

And in that reassessment, the fifty thousand dollars they'd estimated in order to get everything London needed for her sensory room would never fly. They wouldn't even be able to do a scaled-down version.

There was only one solution: Drew would pay for it.

He'd offered to pay for the sensory room before. From the moment he realized just how important it was to London, Drew knew in his heart that he would do whatever he could to make it happen. He could make the donation in his mother's name, or maybe he could ask London if she had a patient she'd lost in the past whom she had been particularly close to. The sensory room could be a memorial to whomever she chose. It was the easiest solution.

But was it the smartest?

He dragged his palm down his face and sucked in a deep breath in an effort to curb his frustration. He knew better than most that throwing money at a situation wasn't always the best solution.

Even if he specified what the donation was intended for, the acceptance and subsequent distribution of monetary gifts would still have to go through the hospital board's approval process. They could choose to reject his gift outright if they didn't agree with the strings he attached to it. Given the way they'd covered up Coleman's malpractice suit, Drew wouldn't put it past them to do just that.

The board's opinion was one thing, but they also had to consider the public's opinion. If it turned out that there wasn't enough money to fund some of the more urgent needs of the hospital, there was no way he could justify a donation being made to finance what many would consider to be his girlfriend's pet project. Not when they could potentially face cuts to basic services that were used by the majority of patients.

Drew couldn't think of a PR firm in the country that could put the kind of spin on this that they would need in order to pull it off.

Fucking Coleman.

That son of a bitch was going to cost London her sensory room after all.

35

Excuse me, are you using this extra chair?"

"Yes," London said to the woman who'd already started carting the chair away from the table. "I'm waiting for someone," she further explained.

Someone who should have been here twenty minutes ago.

She glanced at her Apple Watch again, then up and down Fourth Street. According to April's text, Kenneth was to meet her here at noon. The downtown coffee shop was only a block from his law firm, but London refused to go to his office. Her olive branch extended only so far.

She returned to the journal Samiah had sent her. She hated to admit it, but this shit worked.

London hadn't realized how much the guilt over her nonexistent relationship with her siblings had affected her. She knew it all tied back to Kenneth, of course, but as her pen flowed, a truth she was ashamed to own began to reveal itself.

She'd distanced herself from Nina, Miles, and Koko to get back at her dad. She'd robbed them all of precious time together, thinking that it would hurt him, when in reality, Kenneth was incapable of feeling hurt about something that didn't directly affect him. The only ones who'd suffered were her siblings.

And her.

It wasn't until she began writing down her thoughts that London recognized the pain she'd caused herself by staying away.

She closed her journal. She needed some space between these thoughts and seeing Kenneth face-to-face. If he ever showed up.

Just as she was about to text her stepmom so that April could, in turn, text Kenneth, London spotted him coming up the sidewalk along Lavaca Street. He turned the corner and climbed the concrete steps of Halcyon coffee shop and lounge.

"Over here!" London waved from the table she'd commandeered on the busy outside patio that spanned the front and left side of the building. Kenneth acknowledged her with a nod and pointed to the front door. "Can I get you something?"

London held up her cup. "Another iced coffee. Medium roast with cream and two sugars."

She drained the rest of what she'd purchased when she first arrived, and continued scrolling through her email as she waited for Kenneth. Her thumb arrested on the screen when an email popped up from the head of the fellowship committee at the hospital in Chicago.

Dear Dr. L. Kelley,

It is no secret that my interest in having you join our pediatric cardiothoracic surgical fellowship program remains strong. I would like to personally extend to you an invitation to explore our medical facility in person this coming week. My assistant is cc'd on this email. If you would provide her with the necessary information, she will take care of your flight and lodging arrangements. We have booked a suite at the famed Drake Hotel on Chicago's Magnificent Mile in anticipation of your visit.

Please respond ASAP. As you know, the deadline for accepting the fellowship is quickly approaching, and if you have to unfortunately decline, we would like sufficient time to offer the spot to our next best candidate.

I look forward to meeting you this week in the city that I hope you will soon call home.

Sincerely,
Dr. Bruce Davidson.

"Holy fucking shit," London said.

"Have you always had such a foul mouth?"

She jumped at the sound of her dad's voice over her shoulder.

"Sorry," London said, taking her coffee from him.

She closed out her email and set the phone facedown on the table. She was happy for the distraction meeting with Kenneth would provide. It prevented her from shooting off a quick acceptance of Dr. Davidson's invitation. She needed to think long and hard about the perception it would give if she were to allow the hospital to go to the expense of flying her to Chicago and putting her up in a suite at a four-star hotel. It's possible they would see it as a guarantee that she would accept the fellowship offer, when she was all but certain that she would turn it down.

"So," Kenneth said as he unbuttoned his suit jacket and sat in the chair across from her. "I assume the apology is first."

"Okay," London said.

He stared at her.

She stared at him.

"Okay," she repeated.

"Well, are you going to apologize?" he asked.

"Me? You want *me* to apologize to *you*?"

"Your stepmother said that's why you asked to meet with me today."

What the fuck?

"I did not ask to meet with you. *You* asked to meet up with me. At least that's what April told me. She said you wanted to extend an olive branch."

Kenneth sat back in his chair and folded his hands over his chest. Releasing a weary breath, he said, "Well, it would seem communications were crossed, or, more likely, that my wife is up to something." Annoyance pinched his brows. "I have no intention of being the first to extend an olive branch of any kind. I am *not* the one at fault here. You were incredibly rude and disrespectful to me in my own home. And for no good reason."

No good reason.

"Are you fucking kidding me?" London said.

"London!" He slammed his fist on the table.

"What do you expect me to say to that, *Dad*?"

"I expect you to conduct yourself as a lady should. Using that type of language in front of your own father is beneath you."

"Give me a fucking break," she muttered under her breath. "My language is the last thing you should be concerned about right now. You should be grateful that I'm speaking to you at all, because I vowed I wouldn't anymore."

"And how would that be any different from the way things have been for the past few years?" Kenneth asked.

She huffed out a grunt. "You're right. It wouldn't be different." London studied him as she took a long drink from her coffee. She set the cup down and assumed his pose, crossing her arms over her chest. "Did it ever cross your mind to ask *why* I don't speak to you?"

"Probably because Janette fed you some kind of nonsense about me being a bad father."

London couldn't help herself. She burst out laughing, and once she started, she couldn't rein it back in. Even as several people from neighboring tables openly gawked at them, she still could not pull herself together. She imagined how the two of them looked—Kenneth scowling and confused while she belly laughed to the point that she could scarcely catch her breath—and it caused her to laugh even harder.

Once she was finally able to get a hold of herself, she used a paper napkin to dab at her eyes.

"Are you done?" Kenneth asked in his most condescending voice.

"I think so," London said. She took another sip of her coffee. "I'm just floored that you think I needed my mother to tell me that you were a shitty father. Do you not realize that Janette is the only reason we have a relationship at all? I would have washed my hands of you a long time ago if not for her constantly in my ear about how I should be grateful to still have a father in my life."

"She's correct. And at least you have a father who took care of your needs, and not some deadbeat."

"You do realize that making child support payments was the bare minimum, right? That doesn't get you the Father of the Year Award that you obviously think you deserve."

He jabbed a finger at the table. "I did more than just pay child support. You wore designer clothes throughout high school. I bought you a brand-new car your senior year. I offered to pay off your college loans and to add a porte cochere to your house, but you refused because apparently you're too good for my money now."

"You also skipped my high school graduation for a golfing trip," London said.

"That was a business trip," he countered. "And it was fifteen years ago. Get over it, London."

"I've tried," she said. She shook her head and swallowed down the lump of emotion that formed out of nowhere in her throat. "I have spent countless hours telling myself that it doesn't matter. It's in the past. Just move the hell on."

She pulled her bottom lip between her teeth when she felt that son of a bitch tremble. She wouldn't allow Kenneth to see how much this still affected her.

"I think it's the constant gaslighting that makes it so hard for me to move on. You telling me how great you were as a father when I lived through years of being ignored, and that was before you and Mom divorced. It only got worse as you went through your parade of wives." She toyed with the frayed paper napkin, studying it so that she wouldn't have to look at her dad's face. "If you would just acknowledge that you could have been a better father, maybe I could let it go."

Several moments passed without a word from the other side of the table. When London looked up, the coldness of her father's stare was enough to freeze her eyebrows.

"I will do no such thing," Kenneth finally responded. "I gave you everything you needed."

"I'm not talking about *things*! See, this is the gaslighting! You're a smart man, you know that I'm not talking about the physical things you bought me." London held up a finger. "And since we're on that subject, let's be clear: Even when you gave me those *things*, it was never really about me. You bought me designer clothes because it made you look like a generous parent. The same goes for the car. It was something you could brag about to your buddies on the golf course. It was always about *you*."

His irritated expression bordered on disgust. "After all these years, you are still an ungrateful brat."

"And you are still a clueless, unfeeling father," London said. "I would have rather you throw me a 'good job, London' every now and again than to have a closet full of brand-name clothes and tennis shoes. I had to hear about your compliments secondhand." She shoved her hands in her hair. "I didn't realize you were even capable of paying attention to your children until you finally had a son. Then you suddenly became this ultra-involved parent."

"Are you jealous of a nine-year-old?" The censure dripping from his words made her feel like a recalcitrant child, but London would not allow him to discount her extremely legitimate feelings.

"I'm not jealous of Miles. I'm disappointed in *you*. It's upsetting to see you treating Nina and Koko the same way you treated me. Except this time, your indifference is amplified when weighed against the amount of attention you shower upon your son. Stop treating your daughters like shit."

He steepled his fingers and rested them against his lips. After several uncomfortably tense moments passed, he pointed at her and said, "I can only hope that you one day come to realize just how good you had it, London. Maybe then you'll show me a little gratitude instead of constantly engaging in such vile behavior."

"You know what? I'm not doing this." She threw her hands up. "I'm just not doing it. One way of controlling my blood pressure is to cut down on stress, and this stresses me the fuck out. *You* stress me out, Kenneth."

"I have given you everything, London. I don't know what else you want from me."

She just stared at him as she allowed the sobering reality to sink in. He would never be the father she needed him to be. She'd told herself this countless times over the years. But she had always held out hope that if she ever took the time to truly explain how his utter indifference had affected her, he would acknowledge his role in this fucked-up relationship.

But he wouldn't. He wasn't capable of it.

It was exactly as Drew had said. Kenneth Kelley was a textbook narcissist who simply could not view the world through a lens that wasn't focused entirely on him.

"I don't want anything from you," London said. "I will make sure that my sisters know they are loved and appreciated just the way they are, and that it isn't worth their time to seek any further attention from you."

London pushed her chair back and stood. She did her best to stem the tide of disappointment and utter sadness that rushed through her—at least until she was no longer in the presence of the man who'd caused it for much of her life.

She hadn't expected a storybook ending, but she had hoped to walk away from their talk today feeling as if her dad had finally heard her. She had hoped to mend what was broken.

But some things were not meant to be. It was time she finally, conclusively accepted that.

"London," Kenneth called after her as she walked away from the table.

She didn't look back.

She got behind the wheel of her Mini and held on to the steering wheel in a vise grip. London waited for the tears that had collected in her throat to burst forth, but none fell. Her dad had broken her heart so many times that this final crack barely had an impact.

Still, as she started her car, there was only one destination her brain would even allow her to consider. She turned toward Drew's building, and five minutes later, parallel parked in a spot across the street from the high-rise.

She used the code to take the elevator up to his floor. But when she knocked on his door, it wasn't Drew who answered, it was Samantha Gomez.

"Hello, Dr. Kelley. Come in," Samantha said, stepping aside.

London entered the apartment and stopped short. She had been to funerals with a livelier atmosphere.

She spotted Drew leaning over a laptop on the conference table. His shirtsleeves were rolled up, and whatever tie he'd put on this morning was long forgotten.

He stood up straight when he spotted her. "London."

Trepidation skirted down her spine at the strain she heard in his voice. Something was wrong. Something was very wrong.

"What am I missing?" she asked as Drew approached.

His shoulders dropped in arrant defeat.

"I'm sorry, London. I'm just so, so sorry."

36

Drew tried to swallow but was having a hard time of it. It felt as if his heart were lodged in his throat.

He held his hand out to London. "Come with me. Please."

He didn't want to go into too much detail in front of his team. It was Trident's policy to bring their findings to the client first—in this case, Travis County Hospital's board of directors and upper administration officials—before disseminating the information to other relevant stakeholders. But there was no way Drew could stomach leaving London completely in the dark. It felt too much like lying to her.

He guided her into his room, and they both sat on the edge of the bed.

"We found something today," Drew started. "I can't get very far into it, but a member of the team stumbled across a previously undisclosed financial situation. One that changes everything."

"What do you mean?"

"The hospital is being sued. Or, I should say it *has* been sued. The case was settled, but the payout hasn't happened yet." He looked over at her. "It's a lot of money, London. I need to talk to those in the administration who were involved—"

"Coleman," she said.

Drew sat up straight. "Do you know about the lawsuit?"

She shook her head. "No, but he's the only person at the hospital who would warrant such a cover-up."

"We don't know if the administration was covering up for Coleman," Drew said. "It may have just slipped their minds."

She let out a derisive snort. "Really, Drew?"

"Okay, yeah, they definitely held this from us. It was stupid on the administration's part. They had to have known this would eventually come out."

"My guess is they were hoping the hospital would get sold before anyone had to own up to it," London said. "I wouldn't put anything past them."

Drew was quiet for a moment before continuing. "The fact is, this lawsuit is going to take a large chunk of the budget Trident has prepared for County. Several of our recommendations will have to be scrapped." His heart as heavy as a ship anchor, Drew finally said the words he dreaded saying. "Your sensory room will likely be one of those things, London. I'm sorry."

Drew braced himself for a profanity-laced tirade where she called Frederick Coleman everything but a child of God, but there was none of that. She was calm. *Too* calm. Almost... apathetic.

She flattened her palms on her thighs and nodded. "I understand."

"You do?"

"I knew this was always a possibility." Her small, sad smile crushed him. "I've been conditioned not to get my hopes up from a very young age, Drew. I told you about life with Kenneth." She shrugged. "I'm used to it."

The realization sliced through Drew like a samurai sword. She had been expecting to be let down all along, exactly as her father had disappointed her so many times before.

"London, you have to know that this is the last thing anyone on our team expected to happen, especially me. If I'd known—"

"Drew, it's okay," she said.

"No, it isn't. You worked hard for that sensory room. With all the research you put into it, you deserve to see it come to fruition."

"And maybe I will one day." She hunched her shoulders. "Just not today."

The lack of emotion in her voice destroyed him. He knew how passionate she was about this project. So why did it feel as if this was hurting him more than it hurt her?

Because she never thought he'd follow through on his promise. She'd anticipated his failing her.

There was a knock at the door, followed by Samantha's voice. "Drew?"

"Come in," Drew called.

"Your phone has been ringing constantly for the past ten minutes. I checked the caller ID. It's B. J."

"Shit," Drew whispered. If his partner was repeatedly calling without leaving a message, it had to be bad.

"Go," London said, pushing herself up from the bed. "I need to do the same. It's been a very long day."

"London." Drew grabbed her hand, but he couldn't think of anything else to say to her.

"It's okay," she said.

It wasn't okay. He wanted to fix this for her. He needed to.

His phone started to ring. It was B. J. again.

"I'll see you later," London said.

And then she was gone.

37

London felt as if she would permanently damage her cheek muscles if she was forced to maintain this smile for another second, but she did it anyway. That's just what you did when the person who'd put you up in an eight-hundred-dollars-a-night suite and treated you to a two-hundred-dollar lunch was expounding on all the wonderful things his hospital had to offer.

The first thing London thought when Dr. Bruce Davidson greeted her was that he was tall enough to play center for the Chicago Bulls. She soon learned that he had been a standout collegiate basketball player back in the day, but that losing his younger brother to leukemia had started him on the path of pediatric oncology.

His kind eyes and quiet demeanor were well suited to someone who had surely had his share of tough discussions with scared parents. London took mental notes. She did just fine with the kids but could use some work when it came to communicating with her patients' caregivers.

Although she wasn't sure how much face-to-face communication she would have with patients or their families if she accepted this fellowship. Based on everything that had been covered so far, this position was far more research heavy than any of the others she'd looked into.

But maybe that's what she needed. Research was less stressful than being in the operating room day in and day out. It would do her some good to have less stress in her life for a couple of years.

But she didn't become a surgeon to spend her time in a lab. And while it may be stressful to have a tiny human's life literally in your hands, the reward of a successful surgery that gave that child a longer life was worth all the stress in the world.

She *thrived* in the operating room. It was where she was her most content. Would she even be happy in a fellowship like this one?

"And there she is," Dr. Davidson said.

London turned in the direction he pointed. She didn't have to force her smile this time, not with one of her heroes striding toward her. London beamed as the short Black woman in her mid-sixties approached.

"London Kelley, may I introduce you to Eveline Mayberry."

"It is truly an honor, Dr. Mayberry." London shook the woman's outstretched hand. "I've followed your work throughout medical school and my residency. I wrote several papers on your groundbreaking research on Eisenmenger syndrome."

"I've read them," Eveline Mayberry answered.

London's head snapped back. "You have?"

"Of course I have. Your reputation precedes you, Dr. Kelley." She looked to Dr. Davidson. "Do you mind excusing us, Bruce? I'd like to buy Dr. Kelley a cup of coffee and speak to her one-on-one."

"Not at all," Dr. Davidson said. "In fact, let me do the buying."

He guided them to the hospital's nearby doctors' lounge that made the one back at County look like an abandoned 1950s roadside diner. Everything was clean lines and stainless steel. Dr. Mayberry chose a table next to the floor-to-ceiling windows overlooking the Chicago River.

As they waited for Bruce Davidson to return with their coffees, Dr. Mayberry inquired about London's flight up from Austin and asked if she was enjoying her stay at the Drake.

"Everything has been amazing," London said. "This is my first time in Chicago, so it's a treat to stay in the heart of the city. I'm going to do a little sightseeing once Dr. Davidson and I are done."

"We're not done, are we?" Bruce Davidson asked as he returned. He placed two cups of coffee on the table, along with an extra that was filled with various sweeteners and single-serve nondairy creamer cups.

"No, you're not done," Dr. Mayberry answered. "I'll bring Dr. Kelley to your office once we've chatted a bit."

"Enjoy," he said before leaving their table.

"You know, Dr. Kelley," Eveline Mayberry began as she opened a single pink packet of sweetener and added it to her coffee. "I personally asked Dr. Davidson and the others in the fellowship program to roll out the red carpet for you because I want you on my team."

London's heart began to thump so loudly in her ears that she was sure the other doctor could hear it.

"Um, that's... very flattering."

"You *should* feel flattered, because it's not something I

would normally do. I trust they have rolled out the red carpet for you?"

"Yes." London nodded vehemently. "Everyone has treated me extremely well. It makes the decision I have to make even more difficult."

"That's disappointing to hear," Dr. Mayberry said.

London paused mid-sip. "Excuse me?"

"This decision should be an easy one. Who are we up against?"

It took a lot to intimidate her, but London had to admit that Eveline Mayberry intimidated the hell out of her. All four feet, ten inches of this woman screamed, *Cross me and I will crush you.*

But then London remembered that this world-renowned surgeon wanted her here. She'd instructed an entire team of world-renowned surgeons to pull out all the stops to convince London to accept their fellowship offer.

She decided to be straight with her.

"I've narrowed it down to this fellowship in Chicago and continuing to practice at Travis County Hospital in Austin," London said.

"Hmm," Mayberry murmured. She took a slow, deliberate sip from her cup as she turned her attention to the view outside the window. Then she set the coffee down in front of her and returned that laser focus back to London.

"It will be difficult for you not to take this the wrong way," the doctor continued. "But I'm going to say it anyway. Your talents are wasted at Travis County Hospital."

"Excuse me," London said again, but in a tone totally opposite from her previous one. She had mad respect for a pioneer like Eveline Mayberry, but she was obsessively protective of the hospital that had nurtured her these past five years. She wouldn't allow anyone to shit on County, no matter how much of a legend they were.

"Dr. Kelley, there are surgeons finishing residencies all around the country who can step into your role at the hospital in Austin, and your patients would not suffer one bit. However, there are very few who are worthy of the work my team and I are doing here. *You* are one of them."

"Look." London folded her hands on the table. "I appreciate that you think so highly of my skills. Wait—I'm sorry, that sounded incredibly arrogant."

"Don't apologize. You've earned the right to be arrogant. Embrace it and don't let anyone tell you differently."

London sat up straighter at the older woman's pronouncement. She could only imagine what Eveline Mayberry had faced in her forty-plus years in medicine. How hard she'd had to fight for respect. How many male counterparts she'd come up against who tried to dim her light.

London had been able to shine so bright because of doctors like Eveline Mayberry paving the way. She would indeed embrace that which she had earned.

"Thank you for seeing the value of my work," London said, rephrasing her previous statement.

Dr. Mayberry nodded as if to say, *That's more like it.*

"However," London continued. "I believe that I have been a unique asset to Travis County Hospital. Austin is my home. The people I serve there, some of them have become like family. I also have to consider my actual family," she said. "There are many factors that will go into my decision."

"I understand that," Dr. Mayberry said. "But when I see talent like yours, I'm compelled to fight for it. I want to cultivate every morsel of the gift you've been given so that you can reach your full potential, Dr. Kelley." She drained the rest of her coffee, stood, and indicated that London should do the same. "I will campaign on behalf of this hospital until you make your decision, but no matter where you choose to further your career, I hope you stay in touch." She gestured toward the door to the lounge. "Ah, there he is. I knew Bruce would be lurking."

Dr. Mayberry turned to London and held out her hand. "It has been a pleasure. I hope I can welcome you here soon."

And then she marched her tiny frame out of the lounge, leaving a sense of fear and awe in her wake.

By the time London arrived back at the Drake Hotel hours later, she was both mentally and physically exhausted. She had a ticket for a boat ride on the Chicago River, but her chances of making it were a negative eighty-five. She was going to order ridiculously expensive room service—which she would charge to her own credit card—and binge-watch episodes of *Dateline* on the ID channel.

She had managed to make her way to Navy Pier, both to see the famed tourist spot and to think over the massively difficult decision she had to make. But the crisp Chicago air had done nothing to clear her head. And as she entered the hotel, she wasn't any closer to making a decision than she had been for the past three months.

"Why are you even questioning this?" London muttered.

This was a once-in-a-lifetime opportunity to work with one of the most renowned surgeons in the country—a surgeon fighting tooth and nail to bring London onto her team. Meanwhile, London had a money-strapped hospital with an administration she constantly butted heads with back in Austin. The decision should be the simplest of her life.

And maybe it would have been, if she hadn't received that text from Nina about an hour ago.

Her little sister wanted to remind her about the volleyball match next Saturday. London's first instinct had been to tell her that she wouldn't be able to attend, but there was no way she could disappoint Nina this soon after making the promise to be there for her.

London climbed the stairs leading to the lobby floor of the Drake. She stopped short at the sight of the man sitting on one of the tufted, cream-colored couches.

"Drew Sullivan, what are you doing here?"

38

Drew was on his feet the moment he heard London's voice. His heart lurched in his chest at the sight of her. It had only been two days, but it felt like a millennium.

He had not seen her since she left his apartment Thursday evening, after he'd broken the news to her about the malpractice suit and the impact it was likely to have on several projects at the hospital—including her sensory room. Before he could offer up alternative solutions, Samantha had interrupted with that call from B. J., which turned out not to be as much of an emergency as Drew had first guessed. Although news that the urgent care outfit in Kansas City had chosen Trident over Meacham was a reason for them all to celebrate.

But Drew hadn't been in the mood to pop champagne bottles. Setting things right with London had been the only thing on his mind.

She had been tied up in a string of back-to-back-to-back surgeries the next day, and when he'd texted her an invitation to dinner, she replied with the news that she couldn't because she would be flying up to Chicago the following morning to speak with the hospital that had been courting her for their fellowship program.

It had taken everything within him not to take an Uber to her house. His plan had been to give her these two days in Chicago and then make his case when she returned. But he couldn't wait. He'd caught the first flight he could get on following his meeting with Travis County Hospital's board of directors.

Now, as he met her underneath the massive crystal chandelier that hung above the center of the Drake Hotel's opulent lobby, Drew couldn't believe he'd lasted this long without seeing her.

He wasn't sure how she would greet him, but when her arms went around him in a strong, swift hug, it felt as if every single thing in his world was right. She immediately pulled back and asked again, "What are you doing here?"

"I wanted to apologize," Drew said. "And I couldn't do that over the phone. I needed to see you in person."

She shook her head. "Drew, you don't have to apologize."

"Yes, I do. I—"

"None of this is your fault," she said, cutting him off. She looked around and said, "We can't do this here." Then she took him by the hand and went straight for the elevators.

It looked as if they would have a car to themselves, but at the last minute a couple carrying Bloomingdale's shopping bags boarded, traveling all the way up to the same floor where London's room was located. He and London got off the elevator and walked just a few doors down before they arrived at her room. Drew stood to the side as she opened the door, then he followed her into her suite.

"Wow," was all he could say. He'd visited the Drake before, but only for evening drinks at the Palm Court. Some would consider the heavy, rich wood furnishings and dark carpeting to be out of style, but he liked the old-school grandeur. "They must really want you at this hospital if they went to the expense of putting you up in a suite like this," Drew surmised.

"Yes, they really, really do want me," London said. She set her purse on an intricately carved sofa table and folded her arms over her chest. "I have to admit, today did absolutely amazing things for my ego. One of the most renowned surgeons in the world—a woman I've admired for years—sat down for coffee with me so that she could personally petition me. She wants me on her team."

Drew's steps slowed as he approached her. "What do *you* want?" he asked in a quiet voice.

London pulled her bottom lip between her teeth and shook her head.

"I still don't know." Blowing out an irritated breath, she shoved her hands in her hair—something he realized she did when her frustration was at its highest level. "This isn't like me. This dithering back and forth, not being able to make up my mind? It's the most uncomfortable feeling in the world." She pounded her open palm with her fist. "When I have a decision to make, I sit down and I make the damn decision. I figure out what's most practical and that's what I go with."

"So, what's holding you up? Or, maybe I should ask, what's keeping you in Austin? Is this about your siblings, and you not wanting to disappoint them?"

She huffed out a tired laugh. "You can read me like a book, Drew Sullivan. I'm not sure if I like that."

He shrugged. "You've made it clear how important it is for you to keep the promise you made to them, especially to Nina." Drew knew that they couldn't dance around the reason he'd flown up here. "Speaking of promises, I am sorry for breaking mine, London."

"Drew," she said with a sigh. "I told you, you have no reason to apologize. It is not your fault that County got hit with a malpractice lawsuit. Am I disappointed we're not getting the sensory room? Of course I am. But I don't blame you."

"I can't help feeling as if I let you down," Drew said. "And after hearing about all the times your dad let you down in the past—"

She walked up to him and captured his cheeks between her palms. "Don't even finish that statement. Kenneth Kelley's lifetime of broken promises has absolutely nothing to do with you. Now that I know the *real* you, I would never put you in the same category as my dad, Drew."

"I'm going to fix this," he said. "I haven't figured it out yet, but I'm going to find a way to get you that sensory room." He stared into her eyes. "But will that be enough to keep you in Austin?"

"Is that *your* goal?" London asked. "Keeping me in Austin?"

"I already told you, I can be wherever you want me to be. You have to decide where that is, London. But just promise me this," Drew said. "Promise me that you're making the decision for the right reason. Now that you've been here and seen what they have to offer, does Chicago feel right?"

She pulled her bottom lip between her teeth again. After several moments passed, she said, "No."

Drew's head snapped back. "No?"

"No," she said. She looked at him in amazement, as if she didn't quite believe that she'd said that word either.

"If you asked any pediatric surgeon in this country what they would give to work with Dr. Eveline Mayberry, the majority would say everything. That's just how badass this woman is. She's a living legend. If I were to accept this two-year fellowship, when I'm done, I would be able to demand a salary that matched a surgeon with twenty years of experience. When it comes to deciding where I want to practice medicine, the choice of hospitals vying for me would be endless."

Drew put voice to the word that lingered in the air, unsaid. "But?" he asked.

"But I don't want to do the work they would expect me to do here in Chicago." She shrugged. "It really is that simple. The research Dr. Mayberry and her team are conducting, it's groundbreaking. It's the type of research that gets you on the short list for the Nobel Prize."

"Whoa," Drew said. "And you're willing to pass that up?"

"Seems unbelievable, right? But that's where I am. You know that this ego of mine has never really needed much stroking. And the thought of adding the kinds of accolades that will come with being on this particular research team..." She shook her head and laughed. "Seriously, just pump my ego full of steroids right now."

Then she sobered, her expression turning more earnest. "But it's just not for me. I have so much respect for the doctors conducting research out there. It's because of them and the work they do that I can do my job. But *my* job is in the operating room. I became a surgeon because I wanted to perform life-saving surgeries." She shrugged. "My heart wouldn't be in the work here, and that's what should matter the most. But I just can't do it."

She slid her arms around his neck and cradled the back of his head in her hands.

"Are you still willing to put extra miles on Trident's jet in order to come and see me in Austin?" she asked.

He grinned. "I am, but I don't need a jet to get from Westlake to County Hospital, or to your house in Hyde Park."

"What?"

"I probably shouldn't count my chickens before they hatch, but if the offer I put in on a house in Westlake yesterday falls through, I have several others in mind." Drew hunched his shoulders. "I was going to buy a condo, but I decided it would be nice to have a place with a yard for once. That's one of the reasons my mom loved her house in Hye. Maybe I'll take to gardening the way she did."

London stared at him with an awed look on her face.

"Drew fucking Sullivan," she said. "Who would have ever thought I'd find myself in love with you?"

Drew's heart lurched. "You do realize you just said that you're in love with me, don't you?"

Her smile broadened. "Yes, I do. Because I am."

She lifted her head up and Drew leaned forward, meeting her kiss. It was slow and generous and breathtaking. *She* took his breath away. This woman who claimed to have hated him for years, who had seen him as only a temporary hookup. This woman had just told him that she was in love with him.

"I hope you know that you could have accepted a fellowship in China, and I would have gladly signed up for Mandarin lessons. Well, I would have had Larissa search for the class and sign me up."

London burst out laughing.

"You don't have to follow me halfway around the world, Drew. Just halfway across town, because I'm not giving up my cute bungalow in Hyde Park."

Not yet.

He knew her too well to say those words out loud, but he'd convinced her to come this far on this ride with him. He would eventually bring her around to the idea that just living in the same city wasn't close enough.

Or maybe he'd join her in that chintz-covered house in Hyde Park. He didn't care, as long as he was with her.

39

London readjusted the green-and-white baseball cap that had been in a constant battle with her springy, natural curls since the moment she'd put it on. She stood so that the father and his twin daughters who'd gone to the restroom three times since the start of this volleyball match twenty minutes ago could get to their seat.

Bless his heart—in the true sense of the phrase, not the Southern. This poor man was living testimony that the struggle was real when it came to toddlers.

London settled back in her seat, braced her open palms on either side of her mouth, and yelled, "Here we go, Tigers! Here we go!"

Nina's eyes shot to hers and she made a *cut it out* motion, swiping her hand across her neck.

"Well, excuse me," London muttered. "I was just trying to show some team spirit."

"Did you come here just to embarrass your little sister?"

She looked up and smiled.

"Hey, you," she said to Drew. He took a seat next to her, and she immediately planted a loud kiss on his lips. She'd already embarrassed Nina, so she figured what the hell.

"Apparently, my dear sister thought she was getting a quiet, demure spectator," London said. "That'll teach her to be more careful about what she wishes for."

"I'm sure she is thrilled that you're here, even if she doesn't show it."

London had no doubt about that, even if she'd barely made it in time. She'd spent the morning in the OR—Sarah and Charles Jefferson decided that Ahmad should have his surgery after all, much to Peter Foster's chagrin. But London had been determined to get to the match. She'd arrived at the gym just as the two squads made their way onto the court.

Nina's wave had been short and brief, but her accompanying smile and the joy radiating from her made London's sacrifices to get here worth it. Granted, some of those sacrifices were bigger than others, but they were all still worth it. She knew what it was like to have a parent who couldn't be bothered to spare even the most infinitesimal bit of his time. Neither of her sisters would endure any more of that.

London's most significant forfeiture, by far, was the fellowship in Chicago.

She'd officially declined it yesterday. Her call with Dr. Bruce Richardson had been immediately followed by a call from Dr. Eveline Mayberry. The older woman had not minced words when it came to voicing her disappointment, but she had also applauded London for doing what she thought was right for herself. Which she had then followed with a ten-minute diatribe about why London was wrong about what she thought was right for herself.

They'd ended the call with a plan to meet for dinner when Dr. Mayberry attended a medical conference in San Antonio next month. She cautioned London that she would continue to push her to come to Chicago, but it was also meant to be a way for them to remain in touch.

The Eveline Mayberry was determined to work with her one day. London still could not fully grasp it.

But London felt it in her heart that she *had* made the right choice, despite Aleshia Williams ranting that London was out of her mind and offering to take her place, even though it wasn't her specialty.

London knew she wouldn't have been happy in Chicago. The fellowship she'd accepted from St. David's Children's Hospital here in Austin would allow her to work a number of hours at Travis County Hospital every week, while also studying under the tutelage of Dr. Regina Lewis, another star when it came to Black female doctors. Dr. Lewis also happened to be one of Eveline Mayberry's most lauded students.

Yeah, she'd made the right choice.

"Nice spike!" Drew called.

"Is that what it's called when they pounce on the ball like that?" London asked.

"Do you know anything about volleyball?" Drew asked.

She reached into her pocket and produced the earrings she'd taken out of her ears earlier.

"I came here wearing these," she said.

"These are soccer balls."

"Exactly." She looked over at him and saw the effort he was making not to laugh. "You can laugh."

"I won't," Drew said. "At least not to your face." He wrapped one arm around her and pulled her closer to him, giving her a reassuring squeeze. "The fact that you know nothing about volleyball yet you're here—especially after that long surgery this morning—makes you a contender for the Big Sister of the Year Award in my mind."

"I have a long way to go before I can claim any rights to *that* award," she said with a laugh. "But I can endure a volleyball match if it means Nina will feel that she has someone in her corner. Sometimes, that can make all the difference. Oh, and the spa day I've booked for me, Nina, and Koko will help my chances in the Big Sister of the Year category. I plan to teach them both the importance of self-care."

"As you continue to learn it yourself?" Drew asked.

"Hey." She reached into her bag and pulled out a skein of yarn. "I'm doing a lot better. I'm working on your beanie between matches."

"You're going for the Girlfriend of the Year Award, too, I see." He leaned over and planted a kiss on her lips. "Hey, you mind if we talk about work while we watch the match?"

"Of course not," London said. She tried to ignore the scent of nachos wafting from somewhere behind her as she took a bite of the homemade fruit leather Taylor had delivered to her yesterday. Salty snacks were out; healthy snacks were in. She didn't like it, but she would deal.

"What's up?" London asked, holding out the chewy, strawberry-flavored strip to him.

He declined with a shake of his head and rubbed his hands together. Then he flattened his palms on his thighs. London realized it was the first time she'd seen him in jeans—and she absolutely loved them on him.

"Here's the deal," Drew said. "I'm making a million-dollar donation to Travis County Hospital."

London nearly choked on the fruit leather.

"That's the initial amount," he clarified. "It's the start of an endowment that I'm setting up in my mother's name. It's to benefit cancer patients, and since the pediatric ward treats cancer patients, the multisensory environment room falls under the endowment's purview."

"Drew," she whispered, shaking her head. "No. You know that money doesn't solve everything."

"Except that sometimes it does, London." His earnest expression went straight for her heart. "There are a lot of problems in this world that could easily be solved if those with an abundance of wealth spread that money around. This is one of those issues. The only reason County couldn't get that sensory room built is because it didn't have the money to pay for it. I do. Problem solved."

London knew he'd purposely delivered this news in that pragmatic fashion with the intent of downplaying the magnitude of his gift. It was his nature. But she would not allow him to minimize this.

"That is amazing, Drew. *You* are amazing."

"No, I'm—"

"Yes, you are," she said, cutting him off. She took his hand and brought it to her lips, placing a gentle kiss on his palm. Then she brought it to her chest and held it there. "That sensory room will make such a huge difference for the patients at County, and it will all be due to your generosity."

"And your vision," he added.

Gratitude swelled within her, until it felt as if there were no room for anything else. Except for love. She loved this man with her entire being.

"But this isn't just about one project," he continued. "Although your sensory room *is* the catalyst, make no mistake about that. But, London, I lost my mom because of inadequate health care. My millions couldn't save her, but they could have given me more time with her if her early treatment had been better. This endowment will ensure that others have more time with their loved ones. I honestly can't think of a worthier cause to spend my money on."

"Neither can I," she said. She palmed his jaw and leaned her forehead against his. "Thank you," she whispered. "Those two words are so insufficient, but they're all I can think to say right now. Thank you, thank you, thank you."

"Thank *you* for being the kind of doctor you are. Your patients will never know how lucky they are to have you, London."

She looked into his eyes and was overwhelmed by the love staring back at her.

Love like this was unimaginable to her just two short months ago. Loving *this* particular man like this? Never in this lifetime could she have ever conceived of it.

Never had she been so happy to have been proven wrong.

EPILOGUE

There they are!" London took Drew by the hand as they made their way around the tables at the Asian fusion restaurant in Downtown Austin. She had been surprised when Samiah had suggested this place of all places for their couples dinner tonight. But, in a way, it was fitting. It's where she, Samiah, and Taylor had met.

Who would have thought she'd ever be so damn grateful for that no-good, three-timing asshole Craig Johnson. If their paths were to ever cross again, London would probably give that bastard a hug. His assholery had resulted in the most amazing blessing a woman could ask for, two remarkable girlfriends. And it was the encouragement of those two girlfriends that had forced her to get out of her own way so that she would be open to seeing the good in the man at her side.

Yeah, she would hug Craig Johnson. She'd probably also knee him in the balls for being such an asshole, but a hug would soon follow.

"Sorry we're late," London said.

"Don't worry, we know," Samiah said. "You got held up at the hospital."

London looked to Drew and nodded. "Okay, we'll go with that."

"You two were getting busy, weren't you?" Taylor asked with a sly grin.

London ignored her question as she sat in the seat next to Jamar, Taylor's boyfriend. "Please tell me the Volcano sushi roll has already been ordered," she said.

"Three of them," Jamar said. "I have to see what all the hype is about."

"Believe me, it will blow your mind," London told him.

"We ordered for the table once you texted that you were on your way," Samiah said. "Taylor and Jamar have an early flight to North Carolina in the morning to celebrate her mom's promotion to senior partner, so we can't be out too late."

"Yay for Mama Powell," London said. "Give her a high five from me." London looked to Samiah. "So, what made you choose this restaurant of all places?"

"Well, first, because it's been a while since I had that sushi roll, and I've been craving it."

"Craving?" London asked with a raised brow.

"I'm not pregnant," Samiah said.

"No, she is not pregnant," Daniel added.

"Girl, don't bring that energy around here." Taylor made a shooing motion with her fingers. "Nobody's looking to have babies anytime soon."

"Now, I didn't say all that," Samiah said. "The other reason I picked this restaurant is because it felt like the best place to share this full-circle moment." She stretched out her left hand. "We've decided to do a thing."

A gorgeous diamond ring shone under the lights hanging above their table.

"Bitch, what?" London and Taylor simultaneously screeched.

London reached across the table and grabbed hold of Samiah's hand, tilting it from side to side so that she could look at the ring from all angles. It was stunning. A radiant cut in a platinum setting.

"Way to bring the fire, Dimples," London said.

Daniel Collins's adorable dimples deepened even more. "I took a risk buying it on my own, but I think I did okay, huh?" He looked to Samiah.

"You did an excellent job," she said, pressing a kiss to the tip of his nose.

Even though London was no longer opposed to getting lovey-dovey with one's significant other in public, these two still made her roll her eyes.

"Congratulations, you two!" Taylor crowed. "You're like my favorite engaged couple now." She looked over at Jamar and held up a finger. "I'm not ready yet, so don't go getting any ideas."

Jamar held up both hands. "I wasn't. But eventually, right?"

She gave him a kiss. "Maybe one day, Twenty-Three." She returned her attention to the table at large and said, "Okay, so my news will seem like shit compared to Samiah's, but I'm sharing it anyway," Taylor said.

"Share away, girl," London encouraged.

"I passed all my classes," Taylor said. "All Bs! Because I'm a bad bitch, baby!"

"Gimme some, genius!" London reached over and gave her a high five.

"That's fab, Taylor!" Samiah said.

"And," Taylor continued. "I just signed a lease on a studio in Georgetown. Taylor'd Conditioning officially has its own gym!"

"Congratulations, girl! That's amazing," London said. "I am so freaking happy for both of you. My only news is that I'm out of the danger range when it comes to my blood pressure, but you two are about to send it skyrocketing with all this excitement."

"You're going to be just fine, both with your blood pressure and this new fellowship," Taylor said. "Face it, ladies. We are hot shit."

"The hottest shit," London concurred. She looked at the men at the table. "You three are the luckiest men in Austin."

Daniel, Jamar, and Drew all looked at each other. "We know," they answered in unison.

"Well, ladies." Samiah held her drink in the air. "Here's to good health, fabulous friendship, and living our best lives."

London and Taylor clinked their glasses to hers.

"Cheers to that!"

ACKNOWLEDGMENTS

When I sit down to write a new story, it's just me and my characters. But by the time that story reaches readers so many hands have touched it. My thanks to all who had a role in bringing this book and this entire series to life.

To my editor, Leah Hultenschmidt, and editorial assistant, Sabrina Flemming. You've been so amazing throughout this project. I appreciate your hard work so very much.

To my fellow Disney lovers and the best PR team an author can ask for, Estelle Hallick and Dana Cuadrado. You are both magic. There are no words to express how grateful I am to work with you both.

To Mari C. Okuda and the rest of the production crew at Hachette. My sincere thanks for all the work you put in behind the scenes.

To my agent, Evan Marshall. Sending that single-page query to you in 2005 was one of the best decisions I've ever made in my life. Thank you for always being on my side.

To Kwana Jackson and Priscilla Oliveras. I cherish your friendship. Thanks for the accountability texts and encouraging words.

To my family. Your belief in me is the reason I get to

do this job. I love you all more than anything. We'll get through this.

To Samiah, Taylor, and London. You may be fictional characters, but you've felt so very real to me over these past four years. You three changed my life. Thank you for letting me tell your stories.

Lastly, my heartfelt thanks to all the health-care providers who have sacrificed so much to keep us safe during these scary times. Throughout this series, London has jokingly bragged about the fact that she saves lives, but there is no joking when it comes to all the doctors, nurses, techs, paramedics, EMTs, and others who have given so much of themselves. You save lives every day and we will forever be in your debt.

ABOUT THE AUTHOR

Farrah Rochon, *USA Today* bestselling author of *The Boyfriend Project*, hails from a small town just west of New Orleans. She has garnered much acclaim for her Holmes Brothers and New York Sabers series. When she is not writing in her favorite coffee shop, Farrah spends most of her time reading, cooking, traveling the world, visiting Walt Disney World, and catching her favorite Broadway shows.

You can learn more at:
FarrahRochon.com
Twitter @FarrahRochon
Facebook.com/FarrahRochonAuthor